Love's Grand Sweet Song

by Jennifer Lamont Leo

LOVE'S GRAND SWEET SONG

Published by Mountain Majesty Media, Inc.

PO Box 638, Cocolalla, Idaho 83813

ISBN: 978-1-7337058-9-9 (e-book)
ISBN: 978-1-7378741-0-2 (paperback)
Copyright © 2024 by Jennifer Lamont Leo

Cover design by Hannah Linder

For information on this book or author visit: www.jenniferlamontleo.com

This is a work of fiction. Names, characters, and incidents are all products of the author's imagination or are used for fictional purposes. Any mentioned brand names, places, and trademarks remain the property of their respective owners, bear no association with the author or the publisher, and are used for fictional purposes only.

Library of Congress Cataloging-in-Publication Data

Leo, Jennifer Lamont

Love's Grand Sweet Song / Jennifer Lamont Leo 1st ed.

Printed in the United States of America

For Thomas

Do noble things, not dream them, all day long;
and so make life, death, and that vast forever
one grand sweet song.
(Charles Kingsley, 1856)

Life is one grand sweet song, so start the music.
(Ronald Reagan, 1928)

Books by Jennifer Lamont Leo

Corrigan Sisters

You're the Cream in My Coffee

Ain't Misbehavin'

Wrap Your Troubles in Dreams

Windy City Hearts

Moondrop Miracle

The Rose Keeper

Love's Grand Sweet Song

Novella Collections

Lumberjacks & Ladies

The Highlanders

**Join Jennifer's Reader Community
at https://JenniferLamontLeo.com**

CHAPTER ONE

Christmas Eve, 1915

Seated in the drafty choir loft at the back of Scoville Community Church, Francie Forrester listened with only half an ear as the bespectacled preacher repeated, in his distinctive nasal drone, the familiar story of the birth of Jesus. Her mind was occupied by silently reciting, over and over, the opening notes of the solo she was about to sing. Much as she yearned to concentrate fully on the biblical account, her nerves refused to settle until the solo was out of the way. Only then would she be able to relax and turn her full attention to the preacher's words.

No matter how many times she'd sung in church, no matter how many kind words people said to her afterward, she could never seem to calm the pre-solo jitters.

Gazing over the congregation below, she stopped short when she noticed the back of Chip Hardwick's handsome blond head. Her heart sank a little. What was he doing here? He wasn't a member of Scoville Community. In fact, Francie had never seen him at her church before. And this was Christmas Eve. Shouldn't he have been home with his family in Wisconsin?

Then she saw the reason for his presence, and her heart sank further. Seated next to Chip, her slender shoulder pressed against his, was the even blonder Theresa Van Dell, daughter of one of Scoville's most well-to-do families, members of which filled the rest of the pew. No wonder Chip was spending Christmas Eve in Scoville, months after he'd graduated from Scoville College and supposedly left Illinois. He was keeping company with Theresa.

Months after he'd broken Francie's heart.

Francie's mother, Ramona—called "Ramona" instead of "Mama" by her own choice—had tried to warn her. "I toldja. Romances between college boys and the town girls never work out. He's just lookin' fer a short-term fling to ease his loneliness while he's far from home. You'll see. He'll forgetcha once the term ends. Mark my words and keep yer distance. Stick to yer own kind."

By "own kind" Ramona had meant the mechanics, carpenters, and farmers' sons Francie had grown up alongside. They were sturdy, dependable, hardworking men who could be counted on to bring home a steady paycheck. For Ramona, security meant getting a man to commit to you—something the woman herself, ironically, had never achieved.

But wrapped in the radiant glow of her infatuation with the dashing college senior—her first love—Francie hadn't listened. Her mother hadn't trusted Chip to tell the correct time, but Francie had trusted him completely. She hadn't guarded her heart. And she'd learned the hard way that sometimes, even if only on rare occasions, her mother was right.

Francie tore her gaze away from the dazzling couple, determined to concentrate on the pastor's words. Her black leather music folder trembled in her clammy hands. The rich, spicy aroma of pinesap wafted throughout the greenery-draped sanctuary, tickling her nose. Goodness, she didn't need to be sneezing at a time like this. She needed to be harkening to the Word of God.

She drew her mind's eye back to the inn at Bethlehem, to the stable where the infant Savior lay in a manger, wrapped in swaddling clothes, with angels singing all around. *Of course, it was easy for those angels to sing with joy*, thought Francie with a twinge of resentment. *They didn't have Mrs. Dornbusch for a choir director.* The irreverent thought brought a reluctant giggle to her throat as she pictured the formidable Elsie Dornbusch running the heavenly host through their paces. *Louder, tenors! I can't hear you! Louder!*

A chorus of mumbled *amen*s rippled through the sanctuary, interrupting her daydream. Gertie Pennington, seated next to Francie in the soprano section, poked her in the shoulder. To her chagrin, she realized that her mind had drifted again, and now the entire congregation sat silent and waiting. The preacher raised a questioning brow to the choir loft in hopeful anticipation. Someone coughed, and Mrs. Dornbusch, from her seat on the piano bench, glared at Francie with a "Come along, Francine, we haven't got all day" scowl on her face.

In a cold panic, Francie shot to her feet, stumbled to the railing, and flipped open her music folder, which chose that moment to slip from her grasp and tumble to the floor of the loft. Sheets of music—hundreds of them, it seemed, although it couldn't have been more than a dozen—exploded across the carpet. Gasps from her fellow choir members and muffled twittering from below resounded as Mrs. Dornbusch's facial expression telegraphed deep disappointment. Francie didn't even dare to glance in Chip's direction, knowing that whatever she'd see on his face—whether amusement or pity or indifference—would only deepen her humiliation.

She knelt and scrambled to collect the sheets and return them to her folder right side up and in the proper order. Gertie bent down to help her, but her fumbling assistance only made things more difficult.

More coughs, a few giggles, and a muted murmuring drifted up from the congregation.

Rivulets of sweat forked around her temples. At last she stood, found the correct page, gathered what was left of her dignity, and nodded to Mrs. Dornbusch. As the gray-haired woman plunked out the opening notes on the piano, Francie breathed a quick prayer. *Lord, help me. I don't think I can do this.*

All at once, a snippet of Scripture floated into her mind.

I can do all things through Christ which strengtheneth me.

She heard no audible voice, no direct dispatch from Heaven. But to Francie, it felt as if the Lord had said, *You're not singing for Mrs. Dornbusch. You're not singing for Chip or for all these people. You're singing for Me.*

A warm sense of peace settled over her heart. All her nervousness melted away. At the proper moment—not too early, not too late—she lifted her head, drew a deep breath, and opened her mouth.

And the voice that God had given her—the voice that everyone said was much too big and much too soaring to come from a scrawny little thing like her—rang out and filled the room to its farthest corners with glory to the newborn King.

Forty miles away, in a fashionable church in Chicago's Lincoln Park neighborhood, Henry Jasper sat next to his parents and listened to the satin-robed choir sing a complicated arrangement of the "Coventry Carol." While the harmonies were hauntingly beautiful, he found the bleak lyrics about King Herod's senseless violence against the Hebrew babies an odd choice for a Christmas Eve anthem, bringing to mind recent news reports of Belgian babies brutally slaughtered by the

Kaiser's army. The song only served to darken his mood, which was already somber after the conversation that had taken place over dinner that evening.

"A seventy-five in Latin? Seventy-*five*?" his father had sputtered, waving a card bearing Henry's fall-term grades. "Jaspers don't earn a seventy-five. Jaspers don't earn below a ninety."

"Abbott, please," Henry's mother had soothed, with a quick sideways glance at the maid who was serving the turkey. "It's Christmas Eve. Can't you and Henry talk about this later?"

"I suppose so," his father grumbled. "But we *will* talk about it. This discussion is not over."

And it wouldn't be over—not by a long shot—until Abbott Jasper had pontificated at length and Henry had vowed with equal passion to raise his grade. He hoped the issue wouldn't cast a pall over his entire Christmas break from college.

It wasn't that he didn't appreciate the value of Latin, Henry told himself as the minister launched into a homily about the miracle of the nativity. However dead the language might be to the rest of the world, it was alive and well in the field of law, where Henry's future career lay.

It wasn't that he lacked an aptitude for languages, either. He always scored well in German class, for example. To Henry, German seemed reasonable. Its straightforward rules made sense to him. But Latin was proving to be his Waterloo. The grammar, the syntax—all of it seemed much more difficult to grasp than it apparently had been for earlier generations of Jaspers. Henry hated letting his father down, and all those other Jaspers before him, right down to his cousin Oliver who, despite being only a few years older than Henry, outshone him in nearly every way. Oliver was smart, handsome, athletic, and already making a name for himself at the law firm of Jasper and Jasper.

Father didn't need to speak the words aloud for Henry to hear them in his head. *Oliver would never have gotten a seventy-five in Latin.*

To make matters worse, the war raging in Europe continued to distract him from his work. Even though America was neutral in the conflict, a few of his Scoville College classmates had interrupted their studies and gone over to England to fight alongside the Allies. Henry felt torn. Often, on hearing reports of the carnage, he appreciated President Woodrow Wilson's promise to keep America out of the war. But he couldn't help but admire his friends for doing a good and honorable thing, helping to stop the vicious slaughter of innocents, and he was tempted to join them.

He hadn't voiced any of these thoughts to his parents, who'd surely oppose the idea of their only child going off to fight in a war. For the time being, he'd have to stay in school, and to stay in school, he'd have to get a better grasp on his Latin grade.

I'll just have to knuckle down and try harder, he told himself as the immense pipe organ burst into the opening notes of the recessional, "O Come All Ye Faithful." Henry stood with the rest of the congregation and flipped open his hymnal to see they were to sing not the familiar English version, but the Latin one, "Adeste Fideles."

It figures. With a wry smile at the cosmic joke, he joined in the singing.

CHAPTER TWO

After the closing hymn, the Scoville Community sanctuary erupted with activity as worshippers stood, gathered their belongings and their children, and wished each other a merry Christmas. As Francie descended from the choir loft, a few people remarked on her solo and thanked her for singing.

Such positive comments always made her feel both pleased and awkward. While the praise was sincere and she thanked each commenter, it didn't seem quite proper to take credit for an ability she'd been born with, that she'd done nothing to deserve. She said as much to Gertie in the choir room as they changed out of their robes and slipped into their coats and galoshes.

"But you *did* do something," Gertie countered, wrapping a plaid muffler around her neck. "You worked hard to learn the song, and you practiced it over and over again. You always give it your very best."

"I should have memorized it," Francie said. "If I'd memorized it, I wouldn't have needed to hold my folder and wouldn't have created a spectacle by spilling papers all over the place."

"You're too hard on yourself." Gertie shrugged. "Accidents happen. You recovered nicely." Arm in arm, they entered the bustling foyer at the back of the sanctuary, filled with people wishing each other the happiest of holidays. Gertie turned to Francie. "Look, I've got to go home and help Mother get ready for Christmas dinner tomorrow. We're having turkey and all the trimmings. All the cousins are coming and there'll be quite a crowd. What's your family doing?"

"Oh, the usual," Francie murmured. "You know . . . traditions and things." She cast about for a description of the typical Forrester family Christmas that wouldn't sound pathetic to Gertie's ears. But she needn't have bothered, as Gertie's parents and lively brood of siblings came to whisk her away before Francie could elaborate.

"Merry Christmas," Gertie called over her shoulder as they hustled her out the door.

"Same to you," Francie replied with as much festive cheer as she could muster. Then she turned and scanned the diminishing crowd for her brother. To her relief, those golden-haired lovebirds, Chip and Theresa, were nowhere in sight.

"Excuse me, miss. May I speak to you a moment?"

A woman approached whom Francie had never seen before. She was of indeterminate age, youthful but not young, well dressed in a stylish, tailored wool suit and coordinating hat, an ensemble the fashion magazines would call "smart and sophisticated." In other words, she looked nothing like the typical Scoville Community Church congregant.

"Yes, of course." Francie couldn't help but smile. What the woman lacked in physical beauty she made up for with a warm, attractive demeanor that had nothing to do with looks.

"I enjoyed your singing very much," the woman continued. "Do you sing professionally?"

Francie's face heated. "Why, no," she said, flustered. What a question! As far as she knew, Scoville's only opportunities to sing professionally took place in the local taverns. With this in mind she added, "I'm only seventeen."

"Well, then, may I ask who's your teacher?" Francie's thoughts shifted to her days at Scoville High School, which had ended last year when she needed to work full-time to help support the family. Confused, she wondered which teacher the woman was talking about. Her homeroom teacher, Mrs. Styles? Her math teacher, Mr. Grant?

When Francie didn't reply, the woman added, "Your voice teacher?"

Francie started to say she had no voice teacher, then paused.

"That would be Mrs. Dornbusch, I guess."

"Dornbusch?" the woman repeated, frowning, as if trying to place the name.

"Our choir director here at Scoville Community," Francie said. "We didn't have a real music teacher at the high school," she added, feeling sheepish, as if this omission were somehow her fault.

Everything Francie knew about music—even if it didn't amount to very much—she'd learned from Mrs. Dornbusch. During weekly choir practice she'd learned the basics of how to read the notes on a scale, and that *pianissimo* meant quiet and *forte* meant loud and *People! People!* meant the temperamental director was nearing the end of her tether.

Just then her brother came and stood next to her, his gangly limbs protruding awkwardly from his too-tight jacket and too-short trousers. At nearly ten years old, he almost matched her in height.

"Ready to go?" he asked.

"Ready," Francie replied. She turned to the stranger. "It was nice to meet you, Miss . . ."

"Whitworth." The woman extended her gloved hand toward Francie. "Grace Whitworth."

Francie shook her hand. "Francie Forrester. And this is my brother, Will." She sensed the polite thing to do would be to stick around and make small talk with the woman until her friends, or whomever she'd come with, came to fetch her, but no one did.

"Well," Francie said after a minute, "a merry Christmas to you."

The woman smiled. "You also."

"Who was that?" Will asked as they headed down the sidewalk, their boots crunching on the fresh snow.

"I don't know," she replied. "A visitor, I guess. Probably from the city, by the looks of her."

"You sang good tonight," he said.

She bit back her impulse to correct his grammar. Compliments from her brother were a rare treat. So she said only, "Thank you."

He stopped to form a snowball and hurled it at a stop sign. The projectile reached its target and exploded with a soft thud.

"Good shot," Francie said. "And in the dark, no less."

"I'm going to try out for the baseball team in the spring," Will replied confidently.

"You should. I've no doubt you'll make the team."

Will looked pleased at her acknowledgement of his athletic prowess.

When they arrived home, the shabby clapboard house was dark. Apparently, Ramona had gone out for the evening and, once again, failed to leave the porch light on for her children. Worse, in Francie's opinion, was that theirs was practically the only house on the block without Christmas bulbs lighting the window. The house looked desolate and unwelcoming. Francie wished they could return to the light and warmth of the church.

She nudged her brother. "Let's go around back so we don't track snow through the house."

They circled through the side yard and trudged up the unshoveled back steps.

"She oughta be home by now," Will complained. "It's Christmas Eve." He kicked a snow-covered step with his boot.

"She'll be home soon. I'm sure of it," Francie assured him, even though she wasn't sure at all. She pressed her key into the lock. "Tell you what," she said in a hearty voice meant to lift his spirits. "Why don't you and I make hot cocoa and pop some corn, and we'll light the tree and play Christmas music on the Victrola, and I'll read aloud from that old book of Christmas stories you enjoy. Would you like that?"

He brightened a little and nodded.

"All right." Francie pushed open the back door and flicked on the kitchen light. They hung their coats and hats on wall pegs and kicked off their boots, then Francie went immediately to pull milk from the icebox while Will headed for the front room. As she heated the milk in a saucepan and popped corn in a covered skillet, the opening notes of a familiar carol floated from the Victrola. She thanked God that Will wasn't letting their mother's absence dampen his Christmas joy. He'd been so moody lately, she never knew what to expect. With any luck, Ramona would have the sense to make her way home before she and Will went to bed. Whether or not her presence would be a good thing, of course, would depend on how much "Christmas cheer" she'd consumed over the course of the evening.

Francie stirred sugar and cocoa powder into the milk, watching the mixture to make sure it didn't boil. She shook the skillet as the kernels began to pop, and melted butter in a small saucepan. Minutes later she joined Will in the front room. He'd switched on the single string of electric lights adorning their small tree, and they admired it sitting side by side on the sofa, wordlessly sipping cocoa, munching popcorn, and listening to the music. When Francie had drained her mug, she kept her promise and took a book with a worn red cover off the bookshelf. She flipped it open and began to read aloud.

"Marley was dead to begin with. There is no doubt whatever about that."

A few paragraphs in, Will sighed and leaned against her shoulder, and she kissed the top of his head like she used to do when he was small. At nine years old he was almost too big to snuggle with. Almost, but not quite, as long as his friends weren't around to make fun of him.

By the time they'd finished the story and Will had unfolded his lanky self from the sofa and gone to bed, Ramona still hadn't come home. Francie replaced the book on the shelf, put away the record album, carried their mugs and bowl to the kitchen, and washed them in the sink.

Just before going upstairs, she pulled a couple of wrapped presents from their hiding place in a high cupboard and placed them under the tree: a box of bath salts for her mother and a model airplane kit for Will, along with a small bag of candy for each. She'd purchased the gifts at the five-and-dime with her waitressing tips, unsure if Ramona would buy anything and unwilling for Will to have a presentless Christmas.

She reached to switch off the tree lights, then changed her mind. It was Christmas Eve, after all. And even if it would add a few more cents to the electric bill, the soft glow would greet their mother whenever she finally made it home, and keep her from stumbling in the darkness.

CHAPTER THREE

JANUARY 1916

In the steam-heated stillness of the empty restaurant, Francie paused while filling salt shakers to gaze out the large plate-glass window that faced Main Street. The giant electric "Café Figaro" sign blazing above the door cast an eerie blue glow over the snowdrifts lining the deserted sidewalk. Huge white flakes swirled madly around the streetlamps as a lone figure lumbered past the window, huddled against the wind. Francie's spirit lifted momentarily with the hope that perhaps the pedestrian would come inside for a bite to eat, or even just to warm up, and the entire evening's shift wouldn't have been wasted, after all.

But the moment was short-lived as the woolly creature continued on his way. Francie's shoulders drooped. Who was she kidding? There'd be no customers tonight. Tuesdays tended to be quiet at the best of times. And who'd dare to venture out during a storm like this without a darn good reason?

She caught her reflection in the darkened glass. Staring back at her was a skinny girl wearing a pink-and-white aproned uniform with a ludicrous frilly white cap perched atop her dark brown curls. She sighed, then straightened and chided herself. She ought to be grateful for her uniform. After all, it wasn't any worse than what every other waitress in town was expected to wear. Besides, having a uniform meant she could spend less money on clothes. Fewer clothes for herself meant more cash for necessities, like new trousers for Will, who'd been sprouting up like the proverbial weed.

Francie paused, waiting for the sense of peace and contentment such a self-sacrificing attitude was supposed to bring, according to the pastor. When no such feeling came, she allowed her shoulders to sag. Clearly her peace-and-contentment muscle needed strengthening.

As she resumed filling the salt shakers, the mingled scents of garlic, fennel, and basil wafting from the kitchen made her stomach rumble. The growling was practically the only noise in the room, apart from the hiss and clang of the steam radiators, punctuated by an occasional metallic bang emanating from the kitchen. She began humming a tuneful aria from *Carmen* to dispel the silence and cheer herself up. Her employer, Mr. Figaro, had lent her a thick 78-r.p.m. recording of the famous opera. She knew only snippets of the story set in far-off Spain, and could only mimic the French lyrics, likely mangling them. But the peppy melody lifted her spirits.

The kitchen door swung open and Guiseppe Figaro, the restaurant's owner and chef, poked his leonine head into the room.

"Still nobody?" He glanced around the sea of empty tables as though Francie might have neglected to tell him a hungry customer had arrived, chilled to the bone and eager for a steaming bowl of his locally renowned minestrone soup.

"Not a soul," Francie assured him. "I guess the storm's keeping everyone at home tonight."

"I'm afraid you are right," Mr. Figaro conceded sadly, his vowels heavily seasoned with the accent of his native Italy. "Why you no go home early, Francesca? If some poor soul does wander in, I take care of him myself."

Francie liked when Mr. Figaro called her Francesca. It sounded more intriguing than Francine, like one of those illustrations in *McCall's* magazine of stylish women wearing fashionably narrow skirts and crimped hair. Like the strange woman she'd met at church on Christmas Eve and hadn't seen again since.

She considered her boss's tempting offer for a moment, then remembered that her mother was entertaining a guest that evening—the latest in her string of male companions. Masculine attention was never lacking when it came to Ramona Forrester.

Francie shook her head and unscrewed the top of a saltshaker.

"No, thanks. I'd be just as happy to stay here. Ramona is hosting company tonight." She cast a meaningful glance in his direction.

"Ah." Mr. Figaro nodded in comprehension. They'd talked about Francie's challenging relationship with her mother on previous occasions. "Your mama, she is well?"

Francie shrugged. "Same as usual. She stayed in bed all morning, and I had to give Will his breakfast and make sure he had everything he needed for school. She felt better in the afternoon, though. At least, well enough to keep her date tonight."

"At the greengrocer yesterday, I overhear somebody say she has a new friend. That fellow, Mr. Bailey, who owns the automobile shop."

Francie's chest filled with outrage. "I wish people in this town would learn to mind their own business and find something else to talk about besides my family." Then, remembering who she was talking to, she immediately relented. "I'm sorry, Mr. Figaro. I didn't mean you."

"Is all right," Mr. Figaro said kindly. "Is none of my business." He made a gesture of sealing his lips and tossing away the imaginary key.

Francie pressed her lips together, frustrated at herself for her outburst. The trouble was, it was not just a rumor. The automobile man was sitting in the Forrester front room at that very moment, keeping company with Ramona. And Francie hated the whole idea. She wished her mother would act like other mothers, content to spend evenings reading or sewing or playing Snakes and Ladders with her and Will instead of frequenting The Thirsty Swallow, where she met the likes of Mr. Bailey. And the fellow before him. And the other fellows, all the way back to Will's father, and even Francie's.

As if to change the subject, Mr. Figaro's expression changed to mock dismay. "And why is this, always 'Mr. Figaro, Mr. Figaro'? How many times I tell you, call me Guiseppe, like everyone else? We are friends, no?"

"Yes, Mr. Fig—I mean, Guiseppe." Francie's face warmed. She liked her jovial employer very much, but it felt strange to her to call a man practically old enough to be her grandfather—and her employer, no less—by his first name. It seemed disrespectful somehow. Overly familiar. But, always eager to please, she meant to try.

Names had significance. Francie had been named after a shadowy figure named Franklin Forrester, who had vanished forever very early in her life. Her mother, a teenage beauty herself at the time and thoroughly unprepared to bring up a child on her own, had insisted her young daughter call her by her first name, Ramona, instead of Mama or Mother, thereby giving the impression they were sisters rather than parent and child.

Not that anyone in Scoville was fooled, least of all the sharp-tongued gossips who gathered in small, whispering groups to discuss the unseemly antics of Ramona Forrester.

Will's father's name was Sprague, but Ramona continued to use Forrester after Will was born. Francie was grateful they at least shared the same last name, other familial bonds seeming flimsy at best.

Suddenly Mr. Figaro's face visibly brightened. "I almost forgot. Wait here. I got something that will cheer you up."

He vanished back into the kitchen and returned a moment later carrying a folded sheet of paper, which he handed to Francie. "Some kid give me this when I walk past the college today. Looks like something you'd like, no?"

Francie unfolded the sheet. Beneath a grainy photograph of a pigeon-chested woman wearing a plumed hat and a dignified expression, the name "Beatrice de Bonneville" appeared in bold type, followed by details of a recital the acclaimed soprano would be giving the following Sunday afternoon in Piper Hall, the auditorium of Scoville College. The purpose of the event was to raise funds for victims of the previous summer's disastrous *Eastland* capsizing in Chicago, in which over eight hundred people had died.

Francie's heart skipped a beat. Beatrice de Bonneville, the world-famous opera singer! Right here in Scoville!

Then she noticed the ticket price.

Swallowing back her disappointment, she refolded the paper and held it toward her employer.

"Thank you for showing it to me."

His large hands made a sweeping motion. "No, you keep, you keep. You *go*. A live concert, much better than Victrola machine, no?" His dark eyes, crinkled at the corners from his habitual smile, regarded Francie tenderly. "Maybe hearing this Signora de Bonneville in person will inspire you to follow in her footsteps."

Francie snorted. "Me, become an opera singer? That'll be the day."

Mr. Figaro's expression turned serious. "A voice like yours, it is a gift from God," he admonished. "It should be used to bless others, not hidden away in some, how you say, one-mule town."

Francie smiled in spite of herself. "One-horse town. But one mule works too, I suppose." She looked at the flyer. "If it weren't for the college, Scoville would have no culture at all."

Mr. Figaro pointed an accusing finger at her. "Now you are chang-ing subject. I know you love opera. You borrow all my records."

"I do love opera," Francie said. "Listening to it. But singing it—why, singing opera takes training, and training costs money and time." If she'd learned nothing else from her avid reading of *Opera News*, borrowed from the public library, she'd learned that vocal train-ing was both necessary for any aspiring opera singer, and prohibitively expensive. "Not to mention there are no opera companies in Scoville," she added drily.

He shrugged. "So you move to Chicago. You are young and strong. And you have extraordinary voice. A voice that should be heard by everyone."

She shifted, uncomfortable under his praise.

He pointed again, this time toward the tin ceiling. "Francesca, God gave you that voice. Why you no ask Him how He would like you to use it?" He tapped the flyer in her hand. "In the meantime, stop being foolish and go to that concert. Enjoy."

Outwardly, Francie remained calm, but inside grew a fever of an-ticipation. Opportunities to hear a world-class talent like Beatrice de Bonneville, live and in person, did not come along every day. Especially to someone like Francie. But what would be the point of going? It would only remind her of the glittering musical career she dreamed about but could never have. Besides, she couldn't possibly afford the ticket.

"I'd love to, but . . ." She stopped herself from mentioning the ticket price to her employer, lest he think she was complaining about her wage. He was a generous man. It wasn't his fault that Will was outgrowing all his clothes.

Mr. Figaro lifted his hands. "Whatsa matter? You no work on Sunday." He sounded frustrated, as if Francie were deliberately misunderstanding him.

"I know. Thank you. *Grazie*," she said with a warm rush of immense gratitude toward her boss, the only person who never scoffed or teased her about her dream. She pressed the flyer to her aproned bodice. "I promise to think about it."

"Always thinking." Mr. Figaro shook his head with a what-am-I-going-to-do-with-you expression on his face. "You think too much, Francesca. Sometimes you just gotta *do*."

But there was nothing to think about. When he disappeared back into the kitchen, she crumpled the flyer in her fist and tossed it into the wastebasket. As kind as he had been to think of her, there was no way she could afford the ticket. She had expenses. Responsibilities. Her little household was barely scraping by as it was, and the little bit Ramona brought in from odd jobs here and there didn't help much. By the time the groceries were bought and the rent and the electric were paid and Will had a decent set of clothes that fit his fast-growing body, there was little left over for frivolities like concert tickets.

Even so, as she emptied the coffee urn later that evening, she caught a glimpse of the crumpled flyer and couldn't quite bring herself to bury it in damp coffee grounds. She fished it out and shoved it deep into her apron pocket, where it would likely remain until washday, by which time she would have long forgotten about Beatrice de Bonneville.

CHAPTER FOUR

S everal blocks away, near the ivy-draped campus of Scoville College, Henry Jasper huddled over the scarred wooden desk in his
drafty room at Mrs. Baker's ramshackle boarding house, trying his
best to cram his brain full of Latin vocabulary while ignoring his
scratchy throat and congested head. The plaid wool blanket wrapped
tightly around his shoulders proved wholly inadequate against the
January winds that rattled the window and gusted in through small
gaps in the frame. Snorting with the effort of breathing, Henry cast a
longing glance toward his tidy bed and wished he could crawl under
the covers to die, like some slithering marine creature. But alas, death
was not imminent—it was just a common head cold, after all, no
matter how miserable he felt—while Monday morning's Latin test
loomed large. Professor Ames's examinations were notoriously brutal,
and Henry needed to maintain top grades or risk a repeat of the
paternal dressing-down that had taken place at Christmas break.

Henry cringed at the memory, blew his nose with a honk, and
returned his bleary gaze to the text before him.

From the floor below came the sudden slam of the front door. A
cacophony of male voices blasted up the stairs, followed by pounding footsteps. The door to his room burst open and in surged three
high-spirited classmates.

"Look alive, Jasper. Put down those books and guess the news," said the tall, dark-haired one as he collapsed on Henry's bed. "You'll never guess."

"Then tell me, Greeley." Irritated, Henry set down his pen and twisted in his chair to face the group. "Why do you all look so jubilant? Did you steal Augustana's mascot again?"

Paul Greeley grinned. "Brockton here has asked his fair Peggy for her hand in marriage, and she has accepted."

A general whoop went up, and Pete Brockton's normally pale face reddened with pleasure as his companions clapped him on the back for likely the umpteenth time that evening. Henry pulled himself to his feet and faced his friend.

"Congratulations, Brockton," he rasped. "I'd shake your hand, but I have the most miserable cold and don't wish to pass it on. Please excuse me, and accept my heartiest good wishes to you and Miss Parker. Hope she knows what she's getting into."

"The miracle is that she said yes," Paul joshed, slapping Pete Brockton on the back. "Women are a mystery, eh?"

"Sure are. The best kind of mystery." Pete beamed, looking as if he might levitate at any moment. Henry's chest tightened with a feeling of—of what? Envy? Surely not. Peggy Parker was a nice enough girl, but intent on raising his grades, Henry had no time or inclination for frivolities like romance. He thumped his chest and coughed.

"Gads, Jasper, you sound awful. What'd you do, swallow ground glass?" said Bob Miller, a stocky young man wearing a v-neck sweater and wool scarf.

"Feels like it," Henry croaked.

Bob frowned. "Maybe you'd better call it quits for tonight and hit the hay."

"Can't," Henry said. "Big test Monday in Ames's class. Say, Greeley, you're in that class. Shouldn't you be studying, too?"

Paul grinned from his perch on the bed and tapped his forehead with an index finger. "I've got it all down pat, see?" Then he placed his hand over his heart and fluttered his eyelashes in a comical way. "*Amare, amo, amatum.* To love, I love, beloved." He sprang to his feet and poked Brockton in the ribs, launching a fresh round of hilarity.

"Well, I *don't* have it down pat," Henry muttered, "so if you'll excuse me . . ."

"You get better, old thing," Paul said. "We need you in top shape for the big game next week."

"You heard the man, gentlemen," Bob said firmly, nudging the men toward the door. "Let's clear out so he can study. And get some rest."

"We'll be right down the hall," said Brockton as they all crowded into the hallway. "Picked up a cherry pie at the bakery to celebrate this momentous occasion. Come join us when you take a break."

Henry nodded. Normally he loved any excuse for a party, but in his current state of misery, cherry pie sounded about as appealing as wood glue on toast. He shut the door behind his friends and slumped back at his desk. He found it impossible to concentrate, however, as the men's boisterous laughter continued to float down the hall, soon followed by the twang of Bob's ukelele and a rousing chorus of "Peg O' My Heart."

With an exasperated groan, Henry gathered his books and papers and shoved them into a leather satchel. Then he shrugged off the plaid blanket, put on his coat and gloves, and headed downstairs to the snow-covered street.

Where could a fellow go to find some peace and quiet? The library and student union were closed at that hour, but Henry remembered a small restaurant on Main Street that stayed open late. He tightened his scarf and trudged the few blocks to downtown Scoville, head bowed against the howling wind, boots crunching on the snowy sidewalk.

Main Street, eerily void of pedestrians, glowed under the bright electric lights of Café Figaro. Henry yanked open the glass door. A blast of warm air greeted him, spiced with the enticing aromas of garlic and onion. Even with a stuffy head he could smell that much, and felt oddly comforted. Before him lay a sea of empty tables covered in blue-and-white gingham oilcloth. The place was deserted, except for a pretty brown-haired waitress wearing pink and white, who greeted him with a cheerful smile.

"Sit anywhere you like," she called from a corner station where she was stacking plates into a cupboard. "Nasty night out there, isn't it? Can I get you some coffee? Won't take but a minute to brew some fresh."

Henry grunted his assent and chose a corner table that looked relatively private, so that even if other customers showed up, he could study in peace. He reached into his satchel and pulled out his Latin grammar book. A few minutes later, the waitress set a steaming cup of coffee before him, along with a glass of water. She pulled a pad and pencil from the pocket of her uniform.

"Cream and sugar are on the table. What else can I get you?"

"This will do nicely, thank you." Henry croaked, lifting the coffee cup from the saucer. He tried to take a sip, but sputtered as he hacked loudly. "I beg your pardon," he gasped. He set the cup back down and cleared his throat.

"Say, you don't sound too well." Her gaze was warm with sympathy. "Maybe you should have a bowl of soup, as well. It's minestrone tonight."

"No, thank you. Just coffee."

"Are you sure? Owner's secret recipe," she coaxed, flashing a dimple. "Best soup within fifty miles. And they say it's excellent medicine for a cold."

Henry gave her a wan smile. "Sounds tempting, but I'm afraid I only brought enough money for coffee."

"Alrighty. You let me know if you need anything else." She flipped the pad closed and slid it into her pocket.

Henry thanked her and swallowed another sip, more successfully this time. Ignoring his textbook for the moment, he slid a glance to the waitress, who'd returned to stacking plates. Her dark hair was gathered into a topknot under a ridiculous frilly hat, but a few curly tendrils escaped here and there. She bore an expression that hinted she was always on the verge of bursting into a smile. She had the kind of face that made a fellow feel warm inside on a bitter night.

With reluctance, he returned his attention to his grammar book. Another coughing fit seized him and he shot his hand for the water glass, embarrassed. Jeepers, she was going to think he was some sort of consumptive.

The waitress disappeared into the kitchen. Moments later she reappeared at the table bearing a thick white bowl of dark red, tomatoey-looking soup. She set it before Henry, along with a small plate of soda crackers, a spoon, and a napkin.

"Here you go," she said. "It's on the house."

Henry recoiled slightly. "Oh, you don't have to do that."

"It wasn't me." She jerked her head toward the kitchen. "The cook insists."

He stared down at the bowl. "Tell me the flavor again."

"Minestrone. Trust me, it's delish." Henry started to protest again, but she cut him off. "Hush now. Eat up."

Humbly he laid the napkin on his lap. "Thank you, miss."

She pointed to her nametag. "Francie. Francie Forrester."

"How do you do, Francie. I'm Henry Jasper."

"Nice to meet you, Henry." She nudged the bowl toward him. "Eat up, now." She smiled and returned to her task.

He obeyed and lifted the spoon. The steam eased his breathing and the hot soup slid soothingly down his aching throat. He grunted in satisfaction and took another spoonful while glancing at his textbook.

Seco, secare, secui, sec—

All at once the room filled with the most beautiful sound he'd ever heard. A voice exquisite enough to make him abandon his Latin verbs and sit back in wonder.

The waitress, over in the corner, had started softly singing a song that was growing in popularity on campus.

"Keep the home fires burning, while your hearts are yearning . . ."

And Henry, who'd listened to plenty of singers in his lifetime, swore he'd never heard a voice as sweet and melodic as hers.

CHAPTER FIVE

W hen Francie finished stacking the plates, she began sorting silverware, feeling more cheerful than she had in weeks. Every once in a while, she glanced over at the lone customer. Poor thing shouldn't be out on a night like this with a cold like that. He must not be married, or he wouldn't be sitting in her restaurant on a stormy night, hunched over a bowl of soup. He'd be at home, being fussed over by a caring wife. Probably didn't have a mother to care for him, either. No wife, no mother. So good-looking, too, with honey-colored hair and that cleft in his chin.

Francie's heart tugged, just thinking of the poor, ailing, good-looking man with no woman to take care of him, which brought to her mind a popular, sentimental tune about soldiers, and before she knew it, she'd abandoned *Carmen* for "Keep the Home Fires Burning," the latest hit from Tin Pan Alley.

Singing came as naturally as breathing to Francie. Music of all kinds gave her joy, especially opera, and she almost couldn't help but sing whenever a tune popped into her head. Blessed with what a schoolteacher had once called an extraordinary set of pipes, she sang at home, at work, even while walking down the street. Fortunately for her, Mr. Figaro enjoyed hearing her sing as she went about her work, not least because the customers also enjoyed it. That was a blessing, because

Francie didn't think she would be able to stop even if he told her to. Ever since she was a little girl, singing had helped ease her way through life, especially through the hard parts.

As she neared the end of the song, Mr. Figaro poked his head out of the kitchen and blended his rich tenor voice with hers.

"There's a silver lining, through the dark clouds shining, turn the dark clouds inside out, 'til the boys come *booome*."

Then he gave her a wink and disappeared back into the kitchen. She laughed.

A sudden clapping startled her.

"Well done!" Henry rasped from his table in the corner. "That was absolutely magnificent."

She felt her cheeks turn crimson as she strolled toward his table. "It's a pretty song, isn't it? Makes me think about all those soldiers fighting over in Europe."

He grimaced. "If you believe what you read in the papers, American soldiers will soon be fighting over there as well. There's talk of a draft."

She wrapped her arms around herself, suddenly chilled. "I hope it won't come to that. Mr. Wilson promised to keep us out of it." Even though Will was too young to be drafted, she couldn't help but wince at the thought of other people's brothers, sons, and sweethearts being called up.

"Well, it looks like the Allies might need our help in putting an end to things."

Francie didn't reply. She didn't want to talk about the war, even with this appealing stranger. Her peaceful mood unsettled, she returned to her task, humming a very different tune, a comforting ditty about taking a train to a warm, sunny place far away.

"How about a refill on that soup?"

Absorbed in his Latin grammar, Henry realized with a start that the singing had stopped and the songbird was standing over him, asking a question that apparently required an answer.

"Sorry?"

She repeated her offer.

"Thank you," he rasped, handing her the empty bowl. "It's very good. At least I *think* it is. My taste buds aren't in great shape right now. In any case, you were right about the healing powers. I'm already feeling much better." He grinned at her as she took the bowl from him. Somehow her kindly manner made him feel . . . loved. He blushed inwardly at the presumption. *Loved* was too strong a word. *Cared for*—that was the idea he was searching for. This waitress, a complete stranger, somehow made him feel cared for.

And Henry hadn't felt cared for in a very long time.

"I see you like to read." She nodded toward his book. "So do I. I'm halfway through the latest Mary Roberts Rinehart. Have you read *The Circular Stair*?"

"I'm afraid not," he admitted, surprised to find himself wishing he had.

"Well, it's a good story. What is it you're reading?"

"Oh, this." He glanced scornfully at his textbook. "This is in Latin."

"Latin!" Francie threw her head back with a spray of laughter. "You must be very smart. If I were capable of learning another language, I don't think it would be Latin."

He closed the book, marking his place with a finger.

"No? What language would you choose?"

"Italian," she said firmly. "It's the language of music. All the best operas are written in Italian. It even *sounds* musical. I-tal-i-AN-a. Spa-GHET-ti," she breathed in an overly dramatic accent. "Par-ma-GIA-na."

He laughed, which sent him into a coughing fit. When he got his breath back, he said, "Italian has a lot in common with Latin, you know. And hearing you just now, it sounds to me as if you're speaking it already."

She blushed prettily. "My boss, Mr. Figaro, is Italian, and so is the man who delivers fruits and vegetables. They've both been teaching me a few words here and there. They knew each other back in Italy. Both from the same village. The fruit man's wife is still over there, and he's trying to save enough money to pay her passage to America."

Henry marveled that this young woman seemed to take an interest in everyone, even tradesmen. And sickly customers.

"Well, you make a good case for learning Italian," he said, "but unfortunately, I need to pass Latin in order to graduate."

All at once a shadow passed over her face, like a cloud drifting across a glowing moon. Her smile dimmed.

"Graduate?" A little crease formed between her eyebrows. "Oh, I get it. You're a student. At the college, I suppose." She jerked her head in the general direction of the campus.

"Yes. I'm studying pre-law. Hence the Latin," he replied, thrown off balance by her unexpected change of demeanor. A look of disappointment crossed her pretty face, and he felt his defenses go up. Well, who had she thought he was, anyway, other than a student, with his Latin grammar book and his ink-stained fingers?

"I see." Her manner turned prim. "Well, I'd better go and refill your soup." But all the sunshine had gone out of her voice. She sounded dejected, as if a lovely present had been abruptly snatched out of her hands.

Watching her retreating back, Henry suffered a brief moment of dismay. *What did I say?*

Then he shrugged, wheezed a little, and opened his book. His friends were right. Women were a mystery, impossible to understand. That was all there was to it. No sense in even trying to figure them out.

And he needed to concentrate on his Latin test if he didn't want another nasty confrontation with his father. That trumped even a pretty girl with an angel's voice.

CHAPTER SIX

Francie burst through the swinging door into the kitchen and clattered the soup bowl onto the counter.

"There is a fire that you make such a racket?" Mr. Figaro paused in wiping down the grill to glance over his shoulder at Francie. "Whatsa matter with you?"

"Nothing," she muttered, disappointment flooding through her. She picked up the bowl, stomped over to the big kettle on the stove, and lifted the lid.

"Use a clean bowl, please," Mr. Figaro reminded her. He wiped his hands on his formerly white apron. "He like my soup?"

"Everyone likes your soup." Somehow the statement sounded more like an accusation than a compliment.

"At least we got a customer."

"Only one." She dropped the empty bowl in the sink, took a fresh bowl from a cupboard, and ladled soup into it. Then she slammed it onto a tray, not caring that it sloshed a little.

Mr. Figaro lifted one thick eyebrow. "One is better than none, no?"

"One who can barely afford a cup of coffee."

He turned back to the grill. "So whatsa matter, *cara mia*?"

"He's a *college* man." Disdain dripped from her words. "Studying to be a *lawyer*, of all the pretentious . . ." She didn't bother finishing her thought.

"Ah. I see." He slid her a sidelong glance. "Lawyers are not all bad. Once in a while, they come in very handy."

"I don't mind lawyers," Francie clarified. "I mind college men."

He lifted his hands. "They are not all bad either, you know, college men. Some of them are quite nice, in fact. Like my nephew Carlo, for instance, whom you have yet to meet, even though I think you two would, how you say, hit it off."

Francie tossed him a baleful look as she replaced the lid on the kettle. "College men are bad news. They're all a bunch of stuck-up snobs. Spoiled, too. That fellow out there has probably never done an honest day's work in his life."

Beneath his salt-and-pepper mustache, Mr. Figaro's lips twitched, betraying his effort to suppress a smile. "They are all like that? Every last one of them?" Then, more seriously, "Francesca, you must not judge the whole bushel by one bad orange."

"Apple. One bad apple." She caught the twinkle in her boss's dark eyes and giggled in spite of herself.

He shook his finger. "One day soon, *cara*, you will wake up and you will never think of that boy again."

"What boy?" She avoided his gaze.

Mr. Figaro's face broke into a wide grin. "You see? Already it happens."

His sonorous laugh mingled with her reluctant giggle, but she knew exactly to whom he referred. Chip. She would never forget the shabby way he'd treated her. Never, never, never. And she would never give another college man the time of day, either. Not even a nice one with dimples. *Especially* not a nice one with dimples.

Resigned to her disappointment, she opened a tin of crackers and set a few on a plate.

"You take a jar of this good soup home with you when you go," Mr. Figaro instructed. "And a loaf of bread. And a few cookies for your brother." He shrugged. "Will be stale tomorrow anyway."

"Thank you. *Grazie*." Francie cracked open the door and peeked around it. She watched the customer's square shoulders shake as he coughed, and felt compassion in spite of herself. She sighed and hoisted her tray. "But first, I'd better take this soup out to College Boy," she said. "He's in a bad way."

"Wait, Francesca!" Mr. Figaro called.

She turned. "What is it?"

He hurried toward her, carrying a jar. "The cheese," he admonished as he sprinkled ivory-colored flakes onto the surface of the soup. "You forget always to add the *parmagiana*. Is no good without."

Francie wordlessly served Henry his soup, then found other small tasks to do to keep her away from his table. But she kept glancing back to observe him. Toward the end of the evening, when he closed his book and stood, she was surprised to see how tall he was, and how muscular. With all his wheezing and coughing, she'd gotten the mistaken impression that he was a weakling. Well, maybe he wasn't weak. In fact, he was pretty easy on the eyes. But he was a college man, and unlikely to leave a poor townie girl with anything more than a heart crushed under the weight of disappointment.

And probably a head cold to boot.

CHAPTER SEVEN

B y the time College Boy had paid for his coffee and left, and Francie had helped Mr. Figaro close up the restaurant, it was nearly eleven o'clock. The snowstorm had passed, and snow crunched beneath her boots as she trudged down empty downtown streets. In spite of her sour mood, she had to admit the white stuff was pretty, sparkling diamond-like in the glow of the streetlamps.

Rounding a corner into a residential area, she observed two stalwart, muffler-swathed homeowners shoveling their front walkways. She imagined the other neighbors tucked snugly in their beds until morning, which is where she longed to be. Shoveling their own sidewalk could wait until tomorrow. Nobody'd be coming or going any more tonight.

She spoke too soon. In front of her own house, a black Stutz-Bearcat sat parked at the curb, its wheels buried deeply in a snowdrift. A prickle of irritation ran up her spine. Not only was her mother's visitor still inside, but now he'd likely have trouble leaving.

It wasn't that she disliked Mr. Bailey, exactly. She didn't know him well enough to either like or dislike him. She had no feelings toward him one way or another. He was just one more in a string of her mother's boyfriends who was unlikely to stick around longer than a few weeks or months, thus not worth taking the trouble to get to know.

His one distinguishing characteristic was that he sold automobiles, a fairly recent phenomenon to reach Scoville, and talked about them incessantly—which was the only reason she could identify the black sedan as a Stutz-Bearcat.

Too weary to greet Mr. Bailey and exchange insincere pleasantries, but too cold to wait outside for him to leave, she walked around to the back of the house and slipped into the darkened kitchen as noiselessly as possible without turning on a light.

"Hiya!"

Francie nearly hit the ceiling. At the kitchen table sat Will in his pajamas, a milk mustache gracing his mischievous grin.

"Don't scare me like that," she hissed, placing a hand over her thumping heart. She glanced toward the front room, where scratchy dance music played on the Victrola. "Why are you sitting here in the dark? And what are you doing up? It's late. You should be in bed."

"Couldn't sleep."

"I'm not surprised, with that racket going on." She shrugged out of her coat and scarf and hung them on pegs near the door. From her bag she pulled out the containers of food Mr. Figaro had given her and put them away for tomorrow's supper. Then she turned to her brother. "Have you eaten something besides cookies tonight?"

"I made some milk toast earlier."

"All right. Come on, then. To bed with both of us."

Together they climbed the stairs leading from the kitchen to the upper floor amid shadows cast by a wall sconce. Francie paused outside the bathroom.

"I'll wait while you brush your teeth."

"I already did."

"You just had a snack. Better brush them again."

"Aw." He shuffled into the bathroom. When he emerged, she accompanied him to his bedroom, waited while he crawled into bed, then tucked the blankets under his chin as if he were a small boy. She perched on the side of the bed.

"Did you remember to say your prayers?"

He nodded.

"All right, then. I'll stay until you're asleep."

He closed his eyes. She brushed a lock of hair from his forehead, then moved to a nearby chair on which his half-finished model airplane sat. She set the toy on the dresser and folded a stray sweater that had been tossed there. As she did so, she frowned. The sweater carried a strong scent of tobacco. Their mother did smoke the occasional cigarette in the house, but this smelled stronger, and Francie hoped Will's friends weren't pressuring him to smoke. She made a mental note to talk to him about it in the morning.

As the laughter downstairs crested and ebbed and swelled again, she walked to the window and idly traced the lacy frost patterns decorating the windowpane, sparkling white crystals illuminated by the moon. Her thoughts, however, were not on her mother and Mr. Bailey, nor Will, nor the frost, but on the evening's events and on one customer in particular. She wondered if he, too, was awake at this very minute, looking at the moon from his bedroom at the college. The lyrics to one of her very favorite arias, from the opera *Rusalka*, popped into her mind.

Moon, tell me, where is my lover?

She shook her head and drew back from the window. *Hoo boy. What nonsense*, she sternly chided herself. *Ridiculous. I'll likely never see him again, which is just as well. Remember Chip? All his pretty words and empty promises? Ramona's right. College men are bad news.*

But she couldn't seem to stop thinking about him. She sat on the chair for a while, listening to Will's even breathing. Then she noticed the dance music had stopped drifting up from the front room. Minutes later, the muffled scraping of a shovel came from the street below the window, accompanied by a goodly amount of masculine muttering. Then the cranking of the motor and a few false starts. More muttering. Eventually, the automobile's engine sputtered to life. She waited until its rumble faded, then emerged from Will's bedroom and went down to the kitchen where her mother was rinsing glasses at the sink.

Ramona turned at her approach. "Where ya been, out so late?" she asked. "I was gettin' worried."

Francie doubted that. She could tell by her mother's breath and glassy eyes that she and her visitor had been drinking. Probably heavily.

"I was working." *Someone in this house has to*, she thought but did not say. Sarcasm never improved any situation. Ramona tried her best to keep the family afloat, although she had drifted from job to job for most of Francie's life, never staying at one place of business very long. Currently, she was between jobs, having lost her most recent position at the drugstore for taking too many days off, though she brought in a little money by singing at The Thirsty Swallow on the nights the clientele was sufficient to make it worthwhile. She was a regular fixture at the tavern anyway, might as well make it pay off.

"I got a delicate constitution," she often told Francie, and anyone else who inquired. "I need lotsa rest."

But Francie suspected her "delicate constitution" had more to do with how much she drank and how late she stayed out than how much rest she needed.

"Well, ya shoulda come in and said good-night to Mr. Bailey," Ramona said now, her words slurring together. She patted her bright, bottle-red hair and yawned. "It was rude of ya not to. Clarence woulda liked ta see ya."

So he was "Clarence" now. "Next time," Francie promised without enthusiasm. "Here, I'll finish washing up. You go on to bed."

As her mother weaved up the stairs, none too quietly, Francie finished rinsing the glasses, then went into the front room, where smoke lingered from Mr. Bailey's cigar. Eyes watering, she cracked open a window to let in some brisk, chilly air. She picked up the daily newspaper lying folded on an end table and carried it upstairs, turning out lights as she went. Passing his room, she peeked in at Will, who appeared to be sleeping peacefully. She slipped into his darkened bedroom and adjusted his covers. Then she went to her own room, got ready for bed, and crawled underneath the blanket.

In the circle of light from her bedside lamp, she leafed through the newspaper, skimming the stories about town council meetings, rummage sales, and bridge parties that qualified as news in the *Scoville Scoop*, until she came to the arts page.

She bolted upright, all sleepiness gone. Displayed prominently on the arts page was a celebrity interview with Beatrice de Bonneville, published in anticipation of the upcoming concert. Eagerly Francie devoured the article. Interviewed by the newspaper's music critic, the famous singer went on at some length about her favorite roles and memorable stage anecdotes, then offered wisdom that Francie supposed was meant to be encouraging.

I give lots of advice to young singers, the article quoted her as saying. *Talent is necessary, but it's not enough. You must practice, practice, practice. Work hard every day. Take lessons. Expand your repertoire.*

Francie tossed the newspaper aside in frustration, turned off the lamp, and punched her pillow. How she would love to take singing lessons and practice, practice, practice and expand her repertoire, whatever that was. *If only*, she whispered into the darkness. If only it were possible for a girl like her to sing on a stage, with an orchestra, alongside the likes of stars like Beatrice de Bonneville and Florence Easton and Luisa Tetrazzini.

Closing her eyes, she vowed she would work hard, harder than anybody, if ever she were given the chance. Mr. Figaro seemed firmly convinced that God had given her the gift of an extraordinary singing voice. Francie agreed that her voice was a gift from God. But why had He given it to her, if He didn't intend her to use it, except at church under the disheartening direction of Mrs. Dornbusch?

For a long time, she lay in the dark. Sleep eluded her. At last she gave up, switched on the lamp, and picked up the newspaper to reread the interview, desperate to find some bit of hope, some morsel of encouragement, in the great diva's words. She found none.

Coming to the end of the article, she skimmed the details of Sunday's recital, most of which she already knew from Mr. Figaro's flyer, including the astronomical ticket price. However, this time she noticed an additional line that hadn't appeared on the flyer: *College students, half-price.*

Half price! She could afford, even if just barely, a ticket at half price. But she wasn't a college student. Technically.

Snuggling back under the covers, she thought through this new wrinkle. True, she wasn't a college student. But she was the same age as the students. She looked like one of them. She talked like them, more or less. Could definitely pass as one of them.

Just before drifting off to sleep, she hatched her plan. She would go to the recital on Sunday, pretend she was a college student, buy a ticket at half price, and then bask in the luminous presence and resounding pipes of Beatrice de Bonneville. Guilt over the fact that she'd be lying about her status pricked her conscience.

What would happen if she were found out? But how would she be? It was a risk worth taking.

CHAPTER EIGHT

On Friday evening Henry, having largely recovered from his illness, returned to Café Figaro under the pretext of having a taste for spaghetti. In reality it was to see Francie and figure out if he'd actually said something that offended her, or if she was simply mercurial in temperament, as many women were—although he had to take that last part on faith, not having a great deal of experience with women.

Though the restaurant was busier than it had been on his earlier visit, there were still several empty tables, so he didn't feel awkward about occupying one all to himself. He chose a booth at the back, near the kitchen. His stomach growled. He'd come prepared to order a full meal this time, and to leave a handsome tip, to show that he wasn't some poor student mooching off the restaurant staff's generosity.

Two waitresses were on duty, and Henry was relieved when Francie approached his table. Not that the other one, whose nametag read Sofia, didn't seem perfectly nice, but it was Francie he'd come to see.

"Good evening," she said with chilly politeness. "Would you care for a menu? Or are you only here to drink coffee and use our restaurant as your own personal study hall?"

He gave her an earnest gaze. "Look, Francie. Whatever I said the other night that made you upset—I apologize. I didn't mean it." Especially since he had no idea what it was.

"I'm not upset." Her voice was cool, calm. "You and I aren't well enough acquainted for me to care one way or another about anything you'd say."

"But I'd *like* to get better acquainted," he insisted. "Please, can't we start over?"

"You're welcome to stay here as long as you like, but I have no time to chitchat." She looked at him, pencil poised. "Are you ready to order?"

"What's your favorite thing on the menu?"

"Mine?" She shrugged. "I don't know. Everything's good. Fettucine Alfredo, I suppose."

He grinned. "Fettucine Alf*rrr*edo," he repeated, with an exaggerated rolling of the R. "Sounds *magnifique*."

"Wrong language." A hint of a smile played around her mouth. "I think you mean *magnifico*."

"That's what I'll have then. With a basket of breadsticks. And a glass of red wine."

She nodded, scribbled a note on her pad, and headed toward the kitchen. He took her near-smile as a good sign and cracked open his textbook, stealing glances at her now and then as she waited on tables. He liked to watch her work, admiring the way she smiled warmly at each customer as she took orders or refilled water glasses. She was good at her job.

Shortly after eight o'clock, the door swung open and a blast of cold air fluttered the pages of his book. A striking woman who looked to be in her forties swept in, accompanied by a young boy. She was impossible to ignore, with her brilliant green coat and even more brilliant red hair. It wasn't a shade of red Henry had ever seen before, and he found it hard not to stare.

He glanced at Francie just in time to see her smile collapse. She hurried toward the woman and spoke to her in hushed, urgent tones. From a distance, Henry could only catch snippets of the conversation.

"Ramona," Francie hissed, " . . . doing here?"

"I need . . . watch him . . . a while," the woman responded.

The boy, wrapped in a threadbare coat and muffler, looked miserable.

The two women continued their huddled conversation until Francie lifted her hands in a gesture of helplessness. Her voice grew louder. "Ramona, you can see that I'm working. How can I be watching him as well?"

Henry couldn't make out the redhead's response, but after several more minutes of intense conversation, Francie looked defeated. The woman smiled, then kissed the boy's forehead, leaving a crimson lipstick stain. "Be good, honeybun."

The boy quickly wiped his forehead with the back of his mittened hand.

Not waiting for a further response from Francie, the woman swept out of the restaurant, leaving the boy standing in the doorway.

Francie looked at him and sighed. Her smile seemed a little forced.

"Okay, buddy, let's get you settled." She touched his shoulder and steered him to an empty table at the back of the restaurant, next to Henry's. "Give me your jacket." He shrugged it off, and she hung it on a coat rack. "Are you hungry? I'll bet you didn't get any supper."

"I'm starving."

"Alrighty. Sit here. I'll be back in a minute." She disappeared through the door to the kitchen.

Henry looked at the boy, who looked back at Henry.

"Hi," Henry said.

"Hi." The boy looked down, pulled his napkin from the ring, and started folding it into smaller and smaller squares.

Minutes later Francie emerged from the kitchen, followed by the chef carrying a tray. The man set a plate of spaghetti and a basket of breadsticks in front of the boy.

"Here you go, *Guglielmo. Mangia*," the chef said heartily. "Eat that up, and when you're done, there's some *cannoli* with your name on it."

William. Eat. The Italian language resembled Latin closely enough that Henry could make out some of the words. He had no idea what a cannoli was, though.

The boy grinned and picked up his fork.

"What do you say?" Francie prompted.

"*Grazie!*" he exclaimed. The chef gave a hearty guffaw.

"You see?" he said to Francie. "He is learning, just like you."

"Thank you, Mr. Figaro." Her voice sounded thick. "Please take the cost of his meal out of my week's pay."

"Bah," Mr. Figaro scoffed, looking almost insulted. "*Tuo fratello ha fame.*"

Your brother is hungry. Henry puzzled out the words.

Her brother. *Hmm.* Did that mean the flamboyant woman in the green coat was their mother? That hardly seemed likely. It sounded like Francie had called her Ramona, as one would address a sister or friend. But maybe he'd misheard. He'd been eavesdropping, after all.

"Is the end of the day, anyway," Mr. Figaro continued. "Don't want the spaghetti to go to waste. Or the cannoli either." He winked at the boy.

As the boy swirled his fork in the spaghetti, a tableful of customers seated across the room drew Francie's attention.

"Be right with you," she called. She turned to her brother. "Be good," she said sternly, and hurried away.

Even as he tried to concentrate on his Latin book, Henry remained aware of how the boy eagerly slurped the whole bowl of spaghetti, as if he hadn't had a decent meal in a while. The chef brought him a second helping, and he polished that off too. And then a cylindrical-shaped pastry—the cannoli, apparently—on top of that. After he'd finished eating, he sat back in the booth, looking thoroughly stuffed and a little bored as he spun the metal napkin ring around and around on the table.

Henry closed his book and leaned over from his own table. "*Psst*! Hey!"

The boy looked at him but didn't say anything.

"What's your name?"

"Will Forrester."

"You're Francie's brother?"

Will nodded.

"Hi, Will. I'm Henry Jasper. I'm a friend of your sister." Okay, that was a stretch. But maybe it would be true someday—sooner rather than later. "Do you know how to make a paper airplane?"

Will shook his head.

"Want to learn?"

The boy said nothing, but a flicker of light came into his eyes.

"Come here. I'll show you how."

Soon Henry and Will were sitting in the booth together, heads bent over a sheet of notebook paper that Henry folded into a winged shape.

"Watch this." He sent it soaring toward the waitress station where Francie poured coffee. She caught the paper missile, grinned, and brought it back to them. Henry was relieved to see the grin. She could just as easily have gotten annoyed at their high-jinks.

"Gentlemen, I believe this belongs to you." She handed the paper toy to Will.

Will looked at Henry with shining eyes. "Let me try to make one."

Henry tore a piece of paper out of his notebook and handed it to Will. Then he tore another piece for himself. "Okay, watch closely and follow what I do."

Will frowned in concentration as he folded the paper exactly the way Henry demonstrated. The next time Francie passed their table, her arms loaded with a tray of dirty dishes, he held up his creation. "Look, Francie! Henry showed me how."

"I see." Over Will's head, she gave Henry a grateful smile. "Thank you," she mouthed silently. Gosh, she was pretty.

Henry and Will continued to make airplanes, a whole fleet of them, until nearly closing time. As Will visited the restroom, and Henry bundled into his coat, Francie asked him, "How did you know he's crazy about airplanes?"

"I didn't," Henry admitted. "I just figured, since I enjoy making paper airplanes, that he would too. Most young boys do."

"So you're a young boy, too." She widened her smile, revealing her dimples.

His insides flipped. "At heart, yes. I suppose I am."

"Well, thanks again for keeping Will entertained. I really owe you a favor."

Henry felt himself glow with pleasure. "It was no problem. I enjoyed his company."

"Though I'm sorry he kept you from studying your Latin." She pointed to the book lying on the table.

Funny. He'd forgotten all about it. "Maybe you can make it up to me by drilling me on my Latin verbs before my next exam."

"But I don't know any Latin."

"You don't need to. Just listen to me recite them and check them on the list." He winked. "It might help you improve your Italian at the same time. The Italian language is rooted in Latin, you know."

She laughed. "In that case, I'd be honored to help you."

Will returned from the restroom and slid into the booth.

"Henry's leaving now," Francie told him. "What do you say?"

"Bye, Henry. And thanks."

"So long, Will. Let's do it again soon." Henry turned to the door. As he pulled it open, his heart warmed to hear Francie behind him, humming a happy tune.

Walking to campus, he marveled at her change in attitude. Amazing what showing a little kindness to her kid brother could do. Maybe now she'd be willing to become friends with Henry, maybe see him away from the restaurant. Go to the pictures or something. She liked music—maybe he could invite her to that benefit concert on Sunday. But no, she'd probably feel bored and out of place among that stuffy classical-music crowd. Better to stick to an activity she'd be familiar with, lest she think he was a flat tire who didn't know how to have fun. A flat tire like good old Dad.

The unwelcome thought that Father wouldn't approve of his interest in a working-class waitress intruded into his mind, but he blotted it out just as quickly. His parents had already determined his choice of school, his major, and his career path. They wouldn't get to choose his companions, too.

CHAPTER NINE

O n Sunday afternoon, Francie bundled herself into her coat and scarf.

"Where are you off to?" Will asked. He was seated at the kitchen table, working on his model airplane.

"A concert over at the college. An opera singer." She hesitated, a small stab of guilt piercing her heart. "I'd take you with me, but I'm afraid I can't afford two tickets." Not even one. Not at full price.

To her relief, he wrinkled his nose. "Me, sit through opera music? No, thanks. Those screechy records you play are bad enough."

"You have no taste." She left the house and walked several freezing blocks to the Scoville College campus. There she followed a crowd of well-dressed, mostly older concertgoers to the imposing red-brick auditorium where the recital was to be held. The sign outside read "Piper Hall."

She stood in the cold sunshine for several minutes, scanning the crowd, until she spotted a group of three or four girls around her age walk up the steps and enter the building. She followed them into the steam-heated foyer, where they joined the line for the ticket booth. She slipped in right behind, staying close to give any casual observers the impression she belonged with them. When the girls burst into laughter over something one of them said, Francie grinned as if she, too, were in on the joke.

One by one the girls purchased their tickets. When it was her turn, she slipped her money across the counter to the clerk. "One half-price ticket, please."

"I.D., please," the clerk responded.

Francie blinked at the unexpected requirement. "I beg your pardon?"

The young man looked bored. "I need to see your college identification in order to give you the student discount."

Her face heated. "But—" She pointed to the girls who were now entering the auditorium. "You didn't ask them for identification."

"I know them." He peered at her. "I don't know you."

"Oh." *What now, what now?* "I'm Francie Forrester. How do you do."

He looked at her and waited.

She scrambled for what to say. "I'm sorry. I—I'm new here. I didn't know—I'm afraid I don't have any I.D. with me." Which was truthful, as far as it went. But not far enough for the clerk.

"Look, miss." His tone said he wasn't buying it. "Rules are rules. Without a college I.D. you'll have to pay full price. That's the policy."

"I see." She hesitated, conscious of the line waiting behind her. "Well, I'll guess I'll just go back home and get my I.D. then."

"I'm truly sorry, miss." The clerk's voice softened in apology. "My boss is a real stickler for the rules. You wouldn't believe the number of people who try to get in for cheap under false pretenses, especially to see a big-name star like Beatrice de Bonneville."

Oh, yes, I would believe it, Francie thought, hot with shame at her own deviousness. What had she been thinking? She certainly didn't want to get the clerk in hot water with his boss on her account.

Drenched in disappointment and humiliated at her attempt to skate by with a lie, she turned to leave. As she struggled to pass through the double doors against the tide of incoming concertgoers, she caught sight of a pretty blond usherette handing out programs. Maybe she could at least take home a program as a sad souvenir of her thwarted scheme.

She approached the usherette, then stopped short. The usherette was not just some random college girl—she was Theresa Van Dell, Chip's new girlfriend.

Ugh. Just my luck, Francie thought bitterly. Running into Theresa Van Dell seemed a fitting end to her failed afternoon. But before she could turn away, she noticed the girl's flushed face and glassy eyes. She looked as if she'd been crying.

Theresa held a folded paper toward Francie. "Program?" she said with a quiver in her voice.

"Thank you." Lowering her voice, she added, "Say, are you all right?"

Her gentle comment unleashed a fresh flood of tears.

"Oh, dear." Francie glanced around. People were beginning to stare. Gently she touched Theresa's shoulder and guided her to a bench in a quiet corner of the lobby. She reached into her purse for a hankie, thankful that she'd thought to pack a fresh one before leaving home, and handed it to Theresa, who dabbed her eyes with it.

"Is there something I can do to help?" Francie asked.

The girl shook her head. "I'm s-s-orry," she sobbed. She blew her nose. "It's just that m-m-my boyfriend broke up with me last night. And now . . . he just showed up here with another g-g-girl!" She erupted in a fresh round of tears.

Francie's heart melted in her chest. "Oh, dear," she repeated, feeling helpless. She patted Theresa on the shoulder.

She understood. Boy, did she understand. *Chip Hardwick . . . that creep. Poor Theresa. If I ever get my hands on that faithless Lothario, why . . .*

Like a bolt from the blue, inspiration struck. Maybe she couldn't afford to buy a ticket, but suddenly she saw a way she could *earn* her way into the concert, fair and square, and help Theresa out at the same time.

"Look, honey," she said to Theresa. "You're in no condition to be doing this job today. Why not let me take over for you?"

Theresa stared at her through watery eyes. "You'd do that for me?"

"Sure, I would. I'll stay right here and hand out programs, just like you're doing. I suggest you go home and take a long, hot bath and a nap. Unless you'd prefer to stay and hear the concert, of course."

The girl shook her head. "I hate opera," she admitted. "I only volunteered to hand out programs today because I'm on the arts committee. Besides, I'd never remain in the same room with—with *them*!" The waterworks started to flow again.

Gently Francie took the stack of programs from her hand.

"Go on home. I'll take care of things here."

Theresa looked at her with gratitude. "You're sure?"

"I'm sure." Francie patted her shoulder. "And Theresa?"

"Yes?"

"He's not worth a single one of those tears."

Theresa gave her a weak, wobbly smile, then walked away. Quickly Francie slipped out of her own coat, stashed it behind a potted palm, and stood where Theresa had been standing. She scanned the foyer for the relevant signage so she'd sound knowledgeable in case someone asked for directions to the balcony or the restrooms.

"Care for a program?" she cheerfully asked the next batch of entering patrons, her heart positively aglow with her change in circumstances.

When the overhead lights blinked, signifying the concert was about
to start, she slipped into the darkened auditorium and lingered at the
back to welcome any latecomers. There were no more unoccupied
seats available, but she didn't mind. She was thrilled just to be in the
same room with the famous diva. She could hardly believe her good
fortune. "Thank you, Lord," she whispered into the darkness, "for
making it turn out all right."

The orchestra tuned their instruments. The audience applauded
the conductor as he entered. At last Beatrice de Bonneville glided
onstage, wearing a gorgeous blue silk gown and ropes of pearls over her
ample chest. And when she opened her mouth to sing, it was the most
glorious sound Francie had ever heard, like pure gold pouring over her
whole body. She stood mesmerized, letting the beautiful songs wash
over her, not caring that hardly any of it was in English. The music
carried meaning with a language of its own.

If I could do that, Francie thought, *If I could sing like that, I would
be the happiest woman in the world.*

Though only a few miles apart, Piper Hall was as far from The
Thirsty Swallow as the sun was from the moon.

CHAPTER TEN

As the curtain fell and the applause faded, Francie floated to the lobby to retrieve her coat, her spirit elated by the joy of hearing her favorite diva sing in person. She'd be sure to thank Mr. Figaro on Monday.

"Francie?" A male voice startled her out of her reverie. Who'd be calling her name? She didn't know any men at Scoville College, except for Chip.

Chip. Her spirit sank with a thud. Expecting to see her faithless former beau and his new conquest-of-the-moment, she slowly turned around in her haughtiest manner, ready to freeze him solid with a stare of icy disapproval.

Instead, she saw Henry Jasper.

"Oh!" she gasped in surprise. "It's you."

He stepped back as if startled. "Sorry. I just—I didn't expect to see you here."

She softened her expression. Her mind cast about for a clever response and came up empty.

"I didn't either," she blathered. "Expect to see me here. Or you, for that matter."

Realizing she was making little sense, she clamped her mouth shut. They stared at each other as people brushed past them on their way to the exit.

"So you didn't have to work today," he said.

"No. They do let me out on good behavior now and then."

She meant it as a joke, but Henry looked confused, so she rescued him.

"It's Sunday," she clarified. "The restaurant's closed."

"Oh. Sure." He cleared his throat. "Did you enjoy the concert?"

"Yes, I did. I love opera."

"You do?" His face lit up. "So do I. Love it, I mean. I don't sing or anything."

As they looked at each other, each waiting for the other to speak, a brown-haired woman wearing a tweed walking suit came up beside them.

"Well, hello there."

Francie struggled a minute to remember where she'd seen the woman before, much less what her name was. Happily, the woman's memory was sharper than hers.

"You're Miss Forrester." She extended her hand. "I'm Grace Whitworth. We met at your church around Christmastime."

"Oh, yes, I remember." Francie returned the handshake. "And this is Mr. Henry Jasper."

"Oh, Henry and I are well acquainted," Miss Whitworth said with a warm smile. "He's one of the school's best pianists."

"Now you're exaggerating." His tone was bashful, but he looked pleased.

"Pianist?" Wasn't he just full of surprises? He didn't strike her as the pianist type. Not that she knew any pianists, other than Mrs.

Dornbusch, but male pianists tended to look thin and pale on the pages of *Opera News*. Henry was built like an athlete.

"Miss Whitworth teaches music here at the college," he explained. "Voice, specifically. She ropes me in now and then to accompany her students for recitals and things."

Francie turned to Miss Whitworth with fresh excitement. "You're a voice teacher?" No wonder she'd taken such an interest in Francie's singing at the Christmas Eve service.

"How do you two know each other?" Miss Whitworth asked.

"Miss Forrester here is my tutor," Henry joked. "She has promised to help me with my Latin verbs."

Miss Whitworth cocked her head. "I didn't realize you were a student, too, Miss Forrester. But I only joined the Scoville faculty last fall, so I certainly haven't had the opportunity to meet the entire student body."

"Oh, no, I'm not a student," Francie hurried to explain. "Henry is just kidding. I'm done with school."

"Oh." Miss Whitworth blinked in apparent confusion.

"But I've been wanting to take voice lessons for the longest time," Francie continued.

Miss Whitworth looked pleased. "I would love to work with a voice like yours," she said. "Lucky for you, there's still time to enroll for the spring semester." She reached into her bag, pulled out a staple-bound booklet, and handed it to Francie. "Here's a course catalog so you can see all of the music department offerings, including mine. As soon as you are enrolled, come see me and I'll see to it that there's room in my schedule for you."

"I don't think that will be possible." Francie tried to refuse the catalog, but Miss Whitworth insisted she take it.

"Keep it anyway. Look it over. And pray about it. Sometimes the Lord makes a way when we see no way."

Francie looked at the slim booklet with the Scoville College logo printed in blue on the cover. "Thank you," she said. There didn't seem to be anything more to say.

Miss Whitworth reached again into her bag, pulled out a small white calling card, and handed it to Francie. "I do hope you will come and see me," she said warmly. "And now I must be off. It was nice meeting you. And Henry, I'll be seeing you in the studio very soon. We have the spring recital to prepare for."

"Yes, ma'am," Henry replied.

As Miss Whitworth exited through the double doors, Francie slipped the course catalog and the calling card into her handbag. The crowd had thinned and only a few people remained in the lobby.

"Well." She turned to Henry with reluctance. "I suppose I should be going."

"Me too."

He held the door open for her, and they walked down the cement steps to the sidewalk.

"Say, it's pitch-black out," Henry observed as if this were a startling revelation. "Even though it's only four o'clock."

"Yes," she replied. "It gets dark so early in winter."

"A lady shouldn't walk alone in the dark." He swallowed. "May I walk you home?"

"You may," Francie replied. And a warm sense of pleasure surged all the way from her chest to her hairline.

At the prospect of walking Francie home, Henry leaped into the air, the way he did when his favorite football team scored a touchdown. That is, inwardly he leaped. Outwardly, he merely extended his arm for her to grasp as they strolled down the sidewalk, carefully sidestepping the patches of ice that glimmered under the streetlamps. He was glad he'd had the good sense to wear his overshoes.

"What did you think of the concert?" he ventured by way of conversation. Too late he realized they'd addressed this topic earlier, but in the moment, he couldn't think of anything more clever to say.

"Oh, it was heavenly," she breathed. "I've never heard anything like it. Beatrice de Bonneville is one of my favorite opera singers. And when she sang 'Un Bel Di' from *Madama Butterfly* . . . why, I practically burst into tears right there in the auditorium."

"I got a little choked up, too," he admitted. "I couldn't believe it when I heard she was coming to perform at our little college. But apparently, she's some sort of distant cousin to the college president, and he was able to work it out to have her appear as a fund-raiser."

"Well, judging from the size of the crowd, ample funds were raised." She smiled up at him, her eyes reflecting the sparkle of the moonlit snow.

"It's for a good cause."

"Yes. A very good cause." She added shyly, "I'd give anything to be able to sing like that."

"You *can* sing like that," he insisted. "I've heard you sing."

She gaped at him. "When?"

"At the restaurant." He smiled at her. "You sing when you work," he added, as if the habit had escaped her notice.

"Oh, that," she scoffed. "I'm not a real singer. Not in any public capacity." She paused, then added, "Except for church. I guess church is sort of public."

"It certainly is. And you could sing other places, too. Anywhere you want to. You're that good."

"You're very kind to say that. I-I do love to sing." She seemed to be groping for words. "What I mean is, I don't know if I could function as a person if I couldn't sing. When I sing, my mind shuts off." She giggled. "I know that sounds terrible, but I mean it in a good way. It's like air. I need music to survive. I can't live without air, and I can't live without music."

He didn't know what to say to that. He settled on, "Gosh."

She gave a little laugh. Had he embarrassed her?

"Really, though, I'm just an avid music lover," she continued. "My boss at the restaurant, Mr. Figaro—you've met him—lets me borrow his opera records from time to time, and I listen to them over and over. He tells me I should join the opera." She snorted. "As if it were that simple. 'How do you do, I'm Francie Forrester, and I'd like to join your opera company.'" Her smile flashed in the dark.

"You must be awfully talented for him to say that."

"I have no idea. Some people think so." She spoke so quietly, he could barely hear her.

"Oh, I'm not questioning it." Henry hastened to reassure her. "Not at all. What I mean is . . . well, if you really enjoy music that much, and you have some natural ability, you should definitely try to study with Miss Whitworth. She's the best."

"That's interesting," Francie said. "She said *you're* the best, when it comes to playing the piano."

"I like to tickle the ivories now and then."

"And yet you're studying pre-law," she said. "Not music."

"My parents say a music degree would be impractical. They've always planned for me to become an attorney, like my father and grandfather and uncle and cousin. They tell me the law is in my blood."

"Do you agree with them?"

He shrugged. "Whether I agree with them or not isn't really part of the equation. I love music, but it will have to stay an avocation. But say, I'm serious about your studying with Miss Whitworth. She could really help launch your career."

"My career?" she sputtered. Her tone gained a bitter edge. "Listen. I did enjoy meeting Miss Whitworth, and I'm flattered that she likes my voice. But there's no way I can enroll in college."

"Why not? You look to be about the right age."

"I'm seventeen, if that's the information you're fishing for." She slid him an amused glance. "But it's not a question of age. It's a question of qualifying, for one thing. I never finished high school."

"You didn't?" Other than a handful of people he knew who'd been privately tutored, Henry'd never met anyone who hadn't graduated high school.

"No. I had to work to help support my family," she said without a trace of self-pity. "I love my job, but it doesn't pay nearly enough to cover the cost of tuition and books and all that. Not on top of necessities like keeping the lights on."

Henry didn't reply. He felt embarrassed, somehow, that his parents were paying for his education. And not only for his education, but for practically everything in his life. It dawned on him that there were a great many things in this world of which he knew very little.

Out loud he said, "Never say never. You shouldn't be so quick to give up on your dream." The sentence hung in the air like the bland platitude it was.

She cast him a skeptical look. "In this case, I'm saying never." Her voice was firm.

He thought it best to steer the subject to other channels.

"So, you and Miss Whitworth were acquainted before today?"

"Yes. We met at my church on Christmas Eve."

"What church is that."

"Scoville Community. You?"

"I attend the college chapel, when I'm in town. At home, St. Cuthbert's in the city."

They walked in silence for a few minutes. Then Henry said, "I enjoyed spending time with Will the other day. He sure is a bright kid."

"Yes, he is," she agreed. "And thanks to you, he's been making paper airplanes all weekend. I even had to hide the mail from him. No shred of paper is safe."

"Who was the woman who dropped him off?"

"That was our mother."

"Really?" He failed to hide his astonishment. Realizing that might have sounded rude, he quickly added, "She's very . . . vibrant, isn't she? I thought she might be your older sister or a young aunt or something."

She rewarded him with a giggle. "She would be flattered to hear you say that."

Henry wanted to ask more questions about her family. For example, was her father still in the picture? If not, why not? But he couldn't figure out a polite way to do so without seeming like he was prying. Which, he had to admit, he probably was. But he wanted to learn everything he could about Francie. The girl fascinated him. She was like a multilayered flower. A rose, perhaps. Peel away one petal only to find many more petals underneath. While he was pondering this image, she spoke.

"You don't live in Scoville?"

He shook his head. "Chicago. I only live here while college is in session. I rent a room in a boarding house near campus."

"Oh, I see," she said lightly. "I assume you go home on breaks and holidays."

"Yes. But this summer I'll be leaving Scoville permanently, since I'll be graduating in June and starting law school back East in the fall." For the first time in four years, sorrow struck him at the thought of leaving Scoville. If only he'd met Francie earlier.

"Oh."

Was that a note of disappointment he detected in her response? A tiny flame of hope flickered in his chest that she was starting to care for him and would miss him when he left. But she said nothing further on that score, and he sought to fill in the conversational gap.

"What about you? How long have you lived in Scoville?"

"All my life," she said. "I grew up here. And so did my mother."

"And your father?" There. He'd cracked open a door.

"I don't really know anything about him, other than his name was Franklin Forrester and he was studying at the college when he met my mother. He left Scoville, and us, when I was less than a year old. I don't remember him at all, but I'm pretty sure he's the reason Ramona takes such a dim view of college men." She slid him a sidelong glance. "Present company excepted, I hope."

A warm rush of compassion tugged at Henry's heart. "But you said your mother grew up here. You must have other relatives nearby."

"My maternal grandmother died a couple of years ago. I didn't really know her well either. She and my mother hadn't spoken in a long time."

A great many more questions crowded Henry's mind, but he left most of them unspoken, except for one.

"I noticed you call your mother Ramona. That's a bit unusual, isn't it, to call her by her first name?"

"That was her idea. When I was born, she thought she was too young to be called Mother or Mama or anything like that. She taught me to call her by her first name. When Will came along some years later, she was ready to be called Ma. But by then it was too late for me to change my ways, and 'Ramona' stuck."

"And Will's father?"

"Different fellow, similar story." She was silent a moment, then murmured, "My mother has had a complicated past, you see. And people around here have long memories. She could never escape her reputation, so she's sort of leaned into it, if you know what I mean. Made a whole career out of making tongues wag, if you will. We're cast from different molds, that's for sure." She drew a deep breath. "I'm sorry. I don't know why I'm telling you all this. I hardly know you. You're just so easy to talk to."

"So are you," he assured her. "I like talking to you, too."

"Let's talk about something else. Something more cheerful."

"I agree." He stopped suddenly and turned to face her. "Say! Have you ever been traying?"

"I beg your pardon?"

"Tray-ing." He pronounced the two syllables distinctly, as Prof Biermann did when teaching the class to say something in German.

"Never heard of it."

"It's like sledding, only using trays from the college dining hall in place of sleds. My friends and I do it whenever there's a good snow."

She frowned. "You mean you steal trays from the school? Don't they mind?"

"They're not stolen. We bought several, fair and square, when the school replaced them with new ones." He shrugged. "They probably wouldn't want ours back anyway—they're awfully beat up." He grinned at her. "Come on. It's still early. Not even five o'clock yet. What do you say?"

"Sure, I'll give it a try. I love sledding."

They retraced their steps toward the college. Francie waited outside the boarding house while Henry retrieved two trays from his room, then they walked half a block to campus. He led her to a spot where a moderately steep hill sloped downward from the sidewalk toward the back of the college gymnasium. To his relief, they seemed to be the only people on the hill.

"Are you sure this is allowed?" she asked.

"Positive." He handed her a tray, then set his own on the snow. "You sit on it, like this." He demonstrated. "Then you simply give it a shove and—" He coasted down the hill with a loud hoot, arms raised high above his head.

When he reached the bottom, she still lingered at the top.

"Come on," he urged. "You try it."

She positioned herself on her tray, wrapping her long skirt around her legs. Then she set her gloved hands in the snow, gave a push, and laughed all the way down the hill.

Henry met her at the bottom and helped her to her feet.

"That was fun!" she exclaimed, her eyes sparkling. "Let's do it again!"

"The only hard part is climbing back to the top," he said.

"Race you!" She laughed and took off running.

They climbed the hill and then coasted down several more times. Henry felt like a kid again. When they were tired, he brushed snow from a bench, and they sat and caught their breath.

"This is fun, but I really should be getting home," she said at last.

"I'll walk you." Henry slid both trays under the bench. "I'll pick these up later. No one will disturb them at this hour."

As they walked toward Main Street and through Scoville's small downtown area, he launched into an animated account of the Scoville College football team's successful season, and the logistics behind the stealing of the mascot of arch-rival Augustana College. She laughed in all the right places. She described to him her brother's interest in athletics and proposed bringing Will to watch a college game.

"We're almost there," she said. "We turn left at this corner, then just one more block to my house."

Henry had been so fully absorbed in their conversation that he hadn't been paying attention to their surroundings. Now he realized they'd left the bright lights of the business district behind. With a strange sense of foreboding, he noticed they'd entered an unfamiliar part of town, a shabby neighborhood where the streets and sidewalks were unkempt and the houses older and more ramshackle than those near the college.

All at once, from behind a broken fence, a large, mangy dog lunged and snarled as they passed, held back from leaping at their throats only by a sturdy length of chain. Henry swore and automatically placed himself between Francie and the dog.

"Excuse my language," he muttered, embarrassed, as he hurried her past the danger.

"It's all right," Francie assured him. "That dog does it every time I pass. I like to tell myself he's all bark and no bite."

But Henry shivered nonetheless, unconvinced. He couldn't imagine what it would be like to live in a place like this. The neighborhood was downright unsafe, and it didn't sound like her mother was capable of providing any real protection. His heart ached for Francie.

"What about you?" she said cheerfully, as if being threatened by snarling, snapping beasts was an everyday occurrence, which perhaps it was. "What's your family like?"

He considered this. "Well, my father is an attorney, and so was his father, and *his* father, going back to before the Civil War. So are my uncle and my cousin. Needless to say, there's a place waiting for me in the family firm when I finish law school."

"And your mother?"

"She has her hand in all sort of charitable enterprises. Whenever there's some major function to raise funds for a worthy cause, chances are Diana Jasper is connected to it somehow."

"She must be a very compassionate person."

He pondered this wordlessly. He'd never thought of his mother as compassionate—more like strategic, calculating, and skilled at convincing her wealthy friends to open their luxurious leather wallets in support of her charity *du jour*. After a pause he said, "I suppose she is," and left it at that.

Francie stopped in front of a shabby house with peeling paint and a sagging front porch. "Well, this is it," she said. "Home sweet home." She turned to face Henry. "Thank you for walking me home, and for the sledding. I enjoyed talking with you." She extended her hand to shake his, but before she did so, she removed her glove, and he removed his. Her hand felt small and cold in his, and he rubbed it. It was all he could do to keep from drawing her close for a kiss, but he knew it was too soon. He didn't want to scare her off.

She smiled at him warmly, then gently withdrew her hand. "Well, good-night."

"Good-night." He swallowed "May I—may I come and see you soon?"

"I hope you will." She flashed her dimple. "After all, we need to work on those Latin verbs." Then she turned, mounted the steps, and opened the door. Once inside, she blinked the outside light to let him know all was well.

He strolled down the dark sidewalk, his heart buoyed by the memory of her soft hand in his, walking close enough for their breath to mingle, forming gentle clouds on the frigid night air. She was something special.

It dawned on him that some of his mother's charities focused on raising funds to help poor working girls like Francie rise above their disadvantaged circumstances. If Mother could see the state of Francie's house, chances are she'd soon be organizing a committee to raise funds for paint and carpentry. Maybe she'd even arrange night-school classes for Francie so she could finish high school. Diana Jasper's charities had served many women, young and old, in similar ways. But helping poor women like Francie find better jobs and decent housing was one thing. Accepting one as her son's sweetheart might be quite another.

He imagined Mother turning quite pale at the thought of her son falling in love with a girl like Francie, who'd dropped out of school, lived in a sketchy part of town, and had a mother like Ramona. In stark contrast, his mother had in mind a well-bred girl of similar station in life, from a family known to the Jaspers. A girl like Lila Gladstone, whom he'd known since second grade, and who was pretty and sweet and well brought up. In the Jaspers' social circle, most everyone expected that Lila and Henry would eventually get married. Everyone except Henry, who found Lila nice enough, but also insipid and boring.

Even so, both of his parents were likely to protest loud and long if he brought Francie home to meet them. They'd call her "common."

They'd warn him not to let his emotions overrule his upbringing, not to allow himself to become attracted to an unsuitable woman.

Too late, thought Henry as he strode back to the college, oblivious to the cold. *Too late for that.*

Surely once his parents got to know Francie, they'd think as highly of her as he did.

CHAPTER ELEVEN

F rancie turned over in bed and reached for the Scoville College course catalog on her bedside table. She'd stayed up late studying the promises contained in its newsprint pages, and had come up with a plan. A plan she intended to present to Miss Whitworth at the first opportunity. And if she were going to do so this morning, before her courage faltered and before her work shift started, she'd better make tracks.

Powered by a rush of energy, she bathed quickly, pinned up her hair, and put on her most serious, businesslike outfit—a dark blue skirt and jacket, white blouse, and trim hat. The skirt and jacket showed wear around the cuffs and hem, but their simple lines kept them from looking too dated. She folded her waitress uniform and cap and stuffed them into a satchel to carry with her, since she wouldn't have time to come home and change before her shift began.

As she walked through the business district and on toward the college as quickly as she could on the icy sidewalks, she prayed. *Lord, if You indeed want me to use my voice for Your purposes, please open the door.* Gradually the houses changed from the shabby cottages of her neighborhood to stately Victorians and Tudor-revivals near campus. As she passed the stone pillars designating the entrance to Scoville

College, she held her head high and tried to look as if she belonged there with the other students who were milling about.

Grace Whitworth's music studio, according to her calling card, was located on an upper floor of Piper Hall. A cacophony of pianos, violins, clarinets, and one particularly flatulent-sounding tuba emanated from the practice rooms as she wound her way through a maze of staircases and hallways, following the numbers on the doors until she located the right one. Someone singing scales, punctuated by remarks from a female voice she recognized as Miss Whitworth's, came through the closed door. Not wanting to interrupt a lesson, Francie refrained from knocking, but sat on a bench in the hallway for a quarter of an hour until the lesson ended and the student—a short, red-haired girl wearing a brown coat and a sullen expression—emerged, carrying a set of music scores under her arm.

"See you next week, Adelaide," Miss Whitworth called after her. "Practice those trills." Then she noticed Francie and her eyes widened. "Miss Forrester? This is a surprise. Please, come in."

She ushered Francie into the studio, a small rectangular room with plain white walls and dark wood trim. The chamber barely accommodated an upright piano and a small desk. Only a tall ceiling and a large window letting in natural light kept the space from feeling claustrophobic. The piano took up one wall. Books and music scores spilled from shelves stretching along the opposite wall. More piles of music, folders, and scraps of paper cluttered every flat surface.

Miss Whitworth motioned for Francie to sit on the only available chair, while she took a seat on the piano bench and glanced at her pendant watch.

Francie shifted nervously. "Do you have another lesson coming up?"

"Not for forty-five minutes," Miss Whitworth said pleasantly. "What can I do for you?"

Francie screwed up her courage. "After our conversation yesterday, I've been thinking it over, and I'd really, really like to take voice lessons with you."

The teacher smiled. "I'm pleased to hear it."

"But there's a problem," Francie continued. "I *only* want to take music lessons."

Miss Whitworth frowned. "What do you mean?"

Francie pulled the course catalog from her purse and set it on top of a pile of paper. "I was up half the night studying this catalog. The plain fact is, I don't qualify to attend Scoville College because I haven't finished high school."

"Sometimes applicants can test out of a diploma requirement," Miss Whitworth explained. "If your scores are good enough in English and math—"

Francie interrupted. "It isn't just that. Even if the lack of a diploma weren't a problem, I don't have nearly enough money to enroll as a full-time student, nor do I have the time to attend a full load of classes, English and history and all that, and keep up with my work schedule. But," she concluded hopefully, "I may be able to pay for music lessons—*just* the music lessons—if you'd be willing to take me on that basis."

"I see." Miss Whitworth studied her for a long moment. "You do have an astounding singing voice, judging from what I heard at church on Christmas Eve. Tell me why you want to take lessons."

Francie tilted her head, confused. "What do you mean?"

Miss Whitworth stood and paced as much as the small room would allow. "What do you plan to do with your singing? Do you want to sing professionally? Do you want to become a music teacher? Do you simply want to perform well in your church choir?" She stopped and faced Francie. "Not that that isn't a worthwhile goal. But you need to know what you want to get out of studying music before you make the investment."

Francie hadn't thought about the use of her talent in such practical terms. She only wanted to learn to sing to the best of her ability. She groped for an explanation that would make sense to Miss Whitworth.

"Because I have so much to learn," she said finally. "I want to learn how to read music beyond the simple basics I've learned in church choir. I want to learn to blend harmonies with other voices. I just—" As she struggled to explain her inner compulsion to Miss Whitworth, Mr. Figaro's words returned to her. "I feel my voice is a gift from God," she said. "So I suppose it's more a question of what He wants, more than what I want. I want to develop the gift He's given me, not hide it under a bushel. But in order to do that, I need help. I don't know where to start."

This answer seemed to satisfy the professor.

"You have the right attitude, then," Miss Whitworth said. "There are no guarantees of success, even for those who are immensely talented, even for those who work very, very hard. But if you sense you're following the Lord's leading . . . well, that's the best place to start."

She resumed pacing. "As I told you earlier, your natural singing voice is stunning. But it's an untrained voice. You have far to go in terms of dynamics, intonation, breath control . . . so many shortcomings of which I'm sure you're aware."

On the contrary, Francie had not been aware of any specific vocal shortcomings except being too loud. Miss Whitworth's ready criticism stung. But she tried to look past the sting. After all, that sort of honesty was exactly what she wanted and needed from a teacher.

"I would be willing to train you," Miss Whitworth continued. "However, under the terms of my contract, I am only permitted to work with students who are officially enrolled at Scoville College. Are you quite sure it's impossible for you to enroll? There are scholarships available, you know."

"Yes, I do know." Francie had read about the scholarships. She'd studied the requirements to qualify, once again encountering the stumbling block that she hadn't earned a high-school diploma. And even on the remote chance that the school admitted her on the basis of entrance exams, and she passed them, and qualified for financial aid to pay for tuition and books, she nonetheless would need to keep working full-time to help support her family. She'd have no time available to carry the full load of courses required of a traditional student.

"I'm afraid it's quite impossible." Sadly, she rose from her chair. "I do understand, though. Thank you for taking the time to meet with me."

"Now, wait a minute," Miss Whitworth said slowly. She appeared to be mulling something over. "The college policy says I can't teach un-enrolled students here in the studio, using school resources. But the policy says nothing about teaching students on my own time, off campus. Perhaps I can work with you privately, in my home."

Hope rose in Francie's chest. "Really? You'd be willing to do that?"

"For a voice like yours, yes. On the condition that you would work very, very hard."

"Oh, I would!" Francie breathed, elated at the prospect. Then she sobered. "But—what would these private lessons cost?"

Miss Whitworth studied her intently for a moment. Then she said, "You seem like a sensible young woman. How are you at housekeeping?"

"Pretty good," Francie replied. She'd been doing the bulk of the housework at home since she was nine or ten. Ramona was so often gone from home, or feeling ill, or sleeping off the effects of the night before.

"I'd be willing to give you music lessons in exchange for some light housecleaning chores each week," Miss Whitworth said. "Dusting, sweeping, that sort of thing. How does that sound to you?"

Francie sensed a door swinging open, an answer to prayer. "That sounds wonderful. I'm a very tidy housekeeper. You won't be sorry." She loved the idea of earning her lessons by doing chores, of being genuinely useful to Miss Whitworth. Which indeed she would be, if the condition of the studio was any indication of the teacher's house-keeping skills.

Miss Whitworth smiled. "It's settled then. I'll give you voice lessons at my home, and in exchange you'll do some housekeeping for me."

"It's a deal!"

They discussed the logistics. The only chance for a regular slot was early evening on Thursdays, Francie's weekly day off. They decided that Francie would do the housecleaning chores on Thursday after-noons while Miss Whitworth was at work. Then they'd share a light supper together and begin their lesson.

Miss Whitworth wrote her home address on the back of her card. "We'll give it a try and see how it goes. Maybe ten lessons to start, and then we'll see where we stand."

That sounded good to Francie. The next student arrived, and Fran-cie took her leave, feeling very much like the trajectory of her life had just turned a corner. Voice lessons might just be the first step to the opera, her ticket out of Scoville and as far away from The Thirsty Swallow as possible. A vision of herself on a stage shimmered at the edge of her mind. Herself, wearing a blue silk gown like Beatrice de

Bonneville's and hitting the sustained high note of "Un Bel Di," with Henry Jasper watching from the wings, or perhaps at the piano, his face aglow with admiration.

She hardly dared to imagine such a scene.

But of one thing she was certain. She was not destined to follow in her mother's footsteps.

"Thank you, Lord," she breathed into the frosty air as she high-tailed it to the café to begin her shift.

CHAPTER TWELVE

Francie burst through the door of Café Figaro just as the lunch crowd was descending. She tossed a quick greeting to Sofia and raced into the restroom to change into her uniform. Pinning her frilly cap to her haphazard curls, she popped into the kitchen, where Mr. Figaro was standing at the grill.

"Thanks again for letting me know about yesterday's concert, Mr. Figaro." She'd given up trying to call him Guiseppe, and he'd given up asking her to. "Beatrice de Bonneville was glorious."

Mr. Figaro beamed. "I knew she would be. I'm happy you enjoyed it, Francesca."

"And guess what else?" Francie's excitement bubbled over. "I've arranged to take voice lessons!"

His jaw dropped and his eyes grew wide. "From Beatrice de Bonneville?"

She giggled. "No. From a professor of music at the college. Only she'll be teaching me privately, in her home."

"*Magnifico!*" he exclaimed. He waggled a finger in her direction "You will see. Very soon now you will become a famous diva. We will all come to hear you sing on the stage of the great opera house."

Francie laughed. "I doubt that will ever happen." Despite her wild fantasies during her walk over. "But the lessons should be fun nonetheless."

The day was a busy one, and the hours zipped by. About an hour before closing time, Henry showed up, toting his Latin textbook. Mr. Figaro had given him and Francie permission to work together at the end of her shift, as long as there were no other customers present. Seated at a table, between drills on vocabulary and conjugations, she told him all about her visit to Miss Whitworth and their new arrangement.

"Golly. That took guts on your part." Admiration shone in his eyes. "But it doesn't surprise me that she's eager to work with you. She's extraordinary. And so are you."

She warmed with pleasure at his remark. "I just couldn't pass up the opportunity to study music seriously. I never thought something like this could happen to me."

"Maybe she'll confirm for sure that you have what it takes to sing grand opera."

"I don't know about that," she said modestly, though secretly she hoped so, too. "Now we'd better get back to your Latin vocabulary, or you'll be in *calida aqua* with Professor Ames."

At last Mr. Figaro shooed them out the door, and Henry walked Francie home. As they neared her house, he said, "Do you think your mom will be happy about your lessons?"

"I hope so." But inside, she debated telling her mother at all. Ramona might ridicule her, might poke holes in her precious dream. She'd done it before. On the other hand, she might surprise Francie and show her support for the idea. Either way, Francie concluded she had no choice but to tell her, because taking lessons, not to mention cleaning Miss Whitworth's house to pay for them, would take her away from home more often.

When they reached her front porch, Henry glanced at the window as though hoping for a glimpse inside, but the drapes were drawn. He cleared his throat. "It might be a good idea for me to meet your mother sometime. She probably wonders who you've been spending all this time with."

"No, she doesn't," Francie blurted, a little too quickly. "I mean . . . well, yes, of course I'll introduce you. Sometime. But, well, it's getting late, and . . ."

"Oh, I didn't mean tonight," he clarified. "I just mean sometime."

A time she hoped she could put off as long as possible. A year ago Francie'd been eager to introduce Chip to her mother. And look how that had turned out.

After saying good-night to Henry, she found Ramona sitting in the front room, reading a magazine. She was wearing a robe and slippers, her hair in curlers. Francie was relieved to find her at home for once, that she hadn't gone to The Thirsty Swallow, leaving Will home alone. She'd done that before. And even though Will seemed mature for an almost-ten-year-old, Francie was none too comfortable leaving him unsupervised for long periods. If his friends were encouraging him to smoke tobacco, who knew what other trouble they might get into?

While she'd debated whether to reveal her plans to her mother, in the end she couldn't contain her excitement. "Guess what?" she blurted, dropping to the sofa after she'd removed her coat and boots. "I'm going to be taking music lessons."

Ramona glanced up from her magazine. "Music lessons? Why?"

"So I can study great music and learn how to sing."

"Whaddya wanna do that for?" Ramona lowered the magazine to her lap. "You know how to sing."

"Not in the way the professionals do."

Ramona rolled her eyes. "Francie, if you wanna sing so bad, why not go to The Thirsty Swallow? I tole ya dozens of times, they're always on the lookout for entertainers, and they pay good money too. Once they heard your voice, you'd be hired"—she snapped her fingers—"just like that."

"Because I'm underage, for one thing," Francie retorted. "And also because I don't want to be an entertainer. Not in that way. I don't want to sing at The Thirsty Swallow. I want to sing great hymns. I want to sing grand opera."

"Well, lah-di-dah," Ramona mocked.

"What's that supposed to mean?" Francie asked, disappointed in her mother's reaction even though she'd half expected it.

Ramona set her magazine aside. "What it means, doll face, is that maybe it's time someone pulled the rug out from under your fancy feet. Girls from Scoville don't sing grand opera. Besides, opera music is so boring. It's like that stuff they sing in that church you go to, only worse because it goes on forever." She reached for a cigarette. "Music should be fun. There's nothing fun about opera. Opera is for rich snobs and longhaired artsy types, not for people like us."

"How can you say that?" Francie protested. "Opera is anything but boring. All that gorgeous music. All those stories of battles and treachery and romance. Those elaborate costumes and divine stage sets!" True, she'd never actually seen an opera. But she'd heard Mr. Figaro's records and seen photographs in *Opera News*. And she had an imagination.

But deep down inside she knew her mother had gotten one thing right. The enticing world of classical music seemed firmly closed to poor, uneducated, common people like the Forresters.

Still, she soldiered on in her defense of the art form.

"Mr. Figaro says my voice is a gift from God and that I should use it."

Ramona exhaled a plume of smoke. "So use it at the tavern, Francie. I'm tellin' ya, there's good money in it. I get extra tips every time they let me sing, especially the old sentimental numbers."

Francie frowned. "I don't think that's what the Almighty has in mind. Besides, Henry says I can do anything, even grand opera, if I put my heart and soul into it."

Ramona raised an eyebrow. "Who's this Henry?"

Francie bit her lower lip. She hadn't planned on mentioning Henry to her mother. Not before she was certain their friendship was on solid footing. Especially since things had gone so very wrong with Chip last year. Now she'd slipped and let the cat out of the bag.

She tried to sound casual. "He's just a fellow I met at work."

"He works at Figaro's?"

"No. He was a customer." She drew a breath. "Actually, he's a student at the college." She braced herself for Ramona's reaction, which came right on cue.

"Francie, ain't I tole ya to steer clear of college men?" She stubbed her cigarette in an ash tray. "They'll just love ya and leave ya. Just like that Chip character did last year."

Francie turned her face away. "I don't want to talk about Chip. Henry's nothing like him."

"Don't say I didn't warn ya." Ramona sighed. "So, about these music lessons. I bet they cost a lot. How are ya plannin' to pay for them?"

"We've worked out a deal. I'll do some housecleaning work in exchange for lesson time."

Ramona collapsed back against the seat cushion. "Seems to me you have enough work to do around here, plus your job at the restaurant.

Who's gonna watch your brother while you're off taking your high-fa-
lutin' lessons and cleanin' house for a stranger?"

"I'll schedule things while he's at school, or when you're able to be
home with him." *Which should be the rule, not the exception*, Francie
longed to say, but didn't.

Ramona looked at her for a long moment, then shrugged and rose
to her feet. "Suit yourself. But I truly doubt that this trainin' in opera,
or whatever it is, could be of any earthly use." At the base of the stairs,
she turned back. "I coulda had a singing career, you know," she said,
her tone challenging and harsh. "I was a pretty good singer back in
high school. Everybody said so. If you hadn't come along when ya did,
who knows what I mighta done. I coulda gone places."

She didn't exactly say Francie had ruined her life, or told Francie
she wished she'd never been born. But the dampening effect on her
daughter's heart was the same.

After her mother had gone upstairs, Francie sat alone in the darkened living room, deflated and discouraged. Not that she'd expected
Ramona to react any differently. But it would have been so nice to have
gotten her support for once.

She bowed her head and prayed. *Lord, what should I do?*

Her favorite verse came to her mind. "I can do all things through
Christ that strengtheneth me."

Faith strengthened her. Music strengthened her.

Sitting on the sofa in the dark, she mulled over Henry's words of
encouragement, and also Grace Whitworth's. Those two were in her
corner, along with Mr. Figaro. And maybe even Mrs. Dornbusch,
underneath her critical exterior. If Francie needed to move forward
without Ramona's support, she'd do it. She had her chance, and she
was going to take it before it slipped forever from her grasp.

CHAPTER THIRTEEN

C ontrary to what Francie had so confidently told Mr. Figaro, music lessons under Miss Whitworth's tutelage turned out to be anything but fun. Rigorous, certainly. Challenging, yes. Even rewarding, maybe, in the same way doing calisthenics or swallowing cod liver oil were rewarding, in the sense that they were good for a person. But not fun.

Definitely not fun.

Having never taken a music lesson before, Francie had imagined she'd spend a blissful hour a week singing beautiful music. But Miss Whitworth had other things in mind.

"Classical music is a demanding art form," she had explained at their first lesson. "I feel you are up to the task, but nothing in your background has prepared you for studying in this way. It will take a lot of hard work to overcome your deficiencies."

Francie didn't take offense. She knew the teacher's words to be true. She only wanted to overcome those deficiencies as speedily as possible.

She'd arrived early for that first lesson. After she'd straightened and dusted Miss Whitworth's parlor and scrubbed her kitchen and mopped her floors and swept her carpets, she fixed a simple soup-and-sandwich meal for both of them.

While they ate, Francie shared Mrs. Dornbusch's criticism of her singing. "She says I'm too loud," she confessed. "She says my voice sticks out too much and drowns out other people. I don't mean to do it. I can't seem to control it."

"When singing as part of a choir, it is important to blend with the other voices," Miss Whitworth said. "But I wouldn't feel too distressed about it, if I were you. Sheer power is part of great operatic singing, especially in the most emotionally wrenching roles. I suspect you can probably sing over a full orchestra."

"I have no idea," Francie admitted. "I've never tried."

"That's the most basic qualification of an opera singer." Miss Whitworth gave her a warm smile. "It's quite possible that God has something else in mind for you. Something bigger than the church choir."

A delicious shiver of anticipation ran up Francie's spine. She could hardly wait to get started.

After supper, seated at the spinet piano in the cluttered parlor, Miss Whitworth ran Francie through various vocal exercises, stopping now and then to scribble notes on a pad.

"You have a powerful, rich voice," she said, "but can you move the sound toward the front of your face? You want the energy going up and out."

The front of her face? What did that mean? In spite of her confusion, Francie did her best to comply.

Several minutes later Miss Whitworth commented, "The *pianissimos* have to be *pianissimo*. You've got to keep it light. You can't over-sing." Francie thought immediately of Mrs. Dornbusch's constant pleas for her to "tone it down" and not make a spectacle of herself. But somehow the criticism seemed much more palatable coming from Miss Whitworth.

From that first day on, they fell into a routine. Every Thursday afternoon Francie cleaned the house and fixed supper. Afterward the lesson began with Miss Whitworth leading Francie through scales and octaves, followed by repetitive vocal exercises. She assigned exercises for Francie to do before the next lesson, and Francie did her best, but sometimes her other responsibilities stole away practice time. Somehow Miss Whitworth could always tell if Francie hadn't practiced enough during the week, and made her suffer through thirty minutes of music theory, which Francie loathed, as penance. Here her hatred of math reared its head as she struggled to count out quarter notes and half notes and make sense of time signatures.

The lessons were supposed to last an hour, but sometimes went twice as long as they ran scales and repeated difficult exercises over and over. Even when Francie thought she was doing just fine, Miss Whitworth pointed out many things that were wrong. She never seemed to run out of things to criticize. After several weeks, Francie began to wonder if taking lessons had been a serious mistake, if she were incapable of making any progress at all.

Yet she *was* making progress, however slowly. At church one Sunday, Mrs. Dornbusch noticed. "Well done, Francine," she commented after one Sunday service. "You're learning how to blend in with the others. Finally."

Finally, Gertie mouthed silently when Mrs. Dornbusch turned her back. It was all Francie could do to hold back her laughter.

On Valentine's Day, Francie had to work, as it was one of the restaurant's busiest nights. When she arrived home, exhausted, Will was sprawled on the faded hearth rug, folding the *Scoville Scoop* into airplane shapes.

"Hey, you," she said, half joking—but only half. "I haven't had a chance to read that yet."

He shrugged. "No good news in it, anyway. Just stuff about the war in Europe."

"That's all anyone talks about these days. Let's hope the U.S. stays out of it." She hung her coat on the coat tree by the front door. "Where's Ramona?"

"In the kitchen."

"What'd you have for supper?"

He wrinkled his nose. "Liver."

At least their mother had cooked something. After serving food all evening, Francie wasn't hungry, but she went into the kitchen anyway and greeted her mother, who sat at the kitchen table, sipping amber whiskey from a tumbler. Francie poured herself a glass of milk, took a couple of heart-shaped cookies from the jar on the counter and put them on a plate. Then she sat at the kitchen table and pushed the plate toward Ramona.

"I baked these before work this morning. Have one."

Ramona stared warily at the cookies, as if they were poisonous. "No, thanks, I'm watching my figure." She took another sip of whiskey. Francie's nose wrinkled with distaste at the smell of it.

"Did you go out today?" she asked. "Did you even get dressed?"

Ramona shook her head. "I didn't feel well."

Francie nodded toward the whiskey bottle. "I doubt that's helping much."

"Aw, don't be a nag." Ramona deflected by changing the subject. "Where ya been? Those came for ya." She waved her hand at a vase of roses standing in a shadowy spot on the counter.

Francie gasped and sprang to her feet. As expected, the small white card bore Henry's name. "They're from Henry," she breathed. "Oh, aren't they gorgeous?" She hadn't been able to smell them over the lingering odors of whiskey, cigarettes, and cooked liver.

Ramona glanced up at her and started to say something, then stopped.

"What?" Francie challenged. "What is it?"

Ramona shook her head. "Nothing. It don't matter. Ya won't listen to me anyway."

Francie set aside the cookie, which had suddenly lost its appeal. "You still don't approve of him. Even though I've told you, over and over again, how nice he is, how well he treats me."

"Why should I approve?"

Francie's voice rose. "You're being unfair to Henry. And to me. Why, you don't even know him, and you've already decided you don't like him."

Ramona took another sip of whiskey. "I may not know Henry, but I know his type. You're wasting your time." Her voice carried a bitter note.

"He's not like other fellows," Francie protested. "He's nothing like Chip, if that's what you're thinking."

"Oh, yeah?" Ramona's eyes narrowed. "Tell me, how is he different from Chip, or any other college man?"

"He listens to me," Francie said. "He takes an interest in me and my life, and he says supportive and encouraging things." *Unlike Chip. Unlike you.*

Ramona snorted. "Sure, he says those things *now*. He's just trying to flatter ya. When he gets what he wants from ya, it will be a different story."

Francie sighed. "I wish you would give him a chance."

"How am I supposed to do that, may I ask?" Ramona's voice was laced with sarcasm. "Ya never bring him around to meet your family. It's as if you're ashamed of us or something."

"It's not that." But deep in her heart, Francie knew that it was. Last year, when she'd brought Chip home for dinner, Ramona'd been hitting the sauce pretty hard. She'd acted silly, sloppy, and worst of all, flirtatious. Cringing inside, Francie had tried to laugh it off, hoping Chip would only think her mother was charmingly eccentric and not a floozy. But within a week, Chip had broken off their romance. That could hardly have been a coincidence. Did she dare take a chance of something similar happening with Henry?

Recently, he'd even mentioned that he'd like to meet her mother. But Ramona was rarely at home in the evenings, and when she was . . . well, one could scarcely say to one's escort, *Wait here a moment, please, while I run inside and make sure my mother's dressed and sober before I let you come in.*

"It's just that you're hardly ever here when he walks me home. And when you are . . . well, I can hardly invite him in when you're dressed like this, can I?"

Ramona glanced down at her nightgown and robe, then shrugged. "I tole ya. I been feeling poorly."

Francie bit back a comment about her mother's drinking. No sense throwing fuel on the fire.

If she and Henry were to have a future together, he'd have to meet Ramona eventually. But if they met too soon, under the wrong circumstances, Francie wouldn't have to worry about their future.

Because there wouldn't be one.

CHAPTER FOURTEEN

The forsythia were beginning to bud when Miss Whitworth made a shocking announcement to Francie.

"I've decided I'd like you to sing in the spring recital with my other students," she declared. "College rules may restrict me from teaching a non-Scoville student on campus, but they say nothing about performances. Therefore, I shall include you on the program." Her tone held no room for argument.

Francie must have had a dubious expression, because she added, "The experience will be good for you. Today we will begin working on a song for you to perform."

A song, at last! After weeks of scales and tedious exercises, Francie could have cried with relief.

"What shall I sing?" In her excitement, she thought of the many gorgeous songs and arias she'd become familiar with from Mr. Figaro's opera recordings. Miss Whitworth rummaged through a stack of scores, pulled one out, and handed it to her.

Seeing the title, Francie sagged in disappointment. "Jesus Loves Me?' Really?" she complained. "Why, we sing this in church every couple of months. It's just a simple children's song."

"Simple is exactly what we need," Miss Whitworth insisted. "Simple yet effective. And it's much more than a children's ditty. Did you know the words were written by Anna Bartlett Warner?"

Francie admitted she did not. Nor did she particularly care, but she kept that detail to herself.

"Anna Bartlett Warner's family lived near the military academy at West Point," Miss Whitworth continued. "She taught Bible classes to the cadets. In 1860 she wrote the poem, 'Jesus Loves Me,' which a man named William Bradbury set to music. When the Civil War broke out, many soldiers on both sides of the conflict sang this song and took a lot of comfort and courage from those so-called simple words."

A hot wave of shame swept over Francie as she regretted her snap judgment of the song. She looked with new respect at the score in her hands.

Seated on the piano bench, Miss Whitworth smoothed the accompaniment sheets and switched on the lamp. "Isn't it interesting how knowing the story behind a song deepens our understanding of it? Similar to how it is with people. The more you know of someone's story, the more you understand who they truly are."

Francie pondered this in silence. Out of the blue, she thought of Henry. How much did she truly know of Henry's story? How much did he know of hers?

"Let's run through it, shall we?" Miss Whitworth touched the keyboard. The piano fluttered to life.

Francie drew a deep breath and began to sing the familiar words.

"Jesus loves me, this I know,

For the Bible—"

Miss Whitworth abruptly lifted her hands from the keyboard. "Posture, Francie. Tall posture." She stretched her spine to demonstrate. "Feet shoulder width apart, shoulders in line with hips, hips in line with knees, knees slightly bent."

The position made Francie feel ready to play leapfrog with Will. Nevertheless, she complied. Miss Whitworth played the intro again.

"Jesus loves me, this I know,

For the Bible tells me so.

Little ones to Him—"

The piano stopped again. "Don't lift your chin. Keep it level, neither up nor down. Let's try again."

They lurched along in this manner for the remainder of the lesson, with Francie singing a few lines and Miss Whitworth stopping her to correct something or other. It was an exhausting process. But sometimes—every once in a while—she'd toss out a bit of praise.

"That's it, Francie," she'd exclaim. "You've got it now."

Those morsels of praise were just enough to keep Francie going.

As the lesson drew to a close, she realized how little she really knew about anything at all. Just as her "fun" music lessons were not as fun as she'd hoped, this "simple" song was turning out to be anything but simple.

Saying good-bye to Miss Whitworth and heading out into the clear evening, she wavered in her confidence and was, once again, tempted to give up. But she wanted music more than she wanted to take the easy way out. She determined to work hard and persevere. *This is how a person learns*, she reminded herself. *It's not supposed to be easy.* And she vowed to give it her very best shot, and to practice "Jesus Loves Me" during the week until Will and Ramona begged her to stop.

Henry waited on the sidewalk outside Grace Whitworth's house to walk Francie home after her lesson. He'd fallen into this habit of late. They'd been keeping steady company for two months now, and he wanted to spend as much time with her as he could before graduation and law school forced them apart.

The front door swung open, and Francie appeared, smiling as if she were delighted to see him. Directly behind her stood Miss Whitworth.

"Henry!" the teacher called before either he or Francie could say a word. "Perfect timing. I've just added Miss Forrester here to the program for the spring recital. Can you fit one more song onto your accompaniment schedule?"

Could he! Henry beamed. "You bet I can."

"It's a simple one." Miss Whitworth wrapped her sweater more tightly against the March chill. "'Jesus Loves Me.' I believe you know it."

"Of course." He hesitated. "I'm happy to do it. That is, if it's all right with Francie."

She smiled broadly. "I'd be delighted."

"I'll give you the score at the next lesson," Miss Whitworth said. "Thursday at six?"

"I'll be here."

Miss Whitworth went back inside the house. Elated at the prospect of getting to spend even more time with Francie, Henry reached out and took her hand. She seemed tired but happy to see him.

"That's wonderful news that you've been added to the spring recital."

"I'm excited," Francie said. "But I'm nervous, too. I've never sung in public before, unless you count church services. I hope the audience will like my voice."

"How could they not?" Henry said. "Miss Whitworth must think very highly of you to include you on the program, and she is an excellent judge of ability."

"I hope so. Sometimes she must think I'm the worst student ever."

Henry tightened his grip on her hand. "What makes you say that?"

As they walked through the cool spring mist, she confided her frustrations about the lessons.

"I thought I knew how to sing," she said. "But clearly I've been doing it wrong all my life."

"That's impossible," he said. "I've heard your voice, and there's definitely nothing wrong with it. Or with you." He drew her arm through his and patted her hand.

She gently squeezed his arm. "You're sweet. But I'm talking about technique, and timing, and so many things that have nothing to do with my vocal cords. I have so much to learn."

"And that's why you're taking lessons," he said. "So someday you can take the opera world by storm."

"Sometimes I dream of doing that," she admitted. "But I also dream of having a normal life, of having a home and a family. I don't know that I can do both."

"Why not? If you marry the right fellow, he'll support your dreams. I know I would." His face grew hot. He hadn't meant to talk about marriage or the future or things like that. He'd thought about it privately, of course. He enjoyed pleasant daydreams about spending a lifetime with Francie, what it would be like to marry her and build a home and family. But his own future was too unsettled to even think about taking a wife at this point. He didn't want to raise unrealistic expectations on her part.

She'd confided in him about that Chip Hardwick fellow who'd broken her heart a year ago. Because of that bad experience, it had taken her a while to trust Henry, and he had no intention of breaking that trust by raising her expectations of marriage only to crush them when he couldn't deliver.

Quickly he changed the subject. But the words were already out there, hanging in the air between them. And by the light in her eyes, he knew she'd heard them.

All through the walk home, he wondered how he could backtrack on what he'd said, to make it clear he'd been speaking in general about marriage, not about him and Francie in particular. But nothing he thought of saying would have improved the situation. And anyway, Francie had moved on to talk about other things, so maybe she hadn't taken him seriously. He began to relax. By the time they reached her house, he had forgotten his small gaffe entirely.

But when he looked into her eyes as they said a lingering, unwilling good night . . . those gentle blue eyes . . . he began to think that being married while in law school might not be so impossible, after all. He lifted a hand and stroked her soft cheek.

"I love you, you know."

Gently he kissed her, and by the way she responded, he knew she felt the same way about him.

"About time you got home." Ramona slouched in her usual chair, whiskey at the ready.

"My lesson ran over a little." Francie dropped her music bag on the sofa before collapsing next to it. "It went pretty well, I guess," she continued, as if her mother had asked. "Miss Whitworth wants me to sing in the spring recital." When Ramona didn't react, she added, "It's a big deal. It's a real honor to be asked."

"That's nice." Ramona said in a monotone, swirling the amber liquid in the glass.

"Henry walked me home after."

"The man of mystery. Ya shoulda asked him to come in."

Not in a million years, Francie thought, eyeing her mother's disheveled appearance. Instead, she said, "Well, Henry'll be at the recital. He'll be accompanying me on the piano. If you come, you can meet him there." She paused. "You *will* come, won't you? I'd love it if you'd hear me sing."

"I've heard ya sing."

"I mean, sing what I've been working on. Show you want I've learned."

Ramona sighed. "I suppose so, if it means that much to ya." She sounded bored. She pushed back her chair and stood. "Right now, I'm goin' ta bed. G'night."

"Good night."

Francie went to the kitchen, poured herself a glass of milk, grabbed a cookie, and sat alone at the table for a while, mulling over the situation. Over the months of their growing friendship, she and Henry had told each other almost everything, had shared what was in their heart of hearts. The one fact Francie had held back was her mother. The idea of Henry meeting her both elated and terrified her. Ramona could be charming and effervescent one minute, mean-spirited and rambling the next. How could Francie be sure of introducing Henry to the "good" Ramona when her behavior was so unpredictable?

One thing was for certain. Ramona was wrong about Henry. In fact, he was nothing like self-centered Chip, who had trouble sustaining any kind of conversation that wasn't about himself. Henry took an interest in what was going on in Francie's life, and said supportive and encouraging things. Francie was beginning to think she truly loved him, but worried that they came from two different worlds.

Would she fit into his?

And why would he even want to fit into hers?

With Henry she felt worthy as a sweetheart and as a musician. She didn't have to choose between pursuing her music and pursuing love. With him, she could have both.

But if they truly had a future together, his career would naturally take precedence. Life as a lawyer's wife would be demanding. She could hardly tour the world singing grand opera if she married Henry. But did that even matter? Maybe even as a married woman she could teach music in her spare time. Would that be enough to satisfy her? Was she prepared to adjust her dream of having a big music career in light of being a lawyer's wife?

Laughing at herself, she drained her milk glass. She was jumping the gun on both counts. Outside of her daydreams she had no expectations of even a modest musical career, much less a grand one. And Henry had only said "I love you," not asked her to marry him.

Chip had said he loved her too, and look where that got her.

Briskly she stood, brushed the cookie crumbs off the table, and rinsed both her glass and Ramona's at the sink. Then she headed for bed. On her way to the stairs, she passed a window and noticed the moon shining brightly. She paused and gazed at it.

Moon, tell me, where is my love?

She had a pretty good idea where he was. But what he was thinking . . . well, that was another question entirely.

Of more immediate concern was the spring recital. Would it prove to be a success, another stepping stone out of Scoville? Or a grand opportunity to fall flat on her face?

CHAPTER FIFTEEN

The following Sunday, Henry sat in a pew at Scoville Community Church and basked in the sound of Francie's glorious voice. As the choir loft was located at the rear of the sanctuary, and he was sitting toward the front, he would have had to crane his neck in order to see her. So he made do with just listening to her, which turned out to be even better. He could concentrate on the words and the music and not be distracted by her pretty face.

While he'd originally started attending Scoville Community in order to spend more time with Francie, he had to admit that he'd learned more about Jesus in recent weeks than he had in a lifetime of attending, sporadically, his family's church. The preacher was not a particularly gifted speaker, nor was the choir polished or professional. But Henry would take Pastor Miller's preaching any day over the glib, insipid homilies delivered by silver-tongued speakers at the church in the city. At Scoville Community Church, people believed the Bible and took it seriously. As a result, so did Henry. Or at least he was learning to.

As Francie finished her solo, Henry gazed toward the front of the sanctuary, at the sunshine filtering through the stained-glass window and falling on the simple altar. He felt at home here. No doubt about it, when he and Francie got married, they'd have the ceremony right here at Scoville, instead of at the city church that seemed so cold and impersonal in contrast. His parents might be disappointed in that decision, but Henry would stand firm on it, if that was what Francie wanted.

With an inward jolt, he realized he'd thought *when* he married Francie, not *if*. If it were up to him, they'd be married tomorrow.

But no. That was impossible. He wasn't ready to take on a wife. He still had two years of law school ahead of him. He'd need to work hard, to give every ounce of concentration to his studies in order to graduate at the top of his law-school class. And then he'd need to get established in his father's law practice. It would be three, four, maybe even five years before he'd be ready to take on the responsibility of a wife.

Or he could chuck it all and marry her tomorrow.

But he wanted to become a lawyer. If he didn't, his parents would probably disown him. Or, more likely, they'd only sigh and express their deep disappointment in him—again. He didn't think he could live with that. But he didn't think he could live without Francie either.

What was a fellow to do?

Francie's lessons turned from drudgery to delight with Henry at the piano. As usual, she and Miss Whitworth began with the exercises, scales, and arpeggios, but halfway through the lesson, Henry would arrive to accompany her on her recital song.

She loved every minute of working together, his piano notes entwining with her voice. They made a good team. Even Miss Whitworth's frequent interruptions and corrections became easier to bear, as long as Henry was there. He was capable of clarifying the teacher's comments and suggestions in a way that landed well with Francie, making her feel encouraged rather than deflated.

"All right, you two," Miss Whitworth would command. "Take it from the top, and do it *right* this time." Chastened, Francie would catch a twinkle in Henry's eye and feel reassured. They were in this together. Everything would be all right. And following Miss Whitworth's direction invariably resulted in a better performance.

What did deflate Francie was Mrs. Dornbusch's reaction to her lessons. One evening after choir practice, Francie lingered behind to share the news of her music study. She'd thought the choir director would be thrilled, but instead she pursed her lips.

"Opera is worldly and immoral," she declared. "A celebration of the arts of Venus. I hope you aren't planning to pursue it. The Lord expects us to use our gifts to build His kingdom, not to pander to the public."

"Oh, don't let that old battle-ax get under your skin," whispered Gertie, who'd overheard the exchange. "What does she know about the arts of Venus?"

But even Mrs. Dornbusch's dire statement barely cast a shadow over the rosy days of Francie's romance with Henry. Whenever they could steal an hour or two away from other obligations, they were inseparable. Sometimes they even took Will with them.

On a pleasant spring evening, one of the first truly warm ones of the season, Francie and Henry strolled the several blocks from Francie's house to Le Coq d'Or, Scoville's finest restaurant. Henry's father, Abbott Jasper, had come to Scoville earlier in the day for some business-related purpose, and had invited Henry and Francie to dinner.

Francie, feeling apprehensive about meeting one of Henry's parents for the first time, had taken extra care with her appearance. She'd pinned violets into her hair and wore her prettiest tea gown, white eyelet with a blue satin sash. The lightweight fabric was a little too summery for April, but she'd borrowed a white fringed shawl from Ramona's closet to drape over her shoulders.

"Wow! Don't you look snappy," Will had remarked when she emerged from her bedroom. She'd almost laughed out loud, since it was so unlike Will to comment on the way anyone looked, least of all his sister. She wasn't quite sure that "snappy" was the effect she was going for. But she stifled her giggle and thanked him sincerely for the compliment.

The light in Henry's eyes when he picked her up told her she'd made the right choice. But now that they'd arrived at the restaurant, a blend of excitement and trepidation roiled her stomach to the point where she doubted she could swallow a bite. She was about to meet the man who would maybe, just maybe, become her father-in-law.

After all, Henry had mentioned marriage. He wouldn't have brought it up if he weren't thinking of proposing. Francie prayed he would do so sooner rather than later. In the fall he'd be heading off for Columbia, and she wanted nothing more than to go with him as his wife.

Some would say that a law student didn't need to be burdened with a wife, that they should wait until he finished his studies, passed the bar examination, and started his practice before marrying. But Francie was certain she would be an asset to him. She'd cook his meals and iron his shirts. She'd learn how to use a typewriter and type his papers for him. She'd make sure he took care of his health. She'd—

"Good evening. How may I help you?" A man wearing a black dinner jacket and bow tie poked an imaginary pin into Francie's pleasant daydream, bringing her back to present reality.

"We're with the Jasper party," Henry informed the *maître d'hotel*.

"Very good. Mr. Jasper hasn't arrived yet, but I can seat you at his table." As the tuxedo-clad host led Francie and Henry through the dimly lit restaurant, Francie couldn't help but notice the differences between the cozy, informal atmosphere at Café Figaro and this top-drawer establishment, a wonderland of white tablecloths, gleaming silver, and hushed voices. The thick carpet cushioned every footstep. If Café Figaro had a carpet like this instead of a tile floor, maybe her feet wouldn't hurt so much at the end of a long shift. *But it must be the dickens to keep clean*, she reasoned. *Maybe rich people don't spill things or drop crumbs on the floor.*

Seated at their table, she looked around. Her anxiety over meeting Henry's father was soothed not at all by the formal atmosphere and the array of silverware, plates, and glasses on the table. How on earth would she know which fork to use?

Under the tablecloth, Henry took her hand in his, which had a calming effect on her nerves.

"I'm sorry your mother wasn't home this evening," he said. "It would have been nice if she could have joined us."

"Some other time," Francie said. With any luck, that time would still be a long way off.

A tall, distinguished-looking gentleman approached their table. He wore a finely tailored blue suit, and his thick salt-and-pepper hair was neatly combed back with pomade. The physical resemblance between him and Henry was obvious. Henry stood, and since she couldn't remember if it was proper for ladies to stand or remain seated, she stood too.

"Hello, son." Abbott Jasper shook Henry's hand. He turned to Francie and smiled warmly. "And you must be the Miss Forrester I've been hearing so much about."

Francie felt herself blush, pleased that Henry thought enough about her to mention her to his parents. He must have said something nice about her, since his father was smiling. She returned the smile.

"May I introduce my father, Abbott Jasper," Henry said. "Father, this is Miss Francine Forrester," he added unnecessarily. He must have been nervous, too.

They took their seats and exchanged a few pleasant comments about the weather. The waiter brought menus, and when Francie opened hers, she noted to her dismay that all the dishes were listed in French. As she struggled to decipher words other than *soupe*, Henry chatted with his father about whatever business had brought the elder Jasper to Scoville. Something about contracts and escrow—not a conversation Francie could contribute to.

Henry turned to Francie. "What would you like for dinner?"

"I can't make up my mind," she said. "What are you having?"

He consulted his menu. "I'm leaning toward the Dover sole."

She closed her menu. "I'll have the same," she said, even though she'd never tasted Dover sole, which wasn't on the menu at Café Figaro.

"A fine choice," Mr. Jasper concurred. When the waiter returned, he ordered for all three of them, and added a carafe of wine for the table. Then he turned to Francie.

"Now, tell me about yourself, Miss Forrester."

She was taken aback, not having the slightest clue where to begin. What did he want to know? What did she care to reveal?

Henry came to her rescue. "Francie is a singer," he said. "She's taking voice lessons. In fact, I'll be accompanying her in the college's spring recital."

"Is that right? Voice lessons." Mr. Jasper looked at her with fresh interest. "What sorts of music are you studying?"

"Mostly the fundamentals," she replied. "Scales and exercises. And a couple of songs. Hymns, mostly."

"I see." He sounded vaguely disappointed. "I thought you might be studying more challenging works, German *lieder* and such."

"Not yet, I'm afraid." She vowed to look up *lieder* in the dictionary of musical terms Miss Whitworth had lent her. "I hope to sing opera someday," she added shyly.

"Opera! Well, that's ambitious."

"The recital is next month," Henry said with enthusiasm. "You and Mother should come."

"I'm afraid we'll be traveling to Texas next month," Mr. Jasper said. "I have meetings in Dallas, and your mother is coming along for the sunshine. But of course we'll be back in plenty of time for your graduation."

The rest of the meal passed pleasantly. Francie found the mild flavor of Dover sole to her liking, and the wine, to which she was unaccustomed, took the edge off her nervousness. Having discovered a mutual interest in opera, she and Mr. Jasper discussed the relative merits of their favorite sopranos—Beatrice de Bonneville for Francie, Mary Garden for Mr. Jasper—as though they were comparing race-horses or baseball teams.

Over a dessert of cherries jubilee and coffee, the conversation turned to sailing on Lake Michigan, while Francie sat back happily and listened. She pictured Mr. Jasper captaining—or was it called skippering?—the ship in a white shirt and trousers, while Henry did something brave and swashbuckling with the sails, and she herself poised elegantly on the bow—or was it called the prow?—of the Jasper family yacht, which was named the *Diana* after Henry's mother.

She wondered what it would be like to have a father like Mr. Jasper—or any father at all, for that matter. A small ray of hope flickered in her heart that maybe—just maybe—a father-in-law could care for a daughter-in-law the way a father was supposed to care for a daughter. Unlike her real father, who'd abandoned her so long ago.

"Well, son, we'll just have to try to squeeze in a sail or two before you leave for South America," Mr. Jasper said.

Francie's attention snapped back to the conversation.

"South America?"

Henry turned to her with a look of apology on his face. "I've been meaning to tell you," he said. "My parents are sending me on a tour of South America as a graduation present."

Francie was speechless for a moment. Then she said, "How wonderful. When?"

"This summer."

"But I thought you'd planned to spend the summer in Chicago, clerking in your father's law office."

"I did, but then Mother and Dad surprised me."

Abbott Jasper beamed. "Under normal circumstances, of course, he'd be taking the grand tour of Europe, like most young men his age. But with Europe torn apart by war, these are hardly normal circumstances." He went on to extol the virtues of South America, but Francie had tuned him out. No one of her acquaintance, male or female, had ever taken a grand tour of Europe, much less South America. A grand tour of Indianapolis was the best most of them could manage. But people like the Jaspers seemed to take such voyages for granted, as a matter of course.

How different their worlds were!

After the meal, Mr. Jasper insisted on driving them home in his gleaming silver Rolls-Royce. Francie's house was the first stop. She was excruciatingly conscious of how shabby and run-down her neighborhood must have looked to this sophisticated man, but he gave no indication that he noticed or thought anything of it. He smoothly pulled the car to the curb, and Henry hopped out of the back seat to open Francie's door. She was almost safely home free when, to her dismay, the front door clattered open and Ramona came hurrying down the porch steps, a ratty old cardigan pulled around her torso, flame-red hair flying in the wind. Of all the times for her to be at home!

"Hello! Hello!" she cried in a too-loud voice fueled by liquor. Francie could smell it on her breath. She swallowed hard.

"Ramo-I mean, M-Mother, may I introduce—"

Ramona released a torrent of words that drowned out Francie's attempt at proper manners. "Wow-ee, that's some ride you got there, mister. Hoo boy. My fella sells cars, see. That's how come I can recognize a real peach when I see one. That beauty musta cost a pretty penny. You must be Henry. 'Bout time you came around and showed your face. Say, who's this?"

Abbott Jasper had exited the driver's seat and was approaching the sidewalk. He wore a neutral expression, but the stiffness in his posture radiated disapproval. Francie prayed for the scraggly lawn to open up and swallow her whole.

"Mother, this is Mr. Jasper—Henry's father. Mr. Jasper, this is my mother, Ramona Forrester."

"Mrs. Forrester," Mr. Jasper said in a cool tone.

Ramona sized him up. "So you're the old man, huh? Well, whaddya know? Pleeztameetcha. I guess it's a good thing for you and me to get acquainted, seeing as how our kids are keeping company and all. Wanna come in for a beer?"

"No, thank you," Mr. Jasper demurred. "I must be getting back to the city." He turned to Francie and extended his hand. "It was a pleasure to meet you, Miss Forrester."

"Thanks so much for dinner. I had a lovely time," she replied, as cheerfully as she could under the circumstances. "Good night, Henry."

"Good night, Francie." Henry looked as ill at ease as Francie felt. "I'll see you tomorrow." He slid into the passenger seat and the Rolls-Royce purred off down the street.

"Well," Ramona slurred, sounding impressed, as they watched the taillights disappear. "Yer Henry comes from money. Ya'd do well to hang on to that one."

"I thought you didn't approve of college boys," Francie snapped.

"I don't. But if ya got a rich one on the hook, and ya can reel him in, you'll be set for life."

Exasperated, Francie steered Ramona back into the house and up the stairs to bed. She peeked in on Will, who appeared sound asleep, then got herself ready for bed. Lying in the dark, she went over the evening in her mind. She'd enjoyed dinner with Henry and his father, and hoped desperately that Mr. Jasper wasn't completely horrified by her mother's behavior, but understanding or maybe even slightly amused. Her face burning in humiliation, Francie resigned herself to the idea that the senior Jaspers and Ramona would have had to have met sooner or later, if she and Henry were to have a future together, which Francie deeply hoped they would.

That is, if Henry could stomach having a mother-in-law like Ramona.

But never, vowed Francie as she turned over and punched her pillow, her mother's mercenary advice ringing in her ears—never in a million years would she marry Henry Jasper, or anyone else, for his money.

Abbott Jasper parked the Rolls-Royce at the curb in front of Henry's boarding house. He killed the engine and turned to his son.

"You understand that it's quite impossible, don't you? Continuing to court Miss Forrester as if you had an intention of marrying her."

"But I do have that intention," Henry protested. "At least, I might have it."

His father gave a harsh laugh. "Miss Forrester seems like a nice girl, and appealing in personality. But she's hardly your type. And that mother of hers—" Abbott pinched the bridge of his nose as if warding off a headache.

"She's *exactly* my type," Henry protested. "She's extraordinary."

"She's very pretty, I'll give you that. I can see why you're attracted to her. But you mustn't give her the impression you'll marry her. You'll be leaving town soon. You're doing her a great disservice by leading her on."

"I'm not leading her on," Henry said through clenched teeth.

His father sighed. "Son, when you go off to Columbia, you'll be away from all this. You'll probably never see Scoville again. There are two types of women in this world. There's the kind of girl a fellow dates for fun, for a good time. And there is the kind of girl a fellow marries. Miss Forrester is clearly the first type."

Anger burned in Henry's chest. "That's not true, sir. Francie is smart, she's beautiful, she's kind, she's easy to talk to, she—"

Abbott Jasper interrupted, picking up the thread. "She's a pretty girl who slings spaghetti for a living, whose highest ambition is a career on the stage. She lacks a proper education, proper breeding. She comes from a broken home in a rundown neighborhood. Who knows who or where her father is? And her mother—her *mother*." He shook his head. "I don't even know where to begin. Reputation matters. You don't want to sully your good name by keeping questionable company."

"But, Father," Henry said plaintively. "I love her."

Abbott Jasper looked at Henry for a long minute.

"That, son, is out of the question," he said coldly. "You don't know your own mind."

"I *do* know my own mind, sir."

"A friendship with a girl like that will reflect poorly on you, and on our family." Abbott drummed his fingers on the steering wheel. "Here's how it goes. If you choose to marry Miss Forrester, or anybody else who doesn't meet with my approval, you'll do so at great cost. I will not pay one cent toward law school, nor toward your support. Should you somehow obtain financing elsewhere and pass the bar exam, I will not welcome you into the family law firm. You will be totally on your own."

Henry felt sick to his stomach. "You don't mean that, sir."

"Make no mistake. I do mean it. Every word. Now I want you to go inside and sleep on it. And the next time we talk, I want to hear that you have gently released Miss Forrester back into the wild and moved on to greener pastures."

Trembling, Henry exited the car. He knew there was no point in arguing with his father. No such butting of heads had ever ended in Henry's favor. Now his entire future was at stake. He had to make a choice between pleasing his father or making a commitment to the woman he loved.

He crawled into bed and lay awake for a long time. The strength of family history, the pull of obligation, could sneer at good intentions. It could seize a fellow from behind and shape him at its whim. He didn't think he could live without Francie, but unless he wanted to throw his future in the river, it looked as if he might have to.

CHAPTER SIXTEEN

Francie nervously paced the performers' dressing room in Piper Hall, awaiting the start of the spring recital. All of the other singers were regular students of Miss Whitworth—Scoville College coeds who had the benefits of background and breeding as well as superior training in music. Dressed in laces and silks that made her own simple organdy look plain by comparison, they rustled and shimmered and laughed and chatted among themselves, but toward Francie they exhibited an inhospitable coolness. Once again she felt like an outsider, shy and markedly different from the rest.

Francie didn't know what was worse—being overlooked, or being noticed and whispered about. One girl in particular, dressed in olive silk, occasionally turned her head and peered at Francie through her spectacles.

"Isn't that Chip Hardwick's girl from last year?" she murmured to her friend in a none-too-quiet voice.

"I believe it is," the friend replied. "A townie. Wonder what she's doing here."

Francie shrank into a corner and wished she were at home, or at Café Figaro, or anywhere but here. Why had she let Miss Whitworth talk her into coming?

Only one student, Molly Mulroney, acted friendly and commiserated with Francie's nervousness.

"I can't wait until this whole thing is over, can you?" Molly fiddled with the gardenia pinned to her sash.

Francie could only nod.

At one point, when the tension became unbearable, she tiptoed out of the dressing room and slipped backstage to peek through the curtain at the perfumed and murmuring audience. She scanned the crowd for her mother. Year after year, Ramona had missed Francie's school programs with barely an acknowledgment. "I can't get off work," was her usual reason, but the excuse rang hollow to young Francie, especially since most of the other parents managed to get there. Still, Francie maintained hope that her mother would see her sing on stage in front of an audience. She would hear Francie's voice and be proud of her daughter. The slings and arrows of their difficult relationship would no longer matter. At last Ramona would understand Francie's passion for music, her desire to study it until she mastered every note and nuance. She would understand at last that Francie was worthy of her love.

She'd given Ramona all the details of the event and had been encouraged when she hadn't actually turned her down.

"I'd really like you to be there," Francie half-whispered before leaving the house. If Ramona could just hear some good music, maybe she'd change her mind that it was useless taking lessons.

But Ramona hadn't shown up. On the other hand, Mr. Figaro had. Spotting him in an aisle seat next to his wife, Rosa, Francie wished she could wave at him. But she wasn't supposed to be peering through the curtain, much less drawing attention to herself. She wasn't supposed to be backstage at all. She turned and tiptoed back to the dressing room.

At last the performers were ushered into a hallway behind the auditorium to await their turn, seated on wooden folding chairs. One by one they got up and disappeared into the dark abyss of the backstage area, and from there onto the stage to sing their pieces. Although she couldn't see them from her vantage point, Francie listened carefully to them all. None of the voices were terrible. A few of them were so skilled, so lyrical, that Francie wanted nothing more than to run out of the building and never return. Only the prospect of disappointing Miss Whitworth kept her rooted in her seat. Mentally she ran through the opening notes of her own number, striving to remember Miss Whitworth's many instructions and bits of advice, all of which were now colliding in her head like so many raindrops.

Then it was her turn to sing. She made her way through the backstage area and stepped onto the stage. The electric lights dazzled her eyes, blinding her for a moment. Henry began the piano introduction. When her vision cleared, she looked toward the piano. There he was, smiling at her. He believed in her, believed she could do it, and she drew strength from his certainty. She turned and focused her eyes on where Mr. Figaro had been sitting, and even though she couldn't make him out in the shadows, she knew he was rooting for her. Her nervousness subsided. She drew a long breath and flung her head up, courage and determination tingling over her like an electric shock. She began to sing, her clear, sweet voice reaching to the farthest corner of the room without the slightest tremor.

When she finished, the audience applauded heartily. Stepping offstage, blushing with shyness and delight, she found her hand vigorously clasped and shaken by Molly Mulroney.

"You did it, Francie! The audience loved you."

The other girls whispered among themselves, but Francie didn't care anymore. She'd succeeded, and she knew it. She thanked God for seeing her through.

When the program was over, Henry sought her out backstage, carrying an armload of pink roses. He kissed her cheek.

"Your singing brought tears to my eyes," he admitted. "I'm so proud of you."

Miss Whitworth, too, was very pleased. "You did splendidly, Francie. I knew you would."

Mr. Figaro sought her out in the lobby. "*Bella* Francesca, your singing is better than any one of my Victrola albums."

"*Grazie, signor,*" she effused, aware of the extreme exaggeration of his praise, and loving him for it.

"I'll walk you home," Henry said as the crowd thinned. "But do you mind if we take the slow way? You're not tired, are you?"

"Certainly not." The "slow way" had become their code phrase for strolling across campus to "their" sledding hill, now dotted with apple blossoms and flowering dogwood. Hand in hand, they strolled along the moonlit paths. Francie breathed deeply and looked into the clear sky beyond the budding branches of the trees.

"I'm glad I did the recital," she said. "At first I didn't want to, but I'm glad I did."

"I'm so proud of you," he murmured, and kissed her. "Were you very disappointed that your mother didn't come?"

"Yes," Francie admitted, "but I can't say I was surprised."

"That's a tough break," Henry said with sympathy. "I think parents should encourage their children."

"It's more than that," she said. "Ever since I started taking lessons with Miss Whitworth, I've hoped that music would become sort of a bridge between Ramona and me."

"What kind of a bridge?" He tilted his head.

She cast around to find the right words. "My mother has had so many disappointments. She never caught a break. Frankly, she's had a pretty awful life. Granted, that was largely due to her own poor choices. But to survive, she built a wall around herself. I guess I was hoping to wear that wall down by singing, by reaching her heart through music. By showing her I could do it, I suppose. But it backfired."

"What do you mean, backfired?"

"I mean, she told me she'd been a good singer and could have had a career in music, too. But I came along unexpectedly and ruined all that for her. So now, instead of being happy for me or proud of me, she seems to resent me. She *really* doesn't want to hear about my music now."

"That's not your fault." Henry tightened his arm around her shoulders. "You know that, right?"

She laid her head against his shoulder. "I know. But it doesn't make it any easier to do without her support."

He rested his cheek against her hair. "Well, you have mine."

Much later, when she finally got home, the house was brightly lighted. Ramona was seated in the living room, along with Mr. Bailey and Will. All three looked at her expectantly as she entered. Will in particular wore a strange, dazed look on his face.

"What's the matter with you?" Francie asked him with concern. "Are you feeling all right?"

Before he could answer, Ramona broke in.

"Where ya been?" she demanded. "We been sittin' here waitin' for ya."

"The spring recital. Remember?" Francie replied petulantly. "You said you'd try to be there."

"Was that tonight?" Ramona fluttered her hands. "I musta forgot. Oh, well, I got some much more excitin' news to tell ya."

"What is it?" Francie snapped, annoyed that her mother hadn't even bothered to ask her how the recital went.

Ramona smiled coyly, with a side glance at Mr. Bailey, who grinned like a clown.

"Clarence and I are gettin' married," she burst out, thrusting her hand to show Francie her new diamond ring.

"Married!" The news punched Francie in the gut.

"Yeah. Can ya believe it?" Ramona said.

Francie could not.

"And even better, Clarence is moving all of us—the whole family—to California!"

The room spun. Francie sat down hard on the nearest chair. No wonder her mother'd forgotten all about the recital. By now, Francie had, too.

"California?" She could hardly get the word out. "Why?"

Ramona clapped her hands together like a small child. "Won't it be marvelous? Clarence is taking on a new position in automobile sales in Los Angeles. He's so very good at what he does." She simpered at Mr. Bailey the way a love-stricken schoolgirl might look at a famous vaudeville actor.

Puffing proudly as a peacock, he pulled a cigar from his vest pocket and clipped the end.

Dismay rose in Francie's throat. In desperation she looked at Will. No wonder he seemed so dazed. The news must have come as just as much a shock to him as it was to her.

"What do you think of all this?" she demanded.

Will lifted his skinny shoulders. "I don't know. California sounds pretty neat, I guess. They say the sun shines there all the time, and the weather stays warm even in winter. There's a lot of orange groves. And they say we'll live near the ocean. I ain't never seen the ocean."

None of them had.

He made no comment on the prospect of having Mr. Bailey as a stepfather, a concept Francie couldn't quite wrap her head around. Ramona'd had plenty of boyfriends before, but this was the first time in a long time she'd talked about marrying one.

But much as she didn't love the idea of her mother marrying this man who was a virtual stranger, Francie's more immediate concern was the proposed move to California. What about her job? She couldn't just leave Mr. Figaro in the lurch. And she had to tell Henry. But why would Henry care? He'd be leaving Scoville soon anyway, and he hadn't yet asked her to go with him. What would it matter whether Francie was in Scoville or California or Timbuktu? And what about her music? Her mind whirled, refusing to form a coherent response.

"Ya could at least congratulate us." Ramona's tone soured.

"Sorry. Congratulations." Francie stood, walked over to the sofa on shaky legs, and kissed her mother and Mr. Bailey each on the cheek. "I hope you'll be very happy," she added woodenly. She returned to her chair. She wanted to protest, but Mr. Bailey had given her no solid reason to dislike him, other than she found him to be something of a bore. And besides, Ramona was a grown woman, an adult in charge of her own affairs, even if she didn't always act like it.

Ramona continued to chatter on. "We plan to get hitched within the month, and to leave for Los Angeles right after that. I need to talk to the landlord about getting out of our lease. Perhaps he'll agree to let us sublet the place. Then we'll need to pack all our things and—oh, Francie, there's so much work to be done between now and then. Now that the recital's over, ya might as well stop with those music lessons so ya can be home more to help me."

At the prospect of giving up her music lessons, reality hit Francie between the eyes. Give up her music? Throw away her chance at a music career?

And move even farther away from Henry than she already was? Why, come fall, he'd be off at Columbia Law School in New York City, an entire continent away from California—a miserable fact about which Ramona had shown zero sympathy. "Whadja expect?" she'd sneered one day when she'd found Francie in tears over the impending separation. "I warned ya about getting involved with a college man."

Scoville was close enough to Chicago that they could arrange to see each other when he came home to visit his parents. But California! Well, she hated to even think about it.

As Francie's thoughts reeled and spun, one thing became clear. From now on, she would no longer seek her mother's approval in anything—not her work, not her music, not her affairs of the heart. And not where she was going to live. But she knew she'd have to make some definite decisions, some practical plans, and soon.

But first, Henry would need to make a clear move toward their future together. What in the heck was taking him so long?

CHAPTER
SEVENTEEN

A week before the graduation ceremony, Francie met Molly Mulroney for breakfast at the Scoville Diner. Since Molly's show of friendliness at the spring recital, they'd gotten together a few times and discovered a mutual love of both Puccini and pancakes. In just a few short weeks, they'd become fast friends, something Francie, in her busy, duty-filled life, had rarely experienced since leaving school. Before Molly, her closest friend had been Gertie Pennington, and that was mostly because they sat next to each other in the church choir, not because they had much in common outside of church. Content in the midst of her large, loving family, Gertie failed to understand why Francie would even consider moving away from Scoville. But Molly understood.

"I'm only sorry I didn't meet you sooner," Francie lamented to her new friend as they sipped their coffee at a small table in the bustling café. "Just think, we could have been friends this whole time while you were studying in Scoville. Now you're about to graduate, and I'll never see you again."

Molly laughed. "Oh, you'll see me again. I may be going home to Indiana for the summer, but I'll be in Chicago starting next fall, studying at the music conservatory. That's not very far away."

"It's extremely far if I'm living in Los Angeles with my family, on the one hand," Francie said, "or in New York with Henry on the other."

Molly shook her head. "Golly. Two possibilities a continent apart. You don't do anything halfway, do you?" She gave a mischievous grin. "Has Henry broached the topic of marriage yet?"

"No," Francie admitted, "but I expect him to any day now. Time's running out, and we need to get things settled before he leaves."

Molly's expression turned serious. "I'm happy for you and Henry. Truly I am. But I must confess, I do wish you were coming with me to the conservatory. It would be so much fun to study music together."

"It would, indeed," Francie agreed. But there was no point in even talking about it. If enrolling in Scoville College had been out of the question, enrolling at the prestigious American Conservatory of Music was even more so. Besides, she had Henry to think of, and their plans for the future. She turned the conversation back to her friend.

"What do you plan to do with your music when you finish your education?"

Molly shrugged. "I'm not sure yet. Maybe teach, or compose. Performing doesn't hold much attraction for me. I get terrible stage-fright."

"I never would have known, seeing you at the recital," Francie said. "You looked cool, calm, and collected."

"I managed to get through it all right," Molly said. "But I didn't enjoy it one bit. The point is, I do want to work in the music field, but I don't want to perform in public. Fortunately, my parents are backing me up and letting me go to the conservatory, at least for a year, to try it out."

"I love performing, once I get out onto the stage," Francie said. "The moments just before are torture. But once I'm out there, it's like I feel I'm where I belong."

"Then you should pursue it," Molly said.

Francie shook her head. "I might try to pursue it if it weren't for Henry. But I want to marry him above all else. And being an opera singer isn't exactly compatible with the life of a lawyer's wife."

"I do wish you and Henry all the best," Molly said. "He's a great fellow, and this is nothing against him, but I hope you don't regret it later. Passing up on a music career, I mean."

"I won't ever regret it," Francie said firmly. "Marriage to Henry will be fulfilling enough for me." But deep down inside, a nagging fear she wouldn't admit to eroded her confidence just a little.

The Scoville College commencement ceremony, class of 1916, fell on a steamy Saturday at the end of May. Seated in the audience on the school's wide green lawn, Francie fanned her face with a paper program and longed for the droning speeches to end and the giving of diplomas to begin. The sooner Henry and his classmates got their sweaty palms on their diplomas, the sooner she and her sweetheart could steal away from the crowd.

Her broad-brimmed straw hat did little to shield her pale skin from the unrelenting sun. She glanced down at her forearm. Gertie Pennington had sworn that dabbing on lemon juice made freckles fade.

Francie determined to try it, even though Henry had said he thought her freckles were cute.

The back of her white eyelet blouse stuck damply to the wooden folding chair as she leaned forward slightly. She cast a sidelong glance down the row to see if anyone else found the ceremony as tiresome as she did. If they did, their faces didn't betray it. They all stared at the mayor as if he were spouting some timeless words of wisdom. Which perhaps he was, but in the most monotonous manner possible.

With a sigh, she leaned back. A fly buzzed near her face and she swatted it away. She turned her eyes back to the platform, where the graduates sat in neat rows. She'd counted twenty-two of them. Why, little Scoville College was getting enormous. Even though the graduates were clearly the honored citizens of the day, she felt a bit sorry for them, perched up there in their black gowns and tasseled caps like crows on a telephone wire. If she was sweating in her light cotton blouse, they must have been absolutely roasting. On the other hand, soon they'd be free to flap away and live exciting lives beyond Scoville.

Not that she hated Scoville. It was a decent place to live, all things considered. But there was a wide world beyond, and she was eager to see it, starting in New York as Mrs. Henry Jasper, devoted wife.

Not in California as plain old Francie Forrester, reluctant daughter.

From the platform, Henry caught her eye and smiled. He looked so dignified in his cap and gown, his dark blond hair snipped short around his ears. Unlike some of his classmates, he appeared to be paying polite attention to Mayor Cantwell's remarks, already acting the part of the respectable attorney he'd one day become.

Francie's heart squeezed at the thought of him leaving for New York without her. They'd been spending time together nearly every day, working around her waitressing and music schedule and his end-of-term exams and papers. She didn't know how she was going to cope after he left. She'd miss him so much. Waiting for the next time they could be together would seem interminable. But the waiting would be more endurable if they could become formally engaged before he left Scoville.

Henry talked in terms of marriage and having a future together, but he still hadn't officially proposed. Goodness, if even a jellybean like Mr. Bailey could commit to marrying Ramona, then surely Henry could do the same for Francie.

But he hadn't yet.

She'd half expected a proposal after they'd had dinner with Abbott Jasper. After all, Henry wouldn't have introduced her to his father if he wasn't serious about marrying her. Would he? Her expectation had grown even stronger after the spring recital, and stronger still each time they met at their special spot on the sledding hill. But each time, he'd escorted her home without a ring on her finger. She was tempted to take matters into her own hands, but she'd never heard of a situation where a woman proposed to a man—outside of the comic strips. It didn't seem fitting, somehow.

Maybe tonight's the night, she thought with a delicious shiver. In fact, tonight *had* to be the night, because his bags were already packed for his graduation trip to South America. He would leave by train for the East Coast, and from there board a steamship bound for Venezuela. He'd be gone all summer, then straight off to Columbia Law School in the fall. If they were to become engaged before he left, Francie reasoned, he had to propose to her tonight. The prospect set butterflies loose in her middle.

At last the mayor's speech ended, and the graduates started marching across the platform to receive their diplomas. Francie waited eagerly for Henry's turn.

"Henry Abbott Jasper, the third," the president of the college in-
toned. Henry strode confidently across the platform, his black robe
billowing out behind him. He shook the president's hand and accepted the parchment scroll tied with a black ribbon. Pride swelled in
Francie's chest. He'd done it! Henry was a college graduate.

And, glory be, he was handsome!

Her tummy fluttered again, and she felt a little dizzy, the way she'd
felt on the roller coaster at the county fair the previous summer. As
if she were teetering at the tippy-top of the coaster, about to plunge
down, and there wasn't a thing in the world she could do to stop it.

She glanced at the backs of Abbott and Diana Jasper's heads. They
were sitting a few rows in front of her. She'd tried to talk to them before
the ceremony, but by the time she'd found where they were sitting,
there was no seat left in the row for her. She'd ended up sitting with
Molly's parents, which was fine with her.

After the ceremony had finished and Molly had joined them, she
embraced her friend with enthusiasm.

"I'm so glad I met you," she murmured in Molly's ear as they clung
to each other. "I'm going to miss you so much."

"We'll keep in touch," Molly promised. "And best of luck on . . .
well, you know." Her eyes carried a conspiratorial twinkle. Francie had
confided in Molly that she expected to be engaged by the end of the
day.

Francie said good-bye to the Mulroneys and sought out Henry's
parents. She approached them across the lawn, smiling broadly.

"Hello, there," she chirped. "Well, it looks like he did it!"

If she'd expected Mr. Jasper to warmly embrace her after their
dinner together, she'd have been disappointed. Fortunately, she hadn't
expected that. He was a man of formal manners. But she hadn't
thought a smile would be too much to ask. Apparently, it was.

"Yes, he did it." Mr. Jasper scanned the crowd for Henry. "Fine future ahead of that boy, if he stays focused and doesn't let himself be distracted by anything. Or anyone."

By his tone, Francie wondered if he considered her one of the distractions.

"Abbott," said the tall, regal-looking woman standing next to him. She had upswept silver hair and Henry's gray eyes. "Aren't you going to introduce us?"

"Pardon me for forgetting my manners." His smile seemed forced. "Diana, may I introduce Miss Francine Forrester. Miss Forrester, this is Henry's mother, Mrs. Jasper."

"How do you do, Mrs. Jasper? It's so nice to meet you."

"Delighted," drawled Mrs. Jasper, not sounding particularly delighted. She also didn't make any further remark, such as *It's nice to finally meet you* or *Henry's told us so much about you.*

"Please, call me Francie." Belatedly, Francie realized her remark was misplaced, as Mrs. Jasper hadn't called her anything at all. She thrust forth an awkward hand and Mrs. Jasper gave it a brief, limp shake.

The three of them stood stiffly, making inane small talk about the mayor's speech and the hot weather, until Henry made his way to them through the crowd, still wearing his black gown and mortarboard. Francie wanted to fling her arms around him, but refrained out of respect for his parents.

They congratulated their son, and he glowed in their praise. While their mannerisms seemed stiffer and more formal than Francie would expect between parents and child, she still felt a strange squeezing in her heart—part jealousy, part longing. At least Henry's parents had shown up for his important occasion, in a way that Ramona couldn't be bothered to show up for Francie.

At last it was time to go.

"If you'll excuse us, Francie and I are going to take a walk," Henry told his parents. He turned to Francie. "Is that all right with you?"

"Oh, I'd love it," she breathed.

"All right, son, but don't be too long," his father said. "We have dinner reservations at Le Coq d'Or."

"And you still have to finish your packing," his mother added. Neither of them said anything to Francie. She wasn't clear on whether the dinner reservation included her. Maybe they took it for granted that she knew she was included. In fact, she reasoned with growing excitement, maybe that's where Henry planned to tell his parents of their engagement. Maybe that was the purpose of the "walk" together that Henry had suggested—so he could propose to her in private. And then they'd all celebrate together over lamb chops at Le Coq d'Or.

It was all she could do not to drag him down the street. She forced herself to stroll calmly alongside him, as if it were an ordinary evening, as if she didn't suspect the great surprise he'd planned.

"Let's stop at the boarding house so I can shed this thing." He flapped his arms to flutter the voluminous sleeves of his gown.

"You look like a giant raven," she giggled.

"Hey, I worked very hard to earn the right to look like a raven."

"Yes, you did." She slipped her arm through his. "I'm so very proud of you."

She waited on the porch swing while he darted inside to change out of his cap and gown. Her heart pounded as she considered the possibilities. Was she actually about to become engaged? The timing couldn't have been more perfect. An engagement to Henry would provide the perfect excuse not to move to California with the rest of the family.

While he toured South America, she'd stay in Scoville, continuing to work and save money, maybe finagle an invitation from Gertie to room with the Penningtons for the summer. She'd plan the wedding while he was away, they'd be married when he returned—fall weddings were so pretty!—and then she'd accompany him to New York for law school.

She'd take good care of him and run the household so he'd be free to concentrate on earning his degree. It would of course be a small wedding, right here in Scoville. She'd ask Gertie to be her maid of honor, or maybe Molly, even though they hadn't known each other for very long, and—

"Ready to go?" Henry reappeared, looking sharp in a crisp blue-and-white striped seersucker suit and straw hat.

Francie couldn't help but glance at his jacket pocket, searching in vain for the telltale bulge of a jewelry box.

On the way to the sledding hill, they discussed Ramona's pending marriage to Mr. Bailey and subsequent move to California.

"I hope I don't have to go with them," Francie said for the umpteenth time since Ramona had revealed her plans. "I'm trying to figure out how to stay here in Scoville. California's so far away, you and I will never get to see each other."

"Trains do go there, you know," he teased. "It's Los Angeles, not the moon." A look of concern passed over his face. "I hope you're not serious about staying in Scoville alone. You belong with your family."

I belong with you, she thought. *My place is with you.* Out loud she said, "Well, no. That certainly doesn't sound practical." She shrugged. "I suppose I'll be stuck going to California, no matter how much I hate the thought of it."

There. She'd given him an opening, if ever there was one, to say *Don't worry, darling. It'll only be temporary, because we'll be married soon, if you'll have me.* Or *How does New York sound instead? I want you to come with me to Columbia, as my wife.* Or, really, he could say anything at all. Anything other than what he was saying now.

"Maybe you'll like it more than you think. I haven't ever been there, but I hear it's quite pleasant." He squeezed her hand and gave a slight grimace in sympathy for her plight.

Pleasant, my foot. Her sunny mood began to darken. Could he seriously be thinking of leaving her behind without making any firm commitment toward their future at all?

They reached the sledding hill and sat on their usual bench, hands clasped and shoulders pressed together. Although the lilacs had faded from their peak grandeur, their scent remained strong. Francie breathed deeply, wanting to remember everything about this moment.

"So," she said lightly. "You're about to set off on your grand tour. Leaving little old Scoville in the dust." *And little old me.*

"Yes. New York first, then we sail to Miami, then down through the Caribbean Sea to Caracas. Then Buenos Aires, Cartagena . . ." His voice drifted off. He sounded vacant, distracted. They sat in silence for a moment. Then he cleared his throat.

"Francie," he began, then stopped. He seemed to be struggling for words.

Maybe this was it! "Yes?" she said. Then, to encourage him, "I'm listening."

He turned toward her and took both her hands in his. He locked his gaze on hers.

"Francie, meeting you has been one of the most wonderful things that has ever happened to me."

"Me too," she murmured.

"That's why it's . . . it's so very hard to say good-bye." His voice grew thick with emotion.

"I know." Oh, did she know. "But we won't be apart forever. And you'll always know where to find me."

"Will I?" He looked at her earnestly. "Will you write to me? And send me your address, as soon as you get settled in California?"

"Of course."

"I'll give you the address of the American Express office in Caracas. That's where I'll be getting my mail, at least for a few weeks." He shook his head. "The fact of the matter is, I'll be gone such a very long time. Touring South America this summer, then off to law school in the fall, then . . . who knows after that?"

She frowned. The conversation wasn't going quite as she'd pictured it would.

"But you'll have breaks," she said. "Holidays. Vacations. You'll come and see me then, or I'll come and see you. Right? You just said that you'd come and visit me, even in California."

"Yes, I would. But Francie . . . I can't ask you to wait for me."

Wait—what? It took a moment for his meaning to register.

"Sure, you can," she insisted. "Of course you can. I love you. And you love me." She heard a note of desperation enter her voice, and she hated it.

He sighed heavily. "Oh, Francie. I do love you. I would marry you today, if I were ready to get married. But I don't plan to marry until after I finish law school and get established in practice. That's several years away. Meanwhile, you have your own life to live. You have your music, and you'll be starting a whole new life in California. A brand-new world's opening up for you. Who knows what lies ahead? Whom you'll meet? Where your music will take you? It wouldn't be fair to ask you to wait for me. To tie you down."

"Yes, it would," she blurted. Sudden tears of disbelief, disappointment, and fury pressed against her throat. "I don't want a new world.

I don't want to meet anybody. I want *you*. I want to go with you to New York, as your wife."

"Oh, Francie." He looked stricken. "Francie—no."

She stared at him, horrified at the words that had just spilled from her mouth. This wasn't how she wanted this special moment to go, with her whole heart splayed open in front of him, practically begging him to love her enough to marry her.

"Darling, we have to be practical about this." He looked miserable. "I need to give my full concentration to law school. There's no room in my life for a wife right now. And you have a bright future ahead of you. I refuse to tie you down when my own future is so uncertain."

"But your future's not uncertain," she said, confused. Law school, then joining his father's law practice . . . Henry Jasper had one of the least uncertain futures she'd ever heard of.

She realized he was saying something. Pleading with her. "But I do hope we can remain friends. Please, Francie, let's be reasonable."

Be reasonable? Be *friends*?

Suddenly all became clear to Francie. No proposal would be forthcoming. Not now, probably not ever. The hillside tilted. For a moment she thought she might be sick.

"You're wrong," she said at last. "You're the one who doesn't want to be tied down."

He made no response, just sat there with a hangdog look.

Her throat tightened further, and tears threatened to flow. Well, she had humiliated herself enough already. She wouldn't give him the satisfaction of seeing her cry.

Abruptly she stood. "I'm going home now," she managed to choke out with as much dignity as she could muster. "I need to go home."

His eyes were pleading. "Francie—"

"It's been nice knowing you. I wish you all the best." She turned quickly and started for home.

"Francie, wait." He caught up to her and grabbed her elbow. "Don't be like this. At least let me walk you home."

She flung off his grasp. "I'll be fine on my own," she said with forced casualness. "I always am. You mustn't keep your parents waiting at the restaurant. They must be wondering where you are." Maybe they knew he was ending their relationship at this very moment. Maybe they'd even encouraged him to do it. The weight of rejection was almost more than she could bear.

"Please, Francie."

"I'll be fine," she repeated. "Send me a postcard from South America, if you can squeeze in the time."

"Francie, please don't do this."

"Don't you worry about me. I'll be just dandy."

But she lied. She was anything but dandy. She could scarcely breathe, so deep was her devastation. It was all she could do to put one foot in front of the other while holding her head high, feeling his eyes on her as he watched her go.

Good riddance, she told herself as she strode down the sidewalk. Henry Jasper had talked a smooth talk, but turned out to be just another Chip Hardwick in the end. Just another college boy who'd loved her while it was convenient, then tossed her aside.

But that night, as she sobbed into her pillow, no matter how much her head told her she'd be better off without him, her heart remained unconvinced. Even the moonlight blasting through her window seemed to mock her.

Where is your lover now?

At Le Coq d'Or, Henry sat across the white-clothed table from his parents. While they prattled on about the graduation ceremony and the mayor's speech, he pushed a beef medallion around the plate with his fork. After the terrible row with Francie, he had no appetite.

What a fool he'd been! He'd expected her to be reasonable, to agree with him, to see the wisdom of staying free of romantic attachments until they were both at a place of more stability in their lives. But clearly, he'd miscalculated. And now he had to leave for South America knowing she hated him.

"You're being quiet tonight, Henry," his mother said. "I suppose you're worn out after your big day."

"Yes, ma'am." The last people he felt like confiding in were his parents. After meeting Francie and especially her mother, Abbott had followed up his verbal warning to Henry with a sternly-worded letter repeating basically the same thing he'd said that night in the Rolls-Royce—give up Francie, or give up his parents' financial and moral support.

Henry felt as if he couldn't breathe, caught between his feelings for Francie and his respect for—not to mention dependence on—his parents. He'd thought he and Francie could take a breather without severing ties completely. He'd be free to focus on law school, and she'd be free to focus on her music. Then later, back in the same city perhaps, they could renew their relationship. Pick up where they'd left off.

He'd never expected her to cut him off like he was a scrawny fish on the line.

As his parents droned on about things he must see and do in South America, Henry made a decision. He'd write Francie a letter. He was always more eloquent at writing than speaking, found it easier to express his thoughts on paper. He'd pour out his heart to Francie, explain more clearly exactly what he'd been thinking. She'd read it and understand and forgive him.

Feeling better now that he had a plan, Henry speared a beef medallion with his fork and lifted it to his mouth.

"Wait until you taste the beef in South America," his father said. "There's nothing else like it in the world."

For the first time during the meal, Henry smiled. Somehow, some way, he'd work things out. He'd smooth things over between his parents and Francie, and they'd come to see her wonderful qualities the way Henry did.

Everything was going to turn out all right.

CHAPTER EIGHTEEN

With Henry gone and her heart in tatters, Francie's life seemed rudderless. She had no idea what the distant future held, but her immediate future was clear. With no wedding on the horizon, she had no valid reason not to move to California with her family, even though the idea of it filled her with despair.

Shortly after he'd embarked on his tour of South America, Francie had received a letter he'd sent from shipboard, apologizing again for their last conversation, reassuring her of his friendship, and reminding her to send him her address when she got settled in Los Angeles. He again tried to explain how it was better for both of them not to be tied down with a serious, formal commitment until their lives were more settled, but that he'd like to stay in touch and remain friends.

Francie hadn't answered immediately, intending to reply from California. She wasn't sure that she wanted to remain friends with him, if that were even possible. Her pride had been deeply injured when he'd declined to marry her, and she felt humiliated by her sloppy display of emotion at their last meeting. *He can wait a while for a response*, she thought with a dash of spite. *Let him wait.*

In spite of her aching disappointment and growing sense of hopelessness about the direction her life was taking, she didn't have a lot of spare moments in which to mourn her loss, which even she had to admit was probably a blessing. The next few weeks were a flurry of packing her family's belongings, selling furniture, and getting the old house ready for new renters. In the meantime, she also had to juggle her job at Café Figaro and her music lessons, which hadn't stopped just because the spring recital was over. While the college students were on summer break, Miss Whitworth had wanted to keep on working with Francie, and Francie was more than willing. The busier she was, the less time she had to obsess over Henry.

Now that Miss Whitworth was on break from teaching at the college, she was usually at home on Thursdays when Francie did the housecleaning. So she donned an apron as well, and the two of them worked side by side, an arrangement Francie found most agreeable. Miss Whitworth showed interest in the mundane details of Francie's life, and Francie found her easy to talk to. Much easier than Ramona, who'd responded to the news of Francie's heartbreak with an unsympathetic, "See? What did I tell you about college boys?"

One Thursday afternoon, after she'd had a little time to absorb and reflect on her deep disappointment, Francie poured out her heart to Miss Whitworth.

"I don't know what I'm going to do," she confided as she rubbed a cloth over the piano in the parlor. "I'm going to hate California. I just know it."

"You don't know that for certain," Miss Whitworth soothed. She was seated on a nearby sofa, sorting through piles of music scores in an effort to impose some sort of order on her haphazard filing system. "I hear Los Angeles is a lovely city. Maybe you'll end up liking it more than you think."

"That's what everyone tells me." Francie grimaced. Hadn't Henry said practically the same thing? "Ramona keeps leaving brochures about California lying around the house, filled with tempting photos of beaches and orange groves. But I'm not convinced. I enjoy my job at Café Figaro, and I love taking music lessons with you. I can't stand the thought of moving so far away, but I also don't see how I can stay here in Scoville on my own."

"There are plenty of jobs in California," Miss Whitworth reasoned. "I assume there are plenty of music teachers as well."

"The music teachers won't be you," Francie retorted. "And no employer could be as kind to me as Mr. Figaro's been."

"Funny." Miss Whitworth sounded thoughtful. "It wasn't that long ago you were telling me how you were afraid of being stuck in Scoville forever. Yet here you are with a chance to move to a new part of the country—a sublime part, by all accounts—and you don't want to go."

"At the time, I had thought that Henry and I—well, it doesn't matter what I thought."

Miss Whitworth's expression filled with sympathy. "Often when God closes one door, he opens another. Have you prayed about the situation? About what God might want you to do next?"

Francie sighed. "Perhaps not as much as I should." With a creeping sense of guilt, she realized that while she'd been weeping and feeling despondent over her situation, she'd completely failed to bring it before the Lord. Wrapped up in her own drama, she hadn't stopped to consider God's opinion on the matter, or what He might want of her. She vowed to rectify that situation immediately.

They worked together in silence for a while, then Miss Whitworth said, "Francie, I understand why you don't want to move to California. Really, I do. And I've felt your disappointment over the whole Henry situation. At the same time, I've seen how much you love your music and how hard you've been working at it. How much you'd hate to give it up."

Francie said nothing. Wasn't she in enough pain without Miss Whitworth enumerating all the ways her life lay in shreds?

Miss Whitworth continued. "I've suggested you pray about your circumstances. And I've been praying about something, too." She looked up at Francie with shining eyes. "How would you like to stay here with me for the summer?"

Francie froze in mid-polish and stared at her teacher. "You mean . . . live here? With you?"

Miss Whitworth nodded. "I have an extra bedroom. It's small, but adequate. Instead of paying rent, you can take on some additional chores around the house. That will help you save some money for whatever your future holds. Of course you can keep your job at the restaurant. And we will continue your music lessons, maybe add some extra ones while I'm on summer break from the college. How does that arrangement sound?"

Francie could hardly believe her ears. A rush of different emotions bubbled through her heart. "Gosh, Miss Whitworth. That would be wonderful."

"Well, you think it over and pray about it." Miss Whitworth smiled. "And if it still sounds good to you, let's say we'll try it for the summer and see how it goes. At the end of the summer, you may decide to join your family in California. Or maybe God has another plan in mind for you. In any case, you'll have three months to think and pray about it."

Tears of gratitude sprang to Francie's eyes. "Miss Whitworth, this is the kindest thing anyone's ever done for me. How can I ever thank you?"

"By working hard at your music and doing your very best," her teacher replied. "By using the summer to pray seriously about your future, read your Bible, and ask God what He wants you to do with

your life. And I suppose, if we're going to be housemates," she added
with a twinkle in her eye, "you might as well start calling me Grace."

Ramona Forrester married Clarence Bailey in a simple ceremony at
the county courthouse. Overwhelmed that first Henry, and now her
mother, her beloved kid brother, and apparently everyone she had ever
loved was destined to leave her, Francie somehow outwardly held her
emotions in check. She gripped a nosegay of baby's breath and sang
"O Promise Me" as Ramona and Mr. Bailey stood grinning at each
other before a judge.

When it was all over, Francie kissed them both good-bye, gave Will
an extra-long hug, and waved from courthouse steps as they rumbled
away in the Stutz-Bearcat. That evening she moved all her belongings,
which weren't very many, into Grace Whitworth's house. To her delight, Ramona let her keep the Victrola.

"You use it more than anyone else does," she said.

"We'll be buying a better one," added Mr. Bailey, who'd made a tidy
sum selling his local automobile dealership and stood to make oodles
more in California, according to himself.

Just before slipping under the quilt in her unfamiliar but cozy new
bedroom, she wrote a few lines to Henry, informing him that she
hadn't gone to California after all, but had stayed in Scoville. She
copied down Grace's address, just in case he'd forgotten it, and added a
friendly but impersonal sentence wishing him a pleasant journey. No
need to make him think she was pining for him, even if she was. At
the same time, the jagged edges of her initial heartbreak had mellowed
slightly, and she found herself reluctant to cut off communication
entirely. Satisfied that her brief, noncommittal letter adequately con-

veyed her lack of hard feelings, she sealed the envelope, addressed it in care of an American Express office in Venezuela, and slipped it into her music satchel to mail in the morning.

CHAPTER NINETEEN

F rancie's life became one of near-constant work between waitressing at Café Figaro, cleaning her teacher's house, and practicing her music. But she found that the harder she pushed herself, the
greater her sense of satisfaction. As the sharp pain over losing Henry
faded, she thanked both the Lord and Miss Whitworth for making it
possible for her to remain in Illinois, at least for the time being.

On top of everything else, she added regular Italian lessons with
Mr. Figaro, meeting him early before the restaurant opened, or taking
advantage of slow spells during the workday. If she were going to get
serious about singing classical music, Grace told her, she needed to
become proficient in some other languages besides English, and Italian
seemed a logical place to start.

They prioritized her pronunciation, as that was the most important
thing for a singer to master.

"Like this, you see, Francesca." Mr. Figaro moved his mouth slowly, modeling the Italian vowels and consonants. She did her best to
imitate him and occasionally succeeded, when she wasn't groaning in
frustration or collapsing into a fit of giggles.

Proper pronunciation was followed by learning the meanings of the
words, which Grace indicated was also important.

"A singer needed to understand what she is singing in order to convey the appropriate emotions," she'd said. "Otherwise you risk singing about doom and gloom with a great big smile on your face."

Least important, for Francie's purposes, was being able to express her own thoughts in writing or speech, so they merely glossed over the principles of grammar. She could pick those up later, if she continued to study the language in earnest. For now, they concentrated on simply making her sound competent while singing an Italian song.

In spite of her deep gratitude toward Grace, her lingering gloom over missing Henry spread around her like a shadowy cloak. One sunny July day, in an attempt to cheer up her young houseguest, Grace treated her to an excursion to Ravinia Park, an outdoor music facility some twenty-five miles north of Chicago.

The pair rode the Chicago, Burlington & Quincy to downtown Chicago and checked into a modest but clean hotel near the station, where they'd spend the night. The distance was too great to travel all the way back to Scoville after the concert, so they'd return home the following day.

After depositing their bags and freshening up, they caught the North Shore and Milwaukee train, arriving at Ravinia Park in plenty of time for the eight-fifteen performance. On the way, Grace told Francie what to expect.

"You'll adore Ravinia," she gushed. "It's a beautiful park, filled with flowers, where you'll get to hear great music and enjoy being outdoors at the same time."

"It sounds blissful." Francie sighed.

The only outdoor concerts she'd ever experienced were those given by the Scoville High School marching band on the Fourth of July. She did her best to set aside her bleak mood and looked forward eagerly to this intriguing new experience.

The train deposited them, along with a horde of other concert-goers, at the entrance to the park. A sign arching over the gates read "Ravinia Opera" in huge white letters. Grace secured their tickets, then they entered the park, pushed along by the crowd.

The heavy-timbered, wooden-roofed pavilion, open on three sides and illuminated by large, round electric lights, boasted over fourteen hundred seats facing a small stage draped with blue velvet curtains. While they were making their way to their seats, a tall, distinguished man approached them in the aisle.

"Excuse me." The man bowed slightly. "Aren't you Grace Whit-worth?" Francie thought she detected a slight accent, vaguely European.

When Grace saw who had spoken, her face lit up with a wide smile.

"Why, Reinhard Schreiber, as I live and breathe. How wonderful to see you here." The two clasped hands and he gave her a light kiss on the cheek. Then she laid a hand on Francie's arm. "Reinhard, may I introduce you to Miss Francine Forrester. Francie is one of my best vocal students. A very fine soprano. Francie, this is Herr Reinhard Schreiber, principal conductor of the Windy City Opera Company in Chicago."

"And former classmate of your teacher," Herr Schreiber added. "American Conservatory of Music, class of nineteen-ought-three."

The two of them shared a laugh.

Francie was charmed. She had some idea who Reinhard Schreiber was, having read his name in various music publications. That Grace had once been personal friends with an important conductor im-pressed her. She hadn't ever pictured Grace as being young or having friends, as if her sole existence revolved around teaching music. Being relatively new to Scoville, the teacher didn't lead much of a social life beyond her professional colleagues. To see her light up like a Christmas tree in the presence of such a distinguished personage made Francie's heart glow.

She shivered with delight when Herr Schreiber gently grasped her hand. "Well, well, Miss Forrester. You must sing quite beautifully to garner such high praise from your teacher. I'm glad to hear it. We need fresh young voices like yours in the Windy City Opera." He turned back to Grace. "Speaking of young voices, have you heard that I'm teaching at our alma mater now?"

"In addition to leading the opera company?" Grace clucked her tongue. "My, my, you're a busy man."

"I teach only a couple of classes, in music theory and conducting. Just trying to keep my hand in, nurturing the next generation of musicians. Which reminds me, Miss Forrester." He turned back to Francie. "I hope you will consider entering the Young Artists' Competition coming up soon. From what Grace has said, you'd stand a good chance of winning."

The house lights blinked, indicating the performance was about to begin. Grace and Herr Schreiber exchanged hurried promises to meet again soon for dinner to catch up on each other's lives, and they all found their seats.

As the orchestra tuned their instruments, Grace murmured to Francie, "Reinhard Schreiber and I both graduated from the American Conservatory, and it's an excellent school."

"I know," Francie murmured back. "Molly Mulroney's going there next year."

"You really should think about entering that competition," Grace said. "I received information about it in the mail. Let's discuss it when we get back to Scoville."

Applause signaling the conductor's entrance cut short Francie's reply. The evening's production was Puccini's *Tosca*, with Florence Easton singing the role of Tosca and Antonio Leonardo singing Scarpia. Francie was familiar with the story from Mr. Figaro's opera records, and she had no trouble following the action on stage. While the scenery was minimal, the singing and the costumes transported Francie to Italy during the era of Napoleon.

When Tosca sang "Vissi d'Arte," her prayer asking God why He has abandoned her in her hour of need, tears flowed down Francie's cheeks at the wonder of it all. Even though the story was tragic and sad, Francie felt buoyed by the gorgeous music all during the train ride back to Chicago.

"That was absolutely divine," she gushed to Grace.

"I'm so happy you enjoyed it," Grace answered, "especially since it was the first live opera you've ever seen. It's been often said that a person's first opera will determine whether one loves the art form or hates it for the rest of one's life."

"Well, I already knew I'd love it, because I love Mr. Figaro's records," Francie said. "But seeing it performed live . . ." Her voice trailed off as she grappled to find the words to describe what she was feeling.

"I'm especially glad you were able to hear Florence Easton," Grace said. "She, along with Beatrice de Bonneville, are two of the three finest sopranos performing in opera these days."

"Who's the third?"

"Mary Garden." Grace gave a decisive nod. "If you ever get a chance to hear Mary Garden sing, you must seize it. That's just my opinion, of course. Others may think differently."

But in Francie's view, Grace's opinion counted higher than anyone else's. She tucked the name "Mary Garden" away in her mental file for future reference.

"I thought Antonio Leonardo was splendid in his part, too," she said, "and so handsome." Weeks of living under Grace's influence had Francie adding words like *splendid* to her vocabulary.

"He is both of those things," Grace agreed. "My colleagues close to the opera say he has enormous talent, and a sense of self-importance to match."

"I suppose it must be hard to stay humble when everyone's always telling you you're a wonder," Francie said wistfully. Not that she knew anything about that. She couldn't even get her own mother to attend her little recital. "Oh, Grace. Tonight was absolutely splendid. How can I ever thank you?"

Grace patted her knee. "You can thank me by taking your own singing very seriously and doing your very best with the gifts God has given you."

Settling back in her seat as the train sped through the dark, Francie silently vowed to do exactly that.

As she and Grace got ready for bed in their hotel room, Francie broached the subject of Reinhard Schreiber.

"He seems like a nice man," she prompted, hoping Grace would tell her more about him.

"He is. Very nice. We were fast friends back in our conservatory days." Francie thought Grace sounded a bit wistful, making her wonder about the exact nature of her friendship with Herr Schreiber. But she didn't dare ask such a personal question.

They climbed into their beds, and Grace switched off the lamp on the small table that stood between them and spoke into the darkness.

"Francie, I'm being serious when I say you should enter that competition he mentioned. It's becoming quite the proving ground for young opera hopefuls."

Francie rolled to her side, facing Grace, and rested her head on her arm. "Tell me about it."

"It takes place every summer," Grace said. "Singers come from all over the Midwest to compete in Chicago. Three winners are chosen, and they receive a year's tuition, room and board at the American Conservatory of Music."

"Only three winners?" Francie flopped onto her back. "I don't think I'd stand a chance, do you?"

"Yes, I do. Would I have brought it up if I didn't? Winning such a competition would propel your career. And whether you win or not, the experience of competing would be good for you."

"Maybe. But failure would be so . . . so public," Francie protested. Her fellow competitors would no doubt be accomplished musicians, people who would behave exactly like the unfriendly girls who'd snubbed her at the spring recital. She didn't care to repeat that terrible feeling of being out of place, the proverbial fish out of water.

"You have just as good a chance as anyone else," Grace said firmly. "If singing opera is important to you, I think you should consider it. There's no time to waste, as I believe the contest takes place in August. I have the entry details on my desk. We'll take care of it as soon as we get back."

"August! But that's not nearly enough time to prepare."

"Sure, it is," Grace assured her. "You can perform your recital piece, for one. And in case you make it to the finals, we'll add a couple of other pieces, maybe that little Bohemian aria you like so much. And now, we'd best get our beauty sleep."

Francie lay awake for a long time, mulling over the contest. Singing before a panel of critical judges, she doubted very much that she'd even make it through one song, much less advance to the finals.

But if she won!

Her mind blossomed with imagined scenarios of a successful opera career. Visions of famous concert halls and opera houses took shape in her mind. Audiences applauded her. Conductors praised her. A tuxedo-clad Henry, who'd gone to considerable trouble to track her down in Paris or Vienna, showered her with roses and begged her to dine with him. And there, sitting front and center in the dress-circle of her dreams, sat Ramona, applauding wildly for the smart, talented daughter of whom she was so proud.

But Francie was a realist. Dreams like that had a slim-to-none chance of coming true. In the end, the chance to sing her favorite aria was the dangling carrot that made her overcome her fear and permit Grace to enter her in the competition. When they got back to Scoville, they completed the application form and mailed it in.

And then they set to work on her lessons, harder than they'd ever worked before. If Francie had any chance at all to unlock her future, the judges held the key.

CHAPTER TWENTY

I n the bustling Plaza Bolivar in Caracas, Venezuela, Henry and his cousin, Oliver, craned their necks to stare up at a statue of the great military leader Simon Bolivar sitting astride a rearing horse, looking confident and debonair.

Henry felt anything but confident and debonair. He and Oliver had just come from the American Express office, where Henry had stopped in each day of their stay in hope of receiving a letter with a California postmark, only to leave empty-handed each time.

The ancient capital city surrounded by tall mountains appealed to Henry. The temperate climate, described in his guidebook as "perpetual spring," refreshed and invigorated him after steamy weeks spent in Puerto Rico and the Caribbean. But in spite of the area's beauty, the lack of a letter from Francie left him disgruntled.

He couldn't understand it. How was he supposed to write to her? Had she tried to reach him and the letter had gone astray? Had he given her the wrong address in Caracas? Or was she simply refusing to write to him? He supposed he should take that as a sign that her affection had cooled. Soon they'd be moving on to Cartagena, Colombia. He could only hope that the American Express office would forward her letter—if there ever was one.

The bell in the cathedral tower tolled noon. Henry's stomach rumbled despite earlier having devoured a traditional Venezuelan breakfast of hot chocolate and fried eggs. The high altitude and rigors of sightseeing had given him a voracious appetite.

Oliver gave him a wide smile. "Cheer up, cousin. You look as though you'd lost your best friend."

"Something like that," Henry mumbled.

Oliver clicked his tongue. "It's not a woman, is it?" At Henry's silence, he slapped his palm on the table. "It *is* a woman! Well, come on. Let's go to the *taberna* for lunch."

Henry's hunger persuaded him to follow his cousin to the tavern. A few drinks and a substantial meal later, the good local wine having loosened his tongue, he told Oliver all about his feelings for Francie.

"She's like no one else I've ever known," he said. "Beautiful, yes, but there's something else. She has a sort of sparkle that I've not found in any other girl."

Oliver signaled the waiter for more wine. "And your folks like her?"

Henry stared at his glass. "That's part of the problem. They don't approve."

"Ah." Oliver sat forward, intrigued at the prospect of a family scandal. "Tell me more."

"They don't think she's 'appropriate.' Their word, not mine."

"What is she? A showgirl? A good-time gal?"

Henry bristled. "She's nothing of the sort. She's a perfectly nice girl, and I'm crazy about her."

"I see." Oliver sat back. "Well, there's your problem."

"What is?"

"You care too much. When it comes to choosing a wife, you gotta think about your future, your career, what kind of a woman will fit in.

Until then, well, *que sera, sera*." Oliver clinked his wine glass against Henry's.

"*Que sera, sera*?" Henry mocked, repulsed by his cousin's cavalier attitude toward women.

"What will be, will be." Oliver swirled his glass, then drained it.

"I know what it means," Henry grumbled. Did all Jasper men read from the same playbook? If so, Henry'd never been given a copy. "How would you know, anyway? It's not like *you're* married. You're hardly the voice of experience."

"Ah, but I am." Oliver reached for the bottle and topped off both their glasses. "You might say I'm something of an expert on inappropriate women."

"But what happens when you bring a girl home? Your dad's just as critical as mine."

"That's the key," Oliver said with a self-satisfied smile. "I don't bring them home. When I'm ready to settle down, I'll find the right kind of girl who'll win the parental seal of approval. And so will you. In the meantime, I'm having a little harmless fun. Which is what *you* should be doing."

Henry stared at him in disgust. "I'd never treat Francie that way. Or any woman." Similar words spoken by his father echoed in his mind. Were all Jasper men this callous and uncaring when it came to women?

Oliver shrugged. "Suit yourself. But I suggest you drink up, *amigo*." He reached for the bottle. "If your lady-love can't be bothered to write a letter, my advice to you is to forget her. Look around you. There are plenty of other *señoritas* in the sea."

But Henry didn't want any other *señoritas*.

He wanted Francie.

CHAPTER
TWENTY-ONE

F rancie and Grace again boarded the train to Chicago, this time en route to the Young Artists' Competition. Francie could hardly believe her good fortune. Not only had Grace helped her fill out the application paperwork, but she'd even paid her entry fee—a guardian angel if ever there was one.

On arriving at Union Station, they checked into the same hotel where they'd stayed on their previous visit to the city. In her anxious state, Francie was grateful for surroundings that seemed at least passingly familiar. Why had she let Grace talk her into this?

"It's hardly worth unpacking," she mumbled as she hung her best dress in the closet and smoothed the ruffles. "After the semi-finals tomorrow, I'll be sent home for sure."

"You don't know that." Grace reached for a hanger. "And I don't appreciate your defeatist attitude. We've worked too hard to get derailed by that sort of nonsense."

"I'm sorry. I just wish I shared your optimism."

Grace's voice was brisk. "Well, I'll be optimistic for both of us, as long as you promise me you'll try your very best."

Francie vowed to try. She wasn't being fair to Grace, who'd worked every bit as hard as she had. But her secret wish was to skip the whole ordeal and catch the next train home. She didn't think her nerves could tolerate this dizzying anxiety for a whole weekend.

On Friday, Grace ordered Francie to spend the morning resting her voice. After a light meal at the hotel, of which Francie could scarcely swallow a mouthful, they walked several blocks to the Auditorium Theater on Congress Parkway. Even though the day was warm and muggy, Francie was grateful for the exercise, as it helped her burn off some of her nervous energy.

The Auditorium Theater was grander than anything she'd ever seen, including Piper Hall, which until then had seemed to her the epitome of splendor. The hulking structure was built in what Grace called the "Romanesque" style of architecture. Its pale limestone walls stood out against the darker, sootier buildings surrounding it. Three wide, arched doorways outlined in cream-colored brick indicated the entrance.

In the foyer, colorful posters announced upcoming productions and lead singers. One photograph in particular caught Francie's eye, showing Reinhard Schreiber in action, standing tall and holding a baton. What a thrill to have actually met the man!

Beyond the foyer were more archways, lots of sparkling glass, murals of goddesses holding musical instruments, and chandeliers dripping with crystals. Francie's breath caught in her throat.

"It's like a fairytale palace," she blurted, then blushed at the childishness of the comment.

Grace didn't seem to notice. "It is stunning. No matter how often I've seen it, it never fails to impress."

In the lobby, they hovered near the patron services desk, unsure of where to go or what to do. Near a door marked "Production Manager" was a cloakroom, and a long bar with glasses and liquor bottles lining shelves behind it. *Ramona would feel right at home here*, she thought irreverently, *although these surroundings are a whole lot classier than The Thirsty Swallow*. With a pang of regret, she wished her mother could be there. If she were, maybe this time she'd be impressed to see her daughter on stage. Or, more likely, she'd only disappoint Francie once again.

Dotted throughout the lobby were soft chairs, and Francie longed to sink into one. But before she could do so, a greeter from the committee organizing the competition approached and invited her and Grace to join the other contestants and their families in a side room.

Before the semi-final competition started, the group was given a tour of the building. No hallway, no corner, was left undecorated. Everywhere Francie looked was fancy scrollwork, gilded paint, mosaics, and sculptured images—*bas-relief*, the guide called them.

The four-thousand-seat theater was breathtaking in its size and ornamentation. Hundreds of electric lightbulbs arched across the ceiling and along the walls, casting a golden light over the space. Francie had never before seen so many electric lights in one place, not even at Ravinia Park.

The fanciest lobby, outside the dress circle where the elite people sat, looked especially inviting, with fireplaces and little nooks to sit in. The balcony level featured two enormous oil paintings, one depicting Spring, the other Fall. The very top gallery—the only seat Francie would be likely to afford, if she were ever able to attend a performance—was lofty enough to induce vertigo. The stage far below them had a curved apron, what the guide referred to as a *proscenium*. Francie had never heard the word, just as she had never before heard of *bas-relief* and other unfamiliar terms the guide kept tossing out. She wished she'd brought a notebook in which to copy them down to read about later.

She felt entirely out of her league, and they hadn't even gotten to the competition part yet.

After the tour, the out-of-place feeling only intensified as Francie, now separated from Grace, sat in a large carpeted dressing room with the other competitors. She obviously didn't belong, yet here she was, awaiting her turn to sing amid twenty other would-be opera singers also striving for the grand prize, all of whom looked older and far more self-assured than she was.

The older part didn't surprise her. Contestants had to be between eighteen and twenty-four years old, and Francie'd barely made the cut, having passed her eighteenth birthday mere weeks before. As for the self-assurance, well . . . she hadn't a clue how to go about obtaining something like that. Either a person had it or she didn't.

Winners were guaranteed a year of study at the prestigious American Conservatory of Music. A thriving career was far from certain, but Francie had read in *Opera News* that some recent winners were ranked among the best opera singers in the world. Glancing at the poised and confident men and women seated around her, she believed it.

Some of the other contestants were practicing, running scales, vocalizing, but she couldn't bring herself to sing a note. Her throat felt tight with dread. Across the room, a soprano carried out musical acrobatics with flourishes and flips, and Francie felt sick to her stomach. Grace hadn't taught her to do any fancy vocal work, or *coloratura,* as people called it. They had their plate full just covering the basics. But now she felt totally inadequate, just plain old Francie Forrester from Scoville. It was all she could do not to race out the exit and back to the safety of the hotel.

At last the competition began. Silence reigned in the dressing room as, one by one, singers were ushered into the backstage hallway. Slotted eighteenth of the twenty contestants for her minutes in front of the judges, Francie listened to the others who went before her. She couldn't escape their voices from where she sat, even though the sound came through muffled. From her eavesdropping she'd learned that one contestant had begun vocal training at age seven, another at eight. They'd studied with the country's most prestigious teachers, at Curtls or the Academy of Vocal Arts or other impressive-sounding institutions Francie had never heard of. A male singer performed an aria by Wagner, probably the art form's most daunting composer. The singer's voice floated to a high plateau and stayed there.

Francie broke out in a cold sweat.

She tried to distract herself by silently reciting the lyrics to her performance piece, the same "Jesus Loves Me" that she'd sung at the spring recital. The bare simplicity of the song gnawed at her. Wouldn't the judges and other contestants think it was childish as well? She'd tried to talk Grace into letting her attempt a more ambitious piece, but Grace had stuck to her guns, insisting "Jesus Loves Me" was the perfect vehicle for Francie's voice. Now she concentrated on repeating the words in her mind, letting them transform into a prayer. *Jesus loves me, this I know, for the Bible tells me so.* Jesus loved her, that she knew . . .

But would the judges?

The contestant before her sang a haunting aria from Puccini's *Madama Butterfly* that Francie recognized from both Mr. Figaro's records and Beatrice de Bonneville's recital. The poetic Italian lyrics depicted a lonely woman missing her lover while expressing confidence that, one fine day, he would return to her.

Would he, though? Francie doubted it, thinking of Henry. He should be home from his tour of South America by now, but if so, he hadn't let her know. In fact, he hadn't written to her at all since that one letter. Not even a postcard.

She shook her head to clear it. The last thing she needed to be thinking about right now was her love life—or lack thereof. She needed to focus.

By the time her turn came, she felt as if she were evaporating.

"Francine Forrester," a stagehand said at last. "Please follow me."

She stood, head held high, and followed him, feeling like Anne Boleyn on her way to face the sword.

The walk from the dressing room to the wings meant pushing through doors marked "Do Not Enter," which gave her a sense of foreboding. She walked past a long stretch of gray cinderblock walls. Above her, scaffolding, cables, piping, all rose into dizzying blackness.

Waiting in a tight, dimly lit spot behind tall black curtains, she prayed silently. *Your will, not mine, Lord. If this is meant to be, it's meant to be. Let me sing to the best of my ability. Let me share my voice.*

When her turn came, she stepped out from the wings and into the blinding lights. She willed her rubbery legs to carry her toward the shiny black piano at the center of the stage. Below her the empty orchestra pit plunged like a canyon. No one sat in the darkened main level of the house except the judges, their seven faces floating disembodied like ghosts amid the endless rows.

All of the judges were connected in one way or another to the conservatory, the opera company, or both. The only one who was familiar to Francie was the tenor Antonio Leonardo, whom she'd heard at Ravinia. Reinhard Schreiber was not a judge, but stood watch over all the proceedings.

Grace was seated someplace up in a balcony with the teachers and families of the other semi-finalists. The competition was not open to the public, a fact for which Francie was grateful. She kept her eyes trained on a random point between the tier where Grace sat and the territory of the judges. She felt the solidity of the boards beneath her feet and marveled that she was standing where some of the greatest singers of all time had stood. All the grandeur surrounding her made her feel very small and insignificant.

The pianist played the introduction. Beginning a song felt, to Francie, like getting on a roller-coaster despite having a dire fear of heights. The car climbed higher and higher, and if she handled her dread during those initial seconds, the rest of the ride might go all right. She might be swept along. But if she lost control early, if her nerves started to rise, she would quickly be left wailing, her brain and throat giving way irreversibly to chaos.

Now the piano played the opening rumble of notes, the low tremulous introduction, and then, while the piano went silent, Francie sang her first lines.

She came in on the right note, at the right time. And as her voice soared up and away, to the balcony and beyond, her heart was carried with it.

CHAPTER
TWENTY-TWO

Henry returned from his tour of South America with a tanned complexion, a taste for *carnitas*, a suitcase filled with souvenirs, and a crack in his heart as long as the Amazon. He longed to see Francie again, to hold her in his arms and tell her he was sorry.

He hadn't even been able to write to her over the summer, because she'd never given him her new address in California. He'd received no response at all to the letter he'd sent from on board the ship. Unsure of whether she'd received it, he'd written a second letter from Caracas and posted it to her family's house in Scoville, hoping perhaps they had arranged to have their mail forwarded to their new home, but it had come back marked "Addressee Unknown."

He went over their last conversation in his mind, scrutinizing every word as if he were studying a legal brief. He'd tried to do the right thing, to make the most logical decision possible at the time. But she hadn't seen things the same way, and now her silence told him she'd never forgive him.

On the still, placid waters of the Lincoln Park Lagoon, he sat at the rear of a rented rowboat and pulled the oars at a languid pace. Not a breath of a breeze stirred the air. He stopped rowing long enough to wipe his forehead on the rolled-up cuff of his white shirt and slap away a mosquito. But the heat and humidity of an Illinois August, combined with the exertion of rowing, weren't the only things making him sweat.

Sitting primly in the prow was Lila Gladstone, dressed entirely in pale mint green, a large brimmed hat shading her delicate fair skin from the onslaught of the sun. She, too, was making Henry sweat, the way she simpered and smiled at him as if he were her beau.

He was *not* her beau, but he didn't know how to make that clear to her without being rude or hurting her feelings.

"You'll be leaving town soon," she'd said thirty minutes earlier. "Isn't it time you made plans for something more? A man has to plan for his future." For all her teeth-aching sweetness, she had an aggressive way about her that was disconcerting.

"Just doing well in law school will be enough for now," Henry had said, feeling like a cornered fox with the hounds yapping and the hunting bugle sounding in the distance. This whole excursion had been his mother's idea. She'd pressured him to take Lila out the Saturday before he was to leave for Columbia Law School.

"Please do it, as a favor to both Lila and her parents. And to me," Mother had wheedled over breakfast. "The girl admires you so much."

"Well, I don't admire her," Henry had replied. "At least not in that way. I mean, she's nice enough and all, but she's hardly my type." How much clearer could he be?

"I'm not asking you to marry her," Mother said, "although I do think you two would make an ideal match. But if you could just show Lila a little attention before you leave, it would please both her and her parents. I need them to be in a good mood when I approach them about sponsoring the Fall Cotillion. Besides, Mr. Gladstone is one of your father's best clients. You want to make him happy, don't you?"

"Ah." Henry pushed back from the table. "So there are ulterior motives at play."

Mother gave him a beseeching look. "Please, Henry. Just this once. I promise I won't ask again."

Henry always had trouble saying no to his mother, so he'd telephoned Lila after breakfast and invited her to accompany him for an afternoon at the park. But now he regretted his decision. While she was quite pretty and looked good on a fellow's arm, Lila had little to contribute to a conversation beyond gossip about people he didn't care about and long, involved retellings of who had said what to whom at which society event. He doubted she had ever read a book that hadn't been assigned in school, or looked at anything in the newspaper other than the society pages. Taking a rowboat out onto the lagoon had sounded fun, but now he wished he had chosen to take her to a matinee instead, or some other entertainment where he wouldn't have to struggle to keep a conversation going. He looked at the waning angle of the sun and tried to estimate how soon he could take her home without appearing rude.

How unlike Francie she was. With Francie, Henry had never struggled to find things to talk about. Despite the fact that she wasn't well educated in the traditional sense—the sense that mattered to his parents—she was a reader and stayed well informed. She held definite opinions and could hold her own on a variety of topics. If a subject was unfamiliar to her, she asked intelligent questions about it until she understood.

He'd been such a fool to let Francie go. On the other hand, he couldn't in good conscience ask her to sit around and wait for him for years while he earned his law degree and established a practice. And he certainly couldn't support a wife while he was in law school, especially since his father had made it clear he'd cut off Henry's financial support if he married Francie.

But in spite of all these reasons, he knew the truth. She was the right girl for him. She'd simply come along at the wrong time. Meanwhile, he was stuck in a rowboat with the wrong girl.

But how could he find her again? The only people who might know how to reach Francie in California were Miss Whitworth and Mr. Figaro. If anybody from Scoville stayed in touch with her, it would be those two.

Henry made a rash decision.

He *had* to get in touch with Francie, if only to clear the air between them before he left for law school. He shot to his feet so quickly that he rocked the rowboat, causing Lila to clutch her hat and squeal in alarm.

"I'm sorry, Lila," he said. "I just remembered some important business I have to take care of before I leave for New York."

He rowed them back to shore at unprecedented speed, settled up with the boat's owner, and escorted Lila home, carefully avoiding any kind of familiar talk or emotional good-bye scene that would allow her to think they were anything other than platonic friends. Once she was safely deposited at her family's home, he raced the few blocks home and arrived, panting and sweating, in the back hall where the main telephone was kept. He didn't care if the servants overheard his conversation, but thought it probably best if his parents didn't.

"Operator? Grace Whitworth's residence in Scoville, please." He bounced on the balls of his feet while the phone rang. When he received no answer there, he tried the college, but again received no response, unsurprising on a summer Saturday. Classes wouldn't be in session for another week.

Frustrated that he couldn't ask Miss Whitworth for Francie's whereabouts, he had one option left. Mr. Figaro. Surely he'd be at the restaurant, preparing for the dinner crowd.

"Café Figaro in Scoville, please," he instructed the operator.

After several rings, a brusque voice Henry recognized as Mr. Figaro's came over the line.

"Café Figaro, *buonasera*."

Saturday evenings tended to be busy. Henry'd make this quick.

"Hello, Mr. Figaro. This is Henry Jasper calling."

After a pause, Mr. Figaro said, "Yes?" in a cool tone. Francie must have told him what had transpired between them, the uncertain way things had been left. Perhaps she'd shared her heart with her employer, letting him know exactly how much Henry had disappointed her. He cringed, then ratcheted up his courage.

"I-I'm trying to get in touch with Francie Forrester. Do you happen to know where I can reach her?"

"She no here."

"I know she's not there," Henry said with growing exasperation. "But I was hoping you could tell me where I can write to her."

Mr. Figaro cleared his throat. "I don't know she wanna hear from you."

"Please, Mr. Figaro," Henry pleaded. "I just want to send her a letter. I have something important to tell her."

Another long pause. Then, "I ask her when I see her, next time she come in. If she say okay, I give you her address. You call back next week. Good-bye."

The receiver clicked.

"Wait—what?" Henry shouted into the phone, startling a passing housemaid. "When you *see* her? You mean, she hasn't gone to California?"

But the line was dead.

He asked the operator to retry the number, but Mr. Figaro did not answer again. He then asked her to try Francie's former number, but she informed him it had been disconnected. Finally, in desperation, he tried Grace Whitworth's home again. Still no answer.

Henry leaned his forehead against the wall. Mr. Figaro's response indicated Francie was still in Scoville, not California. This was Saturday evening. He didn't have to leave for New York until Monday. He'd drive out to Scoville first thing in the morning and spend his last day in Illinois tracking her down. He'd get to the bottom of why she hadn't answered either of his letters and try to patch things up with her before he left. Maybe he could salvage something of their tattered relationship after all. Get a fresh start.

It was all he could do to wait for morning.

CHAPTER TWENTY-THREE

F rancie was ecstatic to hear her name called among the finalists invited to return on Saturday.

"I'm so very proud of you," Grace told her over dinner that night at the hotel. "And clearly you impressed the judges."

"I hope so," Francie replied between bites of chicken pot pie. After hardly eating anything all day, her appetite had returned with a vengeance. "But there's still tomorrow to get through. Those other singers are the best of the best."

"And right now, they're thinking the very same thing about you."

Francie's heart melted within her. "You've done so much for me, from giving me lessons to letting me live with you to introducing me to Ravinia, to encouraging me to enter this contest. I hope I won't let you down."

Grace reached across the table and touched her hand. "You know I'll be proud of you, no matter what happens tomorrow. Win or lose, you've made me very proud to be your teacher."

Nonetheless, Francie barely slept that night, and couldn't eat a bite of breakfast.

Saturday's final competition was a repeat of Friday's, with half as many contestants. In the now-familiar dressing room, even those finalists who'd seemed so confident the day before were subdued and quiet as they sized each other up.

Each contestant performed two arias in the finals. The singer picked the first, which in Francie's case was "Vissi d'Arte," at Grace's suggestion. She liked it and was confident she could sing it well, and she did. The judges listened, conferred among themselves for about ten seconds, and chose the second piece from a short list of options that Francie had submitted ahead of time, again with Grace's help.

"'Song to the Moon,' from *Rusalka*," one of the judges called up to her. A rush of relief coursed through her that they'd chosen her very favorite aria, one with which she was intimately familiar. One that, paradoxically, brought Henry to mind.

Henry.

Not now, she told herself sternly. *You can think about him later. For now, just sing.*

Her throat suddenly dry, she drank from a glass of water supplied by a committee member. As she swallowed, she sent up a prayer. *Lord, I don't think I can do this. You take over, please. Make this performance what You want it to be, not what I want it to be. Your will be done.*

As she relinquished the situation to One far greater than she, a peaceful sensation settled over her. She handed the water glass to the committee member and nodded to the pianist. Then she opened her mouth and poured all of her pain over Henry into her song. Her love-struck character inhabited her body, and she *became* the water nymph Rusalka, who falls in love with a human prince. She sang about heartbreak and lost love with authentic beauty and pain.

Moon, where is my lover?

Her culminating note soared above the piano. When she finished, she exhaled with giddy exuberance. Her timing had been exact, her pitch perfect.

Her heart swelled with gratitude, knowing God had carried her through. No matter the results, she knew she'd done well.

The observers in the balcony applauded heartily, as they had for every finalist. She exited the stage, shaking but triumphant, and, speaking to no one, made a beeline for the ladies' room, not emerging until her stomach had calmed, she'd stopped shaking, and her breathing had returned to normal.

Meanwhile, two more finalists took their turns. Then the judges hid themselves away to begin their debating and tallying while the singers waited in the dressing room, reassuring one another that they'd won just by being there, by getting to the finals. Francie tried to believe it. The unceasing chatter was making her dizzy.

An hour and a half after the last performance, a stagehand came into the dressing room and said, "Finalists, please come to stage right and line up." On quaking legs, Francie followed the others down the hall and behind the stage to the wings. At last they filed onto the stage.

"We have three winners today," Reinhard Schreiber announced.

Ten singers in suits and gowns stood in a row, silent and still.

Francie scanned the director's face. She forgot Henry, forgot her pride. He read out the finalists, singer by singer, pausing for applause after each one, pronouncing the names with gravity and excitement. Name by name, Francie heard her chances of winning diminish. This must not have been God's plan for her, after all. *Not my will but Yours,* she prayed as pieces of her dream began crashing to the floor.

He announced a soprano—the one who'd performed the fancy vocal acrobatics. Next a baritone. Her chances diminished to one. She clenched her chest, constrained her breath. It seemed that if she inhaled too loudly, she could miss her name and forfeit her spot. Her fists stayed tight, but she was certain it was finished. She'd lost the competition. She'd let Grace down. Ramona's voice rang in her head. "What'd I tell ya? Those music lessons was just a waste of—"

Herr Schreiber was speaking. "And, last but not least . . . Miss Francine Forrester."

She burst into sobbing, gasping, ugly tears.

Someone touched her shoulder and gently nudged her forward. Someone else thrust a bouquet of roses into her arms. She regained her composure.

Thank You, Jesus. Thank You.

The next hour passed in a blur of congratulations and popping camera bulbs. People who hadn't bothered to speak to her all weekend suddenly sought her out, acting as though they were best friends. Through it all, Grace stood beside her and held her hand.

But despite all the accolades and excitement, deep in her heart, Francie couldn't help but wish that Henry could have been there to celebrate this moment with her. She knew he would have been proud.

That night, she lay awake, staring at the ceiling of the hotel room, too wired to sleep. After her triumph in the competition, the other winners and their families had invited her and Grace to join them in a late-night celebration supper. The combination of excitement, relief, and rich food made falling asleep nearly impossible.

Across the room, Grace snored softly. Francie slipped out of bed as silently as she could. She padded barefoot to the window and looked up at the sky, trying to catch sight of the stars, but the bright lights of the city obscured whatever there might have been. *Moon, where is my lover?* she sang in her mind.

But on this night, the moon, like her lover, was nowhere to be found.

CHAPTER
TWENTY-FOUR

H enry rose very early on Sunday morning and drove his impeccable Pierce-Arrow—a graduation gift from his grandparents—the hour and a half to Scoville. His plan was to arrive in time for the ten o'clock service at Scoville Community Church, listen to Francie sing in the choir, then surprise her after the service with lunch and an entire afternoon together. In his imagination, they'd talk, and laugh, and clear away the strain of misunderstanding that currently hung in the air between them.

Minutes before ten o'clock, he parked in front of the church, bounded up the front steps, and chose a seat with an excellent view of the choir loft. But when the service started, Francie did not appear with the rest of the choir. Henry scanned the pews, but didn't see her anywhere in the congregation. Nor did he see Miss Whitworth. What was going on? The pair of them rarely missed church. Had he misunderstood Mr. Figaro? Had Francie moved to California, after all?

He slumped back in the pew. So much for his grand surprise.

He fidgeted through the service, then immediately afterward made a beeline for Miss Whitworth's house. He rang the bell repeatedly, but no one answered.

Dejected, he headed for Francie's former home. Her family had moved away, of course, but perhaps the new renters had information on where Francie might be, a forwarding address or telephone number. When he rang the doorbell, a short, stout woman answered.

"Excuse me for bothering you," Henry said. "I'm trying to find the Forrester family. Specifically, Miss Francine Forrester. They were the previous renters in this house."

"I'm sorry," the woman told him. "We're new here. I don't know who the Forresters are or anything about them."

Henry apologized again, and the woman closed the door. He stood on the porch a moment, uncertain of what to do next. There was no use looking for Francie at her job, as Café Figaro was closed on Sundays. Where else might she be?

As a last-ditch effort, he looked up Mr. Figaro's home address in the telephone directory and drove over there. His desire to find Francie overcame his trepidation over Mr. Figaro's probable anger when Henry washed up on his doorstep. But there was no answer at the Figaro home, either. Where the heck was everybody?

He parked the Pierce-Arrow on Main Street and wandered the Sunday-quiet streets of Scoville, hoping to run into Francie, or someone who knew her, by chance. He ended up at the college campus. Although he'd only graduated the previous spring, the place looked unfamiliar and strange. It was no longer his school.

She was no longer his girl.

He sat for a while on the familiar bench on the sledding hill, reliving memories of happier times spent there with Francie and kicking himself over how he'd made a mess of everything. A tall maple tree shaded him from the hot sun. Cicadas buzzed in the lilac bushes, now leafy and full, but lacking their sweet-smelling flowers.

His heart ached.

As evening fell, he gave up. His trip had been wasted. He slammed the car door, roared back to the city, and prepared to catch the morning train bound for New York, vowing to put Miss Francie Forrester forever out of his mind.

Elated but exhausted, Francie and Grace slept late, then treated themselves to breakfast at the hotel, checked out of their room, and killed time before their train with a quick visit to the Art Institute. Grace was eager to view a special exhibit there of paintings by Swedish artists. Francie obliged but, still dazzled by the events of the weekend, paid scant attention to the artworks. Finally, on the train for Scoville, she slept during most of the ninety-minute ride.

When they disembarked at Scoville, Grace stopped at a newsstand and purchased one of the last copies of that day's *Scoville Scoop*. Dropping their bags right there on the floor of the station's waiting room, they seated themselves, and Grace flipped through the paper until she found the arts section. She scanned it closely.

"There might be nothing there." Francie rubbed at a smudge on her white glove. Sometimes it took an extra day, or even two, for city news to reach the *Scoop*, if it made it there at all. After all, it was just a little music contest.

But Grace pointed at the page and grinned.

Francie took it from her and read the small item.

Miss Francine Forrester of Scoville, who has been
studying under eminent vocal instructor Grace Whitworth, is among the winners of the 1916 Young
Artists' Competition. This fall she will take her place
in the incoming class at the American Conservatory
of Music, with the additional possibility of securing
the prize that all young singers strive for, namely an
engagement with the Windy City Opera Company.

"That's something to save in your scrapbook," Grace declared with
shining eyes.

"I don't keep a scrapbook," Francie said, dazed at the sight of her
name in the newspaper.

"You'll need to start one now," Grace told her. "A scrapbook
chronicling your grand opera career."

Francie teetered on the edge of tears, deeply touched by Grace's
unflagging certainty that she'd eventually gather enough music-related
notes and photos and clippings and other bits of ephemera to fill a
whole scrapbook. In the meantime, she'd soon be a student at the music conservatory. And if all went well, that credential would eventually
lead to her first engagement with an opera company.

While that might not have been the sort of engagement she'd once
hoped to have with Henry, perhaps this one would turn out to be even
better.

Perhaps she truly was on her way.

Just as they emerged from the train station, a fancy, shiny roadster
roared across the tracks and careened down Main Street in the direction of the highway, leaving a cloud of dust in its wake.

"Goodness, what was that?" Grace exclaimed.

"A Pierce-Arrow, I think." Francie squinted in the setting sun. "I saw a picture of one on the cover of Mr. Bailey's automobile magazine. But I can't imagine anyone in Scoville owning one. Probably an out-of-towner."

"Well, he'd better slow down and watch where he's going, or he's liable to kill someone," Grace muttered.

The next morning, in her little bedroom at Grace's, Francie emptied her music satchel, stuffed full of various materials she'd picked up over the weekend. Musical scores, written remarks from the judges, congratulatory notes from agents and opera patrons and fellow contestants, stacks of orientation material from the conservatory, and strangers' calling cards slid out. Too weary to read through everything the night before, she'd slung the satchel on a chair, intending to sort through it in the clear light of day. She also wanted to write to Molly. She could hardly wait to tell her the thrilling news that she'd be joining her at the conservatory, after all, and asking if she'd like to room together.

Running her fingers inside the satchel one last time for any remaining items, a lump in the inner lining on one side caught her attention. Curious, she held the satchel toward the light and found a seldom-used pocket. She pulled out an envelope and started to add it to the pile on the dresser. Then, recognizing it, she gasped.

It was her letter to Henry, addressed to him at the American Express office in Caracas. The letter telling him she planned to stay with Grace for the summer instead of moving to California with her family. The letter she assumed he'd failed to answer.

He'd never answered—because she'd never mailed it.

CHAPTER
TWENTY-FIVE

As soon as she realized her mistake, Francie picked up the telephone in the kitchen and practically begged the operator to connect her to the Abbott Jasper residence in Chicago. When the connection went through, a female voice answered.

"Jasper residence."

Francie applied her most cheerful voice. "Good morning. Mrs. Jasper? This is Francie Forrester. You might remember me. We met at Henry's graduation."

The brisk voice cut her off. "This is the housekeeper speaking. Mrs. Jasper is unavailable at the moment. May I give her a message?"

"Oh. No. Sorry," Francie said, flustered. "I'm actually calling to speak to Mr. Henry Jasper."

The housekeeper told her that Henry Jasper was not at home.

"Is he still in South America?" Francie ventured, her hope spiraling.

"He has returned to the States, but this morning he left for school and isn't expected back for several months." The housekeeper sounded eager to get off the telephone.

"I see." Francie's spirit shrank. He'd been home for who knows how long, and she hadn't even known. She'd missed him entirely. And he hadn't tried to get in touch with her.

"I'd like to write to him, if I may," she said listlessly. "Do you have his address at school?"

She felt she owed him an explanation about the letter she'd failed to mail, telling him she hadn't gone to California after all. He probably thought she'd ignored his letter on purpose. And here she'd been blaming *him* for not writing, when the whole time it had been *her* fault. Did he even care about her anymore?

"I'm afraid I'm not at liberty to share that information," the housekeeper replied crisply. "But I can ask Mrs. Jasper to return your call when she's available. Perhaps she'll be able to provide more information."

Francie gave the woman her name and telephone number at Grace's, but held out little hope Diana Jasper would return the call. The ensuing days proved that hunch to be true, and she dared not call again.

But there was little time to mope. The start of the new school year loomed, and arrangements needed to be made speedily for Francie's housing and other practical details before she left for Chicago. Grace assisted her as much as she could, helping to pad out her meager wardrobe and coaching her on what to expect from city life. Molly wrote back and expressed her delight that Francie'd be joining her at the conservatory, and that she'd be thrilled to share living accommodations.

On her last day of work at the restaurant, saying good-bye to dear Mr. Figaro was one of the hardest things Francie had ever done.

"I'm losing the best waitress I ever had," he moaned as they sat together in the empty restaurant after Francie's last shift. The mournful expression in his eyes told her his sadness was sincere.

"It's all your fault," she accused him around the lump in her throat. "If you hadn't encouraged my singing and lent me all those opera records, I never would have gotten the burr under my saddle to do something crazy like this."

"A burr under your what?" he asked with a quizzical frown at the unfamiliar saying.

Francie grinned in spite of herself. "Never mind. I'm just saying that I never would have heard Beatrice de Bonneville in person, or thought it was possible for a girl like me to reach for something bigger, something in the big world outside Scoville, if it weren't for you."

"Bah! Is not only me, Francesca. The whole town wishes the best for you, our little star."

"Not everyone," Francie said. "Not Mrs. Dornbusch. She says opera music is of the devil."

He considered this. "Some is, maybe," he conceded, "but more of it is of God. Like any art form, it can be used for bad or for good." He took her hand in his rough one. "Is a big, big world out there, Francesca. You will, how they say, make it storm."

"I think you mean 'take it by storm.'" She smiled through her sudden tears. "I will. I promise."

"And I will come to the opera house to hear you sing," he continued. "When you have finished, I will stand and shout, 'Brava! Brava!' And I will tell everyone I meet, 'I know that grand diva, that Francesca Forrester, she is nice girl, she is fine singer, but watch out in the kitchen. She forgets always the *parmagiana* for the minestrone.'"

They shared a laugh. Then Mr. Figaro gasped.

"Oh, no, Francesca. I almost forgot to tell you."

"Tell me what?"

"That college boy called here looking for you the other day. Henry Jasper."

Francie's blood heated. "Henry called here? When?"

"When you were away at the contest. I completely forgot to tell you."

A wave of wild hope, tinged with rage at poor Mr. Figaro, swept over Francie. She fought to keep her voice calm. "What did he say?"

"Just that he was looking for you. He thought maybe I knew where you were living."

"Did you tell him?"

"No. I did not know if you would want me to. I told him I would ask your permission, and that he should call back later. And then in all the excitement after you won the contest, I forgot all about telling you. I am so sorry."

"That's all right." Francie swallowed her disappointment. Mr. Figaro wasn't at fault. He'd tried to do the right thing. "Did he ever call back?"

"No."

She drew a breath. "Well, then. He must not have been all that interested in finding me."

Mr. Figaro hung his head in apology. "I am so very sorry, Francesca."

She touched his arm. "It's all right. Truly. If he calls again . . ." She faltered. *If he calls again, then what?* "Well, I don't think he will," she said at last. "But Grace Whitworth will always know how to get in touch with me in the future. Should anyone care."

How funny life is, she thought as she walked back to Grace's house. An unmailed letter. A missed phone call. If God had wanted her and Henry to connect, he wouldn't have allowed so many near-misses. She felt a little better knowing Henry had tried to reach her, after all. He hadn't tried very hard, it seemed, but he did try.

What good was that now? He was on his way to New York, and she was headed for Chicago. He'd be immersed in law school, and she'd be too busy adjusting to life at the conservatory to have anything to do with boyfriends. And that was that.

When Henry had told her they were following different paths, he'd been one-hundred-percent right. And yet, a part of her heart would always ache for him—for what might have been.

CHAPTER
TWENTY-SIX

T wo days later, as they waited together on the platform for Francie's train, Grace said, "I want to be honest with you."

That made Francie smile. When had her dear teacher ever *not* been completely honest, even brutally so?

"In Chicago, you will meet many students from more privileged backgrounds," she continued. "Some people may assume you won't be as good. You must understand deep in your bones that you are every ounce as capable as anyone else. More so than many, I daresay."

Francie clung to those words during those harrowing first weeks at the conservatory. On Grace's advice, she registered for classes in voice, music theory, and French. Her summer of Italian lessons with Mr. Figaro paid off, as the foreign-language instructor deemed her accent more authentic than most of the students'. But she was told that French was essential, and next year she would have to study German as well, which sounded intimidating.

She doubted there'd even be a next year, since the scholarship only covered one year, but she put the matter in God's hands and determined not to worry about it.

Her music classes brought a tidal wave of craziness. The clefs and accidentals, the measures and signatures and dynamics of the score were totally strange and mysterious to her. They might as well have been Egyptian hieroglyphs. What did it mean for a note to be natural? And a musical interval? And a chord progression? As competent a teacher as Grace Whitworth was, she and Francie had only worked together for about eight months, barely enough time to scratch the surface of the world of classical music. Francie could follow the notes up and down the score, knew which ones were short and which were held long, and understood the basics of counting out the beat. Beyond that, she was at sea.

The conservatory enrolled her as a so-called "special student" because she hadn't finished high school. This peculiar status was just one more thing that set her apart from her peers and made her feel different. She didn't want to feel different, not in any way. Yet she was behind the others before she'd even started.

Everything about the place and the people screamed "You don't belong here." When she'd passed Reinhard Schreiber in the corridor, he'd barely acknowledged her, not at all the friendly man she'd met at Ravinia Park. He seemed like a man with a lot on his mind.

She received a modest stipend for living expenses, free voice lessons, and artistic coaching, but it didn't stretch very far in an expensive city like Chicago. Thank goodness she was able to split living expenses with Molly Mulroney. Although she, too, had an admirable singing voice, Molly had enrolled at the conservatory to study her first love, the violin. As Francie'd hoped, she proved to be a cheerful, easygoing person to live with. On more than one occasion during that first week, Francie's anxiety convinced her she'd made a mistake in entering the competition and joining the conservatory, and she almost quit, but each time Molly talked her out of it.

"You belong here as much as anybody else," she declared. "Don't let anybody make you feel otherwise."

At an orientation assembly, the head of the conservatory's voice department spoke directly to the aspiring opera students. "With opera, you have these extraordinary works of art, and for the rare person who is gifted to sing in this way—truly gifted—the voice is nothing less than a life force."

Francie agreed that singing was her life force, given to her by God. But as for being rare, she didn't feel rare at all as she looked around at all the other students she deemed more talented and experienced. Only time would tell who would eventually succeed and who would wash out of the program.

The conservatory was a very competitive place, and Molly was her only true friend. They roomed together in a plain, no-frills walk-up on the fourth floor of a rooming house.

"These stairs are going to kill me," Francie panted the day they moved in.

"Climbing stairs is good exercise," Molly panted back. "Good for toning up our breathing."

How like Molly to see the bright side of everything. Her sunny disposition would get them through even the darkest, most homesick days.

Even so, the roommates seldom saw each other. Francie worked all the time, either in classes or studying and practicing on her own. In rare quiet moments, her heart still ached for Henry, but she didn't have much time to mourn over their broken relationship, which was a blessing. She was lonely for Grace, who for Francie had become so much more than a teacher, but also a counselor, confessor, and friend. She missed Will, but she'd received cheerful letters from him that indicated he was enjoying life in California, so she didn't worry about him.

On the other hand, she didn't miss her mother very much, and felt guilty about her lack of feeling whenever Ramona came to mind, which wasn't often. Nonetheless, she sincerely hoped her mother had found happiness at last with Mr. Bailey and sunny California, and prayed for all of them every night.

Her new voice teacher, a stern Frenchwoman named Marie-Louise Clairvaux, was every bit as demanding as Grace Whitworth without any of her warmth.

"Unerring precision and piercing comprehension are critical to operatic singing," she told Francie at their first lesson, in a tone that indicated Francie had neither quality.

To make matters even more awkward, Madame Clairvaux made it clear she thought it unseemly that Francie, as a condition of her prize, might be permitted to sing in the opera chorus without, as Madame saw it, enduring a suitably grueling apprenticeship.

"To train to be an opera singer takes as much time as to train to be a physician." She sniffed. "One doesn't simply *join*, as if it were a school chorus. It simply isn't done."

Francie didn't bother to explain that she hadn't "joined" anything. She'd qualified for her spot at the conservatory by winning over stiff competition, a fact Madame Clairvaux knew full well. And if she did obtain a small part in an opera, it would also be because of hard work and dedication as well as ability.

But in spite of her sour disposition, the woman had a reputation for turning out highly skilled sopranos who were sought after by major opera companies, and Francie did her best to please her. Madame Clairvaux knew the Windy City Opera Company from the inside, having sung as one of its leading sopranos before vanishing from the stage a decade earlier.

They'd gotten off to a rocky start at their first lesson when Francie had attempted to sing, in French, an aria from *La Traviata* that she'd worked on a little with Grace. Before she even made it through the first few lines, the teacher stopped her.

"What language are you singing?"

"French," Francie ventured timidly.

"I didn't understand a single word." Madame Clairvaux seemed to take Francie's lack of language skill as a personal affront. From then on, she made it her special mission to force Francie to learn French, even though she was already enrolled in French class and Madame Clairvaux was supposed to be training her voice, not her language skills.

The haughty teacher showed zero patience. But Francie soon realized that, when it came to dealing with Madame Clairvaux, she'd need all the patience she could muster.

Even that brought thoughts of Henry. Was he struggling in his studies, as busy, as exhausted at the end of each day, as she was?

CHAPTER
TWENTY-SEVEN

Henry emerged through the tall, arched doorway of the red-brick Kent Hall at Columbia University School of Law, squinting in the autumn sunshine. The brisk air felt invigorating after hours spent bent over his books in the third-floor law library. His growling stomach demanded dinner.

"Let's go get some grub," he suggested to his classmate Bill Sykes, a burly fellow from Massachusetts.

"Jasper! Sykes! Wait up."

Jim Lyon approaching them, brandishing a clipboard. Panting, he thrust the clipboard toward Henry, along with a pen.

Henry looked at the page filled with columns of signatures. "What's this about?"

"It's a petition asking the administration to approve a military training camp here on campus," Jim explained. "General Leonard Wood is setting up training camps at colleges all over the country. We think Columbia should have one, too."

"We don't need any military training camps here," Bill Sykes snarled. "Columbia isn't a military college. Leave that to places like West Point."

"Hold on a minute, Bill," Henry said. "I read a newspaper article about these camps. Seems to me they're not a bad idea. They'd give fellows like us some military training, you know, in case we get pulled into the war."

"The war President Wilson promised he'd keep us out of," Bill countered.

"Yes, he did. But more recently he's been saying it's important to be prepared," Henry said. "The U. S. needs to be strong, to be at the ready, just in case."

"That's what this camp would do." Jim tapped the pen on the clipboard. "To support the president's preparedness initiatives. There'd be classes in military science, for example, and training in firearms."

"Firearms," Bill sneered. "That'll never fly."

"Most of the student body is in favor of it, even if some of the faculty isn't," Jim said. "Participation would be voluntary, not compulsory. Plus it would build discipline and respect for authority."

Privately, Henry thought he'd had quite enough discipline and respect for authority drilled into him by his father. But, reluctant as he was to interrupt his studies, the reality of the war in Europe and accounts of the suffering of innocent people never failed to tug at his conscience. He'd been itching to get involved somehow, to actually do something about it instead of complain.

"Don't tell me *you* want to join the military," Bill scoffed. "To slog through mud and follow orders and get shot at."

"I want to do what's right," Henry said. "Besides, it's just a training camp, not enlistment."

He took the pen from Jim and scrawled his signature on the next available line. Then he held it toward Bill, who shook his head. With a shrug, Henry handed the petition back to Jim, who moved off in search of his next target.

"Come on. Let's go eat," Bill said.

Henry complied, though he wasn't feeling too keen toward Bill at the moment. Maybe he could talk to the fellow, persuade him to change his mind.

As they walked away from the building, he glanced back at the words inscribed over the archway.

IUS EST ARS BONI ET AEQUI. *Law is the art of the good and the just.*

"The good and the just," Henry muttered.

"What'd you say?"

"Nothing." It would have sounded awfully corny to Bill.

But Henry aspired to be both.

CHAPTER
TWENTY-EIGHT

A s the weeks passed, Francie's schedule calmed into a routine of
sorts. She found her classes both challenging and stimulating,
but her voice lessons were beyond the pale.

One October day, as they labored over a difficult passage from
Carmen during a particularly onerous lesson, Madame Clairvaux interrupted Francie's singing. She pinched the bridge of her nose. "Do
you not comprehend, Francine?" she asked, pronouncing the name in
the nasally French manner. Her mouth hardened, and below her stiff
pompadour her forehead wrinkled in disdain. Not only did Francie
appear incapable of reading music with the most basic fluency, but she
stumbled badly over the French words, one of opera's most essential
languages. "Do you understand that the stress is placed on the second
syllable?"

"I'm sorry." *The most stress is placed on the head of the hapless student.* She wished they could abandon French and return to the more
patient and comfortable realm of Mr. Figaro's Italian.

"Pronunciation is crucial to opera, even if half the American audience doesn't know the difference," Madame Clairvaux snipped. "To
garble the language is to make a mockery of the art."

"Yes, Madame." Francie looked down at her scuffed shoes.

"Stand up straight. Start again," Madame commanded. Francie did as she was told. But soon the teacher said "Stop," closed her eyes, and rubbed her temples as if Francie's singing caused her physical pain.

"I am constitutionally incapable of rehearsing this beautiful song so full of mistakes," she declared. "You must go home and practice, practice, practice. I'll expect to see some real progress by next week."

Francie slunk out of the studio, ashamed, despairing of ever pleasing her unreasonable teacher. She stepped out into the brisk winds of Michigan Avenue and took a deep breath to clear her head. Then she headed for the Auditorium Theater one block south, where initial rehearsals for the opera company's upcoming production of Richard Strauss's *Salomé* were taking place.

Francie'd learned that one of the stars of *Salomé* was world-renowned Scottish soprano Mary Garden, who would play Salomé to Antonio Leonardo's John the Baptist. She hadn't forgotten Grace's admonition to hear Mary Garden sing if she ever got the chance. She wouldn't be able to afford a ticket to see the actual opera, but sitting in on a rehearsal would be the next best thing.

Rehearsals weren't open to the public, but this wasn't the first time Francie had sneaked into one. She liked to watch the professionals at work. She didn't care if she had to sit on a step or stand in the corridor. She would slip unnoticed into sessions and quietly absorb everything that was going on.

Away from the splendid grandeur of its public spaces, the rest of the Auditorium had an atmosphere as functional and workaday as any office building. Backstage there was a locker room for the staff. In the lower level, below the theater, the floors were cement, the walls made of gray cinderblocks, and the corridors dimly lit by flickering fluorescent fixtures. There was a break room and a bulletin board filled

with notices for the singers and musicians. Another intriguing space
was the paint room, where the artists who worked on the sets tested
paint colors and practiced techniques. But Francie's favorite room was
dedicated to archival storage—posters, stage scenery flats, costumes,
props. She would have liked nothing better than to have a few free
hours to poke around in there to her heart's content. But today wasn't
that day.

The opera schedule was extremely demanding. Over a season last-
ing from mid-autumn through late spring, performances ran seven
days a week. In a typical season over twenty operas would be presented,
with three or four in production and others in rehearsal at any given
time. In the few years that he'd been musical director of the company,
Reinhard Schreiber had been steadily turning Chicago into an internationally recognized opera center.

Taking a seat on a trunk in a dim, out-of-the-way corner of the
rehearsal room, Francie watched him work. The room had tiers of
seats rising to the top, most of them empty since Herr Schreiber was
working only with the principal singers that day. They were doing an
early run-through from the Strauss opera, which would be presented
after *Eugene Onegin* closed. Eagerly, Francie scanned the cluster of
singers seated in the first couple of rows, looking for Mary Garden's
regal profile, but the great diva had not yet arrived.

As Francie waited for the rehearsal to get underway, her stomach
growled. Her monthly stipend didn't go very far in an expensive city
like Chicago, so she saved money by only eating one meal a day, and
a pretty meager one at that. She'd thought about trying to find a
part-time job to ease her strained budget. But she didn't see how she
could add a job and still keep up with her schoolwork, rehearsals, and
practice schedule, plus eat and sleep occasionally.

Suddenly, her name was called. She emerged from her reverie with a start to find Herr Schreiber's piercing blue eyes staring straight at her.

"Miss Forrester," he called again. "Is that you, lurking there in the shadows?"

She gulped and rose. "Um . . . yes." She hoped he wouldn't humiliate her by sending her away in front of everyone.

"Come here," he commanded, pointing to an empty chair directly in front of the podium. "Miss Garden has sent word that she will be unable to attend rehearsal today. Come and fill in for her."

"You want me to—what?" Francie stammered. *Fill in for Mary Garden, the world-famous diva?*

Herr Schreiber frowned. "You are a soprano, are you not?"

Francie nodded.

"Well, come on then. We haven't got all day." He rapped his baton on the podium. "Don't waste our time."

Lightheaded with embarrassment and wonder, she did as she was told. The director handed her a score flipped opened to the proper page. To her great relief, the lyrics were in Italian, not German as she'd expected, given the composer's nationality. She wouldn't understand any of the words, but at least she would pronounce them correctly.

The rehearsal proceeded as smoothly as it could, given Francie's nervousness and inexperience. She hit some notes with energy and sustained them with polish. Other notes brought strain to her voice. She blundered in her timing. Herr Schreiber rapped his baton, and the rehearsal pianist went silent.

"You're coming in too soon. Breathe with me." The director took an exaggerated breath just before Francie was supposed to enter so she could match his inhale and join the piano on the proper beat.

The other singers were kind and patient toward her, and despite Herr Schreiber's frequent criticisms, his comment at the end of the rehearsal was encouraging.

"Well done, Miss Forrester," he said. "I have no doubt you shall soon be giving Mary Garden a run for her money."

Francie felt a glow reach her cheeks. She knew his offhand remark was a wild exaggeration, but she enjoyed hearing it nonetheless.

As the singers filed out of the rehearsal room, the principal tenor, Antonio Leonardo, strode up beside her.

"You sing Italian very well, Miss Forrester," he said. "I'm impressed."

"Thank you, Mr. Leonardo." She smiled, secretly amused by the distinct Brooklyn accent that emerged from his mouth. When she'd first heard his name and listened to his glorious voice ringing out from the Ravinia stage, she'd assumed he was a native son of Italy.

"It's Tony, please," he said. "Have you been working with an Italian tutor to perfect your pronunciation?"

"No. Well, sort of, I guess," she replied. "A friend back home, Mr. Figaro, has been coaching me. He grew up in Italy."

"I see. What province is Mr. Figaro from?"

"Sicily, I think."

"What a coincidence! My parents came from Sicily." He smiled, his teeth white and gleaming. "Say, I have a little time to kill before my next appointment. Would you care to continue this discussion over coffee?" he suggested. "The brew in the restaurant on the first floor is surprisingly not terrible."

"I afraid I can't, Tony," she said, feeling deeply flattered and unnerved at the same time. "I have to get to class."

"Pity." His brown eyes held hers for a moment longer than necessary. She broke the gaze first, flustered. "Another time, perhaps." They parted at the exit. She waved good-bye but he didn't respond. She remembered what Grace had said about the man, that while he was immensely talented, he was also arrogant and full of himself. Francie had noticed this herself, a little bit, in his attitude and demeanor. Even so, he'd been very kind to take the time to pay her a compliment.

"Are you crazy?" Molly gasped later that afternoon when Francie related the encounter. They were sitting together on the front steps of their building, enjoying one of the last fine days of autumn. The sky above them was a brilliant blue, and bright leaves adorned the trees lining the parkway. "You turned down a coffee date with Antonio Leonardo? *The* Antonio Leonardo?"

"I'd have been so nervous, I wouldn't have been able to swallow a sip," Francie confessed. "Besides, he may be a great tenor and all, but I hear he has a swelled head the size of Texas."

Molly giggled. "Don't they all?"

Francie supposed they did—at least those of great talent, forever basking in the presence of an adoring public. That was one thing to be said about Henry, he lacked arrogance. In spite of his intelligence, advantaged upbringing, and musical talent, he remained humble. How different her life would be if things had worked out between them. She hoped New York was treating him well.

The thought made her ache for him all the more.

CHAPTER
TWENTY-NINE

With the October sunshine pouring through his window, Henry sat at his desk and smoothed out the creases on the letter he'd received from Bob Miller, his former Scoville College classmate. Bob was in his senior year at Scoville, and his letter was filled with news of campus goings-on, like football games, dances, and festive bonfires. Henry soaked up the news, feeling nostalgic for past good times and wondering if Bob ever found time to attend to his studies. There were no dances and bonfires at Columbia—not for Henry, anyway. Law school kept him too busy to do much socializing.

The *tramp, tramp* of marching feet punctuated by barked directives drew his attention to the window. Three stories below, a group of midshipmen drilled on College Walk, looking proud and sober in their brand-new uniforms. The university had indeed established a military training program on campus, as Jim's petition had sought. To Henry's disappointment, however, the program prepared students exclusively for the navy, with classes in naval science and even hands-on training in ships and submarines in nearby New York Harbor. As his summer on shipboard to South America and back had made clear his proclivity toward seasickness, he concluded the navy was not for him. Or rather, he was not well suited for the navy.

Nonetheless, a call of duty pricked at his conscience, a sense of honor and desire to protect and defend the weak. Newspaper stories reminded him daily of the devastation being wrought throughout Europe by the evil Huns. And in spite of President Wilson's campaign promises, Henry sensed his own country drifting steadily toward involvement in the war. It was important to be prepared.

Turning away from the window, he picked up Bob's letter again.

> *One piece of news is that the powers that be have decided Scoville's foreign-language department will discontinue German classes, and good old Prof Biermann has been sacked. A sign of the times, I suppose, although I must say, I'll be sorry to see the old man go.*

Henry was, too. He'd done well in his German classes and liked Prof Biermann. He hoped the measure was only temporary and that the professor would be reinstated soon. At his advanced age, it might not be easy for him to find another teaching position. Or *any* position, for that matter.

> *The biggest news of all is that the college is allowing senior men to graduate early if they want to enter the military. So I'll be throwing my lot in with Uncle Sam as soon as I'm through here, and joining the army. What about you?*

Henry set the letter aside and slumped in his chair. What *about* him? The question had been rolling over and over in his mind all fall.

The call of duty beckoned. Duty to his country. Duty to his studies. Duty to his family. So many competing priorities.

At least he didn't have to take a sweetheart into account. Good thing he hadn't made any promises to Francie.

Though he often found himself wishing he had.

CHAPTER THIRTY

At the end of music theory class the following week, Herr Schreiber said, "Francie, can you stay behind a moment, please?"

Afraid she was about to receive a reprimand, Francie wondered what she'd done wrong. She was both relieved and thrilled when the professor said, "I have spots for a few more supers in *Eugene Onegin*. We need to beef up our corps of Russian peasants. Would you like to join us?"

Francie's pulse raced and she gasped. "Would I ever!"

She'd learned that "super"—short for "supernumerary"—was the opera world's term for what theater people called an "extra." She'd also learned that understudies were called "covers," and the stage was called a "deck" *'Cause back in the early days opera companies hired actual ships' deckhands to climb the scaffolds and manage the ropes and rigging.* Molly, enthralled with her stagecraft class, had explained it to her. It seemed to Francie that her musical and theatrical vocabulary was growing more extensive by the hour. Even so, there was always more to learn, and she despaired of ever mastering all of it.

"I've noticed that you like to watch the professionals rehearse," Herr Schreiber continued with a rare twinkle in his eye. He wasn't the twinkling type. "I'd like you to get some experience standing and moving around on the stage."

As a supernumerary, Francie would have no singing part. The director explained she'd need only to shuffle from one part of the stage to another as part of a large crowd scene. Even so, she was thrilled at the idea of appearing on stage, in costume, during actual live performances. Her first appearance on the opera stage!

Rehearsals for the Tchaikovsky opera took place at the Auditorium Theater, which fortunately was located only a short distance from the conservatory so she wouldn't waste a lot of time hoofing back and forth. Her instructors, many working musicians themselves, were understanding about the need for a few absences from class in order to accommodate the extra rehearsals. Nonetheless, Francie's schedule became even more packed than it had before. For the first time in her life, she had to start keeping a diary to keep track of all her various commitments.

As non-singing, non-dancing actors, supers were brought in only during the last few rehearsals before opening night. They were also unpaid, which didn't bother Francie in the slightest. The experience alone would be enough to satisfy her, for now.

During her first practice, the entire cast moved from a rehearsal room in the bowels of the Auditorium to the stage to learn where to stand, sit, and move in a process called blocking. During the long stretches of time that she wasn't needed onstage, she was fitted for a peasant costume consisting of a blouse, petticoat, bodice, and skirt. Thankfully she was spared the heavy wig that many women singers wore. The costume was hot enough under the stage lights without adding a wig as well.

As kind as he'd been to her in private, Reinhard Schreiber was a tough taskmaster at rehearsals, barking orders and issuing scathing criticisms to the singers and musicians. It amazed Francie that they—not to mention she—didn't crumple under the pressure.

Above all, Herr Schreiber had a mania for punctuality. More than once he had fixed his steely stare on some hapless member of the company who'd come in late to a rehearsal.

"Where were you?" he'd demand in a sour tone.

The poor singer or musician would stammer out some excuse. Depending on his mood, the director would either point at an empty chair—"Sit!"—or point at the door—"Out!" Either way, his commands reminded Francie of the way some people spoke to their dogs. If she didn't know, thanks to Grace, what a nice man he really was underneath his blunt exterior, she'd truly be frightened of him. In any case, she vowed to never be late to rehearsal in order to avoid that particular humiliation. Goodness knew there were enough other ways to be humiliated, even in a simple walk-on role like hers. She lived in terror of missing a cue or stumbling on stage or being at the wrong place at the wrong time.

At the close of a rehearsal in November, Herr Schreiber rapped his baton on the podium and requested everyone's attention.

"As has been their tradition for several years, the Chicago Symphony will be performing Handel's *Messiah* at Orchestra Hall during the Christmas season. And, as usual, they've requested our assistance in providing voices for the chorus. This year I'm recommending six of you. All of you will be expected to remain in *Eugene Onegin* too, and if any of you think taking on *The Messiah* on top of that is too much for you, you may choose to decline." He peered at the group over the top of his glasses. "Although I think you would be foolish to do so. And of course, as chorus members you will be paid for your time."

Francie sat forward. To be chosen for *The Messiah* would be a great honor and provide some temporary extra income—maybe enough to buy a few Christmas gifts to mail to her family in California. However, it would be an additional time commitment that she didn't know she could handle.

"Who will be the soloists this year?" asked a man in the baritone section.

Reinhard consulted his notes. "I believe the soloists are Mary Garden, Beatrice de Bonneville, Antonio Leonardo, and Richard Bonelli."

Suddenly, Francie didn't care if extra rehearsals would strain her schedule, if it meant she could share a stage and sing in a production alongside her idol, Beatrice de Bonneville. The other soloists were also world-class. Singing in the chorus behind them could be an opportunity of a lifetime. She held her breath, silently urging Herr Schreiber to get on with his announcement—and to include her name.

"Here are the six I've chosen for the chorus." Herr Schreiber drew a sheet of paper from his notebook and read from it. "Marcus Howard, Patricia Sizemore, Margaret Flanagan, Peter Lindstrom, Steven Dillard, and Francine Forrester." He set down the paper and looked at the chorus. "Congratulations. And remember, you're expected to be at all *Eugene Onegin* rehearsals as well. If you choose to bow out, come and see me after rehearsal."

Francie's chest surged with a mixture of elation and panic.

Once again it was Molly who talked sense into her head as they got ready for bed that evening.

"Are you kidding? It's an honor to be asked to sing in *The Messiah*," she gushed when Francie expressed her doubts. "Herr Schreiber must think very highly of you."

"I don't know about that." But deep inside, Francie hoped her friend's words were true.

At the following day's rehearsal, she told Herr Schreiber that she'd be honored to participate in *The Messiah*.

"I'm glad," he said. "That's good news. Grace Whitworth will think so, too."

Francie was confused. "She knows about it already?"

"I'm going to tell her. We're meeting for dinner this weekend."

Francie felt a surge of delight. "Oh, will she be in town? I'd love to see her."

"No, I'll be driving out to Scoville this time." That piqued Francie's interest. This time? Did that mean there had been other times? Francie couldn't be sure, but she thought his cheeks reddened slightly.

"Oh, I see. Well, please do tell her I said hello." It pleased Francie that her former teacher and current director had begun seeing each other socially. She hoped they were enjoying getting reacquainted. "And if you're looking for a good place for dinner in Scoville, I highly recommend Cafe Figaro," she added with a smile. "I'm afraid there aren't many other options. It's a pretty small town." She steered clear of mentioning Le Coq d'Or which, though fancier and probably better suited to Herr Schreiber's sophisticated taste, held unpleasant associations for her.

"Thanks for the tip. I'll give Grace your greetings," he promised.

But Francie couldn't help but think he sounded distracted, as if he had a great deal on his mind. She hoped the trip out to Scoville, and breathing some clean country air in Grace's charming company, would help him relax and feel refreshed.

A few days later, Francie scurried into the Auditorium for the final dress rehearsal of *Eugene Onegin*. Before she reached the backstage area, Tony Leonardo stopped her in a corridor and beckoned her aside. Under other circumstances she'd be thrilled at being paid personal attention by the handsome singer, but today she was running slightly behind schedule and needed to change into her costume before Herr Schreiber rapped his impatient baton. But she figured she could spare a few moments if he wanted to talk to her.

"Hello, Francine Forrester. How's my favorite little songbird?"

"Hello, Tony Leonardo." She responded in a light, playful tone, even though the "favorite little songbird" bit left her feeling unsettled. What did he mean by it? Did it mean anything at all?

"I was pleased with your work at the *Salomé* practice a few weeks ago," he said. "*Really* impressed."

"Thank you." He'd already told her something similar. She supposed it never hurt to hear such praise twice, although it seemed excessive. Something about the way he said "really impressed" made her uncomfortable, as if he were talking about something other than her singing. But she couldn't identify what bothered her, and wrote it off to her imagination.

He produced two slips of cardstock from his breast pocket. "I have here two comp tickets to the production. I'd like to give them to you, as a thank-you for helping out."

Francie looked at the tickets, astonished. "Tickets for *Salomé*? Oh, gosh. You don't have to thank me. It was a privilege."

"Even so, I'd like you to have them. A serious student of opera can never see too many professional productions." He grinned. "It beats lurking in the shadows at rehearsals, don't you think?"

Francie blushed and accepted the tickets. "Thank you, Tony. That's very kind of you."

"And I suppose there's some young man in your life you'd like to bring with you."

The unexpected reference to her nonexistent romantic life startled her. "Oh, no," she blurted. "I'll probably invite my roommate, Molly Mulroney. Have you met her?"

"Can't say as I have." Tony took a step closer. "No boyfriend? A pretty girl like you?"

A wary sense of something she couldn't name spidered up the back of Francie's neck. She took an involuntary step backward. She didn't want to be rude to the eminent tenor, but she didn't like standing so close to him. Anything to do with boyfriends was still a sore subject, and her personal life was none of this man's business. Yet his lofty and superior status in the company kept her from saying so.

Given what a stickler Herr Schreiber was about punctuality, she knew it was high time they were both moving along to rehearsal. Other singers and musicians rushed past on their way to the backstage area. She felt an irresistible pull to join them.

"Well, we mustn't be late for rehearsal," she blurted, her voice sounding unnaturally shrill to her own ears. "Guess I'd better get in there and find my place."

"What's the hurry?" he asked in his tough Brooklyn accent that seemed so at odds with his suave, cosmopolitan demeanor. "They certainly aren't going to start without *us*." He threw back his head and laughed, but let her go.

Joining the crowd heading into rehearsal, Francie told herself she was being ridiculous. The tenor was just being nice. He had a naturally flirtatious manner. She needed to not be a girl from the sticks, naïve to the ways of the world and quick to take offense. She certainly didn't want to encourage him lest he think she was interested in anything more than a professional relationship.

Even so, she made a mental note to avoid being caught alone with Antonio Leonardo, lest his gift of free tickets come with a cost.

CHAPTER
THIRTY-ONE

That evening when Francie got home, Molly was in the kitchen, frying eggs for supper.

"Want some?"

"Sure." Francie dropped her music bag on a chair. "Say, it's short notice, but Tony Leonardo gave me two tickets to Windy City's Saturday matinee performance. Want to go with me?"

"What's playing?"

"*Salomé*. That's the one I helped them rehearse a few weeks ago. Remember, I told you about it."

Molly smirked. "Oh, I remember. The occasion will be marked forever in your scrapbook as 'The time I refused to let a world-renowned tenor take me out for coffee.' And now he gives you tickets? I think he likes you." She wiggled her eyebrows in a playfully suggestive manner. Then her expression sobered. "I don't know about *Salomé*, though," she said doubtfully. "Wasn't it banned in London or something? It might be terrible."

"It's controversial, that's for sure," Francie said. "Some say it's positively indecent. Others say Richard Strauss is a great genius of a composer, and that *Salomé* could become the greatest opera of the twentieth century."

Molly snorted. "Since the twentieth century has barely started, there's not much competition yet."

"True. Anyway, I didn't really form an opinion during that one rehearsal. At the time I was too scared out of my wits to pay attention to whether or not I cared for the music. And I was only exposed to a small portion of it."

"The biblical story is pretty depressing," Molly reminded her.

"So is *Samson and Delilah*, but you told me you enjoyed the opera version of that one."

"And I do," Molly admitted. "That gorgeous aria about her heart opening like a flower, right before she weasels the secret out of him about his hair. Every time I listen to it, I hope things will turn out differently, but of course they never do." She sighed. "Maybe depressing stories make good opera. Anyway, as for *Salomé*, I suppose since the tickets are free, it would be silly of us not to take advantage of them."

"That's what I think, too," Francie said. "Also, we shouldn't go around criticizing it on the basis of hearsay. We should see it for ourselves and form our own opinions."

Saturday afternoon, they took their seats in the ornate concert hall.

"I'm so eager to hear Mary Garden sing, aren't you?" Molly said as they waited for the production to begin.

"I can't imagine she's any better than Beatrice de Bonneville," Francie said with a surge of loyalty toward her favorite soprano, "but if she's just as good, that would suit me fine."

After the usual interval of instrument-tuning and conductor-applauding, the house lights dimmed and the orchestra played an intriguingly exotic-sounding overture. Then the curtain rose and the opera began with ear-shattering dissonance. Francie tried her best to appreciate the music, even though it was not to her taste, and she found both the scenery and the subject matter dark and depressing. But she reminded herself it was one of the Bible's harsher stories, so she hadn't expected sweetness and light.

Even so, thirty minutes in, she was not having a good time. In the dim light of the theater, she glanced over at Molly, who appeared similarly ill at ease with the spectacle before them. Francie leaned over the armrest.

"We can leave at intermission, if you want," she whispered.

Molly nodded vigorously. But, alas, the production had no intermission.

Only Mary Garden's exquisite singing captured Francie's attention in the early scenes. The middle scenes made her squirm, especially a number called the Dance of the Seven Veils. What started out as a graceful dance, with the diva swathed in veils and only her eyes visible, soon devolved into a sort of striptease act. Francie tried to avert her eyes and just listen to the music.

But it was the ending, with Salomé's deranged monologue over John the Baptist's severed head, followed by her brutal execution at the hands of the Roman guards, that truly stunned Francie. She thought she might be ill. She wasn't the only one. The audience sat in shocked silence for a full thirty seconds before the curtain fell.

When the house lights came up, she couldn't get out of the concert hall quickly enough. Molly was right behind her. When they reached the sidewalk, Francie took in great gulps of fresh air and tried to forget what she'd just seen.

"Well, that was interesting." Molly's extreme understatement brought forth a strangled half laugh-half snort from Francie. Molly looked at her with concern. "Are you all right?"

She took Francie's arm, and they walked back to their apartment, carefully stepping around slushy puddles in a vain attempt to keep their boots dry.

"That was very disturbing," Francie said when she found her voice. "I'm no prude, but honestly, this production was just . . . salacious and attention-grabbing."

Molly gave a rueful smile. "You know Mary Garden. She's always angling for press coverage, and nothing draws reporters out faster than a touch of moral outrage."

"True," Francie agreed. "But even so, it bothered me. The opera should be more . . . more dignified than that. They should have treated the biblical story with respect and decency."

Molly mounted a weak defense. "Well, after all, it is opera, not Sunday school." She shivered visibly. "Still, I agree with you that it was a pretty scandalous spectacle."

Scandalous was too gentle a word, in Francie's opinion. She lay awake that night, wondering whether Mrs. Dornbusch was right. Maybe the opera world wasn't a proper place for a decent Christian woman to earn her living, after all.

But Molly made her feel better the next morning when she pointed to an article in the newspaper. "Looks like lots of people agreed with us," she said. "It says here that *Salomé* lasted for only two performances. The third performance has been called off as a result of a strong protest by the chief of police."

"Thank goodness for that." She wondered what Henry would have thought of the production. How mortified she'd have been if he'd gone with her instead of Molly.

Francie finished her coffee and headed off to class, reassured there was still some decency left in the world. As long as she was in control of her career, she vowed to participate in the kinds of operas that lifted people's spirits and didn't leave them thrashing around in the mud.

CHAPTER
THIRTY-TWO

F rancie's lesson with Madame Clairvaux ran long the following week, and she had to rush to make it to rehearsal on time. The supers were learning their positions and it was very important she be there. She made use of a shortcut she'd discovered through a seldom-used part of the building. Just her luck to turn a corner and hurtle headlong into Tony Leonardo's broad chest.

"Whoa, there." He chuckled, grasping her shoulders to steady her. "Where's the fire?"

She tried unsuccessfully to wriggle free of his grip. "Sorry, Tony. I'm late for rehearsal."

As if he hadn't heard her, he kept his hands on her shoulders. "Hey, you never told me what you thought of *Salomé*. Did you enjoy using the tickets I gave you? Best seats in the house, wouldn't you agree?"

It was the "wouldn't you agree?" part that set off an alarm bell in her head. Was it her imagination, or did he emphasize the fact that the tickets were a gift? Did he now think she owed him something?

"It was most . . . unusual. I've never seen anything like it." She wasn't going to lie and say she enjoyed it. "Thanks again, Tony. And now, if you'll excuse me . . ." She regretted taking the shortcut. She should have stayed where there were other people around.

He stepped closer. "There are plenty more tickets where those came from. And perhaps you'll allow me to escort you next time, instead of your little roommate."

She bristled at his dismissive tone. Molly was not her "little roommate," she was her best friend. "That hardly seems practical when you're up on the stage."

He bent toward her, his breath hot in her face. "I'm not always on stage," he murmured in a suggestive tone.

Oh, yes, you are. "I have to go." She tried again to wriggle free of his grip, which only tightened it. Before she knew what was happening, he'd planted a kiss on her mouth.

Without thinking, she jerked her head back and slapped him hard across the face. He let go of her shoulders and stepped back, dark eyes wide with surprise. Then he tilted his head back and roared with laughter. Furious, she circled past him and ran down the passageway, his laughter ringing in her ears.

From then on, she steered clear of Tony Leonardo, going out of her way to anticipate his movements and make sure she went in the opposite direction. The cat-and-mouse game exhausted her, and she was relieved to see him turning his amorous intentions to another conservatory student, someone she didn't know. Unlike Francie, the girl seemed to relish his attention. More power to her.

By the time the opening night of *Eugene Onegin* rolled around, she'd largely recovered from both upsetting experiences—the shock of *Salomé* and the stolen kiss. Her love of opera had been restored, and she couldn't imagine any place she'd rather be than gathering backstage at the Auditorium with the rest of the supers. At the proper moment, the group shuffled onto the stage and took their places. The curtain rose.

I'm here! I'm really here! Francie's heart felt ready to burst. Here she was, standing on stage during a performance of a professional opera company. She had a role, an actual role, however humble. She had a costume. She had a purpose. She'd remember this moment for the rest of her life. Someday she'd tell her grandchildren that—

Riiiip.

A sharp tug on the hem of her skirt and a sickening tearing sensation at her waist told her something had gone terribly wrong. A fellow peasant had stepped on her skirt! To her horror, the heavy skirt began sliding downward over her petticoat. In an effort to stop its descent, she bent and slammed her elbows against her sides, trying to hold the wayward garment in place.

"What's the matter with you?" hissed the kerchief-clad peasant woman to her right, a plump supernumerary named Judith. "You look like you're having convulsions." She didn't speak especially quietly. Fortunately, her voice was drowned out during a particularly robust chorus number going on at the front of the stage.

"My skirt," Francie hissed back. "It's falling down!"

Judith took quick stock of the situation and grimaced. "Get behind me."

Francie did as she was told, just as the dramatic action called for the cluster of villagers to move clear across the stage. The hem of Francie's skirt was now dragging on the floor, and she kept stepping on it, resulting in more of a stagger than a walk. From the conductor's podium, Herr Schreiber raised a questioning eyebrow in her direction.

The torn waistband had now worked itself free from Francie's elbows and continued its dizzying descent. Desperately she grabbed the fabric with both hands, yanked it back up to her waist, and held it there with her fists. She had no idea whether the audience had noticed the disaster taking place with her costume, but Herr Schreiber certainly had. Francie didn't think she would ever recover from the humiliation.

Maybe she'd even get fired!

To prevent the skirt from crumpling entirely to the floor, she had to stand and walk with her fists jammed on her waist throughout the rest of the scene, elbows akimbo, striking her compatriots right and left and earning strange looks, until the interminable scene came to a merciful end and she could scurry to the dressing room.

The wardrobe mistress clucked her tongue as she assessed the damage, holding the skirt up to the light and examining it as if it contained threads of pure gold.

"What have you done to it?" she demanded.

"It wasn't my fault," Francie protested. "Somebody stepped on my hem just as I took a step."

The wardrobe mistress hurried to fix the tear with needle and thread before Francie's next onstage scene. She fixed the skirt so securely that, when the performance was over and Francie was ready to change into her street clothes, it had to be snipped off her body with a pair of embroidery scissors.

"Mind you be more careful next time," the wardrobe mistress admonished as she carried the garment away to make a more suitable repair.

As for Herr Schreiber, he never said a word about the fiasco. But Francie's fellow supers did. Egged on by Judith, they found the situation hilarious. They teased Francie and urged her to tell and retell the story. To her relief, it did grow funnier with each telling. By the next morning when she told Molly about it over coffee, they were soon doubled over with laughter.

Thankfully, the newspaper reviews of *Eugene Onegin* were mostly positive.

"Forrest Lamont's voice shimmered in the title role," one reviewer gushed, "and Helen Freund positively sparkled as Tatyana Laranova."

The reviewer, a notoriously hard-to-impress woman, went on to praise the production as being of the highest caliber, "although one of the Russian peasant women stumbled often," she sniped, "giving the appearance of having imbibed too much vodka."

"Of course I hadn't had a drop of vodka," Francie told Molly after they'd stopped laughing. "But perhaps the whole experience would have been more tolerable if I had."

"I doubt that," Molly said. "You needed to keep your wits about you. Which you did! I'm proud of you. I'd probably have run off the stage in disgrace."

With a sigh of resignation, Francie carefully snipped the review from the newspaper and pasted it into her scrapbook. Next to it she wrote in her best handwriting, *My first review.* Then she added, in smaller letters, *For the record, no vodka was involved.*

CHAPTER
THIRTY-THREE

On a cold December morning, in a first-class seat aboard the Twentieth Century Limited, Henry read the newspaper as the train sped through the Indiana countryside en route to Chicago. He was eager to get home to spend the Christmas holidays with his parents. But the headlines made him feel anything but merry. Along with news of an explosion in a British munitions factory that killed thirty-five women, there were the usual war reports detailing battles and atrocities committed by the Kaiser's henchmen and accounts of the people's deep suffering.

He stared out the window at the wintry landscape. How much longer could the United States stay out of this ugly war? As Henry saw it, it was a struggle between good and evil. He needed to do his part.

Later that evening, as he took his seat at the long dining-room table with his parents, he'd come to a decision.

"It's good to have you home, son," his father said as he carved the roast. "How long can you stay?"

Henry swallowed. "I'm not going back."

Father paused the carving and stared at him across the table. "Not going back? What do you mean? I thought you were doing well in your classes. Finally."

Henry ignored the dig. "I am doing well. I mean, I was." He drew a deep breath. "I've enlisted in the American Expeditionary Force. I'll leave for training in January."

"The military!" His father's eyes grew wide. "But why?"

His mother's face paled. Her fork clattered to her plate.

"It's clear the U.S. is preparing for war," Henry kept his voice calm, for her sake. "I'd rather fight for my country sooner than later."

"Gads, Henry. Haven't you been reading the papers?" Father exploded. "President Wilson will keep us out of the conflict. His campaign promise was to keep us out of war. Many are profiting from it, yes, in terms of supplying needed materials to the countries involved. But we're not going to enter the fray ourselves."

"With all due respect, sir, I *have* been reading the papers. And what they tell me is that the Germans are bombing civilians. They're using poison gas, for Pete's sake. How can we stand back when such atrocities are being committed?"

"It's a shame to hear what's going on over there. But, son, it's not our war."

But Henry wouldn't change his mind. He acquiesced to his father on many things. Most things, in fact, but not on this. He refused to live in a bubble forever.

After several attempts to dissuade him, his father raised a glass and said, "Clearly your mind is made up. And I must admit . . . while I detest the situation, on some level, I'm proud of you, son."

"Thank you, Father."

Mother buried her face in her linen napkin.

"Please don't cry, Mother," Henry said, unsettled by her tears. It was most unlike Diana Jasper to display strong emotions of any sort. He reached for her hand. "I'll be home for several weeks yet. I'll make sure you get so sick of me that you'll be glad to see me go."

She pulled herself together. Briefly she dabbed her eyes with a corner of her napkin.

"Well, we don't have to let this ruin our holidays," she said briskly. "We can observe all our usual traditions. Heaven knows we need them. You'll come with us tonight, of course."

"Come where?"

"We have tickets to *The Messiah* at Orchestra Hall. We're all going together, as a family."

Henry wasn't enthusiastic, but he would have done almost anything to make his mother smile.

His father frowned. "Diana, it's the boy's first night at home. Let him relax."

"It's not too much to ask, is it, dear?" She reached across the table and grasped Henry's hand. Another glistening tear threatened to overflow. "I want to spend as much time with my boy as possible."

Henry squeezed her hand and released it. "Indeed, Mother. It's not too much to ask." He laid his napkin next to his plate and stood. "I guess I'd better get changed."

"Splendid." She sounded more like her usual self. "And you'll be happy to know, the Gladstones will be there, and they're bringing Lila. She's home on holiday from Bryn Mawr."

"Marvelous," Henry muttered with barely disguised annoyance. Lila Gladstone. Hardly the person he wanted to see on his first day back in town.

The person he most wanted to see was impossible to find.

CHAPTER
THIRTY-FOUR

F rancie paced nervously backstage at Orchestra Hall, stopping now and then to peek through the curtain. The house was packed with people eager to hear *The Messiah*. She scanned the concert hall for Grace Whitworth, who'd promised to come, but Francie worried the heavy snowfall might keep her away.

She also wanted to avoid sitting in the performers' lounge, where Tony Leonardo was likely to be lurking. Ever since he'd acted flirtatiously toward her, she'd tried to keep her distance from him, arriving at the very last minute for rehearsals and scurrying out immediately afterward. She couldn't stop him from looking her way and smiling, but she did a masterful job of pretending not to notice.

But sometimes she thought she'd imagined the whole thing, made up a story in her head, because except for that one conversation, he treated her indifferently, with no more attention than he paid to any other member of the opera company. If indeed she had misunderstood or misread his intentions, then she felt very foolish. He was a distinguished tenor, some said a musical genius. And he was undeniably good-looking as well, for an older man. Why would a man like that take more than a professional interest in her and her career?

Even so, something about Tony carried a whiff of danger. She found she couldn't spend any amount of time in his presence without a flicker of uneasiness.

The orchestra musicians took their places and tuned their instruments. Francie found her spot in the chorus. The audience applauded as the soloists filed onto the stage and lined up in front of the chorus, and they applauded again when the esteemed symphony conductor, Frederick Stock, strode onto the stage.

The performance went beautifully. No matter how many times Francie had sung the familiar "Hallelujah Chorus" in rehearsal it never failed to make her feel as if her heart were leaving her chest and floating to the ceiling. And now, performing it for an enraptured audience who'd risen to their feet *en masse* felt even more intense. The applause at the end of the performance was sustained, loud and long.

Afterward, Francie went to the lobby to seek out Grace. The two finally connected in the crowd and flung their arms around each other.

"I'm so happy you came," Francie gushed. "I was worried when I saw the snow that you might decide to stay home."

"I wouldn't have missed it for the world," Grace said. "It gave me such a thrill to see you up there with the professionals. And I just love *The Messiah*, don't you? What could be more glorious than singing the words of the gospel set to Handel's breathtaking score?"

"I couldn't agree more." They chatted for several more minutes, then Francie asked, "Can you stay and have supper with me? Molly's around here somewhere, and the three of us could have a good catch-up."

Grace shook her head. "I'm sorry, Francie. I'd love to, but I've already made plans to dine with Reinhard Schreiber."

"Oh, I see." The surprising thought that she might not be the only reason Grace braved the snowstorm took Francie aback for a moment.

Yet she was pleased to see her former teacher blush. "Of course, I understand."

"But you'll be returning with me to Scoville tomorrow, right? To spend your Christmas vacation?"

"That's correct."

"Then we'll have time for several good, long chats." Grace continued to pepper her with questions about conservatory life until Herr Schreiber appeared, wearing an overcoat and galoshes.

"Well done, Miss Forrester. You and your classmates did Handel proud."

She thanked him, and he offered his arm to Grace. "Ready to go?"

Grace smiled and nodded. Francie walked with them to the foyer and waited with her while Herr Schreiber hailed a cab. Shivering in the chilly air, she watched from the entrance until they were safely on their way, then returned to the warm, well-lit lobby.

She had the distinct sensation that someone was staring at her. She glanced around with annoyance, expecting to see Tony Leonardo lurking there with his usual smirk, but instead she saw someone else. Someone who made her heart do flip-flops. She did a double take. It was a gentleman dressed in black tie. But not just any gentleman—this one had a familiar face. She could scarcely believe her eyes.

"Henry?"

"Francie!" He strode toward her. "It *is* you." He grasped both her hands in his and kissed her on the cheek. "I couldn't believe it when I saw you up there on stage. I had to check the program to make sure, and there was your name, listed in the chorus."

Francie couldn't speak for a moment. Even when she found her tongue, she scrambled for words. "I-I didn't know you were back in Chicago. I assumed you were still at school."

"I hopped a train the minute my exams were over, and as soon as I arrived home, Mother and Dad shanghaied me into joining them here." He looked earnestly into her eyes. "Now that I see you're here, I'm awfully glad they did. You're a hard person to find, do you know that?"

She gulped. "Am I?"

"Well, sure. I'd assumed you'd gone to California, until—well, never mind. It's a long story."

She wondered if the story had something to do with his call to Mr. Figaro.

"I did try to telephone you," she said, "but you'd already left."

"You did?" It was his turn to gape. "Nobody told me."

"Anyway, I've been here since September. In Chicago, I mean. At the conservatory."

"That's great. I'm happy for you." He sounded genuinely pleased, if a little wistful.

"But—when will you go back to New York?"

"I'm not going back." He stood tall. "I'm enlisting in the AEF."

"You're what?" Francie blurted, even though she'd heard him perfectly well.

"I'll be meeting with a recruitment officer this week, then soon I'll be off for training."

Training. Learning how to kill people, and avoid being killed. Francie's blood ran cold. "But what about law school?"

"Our country is preparing for war, Francie." His voice was gentle yet somber. "I won't be going back to Columbia for a while. Law school will have to wait."

Francie's insides roiled in confusion. There was so much she wanted to say to him, so many things she wanted to ask him. But now was neither the time nor the place. Not in a crowded lobby with his parents hovering nearby.

His parents. Over Henry's shoulder, she saw them standing together, looking as detached and regal as ever. Beside them stood an attractive young woman with curly blond hair. A sister, perhaps, though Francie didn't remember Henry mentioning any siblings.

She turned back to Henry. "I've been meaning to write to you," she told him. "But I didn't have your address at Columbia, and then I started work at the conservatory, and everything's become a blur." She filled him in on the highlights of what had happened since she'd won the competition and her life had changed so drastically.

"As I said, I'm happy for you." His eyes locked on hers. "You're on your way at last."

"Thank you." But on her way to *where* was the question.

"Come and say hello to the folks," he urged. He grasped her elbow and steered her toward his parents. "Mother, Dad, you remember Francie Forrester from Scoville."

"Yes, of course," his mother said in a cool, well-modulated voice. "How delighted we all were to see you on the stage tonight, Miss Forrester. Most unexpected."

His father simply said, "Miss Forrester," and inclined his head. Then he added, "Have you been introduced to Miss Lila Gladstone? Lila is such a dear friend of Henry, I thought you two might have met."

The blonde woman extended her hand. "Pleased to meet you." She turned to Henry and placed a hand on his arm. "Henry, dear, I didn't realize you had a friend in the chorus. You're just one surprise after another."

Francie's heart dropped. *Dear?* The lobby tilted slightly. This woman wasn't Henry's sister. By the way she was acting, she was his sweetheart.

Well, why shouldn't he have a sweetheart? Francie argued with herself. He certainly didn't belong to Francie, was not her personal property.

Still, the realization that he was spoken for came as a shock. To cover her dismay, she pasted on a smile.

After a few more minutes of awkward small talk, the Jaspers left the concert hall. Henry'd said nothing further about calling her or wanting to see her while he was in town. Francie watched them go, feeling dejected. He was gone. Going off to war. And even if he came back one day, healthy and whole, he wouldn't be coming back to *her*. He was lost to her forever—if he'd ever belonged to her in the first place.

CHAPTER
THIRTY-FIVE

JANUARY 1917

D eep in the bowels of Union Station, a train blew its whistle.

"Well, I guess this is it," Henry said to the small entourage gathered around him on the platform. Nervously he glanced past their heads, hoping against hope to see Francie approaching, but there was no sign of her.

After that awkward encounter at Orchestra Hall, with his parents and Lila looking on, he hadn't had a chance to speak to her again. He'd sent her a note in care of the opera company, giving her the details of his departure and telling her he'd love to see her once more. But she hadn't responded, hadn't come to see him off, and now time had run out. Disappointment overrode even his anxiety about heading off to war. A sudden, deep sense of loss spilled over him.

"Good-bye, son." His father grasped Henry's hand with both of his own. "Best of luck to you. Know that we are very proud of you."

Henry swallowed past the lump in his throat. "Thank you, sir."

"Come home safely, darling." Mother kissed his cheek. Her disciplined Protestant upbringing and naturally steely spine wouldn't allow her to cry openly in public, but her eyes glistened with unshed tears.

In contrast, Lila wept openly. "Oh, Henry!" She attempted to fling herself against his chest, but he extended his hand just in time to grasp hers. By holding his elbow stiff, he was able to keep her from collapsing dramatically in his arms like a heroine in a melodrama.

"Good-bye, Lila," he said pleasantly but without emotion. He resented that his parents had invited her along to see him off. The last thing he needed, as he was about to leave for training camp and from there a possible battlefield, was a sobbing limpet around his neck. He prayed that time, distance, and a complete lack of correspondence on his part would dispel the silly crush the girl had developed on him. He prayed she'd find a beau while he was gone and be safely married, or at least spoken for, by the time he returned. But that wasn't very likely, with the vast majority of young men soon to be conscripted to the military.

"All aboard," the conductor shouted.

"That's me," Henry said. His stomach churned. After one last desperate glance around the crowded station for the girl who wasn't there, he said, "Good-bye, all," and turned to board the train.

Standing just a few yards away, Francie watched from the shadow of a tall concrete pillar as Henry boarded the train. In her hand she clutched the note he'd sent which had only reached her that morning when, returning from the Christmas holidays spent with Grace, she'd picked up the mail that had collected in her absence.

She'd hurried to the station, intending to tell him good-bye, but when she saw him standing with his parents and Lila, she couldn't bring herself to intrude, knowing she'd be unwelcomed by those three. Lila's presence in particular gave her pause. How would Francie have felt if she were in Lila's shoes, saying a tearful good-bye to her soldier, only to have said soldier's former sweetheart turn up out of the blue? Francie knew, if the tables were turned, she wouldn't care for that at all. So she kept her distance, and prayed for Henry's health and safety instead.

As the train slowly chugged out of the station and out of her line of vision, carrying Henry off to a military training camp, a piece of her heart went with him.

CHAPTER
THIRTY-SIX

F rancie continued to study hard at the conservatory during the long winter of 1917, as rumors of the United States's possible entry into the Great War swirled around Chicago. She once again appeared in an opera, Puccini's *Madama Butterfly*. This time Francie found herself promoted from a silent walk-on part to a singing role in the opera chorus. The role required wearing a Japanese-style kimono, black wig, and heavy makeup, and attending many more rehearsals than she had for *Eugene Onegin*. She didn't mind, as being busy helped the winter pass more quickly, and with it thoughts of Henry and how he was faring in boot camp.

Francie felt as if she were born to sing on the opera stage. She loved every minute. Well, *almost* every minute. Rehearsals under Herr Schreiber's direction were grueling, but performing onstage in front of an audience, even in relative anonymity as a chorus member, never ceased to thrill her. She loved to watch Mary Garden and Beatrice de Bonneville at work, singing the lead female roles of Cio-Cio San and Suzuki. And no matter how disdainful her attitude was toward Tony Leonardo in real life, she had to admit he played the part of the ne'er-do-well Lieutenant B. F. Pinkerton to perfection.

Come fall, Herr Schreiber indicated, she might be offered a steady contract with the opera company, and he planned to cast her in bigger roles. Some of the other singers mumbled about Reinhard playing favorites, but Molly assured Francie that they were just jealous because Francie was clearly the better singer.

Meanwhile, she continued the classes that had been included in her prize and wondered what she would do with herself come summer, when both the school and opera company went on hiatus. She should probably visit her family in California, but with the exception of seeing Will, the prospect held little appeal, not to mention it would deplete her bank account.

During the customary midwinter break from teaching, Francie's vocal coach, Madame Clairvaux, had attended a series of educational lectures about the role of the physical body in singing and returned with a newfound enthusiasm for exercise. At a lesson in January, she directed Francie to lie on the floor beneath the piano.

"On the floor?" Francie cast an incredulous glance at the studio's scarred wooden floor.

The teacher nodded, and Francie obeyed, lowering herself gingerly to the floor and stretching out on her back. She felt very foolish.

"Now take a deep breath," Madame Clairvaux instructed.

Francie did as she was told.

"Now relax your abdomen," Madame Clairvaux said. "Let your belly puff out. Pouf!"

Belly-puffing was impossible against the firm stays of Francie's corset, which led to the teacher lecturing her on the need for looser undergarments in order to put the diaphragm to full use.

"You will practice breathing for fifteen minutes a day," she ordered. "Fifteen minutes breathing on your back on the floor."

Next, she told Francie to stand. "Now you are going to drop the chain." She showed Francie how to stretch, to let the chain of her skeleton release, link by link, slackening the body in increments from her scalp to the base of her spine, from the backs of her knees to the bottoms of her heels.

From that day forth, they opened each lesson with physical exercise. While she found the antics strange, Francie had to admit they made her feel good, and were a much more enjoyable way to pass several minutes of lesson time than repeating endless scales and arpeggios.

Francie most enjoyed practicing with Molly in the evening. While Molly was studying violin, not voice, she did share some classes with Francie at the conservatory, and they both found it relieved stress and improved their outlook to work on their technique together.

Molly had a gift for finding a humorous angle in just about any situation, and her hilariously accurate imitation of Herr Schreiber made Francie roar with laughter.

One night when they were taking a break from practicing together, singing runs of notes on particular vowel sounds, she tried to demonstrate some of Madame Clairvaux's physical exercises to Molly. They ended up lying on the rug in a heap of laughter. When they'd finally caught their breath, they lay side by side in the warmth of the steam radiator. The streetlight outside their window, filtered by the falling snow, cast graceful dancing patterns on the plaster ceiling.

"What are your plans for the summer?" Molly asked.

"I don't know yet," Francie admitted. "It's hard to imagine summer when the snow's still coming down."

"It'll be here before you know it."

Francie sighed. "I suppose I'll return to Scoville and resume waitressing at Café Figaro. That is, if Grace will let me stay with her again, and if Mr. Figaro hasn't replaced me." She realized those were some big *ifs*.

"Don't you want to do something music-related?"

"Sure," Francie said, "but I have to be practical. I need to make some real money if I'm going to pay for a second year at the conservatory. Most music jobs wouldn't pay enough." *Or would require stepping foot in the The Thirsty Swallow.* Eager to take the focus off of herself and her hazy future, she turned her head toward Molly. "What about you?"

"I'm going to Idaho," Molly declared.

"Idaho!" Francie raised herself on her elbows. "Whatever for?"

Molly turned on her side to face Francie. "My aunt lives there. She owns a music shop in a small town, and she has invited me to come and work with her for the summer. It's supposed to be a beautiful place, with mountains and lakes and things." She resumed lying on her back, gazing up at the water-stained ceiling.

"That sounds wonderful," Francie said with a mix of admiration and envy. Admiration at Molly's bravery to travel to a completely unfamiliar place, and envy that she had a firm plan already. "Oh, well," she said briskly. "I still have some time to think about it. Meanwhile, we're starting rehearsals for the *Saint Matthew Passion*. We're going to sing it at Easter, in German. I can't wait."

Molly frowned. "He's making you sing it in German?"

"Yes."

"That's kind of risky, don't you think?"

"What's risky?"

"Singing in German."

Francie pulled herself up to a sitting position. "What do you mean?"

"I mean, I've been reading that in places like New York and Boston, people are protesting all things German, from German songs to composers like Bach and Beethoven. They've even renamed hamburger. Now they're calling it Salisbury steak. And German measles are called 'liberty measles.' All because of the war, obviously."

"That's so silly," Francie retorted. "What do Bach and Beethoven have to do with the Kaiser?"

"Nothing but having been born in the same part of the world," Molly said. "But people are reacting to all the bad news out of Europe. All the stuff the newspapers are saying about Germans being barbarians over there and committing unspeakable atrocities. It's making things tough for Germans living over here."

Francie lowered herself back down to the floor. "The thing I don't get is, if all Germans are such terrible people, why are we only just hearing about it now? Why hasn't it been common knowledge for years and years?" She frowned at the ceiling. "Sometimes these shocking stories seem more like propaganda than sound news reporting."

"I agree with you," Molly said. "Why, you and I know lots of Germans and they aren't anything like that. Chicago has a huge population of people who are German or have German ancestry, and they're as kind and decent as anyone else. But some people aren't thinking too clearly these days. And that can be very dangerous." Apparently noticing Francie's troubled expression, she added, "Look, I adore the *Saint Matthew Passion* as much as the next person. All I'm saying is, I think it would be less likely to draw unwanted attention if the choir sang it in English."

"Well, that's Herr Schreiber's decision. As a lowly chorister, I can hardly advise the esteemed director on what to do." Francie rubbed her shoulder where a knot had begun to form.

"It wouldn't be unprecedented to change the language. After all, he chose to perform *Salomé* in Italian instead of the original German. Remember?"

"*Ugh*." Francie shuddered. "I don't know whose decision that was. Anyway, I'd rather not think about that dreadful production." She forced herself to her feet and stretched her arms over her head. "In any case, I have a lot of work ahead of me to do justice to Bach. Madame Clairvaux says I need to bring my sound forward. It's too far back in my head." She peered at her head in the oval wall mirror as if looking for the sound. "And she says I have to fix my pronunciation." She sighed. "She nagged me all fall about my French, and now, suddenly German is the problem."

"In more ways than one," Molly remarked.

Francie's thoughts floated to Henry at training camp. She gave an involuntary shiver, sensing that something ominous loomed closely ahead.

CHAPTER
THIRTY-SEVEN

S tanding at attention in front of the barracks, shoulder-to-shoul-
der with his comrades as Sergeant Bingley paced before them,
Henry squirmed under the weight of his stiff, olive-drab uniform.
Long days of monotonous drills, from bugle call to lights-out, learning
how to handle rifles and bayonets, slogging through mud, and being
hollered at had culminated in this moment. The moment Henry had
enlisted for, when he'd be sent overseas to defend America and fight
the Kaiser.

The men seemed unable to remain motionless, shifting constantly
as if they were waiting for a gunfight to break out, united in a common
purpose to beat the Huns.

At last, the sergeant stopped and faced them, rigid as a fence post.
He cleared his throat.

"Gentlemen," he boomed, his voice echoing through the mega-
phone. "As of today, you have all been given orders for your next
assignment. In two weeks, you will be sent to Belleau Wood, where
you will join the front lines in the first American offensive of the war."

The troops fell into a hushed silence. Henry could feel the tension radiating from the men around him, but within himself, a surprising calmness reigned. Or perhaps he was fooling himself about the danger.

"You will be ready to go by then," the sergeant continued, his voice hard. "I expect you all to be prepared. Now, dismissed."

Returning the sergeant's salute, Henry allowed himself a surge of pride. He was fearful, sure, but also determined. In two weeks' time, he would be ready. More than ready.

Heck, he was ready now.

Francie took her seat in the soprano section for the rehearsal of the Easter-season performance of Bach's *Saint Matthew Passion*. Herr Schreiber rapped his baton on the podium.

"Ladies and gentlemen, before we begin today's rehearsal, I have something important to say to you." The members of the company stopped rustling in their seats and gave the director their full attention. "This morning the board chairman of the opera came to me with a special request." He paused and cleared his throat. "He asked me to cancel our performance of *The Saint Matthew Passion* and replace it with something not so . . . well, not quite so German."

Audible gasps rose around the room, followed by loud murmuring. He beat the baton on the podium again. "Quiet, please. The suggestion is ludicrous, of course. A large and important segment of our audience looks forward to our annual presentation of *Saint Matthew Passion* at Eastertide, and we don't want to disappoint them. Not to mention we've worked too hard and too long to cancel it now. But I feel I need to be frank with you. These are dangerous times we are living in, particularly for some of us."

The room went silent, everyone hanging on his words.

Herr Schreiber continued. "The board has suggested that no more German music be allowed at all. Instead, German numbers are to be replaced by patriotic American songs such as 'The Star-Spangled Banner' to prove our loyalty." He began to pace back and forth behind the podium. "Now, please understand, I have nothing against good American music. But we are an opera company, not a brass band marching in a parade. As director of this company, I have determined that German music *will* be performed, as well as the music of America and of other countries that our audiences have come to love and appreciate."

A low hum rose and fell around the room. Herr Schreiber tapped the baton. "Ladies and gentlemen, please. This is serious." He took a sip of water from a glass kept beneath the podium. Francie could tell he was choosing his words with great care. "Music is the universal language. I will not participate in the senseless censorship of all things German. However, setting questions of musical artistry aside for the moment, many of you here claim German ancestry, as do I. Or Austrian. Or Swiss. I need to warn you, we are, all of us, being scrutinized for possible allegiance to Germany. So I beg of you—all of you, German or not. For your own sakes, do not speak German in public. Do not read German newspapers in public. And above all, don't give even a glance or a nod that would indicate that your sympathies might lean toward support for the Kaiser. Have I made myself clear?"

Heads nodded all around the room.

"Good. And now, let us continue." He gave a rueful smile. Then he lifted his left hand. *Stehen Sie auf, bitte,*" he ordered in direct violation of his own stated rule about not speaking German. *A brief moment of rebellion,* Francie thought. The company rose to their feet as Herr

Schreiber raised his baton and the rehearsal began, but the mood remained subdued.

The next morning over coffee in their tiny apartment kitchen—they'd been skipping breakfast to save money—Francie discussed this disturbing development with Molly.

"It appears you were right when you said singing in German would be a risky move," she said. "It hardly seems fair, though. Herr Schreiber has lived in America for many years. Since he was sixteen, Grace told me. This country is his home."

"It's the same all over, people wanting nothing to do with Germany or Germans. Listen to this." Molly picked up the newspaper that lay folded on the table beside her cup and saucer. "It says right here that the other day in Boston, Theodore Roosevelt said, 'No man has any business to be engaged in anything that is not subordinated to patriotism. If the Boston Symphony Orchestra will not play "The Star-Spangled Banner," it ought to be made to shut up.'"

Francie stared at her friend, wide-eyed. Suddenly a smile tugged at the corners of her mouth, in spite of the somber topic. "The former President really said 'shut up?' In front of reporters?"

Molly glanced at the newspaper. "That's what it says."

"Not very dignified." Francie shook her head. "What's the world coming to? We can only hope that this prejudice against Germans is just a passing bit of insanity."

"I hope so, too," Molly agreed, "for Herr Schreiber's sake, and the sake of all the fine German people everywhere."

CHAPTER
THIRTY-EIGHT

O n the evening of March twenty-fifth, the musicians and
singers assembled on stage at the Auditorium Theater for a
run-through of *Saint Matthew Passion* with the full orchestra. After
working on it for weeks with only a pianist, Francie was stunned by the
rich dimension added by the orchestra. She couldn't think of a better
way to spend an evening. She adored this piece of music. Madame
Clairvaux had helped her translate the German words into English so
she'd understand what she was singing. It made her heart both ache
and soar to sing about the death and resurrection of Jesus Christ.

At this practice, Herr Schreiber was being even more particular
about details than his usual exacting self. When he gave the sopranos
a criticism of their timing, Francie carefully penciled a reminder into
her score.

No sooner had they started to sing the passage than the rehearsal
room door burst open and a group of men stormed in. Some were
dressed in business suits, others wearing the dark blue uniforms of the
Chicago Police Department.

The choir stopped singing. At the podium, Herr Schreiber wheeled
around to face the men.

"What is the meaning of this interruption?"

One of the men stepped forward. "Are you Reinhard Schreiber?" he demanded.

"Yes."

"Under the authority of the Bureau of Investigation and the Chicago Police Department, we demand that you step down from the podium at once and come with us."

"Why?"

"For questioning under the Alien and Sedition Act."

"What does that mean?" Francie's seatmate whispered.

"It means they suspect he's a spy," Francie said.

The woman's eyes grew wide. "A spy? Do you think it's true?"

"Of course not," Francie responded in horror. "His only 'crime' is being German."

Meanwhile Herr Schreiber remained calm.

"Can you not wait until the rehearsal has concluded?" he said in the same voice he used to reprimand a recalcitrant musician.

The men murmured among themselves, then the spokesman turned back to Herr Schreiber.

"We'll hold off until the rehearsal is over," he said, "but then you'll need to come with us."

"Thank you." Herr Schreiber turned back to the choir. He appeared calm and dignified, but a slight tremor shook his hand as he lifted his baton, and a glow of perspiration glistened on his face.

The officers positioned themselves strategically throughout the hall, sitting with their eyes fixed on Herr Schreiber until the rehearsal was over. By then the gleam of perspiration had become a trickle. Francie had no idea how the singers and musicians made it through the practice. She could barely sing a note around the tightness in her throat. But somehow, out of respect for their beloved director, they muddled through.

Herr Schreiber laid down his baton. "That's enough for tonight. I will see you tomorrow."

He turned and addressed the officers. "Gentlemen, shall we go to my office?" He walked down the steps at the side of the stage, where the men surrounded him. To Francie's relief they didn't handcuff him or manhandle him. Nonetheless, it broke her heart to see the respected director ordered around like an errant schoolboy. As they passed the soprano section, he appeared to be making every effort to remain cool, but his shaking fingers belied his true inward agitation.

After they'd gone, the company sat in stunned silence. At last Francie found her voice. She rose and faced the group.

"It isn't fair!" she cried. "They have no right to detain him. He's done nothing wrong. Can't somebody do something?"

But nobody said anything, too fearful of sticking out their necks. In quiet groups of twos and threes, they exited the concert hall and left the building.

Francie didn't leave right away, but waited outside Herr Schreiber's office for as long as she could until a police officer ordered her to leave. The men were all still inside, their voices rising and falling, but she couldn't make out the words.

In spite of his confident assurances to the choir of seeing them at the next rehearsal, Herr Schreiber did not return the following day, nor the next, nor the next. Rehearsals were taken over by a guest conductor, one of his colleagues from the conservatory. Much later Francie learned that while he was being questioned in his office, more officers from the police and the Bureau of Investigation raided his home, retrieving correspondence and other papers. The Bureau recklessly pored over personal items, pulled books off shelves, took pictures off the walls and out of their frames, and pawed through drawers, trunks, suitcases, and closets.

Herr Schreiber was kept in a Chicago jail until April sixth, when he was classified as a "dangerous enemy alien." Accompanied by marshals, he boarded the train to a prisoner-of-war camp. Where this camp was located, Francie did not know.

That same day, President Woodrow Wilson declared that the United States had entered the Great War.

Two days later, on Easter Sunday, Francie stood with the rest of the choir on the Auditorium stage, singing *Saint Matthew Passion* under the direction of the guest conductor as tears rolled down her face. She stumbled over the unfamiliar words, which were not what they had rehearsed. For while the opera board had allowed the company to keep their engagement, they had insisted the piece be sung in English.

CHAPTER
THIRTY-NINE

The week after Easter was spring vacation at the conservatory, when classes did not meet. Francie had planned to use her rare time off to stay in Chicago and play tourist. She'd seen precious little of the city's attractions since arriving, due to her hectic schedule.

Instead, she found herself at Union Station saying good-bye to Molly, who was headed home to Indiana, before boarding her own train for Scoville.

"Are you sure you won't come with me?" Molly said as they stood on the platform. She practically shouted to be heard over the hissing and clanging of the train. "Mother and Dad would love to see you again, and the fresh country air at the farm would do you good."

Francie thanked her. "I really want to see Grace and find out how she's doing. I know she cares deeply for Herr Schreiber, and his arrest must be very hard for her."

The two hugged, then Molly scurried up the train steps and disappeared into the car. Francie returned to the waiting room until it was time for her train to leave. With a pang, she saw the pillar she'd lurked behind the previous winter, cowardly to the bone, watching Henry say good-bye to his family. Now that America had officially entered the war, she worried about him every day and deeply regretted not coming out that day to give him a proper send-off, Lila or no Lila.

She tallied the weeks that had passed since that frigid January day. He was through with basic training by now, or close to it. Who knew where he'd be stationed, or how long he'd be gone? Maybe he'd already been sent overseas. Her heart ached with the realization that she may never see him again. But she needed to not think that way. Besides, he was no longer hers to worry about. He belonged to another woman now.

On the journey to Scoville, she read and napped. When she reached her hometown and Grace answered the door, Francie threw her arms around her former teacher.

"Oh, Grace," was all she could say.

"I was so pleased to get your telegram. Let me look at you." Grace held Francie at arm's length. "You've turned into a real city girl. All grown up. There, there. You mustn't cry. You must tell me everything."

Francie wiped her eyes with the sleeve of her jacket. "I will, I promise."

Francie unpacked her suitcase in her former bedroom, then found Grace in the front yard, raking winter's debris from her flower beds. Grabbing an extra pair of gloves and a rake from the garden shed, Francie joined her. They often had their best talks while working together at some chore.

She brought Grace up to date on her classes at the conservatory and her lessons with Madame Clairvaux. Then the conversation turned to Herr Schreiber's arrest.

"I was there when they arrested him," Francie said quietly. "I was fit to be tied, along with everyone else, but he remained calm and serene as if nothing out of the ordinary was taking place."

"That sounds like Reinhard." Grace's expression was grim. "He seems to be doing all right so far, though, judging from his letters."

His letters? Francie leaned against her rake. "You've heard from him?"

Grace nodded. "I've received two letters so far. One postmarked Chicago, the other postmarked Georgia. He says he's housed with other German and German-American musicians at a place called Fort Oglethorpe, and reports that conditions aren't too terrible, considering the circumstances. It sounds like the worst things are the heat and the mosquitoes. But he hasn't been mistreated. Or so he says." She paused. "He's keeping a positive attitude. He expects the whole sorry situation to be cleared up soon."

"It *has* to be cleared up," Francie insisted. "They haven't a shred of evidence to hold him as a spy. Have they?"

"No, of course not," Grace confirmed. "But in his last letter he said they've tried to accuse him of everything from penciling secret code into his music scores to signaling his alleged contacts with the gestures of his baton." Her tone emphasized the ridiculousness of such a spurious accusation.

"Unbelievable." Francie resumed raking with extra vigor. "It would be ludicrous if it weren't so horrifying. I never thought I'd live in a country where this kind of madness could take place, that a person can be put under suspicion and lose his freedom just because of where he was born. Whatever happened to the huddled masses yearning to breathe free, and all that?" Her voice shook. The whole incident hit squarely on her feelings of injustice and being an outsider.

Kneeling, Grace patted the soil at the base of a rose bush. "I want to go down to Georgia to be near him, though I heard they won't let me visit him. Even so, if I could get an apartment or hotel room close by the camp, maybe I could be of some use to him. If he's still incarcerated when the term ends in June, God forbid, I may do just that."

Francie knelt beside her and pressed her gloved hand. "At least in the meantime, you're able to write back and forth. That's something."

"Yes," Grace replied. "That is a blessing. We must look on the bright side and ask God to protect him." She sat back on her heels. "But enough of that. Tell me truthfully how *you're* doing."

Francie poured out her frustration over opera life in general, and over Madame Clairvaux's drill-sergeant instructions in particular.

"And then there was *Salomé*." Francie sighed. "Truthfully, I was never so embarrassed in all my life. The production made an absolute hash of the biblical story."

"The Bible is filled with battles and other gruesome situations. Even a few lascivious ones," Grace said. "However, there's a big difference between the portrayal of violence that is necessary to the plot and the blood-and-guts spectacle that you're describing."

"It was just really hard to watch." Francie stuffed a handful of moldering leaves into a sack. "It made me question whether I should take any part in opera at all."

"Opera is a difficult place to be a Christian," Grace acknowledged as she clipped a dead branch. "Is a Christian obligated to take on roles that are in line with their beliefs? Should they only appear in operas that reflect those beliefs?"

Francie frowned. "I don't know. Should we?"

Grace stilled her shears. "Nobody said the Christian walk would be easy, especially if you're a Christian working in the public eye. Society will constantly look at you for some sort of commentary. They'll watch you closely to find traits to emulate, or to look for a chink in the armor." She resumed clipping. "To answer your question, I'd say you always have to be mindful of the type of roles you take and how those roles help to glorify Jesus."

"So if a director wants me to sing the part of Salome, I should turn it down," Francie said. "Or Jezebel. Or Delilah, for that matter."

To her surprise, Grace said, "Not necessarily. But if you're going to play an evil character, then portray her as evil as you can. Make sure the audience knows she's evil, and recoils from it. The problem comes when evil is portrayed as good, or attractive, or entertaining. That sort of portrayal is a lie, and dishonoring to the truth of who God is."

Francie appreciated Grace's perspective and felt more comfortable about her place in the opera world than she had in weeks. She stayed in Scoville for several days, helping Grace with the spring window-cleaning and sprucing of closets, before heading back to the city.

"Don't worry about Reinhard," Grace said on their last morning together. "He's able to take care of himself, and soon this whole nasty business will be over."

"How can you be so calm?" Francie asked in genuine amazement.

"Simple," Grace replied. "I trust the American justice system to do the right thing, in the end. And I've put the situation in God's hands."

"Simple, but not easy," Francie said.

"Simple when you trust Him." Grace embraced Francie. "And I do."

"So do I," Francie said, her faith bolstered. "I trust God to take care of all of us. Especially Herr Schreiber."

And especially Henry.

CHAPTER FORTY

G race might have trusted in the justice system to do the right thing, but Francie thought it might need a helpful nudge. On the train ride back to Chicago, she vowed to consult a lawyer about what could possibly be done to get Herr Schreiber released.

The trouble was, the only lawyer she knew was Abbott Jasper. Would a man who so disliked her even listen to what she had to say, much less be willing to help her—for very little money?

There was only one way to find out. As soon as she got back to her rooming house, she looked him up in the telephone directory. She found an entry for Jasper and Jasper, Attorneys at Law. Then she used the communal telephone in the hall to call the office and make an appointment.

On the appointed day, she dressed in her nicest gabardine skirt and jacket and walked the few blocks from her rooming house to the skyscraper on LaSalle Street. As she sat in the walnut-paneled waiting room that smelled of beeswax and money, she practiced what she would say. At last she was ushered into Mr. Jasper's office.

"Please wait here," the secretary said. "Mr. Jasper will be right with you."

A collection of framed photographs lined the credenza behind Mr. Jasper's desk. With a pang, she noticed one of Henry dressed in his army uniform. He looked so serious, so strong, so . . . soldierly. Francie had a sudden wild wish to hide the photo under her jacket and make off with it. But she'd never actually do such a thing. Besides, what good would it do? Right next to the photo of Henry was another photo of him and Lila together. It looked as if it might have been taken at the train station the day Francie lurked behind the pillar.

Fresh shame washed over her for hiding in the shadows that day instead of boldly saying goodbye to the man she loved. Flustered, she turned to Abbott Jasper, who had entered the office and was watching her with a chilly expression as she examined the photos.

"Miss Forrester, this is a surprise. What can I do for you?" He gestured to a leather-upholstered armchair and Francie took a seat.

"Have you had any news from Henry?" She tried to keep her tone light, as one would ask of a casual friend, hoping to thaw the frost a bit.

"Only that he successfully completed his basic training, and has not yet shipped out."

"You mean he hasn't been sent overseas?" Francie gripped the arms of the chair as relief rushed through her.

"Not yet," Mr. Jasper said in a clipped tone. "A fact that has been a comfort to his mother and me, as well as to his fiancée, Miss Gladstone. Though of course we expect to receive news of an overseas assignment at any time. Now, what is it I can do for you?"

His fiancée. Francie's spirits sank. She wasn't surprised, after seeing the two of them together at December's performance of *The Messiah*, but actually hearing the word spoken out loud made her breath catch. She averted her eyes from the photograph of Henry and Lila and turned toward Mr. Jasper to state Herr Schreiber's case as succinctly as she could. His demeanor toward her remained polite but cool as he listened.

"So I've come to ask if you can convince the authorities to get him released," she concluded. "Surely a man of your stature in the legal profession would know whom to contact."

"I don't know what kind of power you think I have, but that's not really the kind of law, I practice, Miss Forrester," he said. "I don't think I can help you or your friend. These are dangerous times, and the government can't be too careful about protecting our country from enemy spies."

"I understand that, but he's *not* an enemy spy," Francie protested, anger heating in her chest. "He's an orchestra conductor. Please, Mr. Jasper." Her voice took on a begging tone. "It breaks all the rules of justice to hold law-abiding people without cause or due process. That's not the America we know and love. That's not the kind of country Henry has prepared to fight for. Surely even you can see that."

She knew she was crossing a line. But she'd gone too far to back down now.

Mr. Jasper made no reply. For an endless minute, the only sounds were a ticking clock, muted traffic noises from the street below, and the secretary's typing on the other side of the door. The door which Abbott Jasper was now opening.

"I'm afraid I can't help you," he said, his voice curt. "Perhaps you should try pleading your case with the U. S. Department of Justice."

"But how would I do that?" The suggestion sounded as ludicrous as traveling to Washington, D. C., to demand a meeting with President Wilson himself.

But Mr. Jasper was ready to be rid of her. "Good day to you, Miss Forrester."

Francie rose with dignity and walked through the door, past the secretary's desk to the elevator, through the elegant lobby, and out to the street. It wasn't until she was safely ensconced in her little apartment that she allowed herself the luxury of bursting into tears.

"Fort Oglethorpe? Fort Oglethorpe, *Georgia*?"

Henry knew he could get in big trouble for questioning a superior officer, but he couldn't believe his ears. For weeks he'd been steeling his mind and screwing up his courage to go to Europe, to finally see some real action and perform his sacred duty to fight alongside his compatriots in this war to end all wars. And now he was being sent to Georgia, of all places? The land of cotton? Of magnolias and moonlight? It was all he could do to hold back his sputtering rage in the senior officer's presence.

Fortunately, the officer took a sympathetic view of Henry's momentary insubordination. "I'm as surprised as you, Jasper. The order came through yesterday that you are to remain stateside for now. But look on the bright side. Most men would be relieved to be in your shoes. Guarding prisoners may not be your idea of a choice position, but somebody has to do it." He leaned back against the edge of his desk. "The truth is, Jasper, the Army needs men like you here, at least for the time being. Fort Oglethorpe has recently experienced a huge influx of prisoners of war and suspected enemies from within our borders. Your high scores in languages, particularly German, have made you an ideal candidate for working with foreign entities."

That's what I get for studying my tail off in Prof Biermann's class at Scoville, Henry thought bitterly.

But it didn't matter what he thought. The Army was the Army. And within a week, he was slapping mosquitoes and babysitting a batch of bewildered German POWs in the wet heat of a Georgia spring.

CHAPTER
FORTY-ONE

C oming home late from rehearsal one May evening, Francie opened her mailbox and pulled out a cream-colored envelope, hand-addressed in graceful cursive to Miss Francine Forrester. She opened it and read an invitation to Beatrice de Bonneville's apartment for tea the following Thursday. With growing excitement, she read and reread the invitation.

Whatever could it mean?

On Thursday afternoon after her final class, she took a taxi to Madame de Bonneville's home, a luxurious apartment building in Chicago's Gold Coast neighborhood. The building's windows were huge, floor to ceiling, and led out over an ornate wrought-iron balcony. A manicured lawn surrounded the building, with a fountain in the center courtyard. Elaborate decorations and shining ornamentation graced every window. Francie felt as if she'd been transported to London or Paris.

The lobby smelled of fresh tea and flowers and perfume. The blue-uniformed doorman dialed a telephone and spoke Francie's name to the voice on the other end of the line. Soon she found her way to an elevator and rode up to the penthouse level. Thick carpeting silenced her footsteps, and the brass number on the apartment door glowed like a beacon.

At her knock, the door to the apartment swung open and Francie was greeted by a housemaid, who bade her wait in the foyer. Fighting down her nervousness, Francie stood uncertainly on the marble floor and took in the scent, a sweet mixture of lavender, fine furniture polish, and eucalyptus. The soft ticking of a grandfather clock was the only sound in the gilded space.

Moments later, Madame de Bonneville swept into the foyer, wearing a blue silk dress with her white hair up in an elaborate coiffure.

"Do come in, Francine," she beckoned. She led the way to a richly appointed drawing room. A floor-to-ceiling window bathed the room in natural light. All around were tall vases of waxen white lilies and bowls of soft pink roses. Signed photos of famous singers and conductors graced the shiny black piano.

At Madame de Bonneville's invitation, Francie took a seat on a sofa upholstered in peach-colored silk. The diva seated herself in a matching wingback chair nearby.

"I'm so glad you could join me today, Francine," she began as the maid poured tea from a porcelain teapot into delicate china cups.

"I'm thrilled that you asked to see me, Madame."

"I've asked you here for a reason, of course. I have something important to discuss with you. We may as well get straight down to business."

Whatever her hostess was about to say, Francie was eager to hear it. She took a sip of the fragrant tea to steady her nerves.

"I took notice of you during *The Messiah*, and again more recently during rehearsals of *Saint Matthew Passion*."

The great Beatrice de Bonneville had taken notice of her?

"You have talent, obviously, but more important to me was your professionalism. You came to every rehearsal, on time and prepared to work. In my opinion, you outshone the other conservatory students in your work ethic and demeanor."

"That's kind of you to say," Francie murmured.

"Kindness has nothing to do with it," the diva continued briskly. "I'm just telling you what I've observed. But what most impressed me was your spirited defense of our dear conductor, Herr Schreiber, when he was dragged off by those evil men. I witnessed that and said to myself, this is a girl with gumption."

Francie swallowed back her rising emotions. "He's done nothing wrong. Nothing but the so-called crime of being born in Germany."

"You're correct, of course. And that's the main reason I wanted to see you today. You see, I too am guilty of the same so-called crime."

"You're German? But you don't have an accent. And 'de Bonneville' sounds—"

"—French. I know. But my real name is Gumpenberger. My manager suggested I change it when I was about your age."

Francie could see why. *de Bonneville* looked better on a marquee.

"I was born in Germany and raised in New Jersey," the diva continued. "My parents brought me to America when I was a very young child. But that makes no difference to the authorities. Not in this current climate."

Madame de Bonneville gazed thoughtfully at her teacup. Then she lifted her head and looked directly at Francie. "The fact is, they are watching me, too, to assess my loyalty to this country. Because of my birthplace, they are doubting my patriotism, even though I grew up here. The fact that my two sons are currently serving in the United States Navy means nothing to them." Her voice grew thick, and she took a moment to compose herself before continuing.

"I am sorry," Francie said with sincerity.

With a sweep of her hand, Madame de Bonneville appeared to brush her words away. "I'm not looking for sympathy," she said plainly. "I'm merely explaining the circumstances under which I'm undertaking a summer concert tour of the West, specifically to perform at military bases and camps, as well as the usual venues. I want to support our troops in time of war, to be sure, but also to reinforce my own genuine and heartfelt patriotism toward this country."

"I see," Francie said. "I think that's a marvelous idea."

"I thought that you might," the singer continued. "That's why I'd like you to accompany me as my assistant."

"Your assistant?" Francie nearly dropped her teacup.

"Yes, my assistant. You needn't look so goggle-eyed, Francine. It doesn't become you."

"But—what would I do?" Francie stammered.

"You wouldn't need to worry about my personal wardrobe or luggage. I have a maid for that. What I need is a traveling companion for the entire three-month journey, someone capable who is eager to learn about the business and could see to various arrangements, details, correspondence, that sort of thing. And once in a while, perhaps you will join me on stage for a song or two. After all, you must keep up your vocal training for the fall season. All expenses paid, of course, plus a generous salary."

Francie was so overwhelmed, she found it hard to speak. Apparently taking her silence for indecision, Madame de Bonneville continued,

"You'll need to think it over, of course. While you're thinking, consider the impact such a position could have on your future. I'd be introducing you to important people. You'd make many contacts who could help your career. You'll be singing for them."

Francie found her tongue. "I'm extremely flattered, and grateful for the opportunity. My only hesitation in accepting your gracious offer is that I'd hoped to visit my mother and brother in California this summer."

"Where in California?"

Francie told her.

"That's not a problem," Madame de Bonneville assured her. "We will be visiting Los Angeles on the tour. We will make sure your family is sent complimentary tickets to the concert." Her eyes twinkled. "Perhaps we will even make that one of the concerts where you join me on the stage."

Francie could hardly believe her good fortune.

"Thank you, Madame. Thank you."

Francie left the diva's apartment on wings of air, breathing a prayer of gratitude. She not only had been offered a summer job—she had just been handed the opportunity of a lifetime.

Henry walked the perimeter of the camp, on the alert for any un-usual activity. All was quiet. An early evening breeze swept through, bringing welcome relief from the heat of the day. If he were honest, his assignment to Fort Oglethorpe was turning out to be not so bad, after all.

True, he felt guilty for not embarking to France alongside his fellow recruits from basic training. After weeks spent getting in fighting trim, he was stuck guarding prisoners of war in this camp on the sleepy border of Georgia and Tennessee. A cushy assignment if ever there was one. He felt sidelined, missing out on the real action, although the longer the war dragged on, the better his chances were for being sent to Europe.

Part of him wished for that—the part that had mastered grueling exercises, gas-mask drills, bayonet-thrusting, digging trenches and filling them up again. The prospect of active combat unnerved him, of course, but wasn't that what he'd trained for? Fighting in the trenches seemed the right thing to do, to lick the Kaiser once and for all.

In the meantime, keeping watch over German POWs under the hazy southern sun was not particularly hard labor. The prisoners were docile and compliant. Most of them turned out to be young men not unlike himself, homesick, scared, and caught up in a war that was not of their making.

He rounded a corner past the mess hall and came across a group of prisoners engaged in a rousing game of soccer. He watched for a minute, tempted to join in, then moved on to complete his rounds.

Activities like soccer games and chess matches had surprised him when he'd first arrived. He'd pictured a POW camp as a harsh place, run with strict militancy.

Fort Oglethorpe wasn't like that. Oh, it was a prison, to be sure. The watchtowers, barbed wire, and armed guards assured it would never be mistaken for a vacation resort. But German prisoners on U.S. soil were given the opportunity to work, study, and even enjoy recreational activities in the camps, and Fort Oglethorpe was no exception.

"The way we treat our prisoners of war has a direct effect on how American POWs are treated overseas," the commander explained. "We want to do everything in our power to ensure the safety of our men over there. We treat our prisoners the way we'd want our men to be treated."

The German POWs who inhabited Camp A were the worker bees of the fort. They followed a strict daily schedule, did hard labor like building roads, and were too worn out at the end of the day to cause much trouble.

Camp B, where Henry was currently assigned, was even easier to manage. Nicknamed "the millionaires' camp," Camp B inmates were civilians, mostly German nationals or even American citizens of German ancestry, whose loyalty had been called into question, often simply on the basis of their last names. A few were men of considerable wealth and status who had private rooms, paid for better food, and even hired help from among the Camp A prisoners. As time went on, by treating these men with respect and earning their respect in return, Henry found himself on friendly terms with most of them. Deep inside, he had his doubts about their guilt. Most of the Camp B men he'd encountered didn't seem capable of anything as complex, wily, and steel-nerved as international espionage. But one never knew. His training had taught him that sometimes the most innocent-looking, blinky-eyed people turned out to be the most dangerous.

He was nearly done with his rounds when the unmistakable sound of Vivaldi's *The Four Seasons* reached his ear, wafting on the soft, sultry breeze from an open doorway to a residential building. Someone there must have gotten hold of a Victrola.

Such a luxury was not unheard of. All it took was payment to a sympathetic camp employee to gain access to things like books, musical instruments, and even Victrolas from a secondhand shop in Chattanooga, just over the state line.

Henry found himself irresistibly drawn to stand outside the door and listen. Peering through the open doorway, he saw not a Victrola, but from a group of men who'd assembled themselves into a makeshift orchestra.

When the musicians caught sight of Henry, they stopped playing and averted their eyes.

"*Sehr gut.*" He tried to sound friendly. "*Wunderbar.* Please continue." But the men didn't move.

The principal violinist—apparently the group's leader, or simply the least intimidated—rose and faced Henry.

"We have permission to play music after we've done our work for the day," he asserted in stiff, mildly accented English.

"Of course you do," Henry assured him. "I'm not here to interfere. I was just drawn in by the music." When the violinist did not reply, he tried to establish a degree of rapport. "Matter of fact, I'm a musician myself."

Still cautious, the man slowly approached him.

"You're a musician? What instrument do you play?"

"Piano."

"We have no piano," the man said, sweeping his gaze around the room. "Some of us were allowed to bring our instruments to prison with us. But no piano."

Something about the man's appearance seemed familiar, as if Henry had seen him somewhere before.

"What is your name?"

"Schreiber."

A series of rapid-fire images clicked through Henry's brain. A concert hall last December. Tuxedo-clad men, women in glittering gowns. Handel's *Messiah.* His parents and Lila.

And Francie.

He stuffed down the sudden rush of emotion that filled his throat. "You're Reinhard Schreiber?" he croaked. "The orchestra conductor?"

Herr Schreiber stood tall, looking as dignified as dirty brown trousers and a not-so-white undershirt would allow. No tuxedo tonight. "That is correct. And I would like to have access to a piano."

Henry could hardly believe it. It seemed wrong, a world-class conductor being locked up in this dump on a flimsy suspicion of espionage. A suspicion probably based on nothing more solid than his birthplace and his name. And instead of demanding justice and restitution—he was asking for a piano.

Anger and embarrassment over his government's actions rose in Henry, but he could hardly let these men know that. Rattled to the core, he blurted, "A piano? No matter, you're doing very well without one. Carry on." He stepped back into the darkness, aware of the inadequacy of his glib response and not wanting to cast a pall over their session. They had so few comforts as it was.

As he walked away, the sound of the strings made him both happy and sad. Happy because the music brought a bit of beauty and culture to this bleak place. Sad because he suspected these musicians had done nothing wrong, nothing worthy of being torn from their lives and imprisoned in Fort Oglethorpe. But the Army was the Army. Rules were rules.

And Vivaldi is Vivaldi. He brightened a little at that thought. At least no one could take Vivaldi away from them.

He thanked the Lord for that.

CHAPTER
FORTY-TWO

The summer tour took Francie and Beatrice, as well as a manager, an accompanist, and a maid, to many Midwestern and Western cities, including Des Moines, Lincoln, and Denver. Francie, who'd never set foot outside of Illinois, was amazed by the different types of terrain they traveled through, especially the Rocky Mountains, which she found absolutely breathtaking. Molly was beyond lucky to be able to spend the summer with her aunt in such a stunning locale. Alas, northern Idaho was nowhere near the tour route.

At each stop, crowds turned out to hear Beatrice sing in small theaters and in large ones, as well as many outdoor events. Sometimes Beatrice performed alone; sometimes she invited Francie to join her. The times Francie was invited to sing became more and more frequent. The reviews in the newspapers were almost invariably positive, lauding Madame de Bonneville and the fresh, new talent she was introducing to the music world.

The late nights performing and long days of travel occasionally took their toll on Francie's mood. One morning she slumped in her seat on the train, too tired to think, much less make brilliant conversation.

"One must sacrifice bodily comfort for the sake of results," Beatrice told her, not unkindly, and ordered the porter to bring them both coffee and breakfast. The freshly squeezed orange juice inspired Francie to sit up straighter and improve her attitude.

"You'll find plenty more where that came from when we get to California," Beatrice promised.

Francie faced the prospect of California with mixed eagerness and apprehension. Eager to see Ramona and Will—especially Will—and reassure herself they were truly getting on as well as their letters seemed to indicate. The faint sense of foreboding came from her slim acquaintance with Clarence Bailey. After all, she'd barely had time to get to know her new stepfather before the family left Illinois. But she prayed about the situation nonetheless, and determined to give him the benefit of the doubt. After all, he was part of her family now, whether she liked it or not.

Upon their arrival in California, after performing at military bases near San Francisco and Long Beach, Francie was deeply grateful to Beatrice for an afternoon off and the use of a car and driver.

Ramona, Clarence, and Will lived in a pleasant, recently built neighborhood on the outskirts of Los Angeles, in a white stucco house with a green roof and shutters and a red door. As the driver pulled up to the curb, Francie remarked at the contrast with the shabby gray house back in Scoville.

Ramona flung open the front door even before Francie reached it. "Ya made it!" Francie didn't even have time to assess her mother's appearance before they fell into each other's arms. But as Ramona led her into the living room, she seemed like a different woman—poised, polite, at ease in her new surroundings. She wore a bright cotton dress, neatly pressed. The henna-red hair remained, but now it was attractively styled, and somehow the color looked less garish in the California sunshine than it had back in Illinois.

During a quick tour of the house—which, to Francie's amazement, looked as neat and tastefully decorated as a photograph in *Ladies' Home Journal*—she was startled to glance out a back window and see a small swimming pool surrounded by a white picket fence. In the distance stood a grove of orange trees.

Ramona noticed her staring at the pool. "Practically everybody has one." She sounded almost apologetic. "The weather stays so warm, we can swim year round. Can ya believe it?"

They returned to the living room and sat together on a blue sofa. The open windows allowed fresh air, the scent of orange blossoms, and the cheerful notes of birdsong to permeate the house. The living room was simply and tastefully decorated. No sign of alcoholic beverages appeared anywhere, and Ramona's countenance was clear and bright.

They chatted pleasantly for well over an hour. Francie had outlined her new life in letters to her mother. Now she colored in the details of life at the conservatory and on the opera stage. Ramona listened politely and asked relevant questions that indicated she was paying attention. Francie could hardly believe the transformation from the careless, self-absorbed woman who'd left Illinois the year before.

"The California sunshine has done you good," she remarked. "It does my heart good to see you so happy."

"Very happy," Ramona said. "I guess I didn't realize how much old Scoville was draggin' me down. I mean, I lived there my whole life. Never thought I'd escape, ya know? But out here, it seems just about everybody's come here from someplace else, and people only think about who ya are now, not who ya was way back when. Know what I mean?"

"I think so." Now that Francie thought about it, that had been her experience at the conservatory. "Chicago Francie" was known as a student, as a singer. So different from "Scoville Francie."

"And you! Look at ya, all grown up and living in the big city, and now being on tour with that big-name star. I'm so proud of ya, I could bust."

"Thanks."

"So things turned out good for the both of us," Ramona declared. "Aren't ya glad now that ya didn't run off with that college fellow? That Henry?"

A shadow fell over Francie as though a cloud had passed, but it was only her mood. So far on this tour she'd been too busy to feel sorry for herself over the loss of Henry. But Ramona's statement brought all the hurt rushing back to the surface.

"Honestly? I think about him every single day."

"Aw, dollface. That won't last." Ramona looked down at her hands and fidgeted with her red-painted fingernails. "I'm sorry I was so hard on ya about that college boy. It's just that I thought ya could do so much better. And ya have. Just look at ya!"

Francie heaved a sigh. No point in spoiling their present reunion by rehashing past resentments. "That's water under the bridge," she assured her mother, forcing herself to believe it was true. "He's living his life, and I'm living mine."

"I just didn't want ya to make the mistakes I did. I made so many in my lifetime." Ramona paused, then lifted her head and looked directly at Francie. "Not that *you* was a mistake. I didn't mean it that way."

Francie reached over and squeezed her hand. "I know you didn't." But it healed her heart to hear it, just the same.

At that moment, the front door banged open and Will walked in. Francie squealed and leaped off the sofa. He tossed the tennis racket he was carrying onto a chair and ran toward her. They threw their arms around each other, and she thought her heart would burst with joy. Then she placed her hands on his shoulders and held him at arm's length.

"Let me have a good look at you, little brother," she cried. "Why, I'd barely recognize you if I passed you on the street."

Having not seen him for over a year, Francie was amazed. He'd grown taller, and his muscles were starting to fill out. His skin was bronzed from the sun, and his hair had taken on a golden cast. He was changing from a boy to a young man. But when he grinned at her, she saw the brother she'd always adored.

"California must be good for you, too," she said as they took their seats. Ramona returned from the kitchen with a tray of glasses and a pitcher of lemonade—just plain lemonade, Francie noted with relief after a sip.

The three of them chatted and caught up until late afternoon. Will loved his private school and looked forward to boarding there in the fall.

"I'm on the tennis team and the baseball team, and they've even got an aviation club," he told Francie with great enthusiasm.

She ruffled his hair. "That's wonderful to hear, buddy. I'm glad you're so happy here, and that Mr. Bailey has been so generous to send you to a fine school."

"He told me to call him Clarence," Will informed her.

"I'll call him Clarence too, then, from now on. Will he be home soon?" Francie tossed Ramona a questioning glance.

"I'm sorry he's not here yet," Ramona said. "I was hoping he'd be home from the dealership by now. Business has been good, and things have been really hoppin' over there. Seems everybody in L.A. wants an automobile these days."

"Not just in L.A. Well, that's all right," Francie said, her disappointment tempered by a warm rush of gratitude. Her mother must be finding marriage to Clarence Bailey very agreeable indeed. He must be a man worth getting to know better. She regretted her dismissive attitude toward him back in Illinois and vowed to be nicer to him in the future.

Too soon, with a reluctant glance at the clock, she stood.

"I have to get back to the hotel and get ready for tonight's concert. It's been so wonderful to see you both."

At the door, she hugged her mother.

"You will use those concert tickets I gave you, won't you? I'd love to see you there."

"We'll be there," Ramona assured her. Francie forced herself not to think about the many times she'd said that before and not followed through. This was a new day, and a new Ramona.

She exchanged a tight bear hug with Will. Then she slid into the backseat of the car and spent the ride to the hotel praying and thanking God for taking care of her little family. She hadn't known what to expect, and the outcome was better than she could have imagined.

Part of her wondered what her life would be like now if she'd moved to California. Would she, too, be fit and tanned from playing tennis all afternoon, instead of pasty and pale from being stuck inside all day? Would she have continued with her music, or given it up in favor of tending a rose garden or whatever else it was people did in California? Then she gently closed that line of questioning. She had her life in Chicago, and despite its struggles, she was grateful for it.

No sense in wondering what might have been—in California or with Henry.

That night, from behind the curtain at the Temple Auditorium, she sought out her family and was gratified to see them sitting in their seats.

"Have they arrived?" Beatrice asked, approaching Francie from behind.

Francie nodded, then turned toward Beatrice and shivered. "I'm more nervous than usual, with them out there listening."

"That's because it's personal," Beatrice replied. "But remember, my dear, if you know what you're going to do, you have no reason to be nervous."

Beatrice performed her numbers first, dressed in a green satin gown, an enormous corsage, a dagger of diamonds, and a huge green feathery ornament in her hair. Francie felt plain by comparison in pale blue chiffon with a darker blue sash. But the costume suited her.

When Francie's solo came, she sang better than she ever had before. Thrilled with her sustained final note, the audience erupted into approval. Amid shouts of "Brava! Brava!" she walked serenely off the stage.

Standing behind the curtain, Beatrice took her by the shoulders, turned her around, and gave her a gentle shove. She reappeared on stage to more applause, and glanced once more at her family, just in time to see Ramona put two fingers in her mouth and let loose an ear-shattering whistle, as if she were in a crowded football stadium instead of an elegant auditorium.

The old Francie would have cringed with embarrassment at her mother's inappropriate behavior. But the new Francie only smiled, grateful beyond words that, after a lifetime of waiting, Ramona Forrester Bailey was living happily ever after, and had truly heard her sing.

CHAPTER
FORTY-THREE

I n the camp commander's office, unable to read his superior's facial expression, Henry waited to be called on the carpet with no idea what the infraction was.

The commander held out a piece of yellow paper.

"Can you explain to me what this is, private?"

Henry glanced at the paper. "Yes, sir. It's a requisition, sir."

"For?"

"A piano, sir."

"Care to explain?"

Henry swallowed. "It's for Camp B, sir. They've formed themselves into an orchestra. But apparently they lack a piano."

"Apparently?"

Henry swallowed. "They lack a piano, sir."

"I see." The commander looked at Henry as if expecting him to say more.

Henry obliged. "They're quite talented, sir. I think, with the addition of a piano, they'd be able to entertain the whole camp. Put on concerts and such."

"Is that so?"

For a long minute, Henry feared the commander was going to reject the request. Maybe even reprimand him for supporting the inmates' leisure pursuits with such bubbling enthusiasm. It wasn't very guard-like behavior on his part.

But to his relief, the commander relaxed. "Let them have their music. It'll blow off some steam and keep morale up. When morale goes up, chances of trouble go down."

"Yes, sir." Henry cleared his throat. "And the piano, sir?"

"Isn't there a piano in the officer's mess hall?"

"Yes, sir." He'd played it himself in spare moments, when no one was around.

"Give the men permission to practice in the officer's mess in the evening for one hour before lights-out. One hour, no more, no less. And you will accompany them to and from the barracks and stand guard over them during that time. Understood?"

"Yes, sir."

"All right, soldier. Dismissed." He saluted, and Henry returned the salute.

"Thank you, sir. I know the men will appreciate it."

When he related the news to Reinhard Schreiber, the conductor cracked a rare smile. "That's encouraging news. Now if we only had someone to play it."

"You have no pianist?" Henry asked, confused. "But you said you needed a piano."

"Several of us have the ability to play, of course, but obviously not while we're playing our other instruments." Reinhard cocked an eyebrow. "Earlier you mentioned you play piano. Are you any good? What is your experience?"

The inquisition took Henry aback. He hardly thought Reinhard was in a position to be selective. "I studied classical piano through high school, and accompanied music students at Scoville College. So I guess I'm good enough."

Reinhard's expression shifted. "Scoville College?" He peered at Henry. "Are you acquainted with Miss Grace Whitworth, by chance?"

"Miss Whitworth? Sure, I know her."

Reinhard's expression turned wistful. "Miss Whitworth is a friend of mine. A very dear friend. Have you seen her recently?"

"Not since I graduated from Scoville," he said. Then, "No, wait, I saw her briefly at a performance of *The Messiah* in Chicago last December. But only from a distance. I didn't get a chance to speak to her."

"I see." The conductor cleared his throat, then returned to the business at hand. "What do you say? Will you help us out? With the piano, I mean?"

"I don't know," Henry demurred, still digesting the news that Reinhard knew Miss Whitworth—rather well, it would seem. "I could get in trouble for that." A guard playing music with inmates? It would never fly. He was supposed to be watching over them, not joining in on their recreation.

But this Schreiber fellow knew Miss Whitworth. He liked Miss Whitworth. Maybe even loved Miss Whitworth. He must be a good egg.

Henry let himself be talked into agreeing, and the commander gave his support, as long as a second guard was posted to keep watch while Henry was pounding the keyboard. Pretty soon he was accompanying the musicians in practice sessions several times a week, and loving every minute of it.

He loved it right up until the day Schreiber announced they'd been assigned to accompany a Sunday vespers service in the prison chapel—opening with "Jesus Loves Me."

The last time Henry had played "Jesus Loves Me," he'd been accompanying a certain curly-haired soprano on the stage of Piper Hall. His heart felt heavy with longing and regret at the memory of it.

At the memory of her.

Arriving in Chicago after the concert tour, Francie accepted a ride in Beatrice's car from the station to her apartment and trudged up the stairs, exhausted but gratified. Not only had the tour yielded a good friend and mentor in Beatrice, but Francie had gained confidence about performing, made several professional contacts, and gotten invaluable real-world experience and advice. After much deliberation and discussion with Beatrice, she'd decided not to enroll in the conservatory for a second year, but would give her full attention to performing with the opera company. She would learn what she needed to know from the professionals who were further along in their careers than she was.

She would, however, continue to study privately with Madame Clairvaux. There was always more to learn, and Francie knew she'd benefit from the discipline of working with such an exacting teacher.

Best of all, she'd seen her family and been reassured of their well-being. It gave her deep satisfaction to know they were thriving in Los Angeles. Both Ramona and Will had looked well and happy—Ramona more like transformed. Maybe there was magic in that California sunshine, after all. Now Francie could throw herself into her work without guilt or concern about how her family was faring halfway across the continent.

She set her suitcase on the floor, closed the door behind her, and hastened to open some windows. Her little apartment was stuffy in the late August heat.

Worse, it seemed particularly silent without Molly, who'd written her to say she'd decided not to return to Chicago for the fall term. Having fallen in love with the mountains, she'd remain in Idaho and continue working in her aunt's music shop. Francie understood, and had written back wishing Molly all the best and expressing hope that they'd stay in touch.

With her income from the summer tour and a more secure position with the opera company, Francie's financial position had improved to the point where she didn't need to take on another roommate right away. Still, the apartment seemed a little lonely and she missed her friend. There were so many things she wanted to tell her! A long, chatty letter would have to suffice. But first, she needed to settle back into simply being home.

She made a quick trip to the corner store to replenish a few basic groceries. Then, after a cool, refreshing bath, she wrapped herself in a lightweight cotton kimono and slippers, fixed herself a sandwich, and sat down to read the stack of mail that had accumulated in her absence.

Among the letters was a note from Tony Leonardo. To Francie's dismay, the amorous tenor had been named as Reinhard Schreiber's replacement at the helm of the opera company for the 1917-1918 season. He asked her to meet with him as soon as she could, before the start of rehearsals. He had something important to discuss with her. *Great.* Could she bring along someone else to be a third party? She still wasn't wild about meeting with him alone.

And yet, something had shifted within her over the course of the summer, after meeting so many new people and appearing onstage beside Beatrice. She wasn't the same bashful music student she'd been last spring. She'd grown in courage and confidence. She could hold her own against the likes of Tony Leonardo.

Even though he now held her career in his hands.

She set aside the note and flicked through the rest of the mail. A shard of disappointment stabbed her that there was no letter from Henry. And why would there be? She hadn't written to him, either. Still, the hope that he'd want to stay in touch was ever present, deep within her heart.

At the very bottom of the pile was an envelope with a return address of Jasper & Jasper, Attorneys at Law. Could this be news of Henry? She ripped it open.

Dear Miss Forrester,

Following our recent conversation, enclosed please find the name and address of an acquaintance of mine who works at the Department of Justice. Perhaps he can advise you on the case of your friend.

Sincerely,

Abbott Jasper, esq.

She withdrew from the envelope a small white calling card bearing a name and address at the Department of Justice.

It wasn't much to go on.

But it was something.

CHAPTER FORTY-FOUR

On a balmy evening at Fort Oglethorpe, after orchestra rehearsal had concluded, as the other musicians packed up their instruments and followed a guard back to the barracks, Reinhard cornered Henry.

"She's coming," he whispered, eyes bright and voice eager. "She's on her way."

"Who?" There was only one "she" Reinhard ever talked about. "You mean Miss Whitworth?"

Reinhard nodded. "She wrote to say she's coming to visit. Coming on the *train*," he added, as if the conveyance were something spectacular. Clearly the man was smitten.

Henry frowned. "That could be a problem. I don't think you're allowed any visitors."

"That's where you come in."

Henry pointed to his chest. "Me?"

"We're hoping you can help her find a place to stay. And a way for her and I to . . . to meet. To see each other."

Henry sighed. He was just a lowly guard. His power to work miracles was vastly limited.

But the hopeful, pleading look on Reinhard's face spoke volumes. Henry sighed again. "I'll see what I can do."

That night in his bunk, he prayed about the situation. *Lord, if it's Your will for this couple to be together—and I believe it is—then show me what I can do to help.*

Then, as usual, he added a prayer for Francie. She was no longer his girl, but she still held a piece of his heart.

A bigger piece than he cared to admit—even to himself.

Less than a week later, on his evening off from guard duty, Henry met Grace Whitworth's train, then took her to a Chattanooga restaurant.

After they'd exchanged some light small-talk and a waitress had served the soup, the conversation turned to Reinhard's case.

"Do you think they'll let me see him?" Grace asked.

"Probably not," Henry admitted. "But I have an idea."

He revealed to her his plan for getting her admitted to the fort grounds. She agreed it was a good plan, if risky.

Then, trying to sound casual, Henry worked up the courage to ask the question that had been smoldering in his heart all evening.

"What do you hear from Francie?"

"She's doing well, I think." Grace tasted the soup and reached for the salt shaker. "I've only received one or two letters from her this summer. I suppose Beatrice keeps her too busy to write."

"Who's Beatrice?"

Grace lifted an eyebrow. "Beatrice de Bonneville?"

"Oh." Caught by surprise, Henry scrambled to make sense of Grace's statement. "Has Francie been studying with her?"

Grace set down her spoon. "I assumed you knew. Francie went on tour with Beatrice this summer, all over the Western states. It's been in the papers."

"I don't have much time to read the headlines, much less the arts section." He took a moment to sort his jumbled thoughts, including a ridiculous image of Francie dressed in chaps and a ten-gallon hat. Had she met any good-looking cowboys on this tour? The thought made his chest burn. Finally he spoke.

"Sounds like she's getting her shot at the big time. Good for her."

"Well, she hasn't hit the big time yet." Grace's emphasis on *yet* implied stardom lay just over the horizon. "But surely it's an excellent boost for her career. Though I daresay a diva like Beatrice must be running her ragged."

"She's on her way." The words sounded hollow. Henry had done the right thing by setting Francie free to pursue her dream. So why did his heart feel like a lead weight in his chest?

His thoughts drifted back to Beatrice de Bonneville's recital at Piper Hall. Not so much the concert itself as the joy of going sledding with Francie afterward, on "their" hill. The way her cheeks reddened with the cold and the snowflakes sparkled on her eyelashes. It seemed a world apart, a lifetime ago.

He realized Grace was still talking and jerked his attention back to the present.

" . . . and she was able to see her family in California. She wrote me that her mother's marriage is a success and her younger brother is flourishing in his new school. So she no longer has to worry about them."

"That's nice." A happy memory resurged of the young boy with whom he'd made paper airplanes. What a good time he'd had, on that cold winter night.

"The truth is, winning that singing competition changed her whole life . . . more than any of us realized it would at the time."

Henry forced himself to smile. He was glad for Francie. Truly. But deeply sorry for himself, as though he had let something very precious and irreplaceable slip from his grasp.

After their meal, they left the restaurant, and he took Grace to the room he'd rented on her behalf in a slightly rundown section of Chattanooga.

"It's a little small," he said by way of apology, "but seems to be all that's available right now to rent by the week. And it's furnished, more or less." He looked askance at the shabby jumble of furniture.

Grace put a hand on his arm. "It's perfect."

"How long will you be staying?"

She shrugged. "I don't know. Until the fall term starts, I suppose. As long as Reinhard cares."

"Oh, he cares," Henry assured her. "He cares very much."

She seemed encouraged by that answer.

Henry had forfeited his chance at love. But Reinhard and Grace didn't have to. Thanks to Henry's behind-the-scenes machinations, soon a dark-haired "lady piano tuner" was brought onto the fort grounds to "fix a problem with the piano."

Of course, to do so properly, she needed to confer with the leader of the orchestra.

In private.

With Henry standing guard outside, to make sure no one disturbed them.

A few days after Francie's return, after posting an earnestly worded letter to the Department of Justice on Herr Schreiber's behalf, Francie went to the Auditorium to meet with Tony Leonardo. In spite of her trepidation of their meeting, after so many weeks on the road, entering the massive building felt like coming home. It made Francie smile to think how cowed she'd felt by its grandeur only a year earlier. So very much had happened in that year.

"Mr. Leonardo is in the office today. Perhaps he can see you now," the bespectacled assistant said in response to her inquiry. "Wait here."

Francie snorted in annoyance. *Perhaps?* He was the one who'd requested the meeting.

As she sat in the waiting room she picked up a newspaper lying on a table. Flipping to the arts section, a photograph on the society page caught her attention. It showed a smiling blond-haired woman holding an oversized check made out to some charitable organization. The woman looked vaguely familiar, but it wasn't until Francie read the caption that the true picture clicked into place.

Lila Jasper, nee Gladstone, accepting a generous donation on behalf of the Something-Or-Other Society . . .

The rest of the caption fell away.

Lila Jasper.

Lila *Jasper.*

A chill settled over Francie's heart. So he'd done it. He'd actually done it. He'd gone and married Lila, just as his father had indicated.

Oh, Henry. A quiet sob escaped her lips. Then she composed herself.

Well, what had she expected? He'd married the person his parents wanted him to marry, someone who suited his station in life. And that was that. The only thing left to do now was to wish them well. To pray for their happiness.

Which I'll do later, she told herself. *I can't quite bring myself to do it now.*

By the time the assistant returned, she'd swept together the bits of her broken heart and locked them deep inside, where no one would ever see them.

No one but her.

"Come with me, please."

She followed the young man into Tony Leonardo's office, which she still considered as Herr Schreiber's. Surely he'd be back at the helm of the opera someday, when this whole ridiculous mess was straightened out.

Tony stood when she entered. She extended her hand, and he grasped it in both of his and gave it a kiss. She fought the urge to wipe it on her skirt.

"Ah, Francie, thank you for meeting with me so promptly. I understand your tour went well?"

Still on her guard, she kept her answer short. "Yes, very well, thank you."

He motioned for her to take a seat, and he sat as well. To her relief, he got straight to the point.

"Francie, I've been following your tour with interest. Glowing newspaper reviews and a positive recommendation from Beatrice got back to Chicago faster than you did. It's my opinion that you're ready to take on some larger roles," he said.

"Thank you." Francie's face heated with gratitude, but that gratitude was measured. What would he expect in return? Not only did she not trust him, but a summer spent listening to Madame de Bonneville's tales of backstage life had cured her of any remaining idol worship of famous conductors, singers, and musicians. No matter how famous, they were just people like her, nothing more.

Well, except for Caruso, she thought at random. Francie would still give anything to sing with Enrico Caruso. But the world-famous tenor remained firmly ensconced in New York, and her pipe dream remained just that.

The assistant brought her a cup of tea. "Lemon?"

"No, thank you." She brought her mind back to what Tony was saying. Tony, who was perhaps as talented as Caruso, but not nearly as classy. "What sorts of roles do you have in mind?" Her imagination began to soar as she pictured herself being cast in leading roles. *Cio-Cio San. Carmen. Tosca.*

"An evil stepsister."

"I'm sorry. What?" Had she heard him correctly?

"I'm casting you in the children's opera," he said, bringing her expectations back to earth with a thud. The children's opera wasn't nearly as prestigious and impressive as grand opera. Francie chided herself for her outsized expectations. She was still a beginner, after all.

"This fall we're doing *La Cenerentola* by Rossini," Tony continued. "You're familiar with it, I assume?"

She was. Not only was she familiar with the Cinderella story from childhood, but she'd listened to the opera many times on the Victrola. She found the score both beautiful and challenging. And it was to be performed in Italian, the most comfortable of her foreign languages. Her mood brightened.

"I'm casting you as Tisbe," he continued, naming one of the step-sisters who make life miserable for Angelina, the name given to Cinderella in the opera. "It's a secondary role, to be sure, but an important one. I think you'll do well in it."

"Thank you," she said, genuinely grateful for his praise. Even a secondary role in a children's opera was a step up from the chorus. "I'll do my best."

"I'm sure you will."

She rose, thinking the meeting was over. But Tony motioned for her to sit, and she sat back down and reached for her still-full teacup.

He looked at her thoughtfully across the desk.

"It's time to start thinking about your career as a whole," he said. "Your reputation in the industry. Your branding, as it were."

"Oh?" Reputation was something Francie understood. Branding, on the other hand, she associated with cattle or washing powder. Where was he going with this discussion?

He minced no words. "I'd like you to consider changing your name."

"My name?" How dare he suggest such a thing? "What's wrong with my name?"

"It's very ordinary." He waved his hand dismissively. "So plain and Midwestern. Audiences are attracted to artists with sophisticated European names. I'm thinking you might take on a stage name. Something like . . ." He tapped his lips with a forefinger for a moment. "Francesca de la Firenza." He pronounced the name slowly with a great rolling of Rs, looking upward as if reading it on a theater marquee.

Francie nearly sputtered her tea. "With all due respect, Tony . . . you do realize how ridiculous that sounds, don't you?"

He looked wounded. "What? 'De la Firenza' means 'of the forest.' Like Forrester. Get it?"

She couldn't help but laugh. "Oh, I get it. I just don't like it."

He raised his eyebrows. "I think it quite suits you. You want to sound European. Sophisticated. Continental. Like how Beatrice Gumpenberger has become Beatrice de Bonneville."

She snorted at Tony's suggestion. "I want to sound like me. Francine Forrester will do quite nicely, thank you very much."

"Bah. Francine sounds so . . . common." He sniffed.

She didn't care for the way he said her name, drawing out the last syllable in an exaggerated, almost mocking way. She looked him square in the eye. "I *am* common," she reminded him. "Just a plain girl from the Midwest, as you said." *Same way you're just a boy from Brooklyn*, she added silently.

He threw back his head and laughed. "Yes, you are, but you needn't hit people over the head with it."

Indignation rose in her chest. "I'm not going to pretend to be something I'm not." She paused. "Besides, only one person has ever called me Francesca, and you're not him." Thoughts of Mr. Figaro brought a lump to her throat. What would her former employer think if he could eavesdrop on this conversation, see her arguing back to a distinguished opera tenor? And now conductor? He'd think she'd gone completely *pazza*. Crazy.

Tony didn't take offense. He merely shrugged. "Suit yourself. But I don't know how you expect to take the world by storm if you keep your head stuck back in Nowheresville."

"Scoville," she corrected testily.

He laughed. "Right. Scoville."

He stood, signaling the meeting was over. "See my assistant on the way out. He'll provide you a score you can study ahead of time. Rehearsals begin the fifteenth of September."

"I'll be ready." She stood and pulled on her gloves. "Thank you for this opportunity, Tony. You won't regret it."

He gave her a chilly smile. "I hope not, Franc*iiiiine*."

Francie decided then and there, he was one of the most unpleasant men she'd ever had the misfortune to meet.

She was proud of herself for not caving to his whims. There was nothing wrong with the name Forrester. Nothing to be ashamed of.

True, she would have loved to become Francine Jasper. But that dream was impossible now, something to pack away with other girl-hood memories in a box marked *Once Upon a Time*. She needed to look forward, not back.

Surely God had something else in mind for her. Something better.

But she'd have to trust Him on that. Because she could not for the life of her imagine what it could be.

CHAPTER
FORTY-FIVE

T he autumn passed in a blur of rehearsals, costume fittings, and grueling coaching sessions with Madame Clairvaux. In November, the production of *La Cerenentola* was a rollicking success, from Francie's point of view as well as the critics' responses. She adored singing the role of Tisbe, which called for a lot of exaggerated, comical gestures and facial expressions. She discovered a latent talent for comedy that she hadn't known she possessed, and she found great delight in playing the fool, especially before an audience filled with children. And the singer who played the other evil stepsister was equally high-spirited and mischievous, which made the experience extra fun. Yet it was the kind of opera she could perform and still maintain her dignity, which was important to her. She vowed to always be selective in the roles she accepted, even if it cost her something in career advancement.

She worked at an astonishing pace, singing eight times every two weeks, with rehearsals in between. Francie loved nearly every minute of it.

In addition, on the advice of a sympathetic clerk who'd finally replied to her inquiry at the Department of Justice, she rallied her fellow music students and faculty to sign a petition for Herr Schreiber's release. If she gained enough signatures, according to the clerk, the department might take another look at the case—although there were no guarantees, he added as a note of caution. So far most everyone had agreed to sign the petition. Herr Schreiber was a popular figure in the music community, and deservedly so.

The Christmas holidays brought another well-received performance of *The Messiah*, but this time, instead of being in the chorus, Francie was one of the soloists. Sitting on the stage of Orchestra Hall, she wondered if Abbott and Diana Jasper were in the audience as they'd been the previous year, but she didn't care to seek them out. She had Abbott to thank for giving her the tip about the Department of Justice. Still, his lack of interest in Herr Schreiber's legal case irked her, and other than satisfying her curiosity about Henry's well-being, she didn't see any reason to speak to them. And she certainly didn't want to risk running into his new wife.

God must have had other plans, because the elder Jaspers were the first people Francie spotted in the lobby after the performance, laughing and talking with another couple. She turned away, pretending she hadn't seen them, certain they were no more eager to converse with her than she with them.

She hadn't bargained on their friends.

"There she is," the man of the other couple exclaimed, and he and his companion hustled over to Francie.

"Oh, Miss Forrester," the woman effused, grasping Francie's hand in both of hers. "We were so delighted with your performance. Of all the soloists who sang this evening, I do believe you were my favorite."

"Th-thank you," Francie stammered, feeling the Jaspers' eyes on her. Out of politeness she lifted her head and returned Diana Jasper's gaze. "Mrs. Jasper. Mr. Jasper."

Their friend's eyes widened as she looked from Francie to Diana. "You are acquainted? Oh, how delightful."

Diana's response was cool. She introduced the couple as Mr. and Mrs. Diamond, then added, "Miss Forrester was an acquaintance of Henry's at Scoville College."

Francie didn't bother to correct her. "So nice to see you again, Mrs. Jasper. Have you heard any word from Henry?"

"He writes us that he's doing well."

Francie already knew this, thanks to Grace. She was grateful Mr. Jasper didn't mention Lila, even though she had questions. Had Henry come home on leave to be married? Had Lila traveled to Georgia? Was she living down there now? Or would she remain with her family until the war was over and she and Henry could live together as husband and wife—a thought that made Francie's stomach clench?

But she asked none of these things. The answers would make her too sad. Better to pretend she didn't care. Besides, Henry's marital status was none of her concern.

At least, that's what she told herself.

"When you write to him, tell him I said hello." She kept her voice light and airy.

Before either Jasper could make such a promise, Mrs. Diamond interrupted. "Oh, I do look forward to hearing more of your splendid voice, Miss Forrester. Tell us, when will you be performing next?"

Francie gave the woman a gracious smile. "I'll be appearing in *Lucia di Lammermoor* in March, and *Tosca* in May. Both minor roles, but I'm happy for the experience."

"Well, we are season ticket holders, and we will be watching for you," Mrs. Diamond said. "Based on what we heard here tonight, we predict you have a wonderful career ahead of you."

"Thank you." Francie's heart warmed at the encouragement.

As the foursome turned to walk away, she placed a light hand on Abbott's arm.

"Have you given any more thought to the Reinhard Schreiber case?" She spoke as quietly as she could given the noisy environment.

His demeanor was stern. "If I had, I would have contacted you."

She withdrew her hand. "Of course." After all, he'd made it clear he couldn't help her.

"Did you take my suggestion to contact the Department of Justice?" he gruffed.

"I did." She noted his look of surprise. What had he expected? That she'd sit on her hands when there was something to be done, no matter how small? "Someone there suggested I get up a petition. But it's taking forever to get the required number of signatures."

His expression softened slightly. "Patience, Miss Forrester. These things take time."

Mutely she nodded. She wanted to be patient, but it was hard.

He looked at her with curiosity. "I must say, I admire your commitment, Miss Forrester. Where is this petition of yours?"

She blinked. "You mean you'll sign it?"

He nodded. "And so will my wife. And so will the Diamonds."

"Wait here." While Abbott explained the purpose of the petition to his wife and friends, she retrieved the clipboard from the choir member who was circulating it among the crowd. When she returned with it, as promised, they all affixed their signatures to it.

Francie clutched the clipboard to her chest as she watched the foursome walk away, until another audience member drew her attention, wishing to compliment her performance. She gave the expected polite responses to the woman's effusive praise, but her mind was far, far away.

People were such a surprise sometimes. You just never knew.

After completing *The Messiah*, Francie left for the West Coast to spend a sunny, relaxing Christmas with her family. Upon her return, rehearsals began for *Lucia di Lammermoor* and *Tosca*, in which Francie had minor but challenging roles that stretched her abilities and her repertoire.

Eastertime brought the traditional *Saint Matthew Passion*—in English, of course—followed by *Aïda* and *Faust*. Letters flew between Illinois and Idaho as she and Molly kept up a brisk correspondence. And on a few occasions, much less often than she would have liked, she took the train to Scoville to visit Grace, or Grace came into the city to visit her. Grace also made good on her promise to travel to Georgia on her breaks from teaching, and rules had relaxed enough to permit her to visit Reinhard at the prison without the ruse of playing a "lady piano tuner."

"He seems to be holding his own, doing as well as could be expected," she told Francie in May, when she came to hear *Tosca*. "He says the detainees are being treated humanely. There are so many musicians in his barracks, their little orchestra has grown. They're even giving concerts to the townspeople. Of course, in spite of all that, he's eager to be released."

"I'm grateful he's not suffering too badly," Francie said, "but it doesn't change the fact that he doesn't deserve to be imprisoned at all. The whole situation is grossly unfair. I wish I had good news from the Department of Justice to share with you, but I sent the petition to them months ago and haven't heard a peep."

"These things take time," Grace assured her. Francie admired her former teacher's patience and fortitude.

When summer arrived, Francie was invited to appear as one of the starring attractions at Ravinia Park, which she was more than happy to do, especially since the offer was accompanied by a sizeable boost in pay. She loved Ravinia Park for the fond associations it held with Grace and Herr Schreiber.

One sultry August afternoon as Francie stood in a practice room at Ravinia Park, running through some warm-up vocalization exercises before a performance, an assistant came into the room and motioned to her.

"You have a visitor."

Francie emerged into the empty pavilion to find Grace waiting for her.

"Grace! How lovely to see you." Francie embraced her. "I thought you'd stay in Georgia until fall term. Have you come to hear the concert?"

"Yes, but primarily to see you." Eyes shining, Grace pulled her aside. "I have the most wonderful news. I received a telegram from Reinhard. He's being released from Fort Oglethorpe. Thanks in no small part to your petition, I'm sure."

Released! "It would have been nice if my contact at the Department of Justice had bothered to let me know," she muttered, but her resentment was swiftly swept away by a tidal wave of joy. Herr Schreiber was being released!

"There's a catch though," Grace said.

"What catch?"

"He's being released on the condition of being deported back to Germany."

"Deported!" A mix of despair and hope roiled through Francie's chest. "I'm thrilled he's finally being released but . . . deported!"

"Yes," Grace said. "It's horrible. But here's the exciting part. He's coming through Chicago on his way to New York. He wants to see us both while he's here."

"Of course."

Grace gave Francie the place and time to meet, naming a church in Chicago.

Francie frowned in confusion. "Why there?"

"Because it's near the train station," Grace explained.

Francie shook her head. "I still don't understand."

"For our wedding," Grace confided with a conspiratorial wink. "We're going to be married, and you're to be one of our witnesses."

After recovering from her initial elation over the news—followed by shock and dismay that Grace would be moving to Germany with her new husband—Francie got into the spirit of planning. On the appointed day, she and Grace met the minister at the church near Union Station, then Grace waited at the church while Francie went to meet Herr Schreiber's train.

The train chugged in right on schedule. Francie scanned the exiting passengers until Herr Schreiber emerged from a car, looking thinner and paler than she remembered, but smiling. She waved and ran toward him, and they embraced.

"Francie Forrester," he exclaimed. "Aren't you a sight for sore eyes."

"Welcome home," was all she could choke out through her tears of joy.

Herr Schreiber glanced around. "Where's Grace?"

"Waiting for you at the church. We'd better hurry. Have you any baggage?"

"Just this." He lifted a valise he'd been carrying. "Oh, and him."

Francie followed his pointed finger to a tall, well-built man with a serious expression on his rugged face.

"Daniel Gregson," the man said, still not smiling. "U. S. Marshal."

Herr Schreiber shrugged. "My constant companion from Fort Oglethorpe until I'm safely aboard the ship in New York Harbor."

Mr. Gregson consulted his pocket watch. "Don't have much time. Train leaves in an hour."

"We'd better get cracking then," Francie said. "Congratulations, Marshal Gregson. You'll be the sole wedding guest." She slipped her arm through Herr Schreiber's and led him out of the station, the marshal dogging their steps.

"How's everything with the opera company?" Herr Schreiber asked as they hurried along the street.

"Oh, the usual," Francie told him. "When I left, five sopranos were clashing over who will sing Violetta, and three were arguing about who would play Carmen."

She was exaggerating, of course, but not by much.

His laughter was a joyous sound to hear.

At the church, Grace and Reinhard clung tightly to one another while the minister waited. Marshal Gregson cleared his throat, and Francie sniffled. The marshal said, "Forty-five minutes," and everyone collected themselves.

They faced the minister, who began an abbreviated form of the wedding service at a breakneck pace. Vows were said, rings were exchanged, the marriage was pronounced, kisses and hugs and congratulations were shared in a great rush.

Reinhard said, "Thank you for supporting Grace and me through this whole ordeal. War and music never did mix, and never will. But love and music, now there's a combination." He smiled tenderly at Grace and squeezed her hand. "We owe both you and Henry so much," his voice caught with emotion. "How can we ever repay you?"

"By living happily ever after," she assured them both.

He turned back to Grace. "Ready?"

"Ready."

When Grace and Reinhard—followed by Marshal Gregson—started out the door, Francie's instinct was to follow, but the minister called her back.

"Just a moment, Miss Forrester. As a witness, you need to sign the wedding certificate. You too, Mr. Gregson." He called the marshal back.

Francie let Mr. Gregson sign first, so they could hurry on their way. Then, as she signed her own name to the certificate, the minister spoke.

"Well, that was one of the more unusual weddings I've ever had the pleasure of officiating."

"It's not over, you know," she said.

He looked at her with trepidation. "What's not over?"

"Situations like Herr Schreiber's. There are many more so-called aliens still incarcerated on what we've come to believe are false charges. And there's still a war on, with tensions running high and suspicions abounding. But we plan to keep fighting for justice." She looked at him. "It's like they say about the starfish."

A crease formed on his brow. "Starfish?"

"It's an old story a teacher once told me," she said. "A man and a boy were walking along a beach filled with stranded starfish. The boy picked one up and threw it back into the ocean. 'Why do you bother?' the man asked. 'You can't save them all.' 'No,' the boy replied, 'but I could save that one.'" She looked up at the minister. "We were able to help one man. A man very dear to me. That's better than none."

The minister rubbed his chin. "Thank you, Miss Forrester."

"For what?"

"For giving me an inspiration for next Sunday's sermon."

CHAPTER FORTY-SIX

As rehearsals got underway for the 1918-1919 season, Francie's heart was heavy over the permanent loss of Herr Schreiber as the company's director. She, along with most of the music world and the opera-loving public, thought his deportation was a tremendous loss to Chicago's status as a world-class music capital. But Grace's letters reassured her that she and Reinhard had found true love in each other at last, and they were starting a new life together in Munich. Francie was deeply happy for her friends.

Even so, her heart ached for herself. Two more people who were dear to her had gone away. Was she destined always to lose the people she loved most?

In the first opera production of the season, Bizet's *Carmen*, Francie was thrilled to be assigned the title role opposite Forrest Lamont's Don José.

In early September, a contract dispute between Tony Leonardo and the opera board took some time to be resolved, delaying the start of rehearsals by a few weeks. The situation was settled, and then rehearsals began with a vengeance to make up for getting a late start. Sometimes the company didn't stop rehearsing until one in the morning, and Francie didn't get to bed until a quarter to two.

Tony's style of conducting was very different from Herr Schreiber's, but Francie tried hard to not compare the two. Hardly anyone mentioned Herr Schreiber anymore, although patriotic American songs had become part of the company's regular repertoire as if to forestall any future visits from government agents.

On a typical day, Francie would get up in time for an interview with the press or an appointment with the wardrobe mistress at eleven o'clock, followed by a quick lunch. At two or two-thirty she might pose in costume for a photographer, or take her voice lesson with Madame Clairvaux. Rehearsal started at four o'clock, and the grueling routine would begin again.

She had very little time to read the newspaper, much less do anything else, but she made it a point to check the daily headlines for war news and never failed to pray for Henry's well being. Although she hadn't seen him in a year and a half, since she'd caught that last glimpse of him at the train station, he was never far from her thoughts and prayers.

On the morning of September twentieth, an item on page nine caught her attention.

Naval Camp Under Strict Orders to Stamp Out Spanish Influenza

The article reported on the strange, powerful new virus sweeping through Great Lakes Naval Training Camp.

"The chief danger is not from the influenza itself," an official was quoted as saying, "but from pneumonia, which is likely to follow."

So far, out of some sixty-six thousand sailors and personnel on the base, twenty-five people had died. All weekend liberty was revoked, and sailors were forbidden from leaving the base in an effort to contain the disease.

Thoughts of Henry prompted a quick prayer of gratitude that he was not stationed at Great Lakes. But who knew how many more military bases were infected? She prayed that he would be spared from this deadly virus.

A few days later, more cases of influenza were reported at Northwestern University in suburban Evanston, and then in the public at large. Each day's tally of cases and deaths was worse than the last.

Rehearsals for *Carmen* continued at a frantic pace, but they needn't have tried so hard, because before long, all opera houses, along with theaters and other public venues, closed throughout the state of Illinois, delaying the opening of the season for an indefinite period. Francie found herself with unexpected time on her hands, time to walk about the city in the cool October sunshine and worry about her family and Henry. Would they all survive the pandemic unscathed? The temptation to travel to California was strong, but the ban on unnecessary travel was stronger. Besides, she couldn't abandon the company mid-season.

The ban was lifted in early November, and *Carmen* opened to crowds that were just as robust as before the pandemic. The first performance got off to a good start. Francie enjoyed playing the flamboyant character, loved Bizet's musical score, and felt confident in her role.

After intermission, though, she came off the stage feeling sick. A burning sensation torched her throat, and her head ached. She drank a glass of water in her dressing room, then popped a horehound lozenge into her mouth and let it dissolve down her fiery throat.

When it was all over, Tony Leonardo was not pleased with her performance, and let her know it.

"What was the matter with you tonight?" he barked in her dressing room after a lackluster curtain call. Francie had no excuse to offer him. She continued wiping her makeup off with slow, methodical strokes of cold cream, which felt cool and soothing against her flushed skin.

"I don't know," she said with clear honesty. "I've been feeling rotten all evening." Her voice sounded reedy and thin.

"Well, whatever it is, don't let it affect your work. We need you to be at your best," the conductor said without sympathy. He turned on his polished heel and left the room.

That night she slept poorly, drifting in and out of strange, disturbing dreams.

She dragged herself to the kitchen the next morning with the intention of making coffee, but every step involved in that process—the grinding of beans, the measuring of water—seemed like an insurmountable obstacle. She settled for a glass of water while she glanced at the newspaper.

The reviews of *Carmen* were not kind.

"Francine Forrester was expected to make a shimmering debut as Carmen, but was not well received," the *Tribune* critic commented acidly. "She was not in good voice and seemed to lack vocal control, and there was a harsh character to her higher notes."

Under normal circumstances, Francie would have been devastated by the criticism. But these were not normal circumstances. She actually didn't feel much of anything at all, except exhausted. Too listless to react with any kind of emotion, she felt weak, shaky, and hot. She set the newspaper and her water glass aside and went back to bed.

Shivering under the covers, she squinted at the alarm clock on her bedside table. *Today is a workday. I must get up in time for my lesson.* She reached for the clock to make sure the alarm was set, but it eluded her grasp in the most maddening way, like trying to capture a slippery bar of soap underwater. She gave up. Why was she so tired? She must get up.

Must get up. Must get up.

And that was her last coherent thought.

CHAPTER
FORTY-SEVEN

E ven before she cracked open her eyelids, she knew she'd been asleep for a long time. Inch by inch she crawled out of the dark cavern of sleep. Someone was calling her name.

"Francine? Francine? Are you awake? Can you hear me?"

Beatrice de Bonneville. What was Beatrice doing in Francie's bedroom?

Wait a minute. This wasn't her bedroom. Whose bedroom was it? She ran the fingers of one hand over the soft, downy covers, touched the unfamiliar lace-trimmed collar of the silk nightgown covering her body. The other hand was—where was her other hand?

She opened her eyes. A narrow streak of sunshine poured through a crack where the heavy drapes met in the middle. Beatrice was sitting next to the bed in a circle of lamplight, holding Francie's hand, while a man in a white coat hovered over her, peering at her through thick eyeglasses.

"She's over the worst of it," the man pronounced. "Now we'll just wait and see."

Francie blinked heavily. Wait and see what?

"Thank you, doctor," Beatrice said.

What was a doctor doing here?

Francie's throat burned. "Thirsty," she croaked.

Beatrice reached for a glass on the bedside table. She helped Francie sit up, then pressed the glass to Francie's lips. "Good girl. Drink up."

After several sips, Francie lay back against the pillows.

"Where am I?" she managed to ask.

"You're at my home, dear." Beatrice smoothed Francie's forehead with a cool hand. "You're in my guest bedroom. And now you must lie still and not talk and try to sleep."

Francie was happy to comply. Just before she closed her eyes, she looked at the doctor, desperate to find some spark of reassurance in his eyes.

"It's a good sign that she wants water," he said. "She may make a full recovery yet."

Beatrice looked up to him. "And her voice?"

"I don't know that she'll ever sing again," he said sadly. "We'll just have to wait and see."

In November 1918, Henry found himself stationed temporarily in Washington, D. C. Two days after the armistice was signed, joyful crowds still milled around on the streets. Henry elbowed his way through the crowd, intent on completing an errand for his commanding officer.

While waiting for the prescription to be filled, he picked up a newspaper and, as was his habit, flipped to the arts section in case there was any news of Francie. Ever since the success of her summer tour, he'd made a point following her career from a distance. It warmed his heart to watch her dreams coming true.

But this time, a headline gripped his attention. A notice said that the soprano Francine Forrester, rising star at Chicago's Windy City Opera, had been taken ill and was recovering at the home of diva Beatrice de Bonneville.

Concern for her creased his brow. Leaving the pharmacy, Henry hustled into the nearest florist shop and ordered flowers to be sent to Beatrice de Bonneville's home. He signed the card simply, "Yours forever, Henry."

Either she'd remember him, or she wouldn't.

Either way, she'd always have a place in his heart.

As Francie began her slow recovery from influenza, she spent hours resting and reading in Beatrice's sunny guest room, which was fragrant with floral arrangements sent by friends at the conservatory and members of the company. A gentle knock sounded at the door and she set down her book.

"Come in."

"Here's another one. Just arrived." Her hostess carried in a sweet arrangement of roses and lilies in a glass vase and nestled it among the others on the dressertop. "Gracious, what a popular girl you are!" she remarked with a smile. "We're beginning to look like a florist shop."

Francie sat forward. "Oh, how lovely. Who sent it?"

Beatrice brought her the small white card. Francie read the name and her heart flipped over. "Oh!"

Beatrice perched on a nearby armchair. "You sound surprised. Do tell!"

"It's—it's from an old friend." She ran her thumb over his signature.

"A special friend, it sounds like."

"Yes." Francie found it hard to speak, filled with nostalgia for their lost romance. "But—"

"But what?"

"Oh, it's nothing. I'm just surprised, I guess. Surprised and pleased."

Charmed by the gesture, she was nonetheless troubled by the card he'd enclosed. *Yours forever*, he'd written, along with his name alone instead of *Mr. and Mrs. Henry Jasper*, or even the more intimate *Henry and Lila*, either of which would have been more appropriate. Not that Francie was a stickler for etiquette, but what would Lila think of his sending flowers to an old flame? Perhaps it would be better to have an opera company secretary acknowledge the flowers on her behalf, instead of writing to him herself, lest she risk opening something that God intended to remain closed.

But these were not things she cared to discuss with Beatrice. She set the card aside to think about later.

"By the way," Beatrice said. "Marie-Louise Clairvaux telephoned earlier, asking how you're feeling."

"She did?" It hardly seemed characteristic of Madame Clairvaux to care about other people's well-being, least of all Francie's.

"Why do you sound surprised? After all, she rescued you, in a way."

"What do you mean? My memories of that day are pretty hazy."

"Well, as I understand it," Beatrice said, "she had a hunch something was amiss when you didn't show up for your lesson. She said you're as regular as clockwork and have never missed a session. Which is quite impressive, I must say."

Best to let Beatrice think she was simply a dedicated student and not admit to being scared half to death of Madame Clairvaux.

"So she sent another student to your rooming house to check up on you," Beatrice continued.

"I think I remember that," Francie said. "Someone knocked on the door, and I said for them to come in because it wasn't locked. Molly would have wrung my neck for that if she'd known. I didn't know the person who came in, but she looked harmless, not like a criminal or a madwoman. She must have introduced herself, but I don't remember much after that."

"Well, the student told the landlady what was going on. The landlady panicked at the thought of germs living under her roof and wanted you taken to the hospital straightaway, but the nearest hospitals were overcrowded and couldn't take you. Then Tony got word to me and I insisted you come here and be treated under the care of my own physician."

"That was very kind of you." Francie said, humbled by the enormous amount of trouble had been taken on her behalf.

"It's for the good of the company," Beatrice said. "We can't have our rising-star soprano lying in a hospital bed with all those other sick people around, can we? Tony wouldn't have stood for it. The singer who covered you as Carmen didn't do nearly as well as you would have, and we're all dying for you to return. Anyway, here you are. And here you shall stay, until you are completely recovered."

Francie thanked her again, then picked at a piece of lint on the bedcovers. "Do you think the doctor was serious when he said I might never sing again?"

"Never mind about that," Beatrice said briskly. "Doctors don't know everything." She rose. "Now get some rest. I'll have Bridget bring your lunch at one o'clock."

Francie slipped back under the covers. Beatrice was dodging the question, but Francie chose not to pursue it. She didn't bring it up again, but rolled it over and over again in her mind and laid the matter before the Lord in prayer.

What on earth would she do with her life if she could no longer sing?

Francie remained at Beatrice's apartment through the holiday season, then ventured back to her own place in January after ringing in 1919. The doctor declared her healthy, and she felt well, if weaker than normal. She began taking daily walks when the weather was clear, to build up her strength.

She had not yet dared to try to sing. She was petrified of what would happen if she opened her mouth and no sound, or some terrible honk, came out.

She screwed up her courage to meet with Madame Clairvaux again.

"We will start small," the teacher advised, displaying a sympathy Francie had not known her capable of. "No big voice. Not yet. We'll work our way up and see what happens." They returned to basic vocalization exercises and breathing techniques. The breathing was the worst. Francie's lungs had taken a beating. Walking helped, and so did the breathing exercises.

By March, Tony Leonardo was starting to apply pressure, lightly at first, then more strongly. He didn't want to push her, he said, but would Francie be ready to sing in *Samson and Delilah* in the spring?

She wanted to be ready. She missed her music. She convinced Madame Clairvaux to let her try an aria.

"If you think you're ready." The teacher sounded doubtful.

Francie's hands trembled as she pulled the score to "Song to the Moon" from her music bag. Madame played the first few gentle chords, then Francie began to sing, her voice low and quiet. So far, so good.

The second stanza caused a hitch in her voice. Madame Clairvaux looked up in alarm, but Francie cleared her throat and made a circular motion with her hand. *Keep going, keep going!* Gradually she built her volume, then built it some more.

Finally, on the peak passage, she gave it all she had. Her voice rang out through the studio.

"There it is!" Madame Clairvaux clapped her hands. "There it is. It is back."

Francie collapsed on the sofa, triumph wringing in her ears.

God hadn't let her down. Her voice was back.

She was back.

After a lot of hard work and prayer, Francie was strong enough to take on the role of Delilah in May. The music-industry press was abuzz with the news of her return to the opera stage.

The propriety of playing the renowned villainess made Francie nervous. She reminded herself of what Grace Whitworth had advised her—to play the villain to the hilt, so the audience would see and feel her deep betrayal for what it was. That was the way to stay true to the story.

On opening night, she held the crowd spellbound. She was at the height of her dramatic performance when a disturbance occurred somewhere out in the audience. She did her best to ignore the come-uppance, certain that opera security would take care of the matter.

But as the people muttered and pointed, the orchestra faltered and sputtered into silence.

So did Francie.

Through the darkness came a voice she knew, "Lemme go. Lemme go! That's my daughter up there, I tell ya."

A woman stood in the middle of the aisle, surrounded by security guards, one shaking finger pointing at Francie.

Ramona.

A very disheveled, and very drunken, Ramona.

CHAPTER
FORTY-EIGHT

W ith the rest of the well-trained cast, Francie froze in place on stage, though it took all her strength not to run to Ramona. In a blur of activity, the security guards subdued the distraught woman and hustled her out of the auditorium.

"She's speaking the truth!" she stage-whispered to the baritone playing Samson. "She really is my mother. Where are they taking her?"

His expression of disdain turned to sympathy. "They'll probably take her to your dressing room and hold her there until we're done."

The production resumed, but Francie's mind was only half on her performance, vaguely aware that the next morning's reviews would likely skewer it, but more worried about Ramona. The second her curtain calls were completed, she hastened to her dressing room, where her mother was indeed being held. Through Ramona's sobbing, the truth poured out.

Clarence had died of influenza.

By midnight, Francie had gotten the full story out of the distraught Ramona. "And the creditors keep coming around, and I didn't know who else to turn to," she wailed. She stank of sweat and gin. Good grief. Where had she gotten liquor, now that all the bars had been shut down by Prohibition? When had she last bathed?

"You did the right thing in coming to me," Francie said firmly, even though her voice shook with a roiling mix of shock, anger, and concern.

Assured that Will was still safely ensconced at boarding school, she continued to soothe Ramona.

"You can live with me, of course," Francie said. "Will can join us on school breaks."

"I'll have to pull him out of school." Ramona sniffled and dabbed a soaked hanky to her eyes. "I can't afford it."

"I can," Francie insisted, although at the moment she wasn't at all sure she could. She'd figure something out. "And maybe he can apply for some scholarships." She took her mom's hand and squeezed. "There's just one condition."

Ramona's eyes widened. "What's that?"

"That you stop drinking. Immediately. I mean it. Not one drop."

And please, God, give her the will and the power to do it.

Upon his honorable discharge from the Army, Henry returned to law school in New York, where he continued to keep track of Francie's career from afar. He saw the news about her triumphant return to the stage after her illness and was tempted to write to her. But he felt he had little to offer her at this point, with her star on the rise. After all, the only acknowledgement of the flowers he'd sent to her had been a impersonal, formally worded note on stiff stationery, signed by some functionary at the opera company. *Miss Forrester wishes to extend her gratitude*, etc., etc. Likely just one of dozens of thank-you notes she'd written for flowers and gifts sent from adoring fans. Poor thing probably had writer's cramp. After all, Francie Forrester was a big star now.

He got the message. Loud and clear. He was no different from any other fan who read about her in the newspaper. She had no interest in maintaining their friendship. At best, she considered him an old flame, a fleeting memory from her youth.

Clearly, she didn't want him in her life. And if she didn't want him, well, he didn't want her. She was probably acting like a diva by now, swanning around, ordering underlings to do her bidding. On the basis of a single impersonal thank-you card, his wounded pride conjured a picture of Francie that was far from the sweet girl he'd known in Scoville.

But, deep down, his aching heart didn't believe it for a second.

CHAPTER
FORTY-NINE

As the 1920s began to roar, so did Francie's career. Following her triumphant return to the opera stage after recovering from the Spanish flu, she won the hearts first of Chicago's music lovers, then San Francisco's, then New York's. In 1923 she made her debut at LaScala in *Lucia di Lammermoor*. In 1925 she conquered the Opera-Comique in Paris as Violetta in *La Traviata*.

Ramona traveled with her, gradually carving out a role for herself as a combination personal assistant/wardrobe mistress/company court-jester, an arrangement that worked out surprisingly well. Ramona turned out to have a good head for organization, once she'd sobered up and set her mind on more serious matters. She even participated in the occasional production as a supernumerary, which she loved.

In return, Francie supported both her and Will. She provided for Will's private school tuition through twelfth grade, and as he prepared to graduate, she helped him apply to a number of good aviation schools.

In the spring of 1927, Francie and several other members of the company traveled by train to New York to participate in *Madama*

Butterfly at the Metropolitan Opera. Francie had the starring role, and was thrilled to be back on the Met stage, where so many great singers had stood before her. Her biggest thrill—the thrill of a lifetime for a girl from Scoville, Illinois—was playing Cio-Cio San opposite the great Enrico Caruso as Lieutenant Pinkerton.

During the final rehearsal, she'd felt the stirrings of a case of stage fright—her first in years—but reminded herself of Beatrice de Bonneville's wise counsel. "No need to be nervous when you're sure of what you're doing." Francie was very sure of herself in *Madama Butterfly*, having played one or another role in the perennially popular opera over the years since her student days at the conservatory.

On the morning of the opening performance, in her suite at the Waldorf-Astoria, Francie was signing checks presented to her by Ramona. A maid padded around them, dusting furniture and plumping sofa pillows.

Francie pointed to the top check on the pile.

"What's this one for again?"

"The war widows' home. And try to quit talkin'," Ramona said briskly. "Ya need to guard your voice for tonight's performance. Ya still got that tickle in your throat? It's got me worried."

Francie shook her head, but pantomimed buttoning her lips. She signed the check, set it aside, and looked at the next one in the pile.

"That one's for Will's tuition."

Francie nodded and signed.

A knock sounded at the door and the maid answered it. She returned carrying a large basket laden with gifts, which she set on the coffee table.

"From the Van Hoppers," she read from the attached card, "to welcome you to New York."

"That was kind of them," Francie said. She couldn't picture the Van Hoppers in her mind, but knew from financial records that they were major patrons of opera.

"Francie, quit talkin'," Ramona ordered. She walked to the basket, surveyed the contents, removed a bottle of bootleg champagne, and handed it to the maid. "Please get this outta here. Thanks."

Francie's heart warmed. Ramona had agreed to stop drinking as a condition of living with her, and both of them made every effort to keep alcoholic beverages far away. No sense in risking temptation.

"Please send a thank-you note to the Van Hoppers," she whispered to Ramona, who jotted it on her pad. They returned to the checks.

"This next one is—"

The telephone jangled on the desk. Ramona picked it up. "Miss Forrester's suite. Yes. Yes. One moment." She put her hand over the mouthpiece. "Someone from Scoville College wants to speak to ya."

"If it's about a donation," Francie murmured, "tell them to send their request in writing."

"He's insistin' on talkin' to ya."

Francie sighed and accepted the phone. "This is Francine Forrester."

"Miss Forrester, this is Dean Carlisle at Scoville College. Thank you for taking my call."

"Yes, Dean. What can I do for you?"

The dean cleared his throat. "First of all, please accept our condolences. All of us here at Scoville College were deeply saddened by the news."

A cold stone dropped in Francie's stomach. "What news?"

"Of Grace Whitworth's death."

The floor slid out from beneath her feet. Grace, dead? It couldn't be.

"Oh," she managed to whisper.

"What is it? What's wrong?" Ramona began fluttering around Francie's chair. Francie put a finger to her lips.

"I-I'm sorry to be the bearer of such bad news," said the dean, sounding apologetic. "I assumed you knew."

Francie fought to pull herself together. "That's all right," she said. It *wasn't* all right, not at all, but that was hardly the poor dean's fault. "How did it happen?"

"She was killed in an automobile accident in Germany. Her husband was driving. He survived, but Grace succumbed to her injuries."

Francie's insides turned to mush. Poor Reinhard! Tears pooling in her throat, she moved to get off the phone quickly.

"Thank you for telling me, Dean Carlisle. Truly. I appreciate being told in person, rather than reading about it somewhere. Now I'm afraid I must be going. Good-bye."

"But that's not the reason I'm calling," the dean broke in.

Francie brought the receiver back to her ear. What else could the man possibly have to say?

"Yes?"

"Miss Whitworth's—I mean, Mrs. Schreiber's lawyer contacted us. As part of her will, she'd left the bulk of her estate to set up a music scholarship for needy students at Scoville."

Francie's heart squeezed. How like Grace to be so generous.

"That's marvelous. I'll mail a donation immediately," she promised. "Should I address it to your attention?"

"There's more," he said. "In her bequest letter, Grace specifically asked that you be contacted about performing a benefit concert here at the college, to let people know about the scholarship and to raise additional funds."

"A benefit concert?" Francie's mind floated back to that first, magical time she'd heard Beatrice de Bonneville sing in person, at a benefit concert at Scoville College. She couldn't think of a more fitting way to honor Grace's memory than to provide such a concert herself.

"Of course. I'd be happy to do it." She shifted the receiver to her other ear.

"Oh, splendid." The dean sounded relieved.

From her perch on the nearby sofa, Ramona's eyes grew wide with concern. She hated when Francie made commitments without checking with her first to make sure the calendar was clear. Francie shrugged in apology and turned back to the phone.

"I have three conditions, though."

"Oh?" Apprehension crept into the dean's voice. "What are they?"

"First, I'd like to present the concert twice—once on Saturday and once on Sunday. That will give busy working people more opportunities to attend." She specifically had Mr. Figaro in mind. If Café Figaro hadn't been closed on that long-ago Sunday, she might have had to work and never seen Beatrice de Bonneville.

"That's certainly possible," the dean said agreeably. "And the second condition?"

"Instead of a firm ticket price, I'd like people to pay whatever they wish to, at their discretion."

"But—but it's meant to be a fund-raiser," the dean sputtered.

"I understand," Francie replied calmly. "But I don't want anyone to be left out because they can't afford a ticket."

"Well, really, I don't see how that will work."

"In my experience, when you explain the purpose of the funds and leave the ticket price open, those concertgoers who can afford to will give generously, far above a stated ticket price," she explained. "The college will likely end up with more donations than they would have

had a ticket price been stated. Meanwhile, those who can't afford it
will give whatever they can, and still get to enjoy the concert."

"I see. Well, I'll take it to the committee and see what they say."

"That's fine," Francie said. "Be sure to tell them it's a firm condition."

The dean sighed. "All right then, agreed. What's the third condition?"

"I must be allowed to sing at least a portion of the program in
German."

A long moment of silence hung in the air. Francie waited until the
dean spoke.

"Some of our patrons won't like it."

"Some of your patrons needn't come then."

More silence. "All right. You may perform up to three songs by
German composers."

"In German."

He sighed again. "In German."

Francie smiled and winked at Ramona, who looked incredulous at
all the wheeling and dealing taking place.

"The thing is," the dean continued, "we need to hold the concert
quite soon if we want it to take place before the term ends. I think
that's necessary to get the word out, so the first scholarship students
can start in the fall."

"I understand. What dates do you propose?"

The dean named a few possible dates, and Francie jotted them
down on a scrap of paper. By now Ramona was gesticulating wildly.

"I'll review my schedule and check back with you in a few days,
Dean. Will that be all right?"

The dean agreed, and thanked her again.

She replaced the receiver and looked at Ramona.

"Grace Whitworth died."

Ramona's face registered surprise. "Oh, dear. Your old music teacher? How sad. I remember ya liked her a lot. It's a shame I never got to meet her."

You could have met her if you'd bothered to come to my recital. Francie bit back the sharp retort, but she felt a fresh sting of disappointment at not seeing her mother in the audience that long-ago day. Then she let it go. She'd long since forgiven her mother for her lapses in parenting, the way God had forgiven her, and forgiveness meant forgiveness, not dredging up old hurts and resentments from the dark recesses of the human heart. She loved Ramona, faults and all, and knew that Ramona loved her—faults and all.

She filled her mother in on the dean's request and handed her the list of possible dates. "Let's look at the calendar and see where we can fit it in."

"I don't see how." Ramona scanned the list. She reached for a leather-bound notebook on the desk and flipped through its pages. "After New York, you're totally booked back in Chicago for the next several weeks, and then there's the Bayreuth Festival in Germany this summer. You're scheduled to sail on the *Savoie* in June."

Francie placed a hand on Ramona's arm and gave her a pleading look. "Please. I really want to do this."

Ramona's expression softened. "Of course, doll. If ya really want to do it, we'll make it work. Now stop usin' your voice."

Francie shot her a look of gratitude.

Ramona made a notation, then set the notebook aside. "Now, let's get back to the checks."

"Can we do this later?" Francie whispered. "I'm suddenly very tired."

"Of course, doll." Ramona stood. "Get some shut-eye. I'll wake ya in time to get to the opera house." She headed off to her own room, taking the financial records with her.

Francie lay on the bed and stared at the ceiling. She thought about Grace, about the many kindnesses she'd shown her, how she'd invested herself in Francie's career and even stepped in as a mother figure when Ramona hadn't been up to the task.

Although Francie hadn't seen Grace since she and Reinhard had left the country, letters flew back and forth between them at frequent intervals. Grace had sounded so happy with Reinhard, so delighted with their home in Bavaria. Francie pictured a cheerful half-timbered house like something from a fairy tale, bright red geraniums spilling from every window box.

Grace and Reinhard shared everything, including their music. Reinhard had taken up a position as a conductor for a regional opera company, and Grace sang in the chorus of some of his productions. They sounded deliriously happy. And Francie had been eagerly looking forward to a glorious reunion with both of them at the Bayreuth Festival.

Now no such reunion would take place.

She'd never see Grace again.

She turned on her side, punched the pillow, and let the tears flow at last.

CHAPTER FIFTY

I n a skyscraper high above LaSalle Street, in the well-appointed offices of Jasper and Jasper, Henry sifted through the morning mail brought to him by his efficient secretary.

"Coffee?" she chirped.

"Yes, please, Miss Anthony."

"Be right back." Turning to leave, she nearly bumped into Oliver, who hovered in the doorway. "Oops, sorry, sir."

"My fault entirely." Oliver stepped aside so she could pass. "'Morning, cousin. Just wanted to remind you of that charity golf tournament out in Hinsdale this Saturday."

Henry winced.

"I know you hate golf, but clients come first. Gotta keep 'em happy."

"I know. I'll be there."

Oliver vanished. Wielding a silver letter opener like a weapon, Henry sliced open each envelope, skimmed the papers within, scribbled a brief instruction for Miss Anthony, and put most of the correspondence in his outbox for her to take care of. A couple he kept for himself, those that referenced more complicated matters needing his personal attention.

When the secretary returned with coffee, he set the letters aside and reached for the daily newspaper. As he sipped his coffee, a huge headline captured his eye.

LINDBERGH LANDS IN PARIS

Gazing up at him was the photograph of the famous aviator and his plane, the *Spirit of St. Louis*. The photograph unexpectedly jarred his mind to a brief memory of making paper airplanes with young Will Forrester who had been fascinated by aviation. *What's he doing now?* The boy would be around twenty years old, if Henry's calculations were correct. Hardly a boy anymore.

As for Will's sister, Henry didn't need to wonder what Francie was doing. The newspapers were full of glowing reviews of her triumphal performances in New York, Rome, and Paris. Henry occasionally caught her performances when she was in Chicago, where she still made her home base with the Windy City Opera Company. But since she'd rebuffed his flowery attempt to reignite their friendship, he was careful not to make his presence known to her, and simply enjoyed hearing her sing from an anonymous spot in the balcony.

Caught up in the coverage of Lindbergh's historic flight over the Atlantic, Henry didn't hear his father enter his office until the door shut behind him.

"Pretty exciting day, isn't it?" Abbott gestured toward the newspaper. "It wouldn't surprise me if soon crossing the ocean will be as easy and commonplace as boarding a bus."

"That's for sure." Henry folded the paper and set it aside. "What can I do for you, Father?"

"I just wanted to make sure you were on top of the Ryerson case," his father said. "There has been a new development, as the lead prosecutor on the case died suddenly of an apparent heart attack."

"I received the news this morning." Henry pointed to one of the letters on his desk.

"Very good. Let's meet over lunch and discuss our strategy." His father shook his silver head. "I was just reading the poor fellow's obituary. Left behind a wife and two kids."

"I'll have Miss Anthony send a floral arrangement on behalf of the firm."

"Very good." Abbott stood. "Oh, and Henry . . .," he added.

"Yes?"

"You might want to take a look at the obituary section. There's a mention of your college. One of the professors passed away. Forgot the name, but perhaps you'd have known her while you were there. See you at lunchtime."

Henry flipped through the paper. There it was. Grace Whitworth's obituary.

Miss Whitworth. The print blurred as unexpected moisture sprang to his eyes. He hadn't thought of her in years, apart from the occasional Christmas card. Now it seemed like yesterday that he'd helped facilitate the romance between her and Reinhard at Fort Oglethorpe. And even before that, when he'd played the piano for her students.

For one student in particular.

He took a sip of coffee to settle his emotions. The article mentioned that funeral arrangements were private, but that two benefit concerts would be held at Scoville College. The purpose of the concerts—one on Saturday, one on Sunday—was to raise money for a scholarship for music students in Miss Whitworth's name.

And the featured performer? A world-renowned opera singer named Francine Forrester.

His blood pulsed hot in his temples. He'd told himself he was through with Francie. But Miss Whitworth's death changed everything. Now he had to see her, if only to put the past to rest.

He pressed the button on his desktop intercom.

"Miss Anthony," he said when the secretary answered. "Please send my regrets for the golf tournament on Saturday. Something's just come up."

CHAPTER FIFTY-ONE

F rancie peered out the spotless window of the sleek black limousine as it purred through downtown Scoville.

"There it is, on the right," she told the uniformed driver. He pulled to the curb in front of Café Figaro and cut the engine. Then he circled the vehicle and opened Francie's door. She stepped out onto the sidewalk. A gentle, early evening breeze ruffled her hair, and she pulled her watered-silk wrap more tightly around her shoulders.

"They're waiting for you at the college, Miss Forrester," the driver reminded her as he pulled open the door of the restaurant.

"I'll just be a few minutes," she promised, and entered the building.

This being a Saturday night, nearly all the tables were occupied. She felt many eyes on her as she stood in the doorway, and heard murmuring over the muted clatter of china and silver. Starched white tablecloths had replaced the blue gingham oilcloth of her day, and a flickering candle now graced each table. Gone were the linoleum floor and the bright overhead lights. The wait staff was dressed in head-to-toe black. *At least the uniforms have improved*, Francie thought, *along with everything else*. She was glad to see Café Figaro was prospering, for Mr. Figaro's sake.

A hostess approached her. "Welcome to Café Figaro. How many in your party?"

"I've come to see Mr. Figaro," she replied. "Is he available?"

"He's in the kitchen." Curiosity filled the hostess's glance. "May I tell him who's asking?"

"Francie Forrester."

If the name meant anything to the hostess, she didn't let on. "Wait here a moment, please." She disappeared into the kitchen. A few moments later, she returned.

"Mr. Figaro asked if you'd come to the kitchen."

Francie smiled. "I most certainly would." She walked through the restaurant, past the curious onlookers, and pushed open the kitchen door.

There stood Mr. Figaro in his white apron, a look of incredulity on his face.

"Francesca," he breathed, his eyes glistening. "I can't believe it. Is it really you?"

"It's really me." She held out her arms. They embraced warmly, then Mr. Figaro held her at arm's length.

"Let me look at you. *La mia bella* Francesca. I knew you were coming to Scoville—" he pointed to a flyer tacked to the wall above the sink—"but I never dreamed you'd find time to drop in on your old boss."

Her heart melted at the memory of the flyer he'd shared with her so long ago, advertising Beatrice de Bonneville's recital. The flyer that had opened up a whole new world, a whole new life, for Francie.

"And dressed so fine . . ." Mr. Figaro continued, shaking his head. "Make sure you no splatter marinara sauce on that beautiful gown."

She laughed. "If I did, I would wear it with pride. It's good to see you, Mr. Figaro."

He pouted. "Still you no call me Guiseppe."

She smiled. "Guiseppe."

"You've come for a good dinner? I fix you anything you like."

"No. I've come to give you these." She pulled several tickets out of her evening bag. "These are for tomorrow's matinee performance at the college, for you and your family. You still close the restaurant on Sundays, don't you?"

"*Si, si.*" He took the tickets and gazed at them. "We would not miss it." He grinned. "My granddaughter, she buys all your records. All day long, *Madama Butterfly, Madama Butterfly.*" He rolled his eyes in mock annoyance.

"That's wonderful to hear." Francie's eyes misted. "I can't thank you enough for everything you did for me. I don't think I'd be where I am today if it weren't for you."

He waved his hands. "You would have found a way. What did I always tell you? When God has a plan, He makes a way."

A young waitress whom Francie didn't recognize burst through the door and, seeing her employer had a visitor, stopped short and stepped back uncertainly. "Um, Mr. Figaro . . . table nine is asking..." She shifted her weight and stared awestruck at Francie.

"Is okay, Susan," Mr. Figaro reassured her. "Their order, it is almost ready."

"I'm taking up your time," Francie said. "I'll see you at the matinee tomorrow. And I'd be honored if you'd allow me to take you and your family to dinner afterward. Somewhere where you don't have to cook."

He laughed. "Is a deal. *Grazie*, Francesca. I am so very proud of you."

Francie returned to the limousine and slid into the back seat. As they drove the few blocks to the college, she gazed out the window and thought wistfully about Mr. Figaro and the family he loved so much, about the blessings of a kind of life she had missed out on. But she made her choice—and she'd chosen music.

The driver left her at the entrance to Piper Hall. She entered the familiar building, which still smelled of varnish as it had so many years ago. A member of the concert committee met her at the door and ushered her to the performers' lounge.

With time to spare before the performance, she took a few moments to walk upstairs and find Grace's old studio. It was unlocked and empty, so she went inside and flicked on the light. Long gone were the piles of paper and stacks of scores. The room looked as if it were no longer used, but the upright piano remained. Francie pressed a few keys and performed her warm-up vocal exercises, all the while thinking of her beloved teacher. Then she turned off the light, closed the door, and returned to the lounge to wait.

At last it was concert time. As she had at her very first recital, she walked through the dark backstage area and emerged into the brilliant lights of the stage. Applause rang out. The orchestra began with a low quivering that built and built. The music swelled. She opened her mouth. She came in on the right note.

Then she shook Piper Hall to its very foundations.

About midway through the concert, during a break for applause after she'd sung "Song to the Moon," she thought she saw a familiar figure seated on the balcony level. She squinted.

Henry?

But what would Henry be doing there? She nearly missed a cue. *Better concentrate on my singing.* She closed her eyes for a moment. They were tired. They were playing tricks on her. The lights were too bright, causing her to see things that weren't there. Of course Henry wasn't there. Why would he be? It was that song. That song, and simply being back at the college and back on the Piper Hall stage, making her think of him. Again.

After the concert, as she accepted congratulations and good wishes, signed programs, and posed for photographs, she kept glancing at the crowd to see if she could pick out the man whom she'd mistaken for Henry, curious if there truly was a resemblance. But she didn't see any such person, much less the genuine Henry. She shrugged it off as the vain imaginings of a weary mind.

When most of the crowd had gone home, she exchanged a few minutes' pleasant conversation with the event's organizers. Someone invited her to a late-night supper, and she begged off, citing fatigue and the need to rest up for the following day's matinee performance. The evening had left her emotionally drained. She said her good-byes, gathered her belongings, and walked out into the beautiful May night, warm and fragrant in the moonlight. She breathed deeply. After tomorrow's matinee, who knew when, or if, she'd ever return to Scoville?

The driver opened the rear door for her.

"To the hotel?" he asked as she slid into the back seat.

She shook her head. "It's such a lovely night," she murmured. "I'd like to make a brief stop first."

She directed him to the other side of the campus, to the sledding hill. "Wait here, Allen," she instructed. "I'm going to take a short walk."

"Do you think that's a good idea, ma'am?" the driver asked with a frown. "It might not be safe, walking alone in the dark. Would you like me to accompany you?"

"I'll be fine," she assured him with a smile. "This is Scoville, not Chicago."

Allen looked uneasy, but nodded and shut off the engine.

Gathering the hem of her gown, she strolled down the familiar path to the bench she'd shared with Henry a decade earlier, gratified to see it was still there. Little had changed. The lilac bushes surrounding it were in full bloom, and their heady perfume nearly took her breath away. She seated herself and let her mind sift through sweet memories. She thought of the hours she'd spent in Henry's arms and couldn't help but wonder if it had all been real. It was as if they had been living in an enchanted garden for those few months in 1916, but since then real life had intervened and wedged them apart.

Looking at the moon, she sang, in her mind, the aria from *Rusalka* that had become, over the years, her signature piece.

Moon, tell me, where is my lover?

Hidden as she was amid the lilacs, the few people strolling through the area paid no attention to her. She lost track of how long she'd been sitting there lost in her reverie, but then a figure approached the bench from behind. A prickle of irritation ran up the back of her neck. Could she not have a few quiet moments to herself without someone making demands?

She tried not to sound as impatient as she felt. "Allen, I told you, I'm fine. I'd like to be left alone for a while, if you don't mind."

"But I do mind," said a voice that was not Allen's.

She turned her head, and there he was, the man of her dreams.

"Henry?"

"Hello, Francie."

She rose, disoriented, as if the memories she'd just been mulling over had suddenly become real.

They stared at each other for a long moment. In the light from a nearby streetlamp, she marveled at how well he looked. Slightly older—as was she, of course—and looking every inch the successful lawyer in a fine wool suit and silk tie.

He took her hand in his. "Let's sit a moment, shall we?" His voice thickened with emotion.

They sat together on "their" bench, as they had so many times before.

"Why, Henry, I never expected—is it really you?" she stammered.

"Yes, it's me," he whispered.

"I'm so glad to see you. It feels right, somehow, your being here. But what are you doing here?"

"I was so sorry to read about Miss Whitworth's death, and I was pleased to learn about the scholarship being set up in her name. And then . . . well, when I saw that you'd be giving the benefit concert, the decision was made."

She swallowed. "I thought I caught a glimpse of you in the balcony, but then I convinced myself I must have been imagining things. This place, this town, brings back so many memories."

"That it does." He glanced around them. "So much time has passed, and yet everything looks the same."

Cold reality poked its way into Francie's brain. Gamely she asked, "Is your wife with you?"

"My wife?" He gave her an odd look. "What wife?"

"I understood you'd gotten married to Miss Gladstone."

His brow crinkled. "Where'd you get that idea?"

Amid her confusion fluttered a tiny spark of hope. "From your father, who called her your fiancée. And from the newspaper, who called her Lila Jasper."

"Oh, I see," he said. "I can see why you'd think that. I received a lot of pressure from Lila, her parents, and my parents, to marry her. But I just didn't have those kinds of feelings for her."

"Oh, I'm sorry," she said, untruthfully.

"I'm not. In spite of what my parents thought, Lila and I were entirely unsuited for each other. The marriage would have been a disaster. After I'd gone off to basic training, she ended up marrying my cousin, Oliver."

"Oliver Jasper?" She didn't know whether to laugh or cry.

"The one and only. They seem to be very happy together, or at least well matched." His eyes widened. "So you thought I was married. Is that why you didn't acknowledge the flowers I sent you?"

"Yes," she replied, feeling very foolish. "I didn't know what your expectations were."

"If I were a married man, I'm certainly not the kind who would step out on his wife."

"Of course you aren't," she said. "But after your father told me you were engaged . . . oh, how did everything get so mixed up?"

"My father?"

She raised her hand. "It was long ago, when I approached him for legal help on a different matter. The matter of Reinhard Schreiber's release, in fact." Whose release had made possible his marriage to Grace. Grace, whose death had brought Francie back to Scoville—to this moment.

To Henry.

"I see." He took her hand in his. "We can't change what's been done or said, so why talk about it? It's the past. But we could look to the future." He paused. "What about you? Is there someone special in your life?"

Francie shook her head. "I've been much too busy with work, travel, with taking care of my mother and brother to add another commitment to my life."

They sat in silence for several minutes.

Then Henry spoke, his voice husky. "Not a day goes by that something doesn't make me think of you. A snippet of a song. The scent of a flower." He reached over her head, snapped a slender lilac sprig from its stem, and tucked it into her hair.

Her breath caught in her throat. "It's the same for me."

He touched her cheek, his eyes searching hers. "Can't we try again?"

She swallowed. "What is it Grace used to always tell us? 'All right, you two. Take it from the top—'" She stumbled on the words.

He finished for her. "—and do it right this time."

The years melted away in the warmth of his kiss.

When at last they parted to take a breath, she caught a glimpse through the lilac branches of the moon glowing overhead.

Moon, where is my lover?

He's right in front of you.

She giggled as if she were seventeen again.

He traced her jaw with his fingers. "What's so funny?"

"I'm just so happy."

"I'm happy, too." he said. "And starving. How about you?"

Shivering with joy and wonder, she smoothed her silk wrap over her shoulders. "It's late, but if Mr. Figaro is still at the restaurant, maybe he would be kind enough to rustle up a bowl of soup."

Together they walked to the limousine, where Francie told the driver he could return to the hotel, that she wouldn't need the car anymore that evening. Allen looked uncertain, gave Henry the once-over, then touched the brim of his hat. "Very good, miss," and drove away.

Francie and Henry didn't speak much as they ambled arm-in-arm through the quiet streets. Francie had much to say, but to her surprise, was in no hurry to say it. They had time together now. An entire evening to themselves. There was no need to rush, only to savor the moment and the joyous feeling of her arm looped securely through his.

They approached the darkened restaurant from the alley, and just in time. Mr. Figaro had his hat on and was about to lock the kitchen door.

"So sorry to bother you, Mr. Figaro," Francie said by way of apology, "but we're famished. Would you mind if we helped ourselves to some bread and cheese?"

The chef looked amused as he opened the door and flicked on the kitchen light. "Is not a problem. You like I fix you a meal? Some nice linguini with clam sauce, perhaps?"

"Oh, no," Francie said. "We don't want to keep you from getting home to your family. We'll just get ourselves a quick bite and then lock up, if that's all right with you."

Mr. Figaro gave the two of them an appraising glance. He frowned and pulled the lilac sprig from Francie's hair. Then his dark eyes glowed with understanding, and he smoothed his mustache, barely concealing a smile.

"I see. Of course is all right. I just put a pot of minestrone in the icebox, probably not even cold yet. And there is good bread in the cupboard, the kind you like best. You remember how to lock up, *si*, *Francesca*?"

"*Si, si. Grazie.*" She'd sang in so many operas, the Italian response rolled effortlessly off her tongue.

Mr. Figaro kissed her hand and went on his way.

Francie found everything they needed, delighted that he'd kept the kitchen organized exactly as she remembered. She heated the fragrant soup on the stove while Henry sliced the bread. When the soup was steaming, she set the pot on the table, along with two bowls. Henry found a candle and matches in a drawer, lit them, and switched off the overhead light. At her questioning glance, he grinned and said, "Atmosphere."

Then, still wearing their elegant evening clothes, they settled at the scrubbed kitchen table to enjoy their feast, and the nearness of each other, by candlelight. As Francie ladled the soup into bowls, she marveled that the Lord had reunited her with her one true love. She did not know what the future held, but she knew for certain that Henry would be a part of it.

And she did not even forget the *parmagiana*.

EPILOGUE

D ATELINE: 30 April 1942 CHICAGO
      FORRESTER TO HEADLINE AT BENEFIT CON-
CERT
      FOR RED CROSS

Internationally renowned soprano Francine Forrester, one of the opera world's most beloved stars, will be the principal singer in a benefit concert to raise funds for the American Red Cross, this Saturday at the Auditorium Theater.

The recipient of the prestigious 1916 Young Artists' Award which launched her career, she has, over the ensuing decades, earned international recognition on some of the world's leading stages. This fall she returns to Chicago's Windy City Opera Company in a new production of the Verdi opera, *Tosca*. This is a particularly meaningful appearance to Miss Forrester, as she first appeared at Windy City Opera in a 1916 production of *Eugene Onegin*.

While growing up in Scoville, Illinois, Miss Forrester enjoyed singing in church, but had little knowledge of the world of grand opera. That all changed when, while working in an Italian restaurant, her employer lent her some recordings of the Metropolitan Opera. "I listened to those records over and over again," she recalled. "I memorized my favorite arias, even though I didn't understand a word of what I was singing."

She studied first under Grace Whitworth, then under Marie-Louise Clairvaux. Winning the Young Artists' Award opened a spot in the chorus of the Windy City Opera, and the rest, as they say, is history. Her acclaimed recording for the Victor Talking Machine Company of the opera *Rusalka*, with costars Antonio Leonardo and Beatrice de Bonneville, remains a bestseller since its 1926 release.

In her private life, Miss Forrester is Mrs. Henry Jasper. Between seasons, they tour military bases in the U.S., supporting the troops. She supported her mother and brother and underwrote her brother's studies at Embry-Riddle Aeronautical University, where he has trained to be an aviator. Maj. William Forrester is currently serving in the South Pacific.

When asked for the secret of her success, Miss Forrester said, "There is no secret. Just strong lungs, a musical ear, and a lot of hard work. The rest is up to God. The only way forward in this world is with faith. God has called us to offer our bodies as living sacrifices, so I see my work in the opera just as much as worship as everything else in life."

The benefit concert will take place Saturday evening at eight o'clock p.m. At the request of Miss Forrester, all military personnel, and all patrons under the age of twenty-one, may purchase tickets at half-price.

And on Sunday afternoon, weather permitting, she will perform outdoors in Grant Park, free of charge, for all who care to come and listen.

La Fine

AUTHOR'S NOTE

Readers of historical fiction often like to know which parts of a novel are fictional and which took place in real life. *Love's Grand Sweet Song* is a work of fiction, with invented characters, settings, and details.

God planted this story in my teenage imagination years ago, when I studied violin at the American Conservatory of Music. On Saturday mornings, I rode the train from the suburbs to downtown Chicago for my lessons. While I didn't love the lessons, I did love the conservatory building, with its creaking staircase, thick plaster walls, and snippets of music pouring forth from the practice rooms. My dalliance with the violin was mercifully brief, but I never forgot the joy of exploring that building.

Scoville, Illinois, is fictional, as is Scoville College (though readers in the know may notice that "Piper Hall" bears a strong resemblance to "Pfeiffer Hall" on the campus of my alma mater, North Central College in Naperville, Illinois).

The Windy City Opera Company is fictional, but the American Conservatory of Music was a real institution that taught students from 1886 to 1991. The Auditorium Theater hosted opera performances from 1889 until 1929, when the Civic Opera House (now the Lyric Opera House) opened. Today the Auditorium Theater, a National Historic Landmark on the campus of Roosevelt University, features a wide variety of musical and other performances. Ravinia Park opened in suburban Highland Park, Illinois, in 1904, and the Ravinia Festival continues to attract some 600,000 music lovers each year.

All of the Scoville residents and most of the conservatory and opera characters are products of my imagination. A few real-life opera singers mentioned in passing include Mary Garden, Forrest Lamont, Helen Freund, Tatyana Laranova, and Enrico Caruso.

In the United States during World War I, anti-German sentiment was strong. Roughly 2,300 U.S. residents, mostly of German heritage, were incarcerated as "enemy aliens." Most were held at Fort Oglethorpe, Georgia, or Fort Douglas, Utah. While Reinhard Schreiber is fictional, his story is very loosely based on the experience of Karl Muck, a German-born conductor with the Boston Symphony. Muck was detained at Fort Oglethorpe as an "enemy alien" in 1918 after being falsely accused of espionage based largely on his German heritage. His "trial by media" started when a newspaper editor accused him (mistakenly) of refusing to play "The Star-Spangled Banner" before a concert. His home and papers were ransacked, and even the markings he penciled into the score of the *St. Matthew Passion* were suspected of containing coded messages. He was eventually released on the condition he return to Germany, which he did.

In a similar vein, the character of Beatrice de Bonneville, while fictional, bears a passing resemblance to the acclaimed contralto Ernestine Schumann-Heink. Mme. Schumann-Heink sensed that she, too, would be under scrutiny based on her Austrian heritage, despite having two sons active in the U.S. military. In part to reassure the authorities of her loyalty, she offered concerts of patriotic music for U.S. troops and raised funds for organizations like the Red Cross and the YMCA.

IN GRATITUDE

To God be the glory.

I offer my deepest thanks to:

Pegg Thomas, patient editor and storyteller *par excellence*;

Anita Aurit, Terese Luikens, and Grace Robinson, cherished writer friends and all-around smart cookies;

Linda Nelson and Diedre Osman, first readers, who navigated the almost-but-not-quite-a-book stage with style and grace;

The women of the Thursday night Bible study at Kootenai Church, who got me through many a dark moment during the writing of this book;

My late parents, Donald and Patricia Lamont, who encouraged and nurtured my love of classical music;

And especially my husband, Thomas Leo. You are the song of my heart.

And thanks to you, dear reader, for taking a chance on my book. Please visit my website at http://jenniferlamontleo.com to sign up for my newsletter or drop me a line. I'd love to hear from you.

SNEAK PEEK

If you enjoyed *Love's Grand Sweet Song*, you'll also love the other books in the Windy City Hearts, stories of courageous women surviving and thriving through tough times. Here's a sample of the first book, *Moondrop Miracle*. Enjoy!

MOONDROP MIRACLE

S leet slashed against the tall damask-draped windows of the Gold Coast apartment, casting gloomy shadows over Constance Sutherland's face as she sat at her dressing table. Already she regretted her decision to speak at the Young Entrepreneurs of Tomorrow banquet. The miserable evening would be much better spent in the coziness of her own firelit library than shivering in some drafty banquet hall. Now, making matters worse was a notice in the newspaper that a local TV station would be featuring, on this very evening, a retrospective of the films of the late Gilda Miller, Connie's favorite actress. She'd have to miss it. *Hell's bells.*

When her dear friend Sonja Atwater had called and asked Constance to speak, whatever had possessed her to say yes? What nugget of wisdom could she possibly offer these vibrant young women about to sail forth with their freshly minted degrees, ready to conquer the world? The very vitality of today's young women made Constance feel old and well past her prime.

Or perhaps it was just the incessant rain that was making her feel like a bowl of yesterday's oatmeal. The pounding of it against the windows carried her mind back to a similar storm, nearly seventy years earlier, on a dark Tuesday that had changed her life forever.

She turned away from the window. Mustn't dwell on the past. Mustn't let her mind slip away. Mustn't give in.

In any case, she'd given her word. And even though one would hardly blame an octogenarian for declining to go out on such a blustery evening, Constance was not one to shirk a commitment.

With a sigh, she lifted her tortoiseshell comb as if it were a weapon and gave a few firm strokes to her silvery hair, still shiny and falling into the soft chin-length waves that had been her signature style for years.

A gentle rap sounded at the door, and the housemaid carried a tray into the bedroom and set it on the dressing table. "I thought you might appreciate a hot cup of tea, ma'am, before you head out."

"Thank you, Elsa. That's very thoughtful."

"Are you sure you ought to go?" Elsa frowned at the dripping windows. "Looks right nasty out there."

"Of course I'll go," Constance said with a note of mild disapproval, as if she hadn't just been entertaining those exact thoughts herself.

"You look lovely. I remember how much your husband liked you to wear blue."

"Yes, he did." A bittersweet pang tweaked Constance's heart. She handed Elsa the newspaper. "If you're staying in, you might want to catch this Gilda Miller film festival on television. I'm sick about missing it."

Elsa took the paper and glanced at it. "You don't have to miss it. Just record it to watch later. That's why your son gave you that VCR last Christmas."

Constance waved her hand impatiently. "I can't ever get that darned gizmo to work right. Too many buttons."

"Don't worry. I'll set it up for you," Elsa promised. "You can watch it later when you get home, or tomorrow. I know how much you liked Gilda Miller."

"Thank you." As Connie took a grateful sip of the steaming tea, a buzzer sounded from the front hall. The cup clinked as she set it in the saucer.

"That will be the doorman to tell us the car is here. Please call down and have him signal the driver I'll be ready momentarily." Under her breath she added, "I do hope the Young Entrepreneurs haven't sent along a chatterbox this time."

"Yes, ma'am."

After Elsa left the room, Constance took another sip of tea, checked her evening bag for the index cards on which she'd jotted some notes for her speech, and glanced once more at the mirror. At eighty-one, she was still blessed with the graceful, almost regal bearing of her youth. Above a long pale blue silk shantung skirt, her silver-and-blue beaded top shimmered in the lamplight and nicely complemented her coloring.

Before leaving the bedroom, she applied one final swipe of lipstick and slipped the tube into her bag.

"Remember to sparkle, old girl," she told her reflection and smiled in spite of herself.

Within moments of pulling away from the curb, it became apparent that the Young Entrepreneurs had indeed sent a chatterbox.

"Oh, Mrs. Sutherland, I can't even tell you what an honor it is to meet you in person." The red-haired, alabaster-skinned driver blurted the words as she weaved the Volvo in and out of city traffic on rain-slick streets.

Constance clung to the armrest and tried not to flinch visibly as the side-view mirror of a cab passed within a hair's breadth of her window.

"When Mrs. Atwater asked for a volunteer to pick you up for the dinner, I begged and begged and begged to be chosen."

"How kind," Constance said, wishing she'd do a little less begging and a little more steering.

"I can't wait to hear what you have to say. Why, you're simply a legend."

What should have been a fifteen-minute drive took no more than ten, thanks to the woman behind the wheel, who drove as fast as she talked. Constance could hardly keep up with the woman's plans to start some sort of a computer technology business. Fortunately, the girl accepted her noncommittal responses without question, hardly stopping to breathe. The car lurched to a stop at the curb in front of the elegant Palmer House Hotel. The legend emerged shakily and gratefully accepted the capable arm of a uniformed doorman, who escorted her into the lobby while the driver handed the keys to a parking valet. In the light and warmth of the gilded lobby, she regained her bearings, glad to be back on *terra firma*.

"This way, Mrs. Sutherland." The redhead caught up to her and gestured toward an escalator rising to a crimson-carpeted mezzanine. Together they rode the escalator, Constance stepping careful to keep the hem of her long skirt from catching in the machine's gnashing teeth. It would never do to fall and break a hip in front of all these people.

The mezzanine was crowded with women milling around outside the ballroom. Some of them gathered in small whispering clumps, sliding glances her way, and she looked down at her outfit to make sure nothing was askew. Several ladies murmured greetings as she passed. Some of their faces looked familiar, but her escort hustled her along before she could place any of them.

"They're waiting for us."

Constance halted. "Miss—MacDonald, did you say? Before we go in, I'd like to stop and powder my nose."

"Oh, um, sure. The restroom is right down that hallway." The girl hesitated. "Do you want me to go with you?"

"I'm not *that* elderly, dear." Constance added a smile to soften the words and headed toward the ladies' lounge.

Satisfied that her appearance was in order, she let Miss MacDonald guide her through the ballroom to the speakers' table. In the low light of the room, she made out her place card. She'd only been seated a moment when a shrill voice pierced through the dusky gloom.

"Connie, darling! I'm so glad you've come, and on this beastly night, too."

"Sonja." Constance's heart lightened at the sound of a familiar voice. An elegantly dressed woman not much younger than herself, but apparently a good deal more spry, slid into the empty chair next to her and the friends embraced. "Thank you for inviting me, although, truth be told, I don't know what I have to say to these young women that they haven't heard a thousand times before."

"You're too modest." Sonja grasped Constance's hand and squeezed it. "Why, the girls insisted I invite you. You're a legend in your own time."

There was that word again. *Legend.*

Introductions were made around the table. The other speakers for the evening, both decades younger than herself, included a prominent neurosurgeon who'd founded a medical technology company and a banking executive whose name Constance had seen on the business pages of the *Tribune*. Four bright-eyed members of the Young Entrepreneurs' board, including Miss MacDonald, filled out the table of eight.

Over shrimp cocktail and French onion soup, Constance and Sonja got caught up. Sonja explained her mentoring role with the Young

Entrepreneurs of Tomorrow, a position she'd taken on after retiring as professor *emeritus* at a local university.

"Goodness, you're as busy in retirement as you ever were," Constance remarked.

"Oh, I love working with the young women." Sonja's eyes sparkled. "They have the whole future ahead of them. Kind of makes me feel young again. And what about you? I'm *dying* to hear about the new Pearlcon facility that just opened in Hong Kong."

Connie started to explain, but just as the entrée was served, Sonja was called away to look after some detail of the production. Connie turned her attention to the conversation elsewhere at the table, which had turned to higher education.

"More women should be encouraged to major in STEM fields," the banker said.

"STEM?" Constance tested the unfamiliar acronym on her tongue.

"Science, Technology, Engineering, and Math," the neurosurgeon explained. "It's a new acronym gaining traction in the universities. Too many women today are opting for the liberal arts, taking the easy way out. How can we ever make headway in a man's world if we don't tackle the same hard subjects they do?"

"Women are trapping themselves in a pink-collar ghetto," the banker asserted. "This alarming situation needs to change. What do you think, Ms. Sutherland? It is Ms. Sutherland, isn't it?"

"*Mrs.* Yes, that's the name I use professionally." It was simpler that way.

"Well, what do you think? Do you agree that women are trapping themselves in a pink-collar ghetto?"

"*Ghetto* seems a strong word, don't you think?" Constance said. "Not all women are cut out for science and math. Not everyone wants to compete toe-to-toe with men."

"Women who shirk doing a man's work are letting down the sister-hood," the neurosurgeon declared. "Of course, you made your fortune in a pink-collar field," she added with a nod toward Constance. "But times have changed. STEM is the wave of the future."

Feeling a bit pounced upon, Constance straightened and addressed the woman directly. "While it's true that few fields are more 'pink-collar' than the cosmetics industry, there are of course a great many women scientists working in Pearlcon laboratories around the world. We wouldn't have much of a company without them, would we?" She dabbed her lips with a white linen napkin, taking a moment to plan her next words. "Many women can and do excel in science and math. But a woman shouldn't feel she has to become like a man to achieve success."

"We don't need to become *like* them. We need to become *better* than them," said the banker with what sounded like a sneer.

"What field did you take your degree in, Mrs. Sutherland?" asked the neurosurgeon.

"Oh, I never went to college," Constance said. "After high school, I attended a year of finishing school. Then I married and had a child. I didn't start my career until later."

"Finishing school?" The neurosurgeon could not have looked more astonished if Constance had claimed Stateville Prison as her alma mater. The doctor and the banker exchanged a glance, clearly wondering why such an undereducated woman was speaking at an event aimed at soon-to-be college graduates. Constance wondered herself. "It's a wonder your business succeeded as it has," the neurosurgeon concluded.

"I didn't know it would succeed at the time. All I knew was that I had to do it. And eventually, I became most interested in offering women opportunities that didn't seem to exist anywhere else."

All at once, the face of an old classmate flitted across Constance's memory. *Julia Harper. That's who these women remind me of. Good old Julia with her no-nonsense leather brogues, mannish hats, and leaflets proclaiming the rights of women and whatnot.* The memory amused Constance so much, she almost missed what the banker was saying. A few minutes later, she wished that she had.

"Thank goodness times have changed," the banker said. "Maybe foregoing a proper education was acceptable back then, but it certainly isn't a viable option these days. After all, very few people have a rich daddy to bankroll their business. Most of the young people here tonight are not women of privilege, such as yourself."

The woman had hurled the word "privilege" as if it were an accusation. *Rich daddy, indeed.* Heat rose in Constance's chest and spread to her face. Why were these rude women attacking her? Where was Sonja? Whatever was keeping her? Constance felt her sparkle melting faster than the ice cream served for dessert. It took everything she had not to snap back some witty barb and put the women in their place. In her mind she heard Aunt Pearl's voice say, *Don't stoop to their level, Connie. A gentle answer turns away wrath.* So she said simply,

"Apparently, you haven't heard my story. Perhaps my speech will fill in some of the gaps for you. I suggest you listen carefully."

Before her tablemates could respond, the lights dimmed. Sonja stepped behind the podium and introduced the neurosurgeon as the first speaker.

The room grew warm. Constance slipped out of her wrap and folded it over the back of her chair. It was too dark to read the index cards in her bag, so mentally she reviewed her speech, noting portions she could skip if the hour grew late but reminding herself of the one point she absolutely had to make to these impressionable young females.

For heaven's sake, be glad that God made you a woman.

As the neurosurgeon droned on about entrepreneurial opportunities around today's highly specialized wellness environments—apparently no one called them "hospitals" anymore—Constance let her mind drift back to her own youth.

She had not cared about college. At twenty-one, she'd had no greater purpose in mind than marrying Winston Sutherland III and having fun. Lots and lots of fun. Aunt Pearl had been the one who had longed to go to college—and been denied the opportunity.

But God had other plans for both of them.

Like it so far? Keep reading! Pick up your copy of Moondrop Miracle today.

WHAT'S THE BUZZ?

Reviews are pure gold to an author! If you enjoyed this book and want to help spread the word, post reviews on book-oriented websites like Amazon, Goodreads, and BookBub. Reviews can be short or as long as you like. And please talk about the book, in person and on social media. Word-of-mouth is still the best way to promote just about anything!

Let's stay in touch. Please stop by and say hello.

JenniferLamontLeo.com (Join my Reader Community for book news, exclusive content, and more)

Facebook

Goodreads

BookBub

Amazon

A Sparkling Vintage Life (My podcast! Listen online at JenniferLamontLeo.com or subscribe in your favorite podcast app)

Made in the USA
Monee, IL
04 April 2024

56356937R00204